'An accomplished novel . . . The plot twists and grips like an octopus. *The Sculptress* is crime choice of the year'

DAILY TELEGRAPH

'Minette Walters has triumphed with *The Sculptress* . . . enthralling right to the final paragraph. Game, set and match to Ms Walters'

SUNDAY TELEGRAPH

'An exceptionally powerful and absorbing story with a puzzle that twists to the last paragraph'

MAIL ON SUNDAY

'Walters cranks up the suspense throughout, down to the brilliantly unnerving ending. This is one of my books of the year'

SUNDAY TIMES

'A devastatingly effective novel with a chilling ambiguity at the end'

OBSERVER

'A gratifyingly superior novel . . . Walters is a quirky, powerful and unusual talent'

THE TIMES

'I have been spoilt for choice in selecting a best book but must give pride of place to *The Sculptress* by Minette Walters'

EDWARD FRENCH, PUBLISHING NEWS

Also by Minette Walters in Pan Books

The Ice House

The SCULPTRESS

MINETTE WALTERS

PAN BOOKS
in association with
MACMILLAN LONDON

First published 1993 by Macmillan London Limited

This edition published 1994 by Pan Books Limited
a division of Pan Macmillan Publishers Limited
Cavaye Place London SW10 9PG
and Basingstoke
in association with Macmillan London Limited

Associated companies throughout the world

ISBN 0 330 33037 3

Grateful acknowledgement is made to Encyclopaedia Britannica,
Inc., for permission to quote from *Encyclopaedia Britannica*, 15th
edition (1992), 12:535.

1 3 5 7 9 8 6 4 2

A CIP catalogue record for this book is available from
the British Library

Phototypeset by Intype, London
Printed by Cox & Wyman Ltd, Reading, Berkshire

For Roland and Philip

PROLOGUE

Dawlington Evening Herald, January, 1988

TWENTY-FIVE YEARS FOR BRUTAL MURDERS

At Winchester Crown Court yesterday, Olive Martin, 23, of 22 Leven Road, Dawlington, was sentenced to life imprisonment for the brutal murders of her mother and sister, with a recommendation that she serve twenty-five years. The judge, who referred to Martin as 'a monster without a grain of humanity', said that nothing could excuse the savagery she had shown to two defenceless women. The murder of a mother by her daughter was the most unnatural of crimes and demanded the strongest penalty that the law could impose. The murder of a sister by a sister was no less heinous. 'Martin's butchery of the bodies,' he went on, 'was an unforgivable and barbarous desecration that will rank in the annals of crime as an act of supreme evil.' Martin showed no emotion as sentence was passed. . . .

Ground-floor plan of Number 22, Leven Road, Dawlington, Southampton, as it was at the time of the murders. Drawn by the present owner for Miss Rosalind Leigh.

ONE

It was impossible to see her approach without a shudder of distaste. She was a grotesque parody of a woman, so fat that her feet and hands and head protruded absurdly from the huge slab of her body like tiny disproportionate afterthoughts. Dirty blonde hair clung damp and thin to her scalp, black patches of sweat spread beneath her armpits. Clearly, walking was painful. She shuffled forward on the insides of her feet, legs forced apart by the thrust of one gigantic thigh against another, balance precarious. And with every movement, however small, the fabric of her dress strained ominously as the weight of her flesh shifted. She had, it seemed, no redeeming features. Even her eyes, a deep blue, were all but lost in the ugly folds of pitted white lard.

Strange that after so long she was still an object of curiosity. People who saw her every day watched her progress down that corridor as if for the first time. What was it that fascinated them? The sheer size of a woman who stood five feet eleven and weighed over twenty-six stones? Her reputation? Disgust? There were no smiles. Most watched impassively as she passed, fearful perhaps of attracting her attention. She had carved her mother and sister into little pieces and rearranged the bits in bloody abstract on her kitchen floor. Few who saw her could forget it. In view of the horrific nature of the crime and the fear that her huge brooding figure had instilled in everyone who had sat in the courtroom she had been sentenced to life with a recommendation that she serve a minimum of twenty-five years. What made her unusual, apart from the crime itself, was that she had pleaded guilty and refused to offer a defence.

She was known inside the prison walls as the Sculptress. Her real name was Olive Martin.

Rosalind Leigh, waiting by the door of the interview room, ran her tongue around the inside of her mouth. Her revulsion was immediate as if Olive's evil had reached out and touched her. *My God*, she was thinking, and the thought alarmed her, *I can't go through with this.* But she had, of course, no choice. The gates of the prison were locked on her, as a visitor, just as securely as they were locked on the inmates. She pressed a shaking hand to her thigh where the muscles were jumping uncontrollably. Behind her, her all but empty briefcase, a testament to her lack of preparation for this meeting, screamed derision at her ill-considered assumption that conversation with Olive could develop like any other. It had never occurred to her, not for one moment, that fear might stifle her inventiveness.

Lizzie Borden took an axe and gave her mother forty whacks. When she saw what she had done, she gave her father forty-one. The rhyme churned in her brain, over and over, numbingly repetitive. *Olive Martin took an axe and gave her mother forty whacks. When she saw what she had done she gave her sister forty-one . . .*

Roz stepped away from the door and forced herself to smile. 'Hello, Olive. I'm Rosalind Leigh. Nice to meet you at last.' She held out her hand and shook the other's warmly, in the hope, perhaps, that by demonstrating an unprejudiced friendliness she could quell her dislike. Olive's touch was token only, a brief brush of unresponsive fingers. 'Thank you.' Roz spoke to the hovering prison officer briskly. 'I'll take it from here. We have the Governor's permission to talk for an hour.' *Lizzie Borden took an axe . . .* Tell her you've changed your mind. *Olive Martin took an axe and gave her mother forty whacks . . .* I can't go through with this!

The uniformed woman shrugged. 'OK.' She dropped the welded metal chair she was carrying carelessly on to the floor and steadied it against her knee. 'You'll need this. Anything else in there will collapse the minute she sits on it.' She laughed amiably. An attractive woman. 'She got wedged in the flaming toilet last year and it took four men to pull her out again. You'd never get her up on your own.'

Roz manoeuvred the chair awkwardly through the doorway. She felt at a disadvantage, like the friend of warring partners being pressured into taking sides. *But Olive intimidated her in a way the prison officer never could.* 'You will see me using a tape-recorder during this interview,' she snapped, nervousness clipping the words brusquely. 'The Governor has agreed to it. I trust that's in order.'

There was a short silence. The prison officer raised an eyebrow. 'If you say so. Presumably someone's taken the trouble to get the Sculptress's agreement. Any problems, like, for example, she objects violently' – she drew a finger across her throat before tapping the pane of glass beside the door which allowed the officers a clear view of the room – 'then bang on the window. Assuming she lets you, of course.' She smiled coolly. 'You've read the rules, I hope. You bring nothing in for her, you take nothing out. She can smoke your cigarettes in the interview room but she can't take any away with her. You do not pass messages for her, in or out, without the Governor's permission. If in doubt about anything, you refer it to one of the officers. Clear?'

Bitch, thought Roz angrily. 'Yes, thank you.' But it wasn't anger she felt, of course, it was fear. Fear of being shut up in a confined space with this monstrous creature who stank of fat woman's sweat and showed no emotion in her grotesquely bloated face.

'Good.' The officer walked away with a broad wink at a colleague.

Roz stared after her. 'Come in, Olive.' She chose the chair furthest from the door deliberately. It was a statement of confidence. She was so damn nervous she needed a wee.

The idea for the book had been delivered as an ultimatum by her agent. 'Your publisher is about to wash his hands of you,

3

Roz. His precise words were, "She has a week to commit herself to something that will sell or I shall remove her from our lists." And, though I hate to rub your nose in it, I am within a whisker of doing the same thing.' Iris's face softened a little. Berating Roz, she felt, was like beating your head against a brick wall, painful and completely ineffective. She was, she knew, the woman's best friend – her *only* friend, she thought sometimes. The barrier of barbed wire that Roz had erected around herself had deterred all but the most determined. People rarely even asked after her these days. With an inward sigh, Iris threw caution to the winds. 'Look, sweetheart, you really can't go on like this. It's unhealthy to shut yourself away and brood. Did you think about what I suggested last time?'

Roz wasn't listening. 'I'm sorry,' she murmured, her eyes maddeningly vacant. She saw the irritation on Iris's face and forced herself to concentrate. Iris, she thought, had been lecturing again. But really, Roz wondered, why did she bother? Other people's concern was so exhausting, for her and for them.

'Did you ring that psychiatrist I recommended?' Iris demanded bluntly.

'No, there's no need. I'm fine.' She studied the immaculately made-up face, which had changed very little in fifteen years. Someone had once told Iris Fielding that she looked like Elizabeth Taylor in *Cleopatra*. 'A week's too short,' Roz said, referring to her publisher. 'Tell him a month.'

Iris flicked a piece of paper across her desk. 'You've run out of room to manoeuvre, I'm afraid. He's not even prepared to give you a choice of subject. He wants Olive Martin. Here's the name and address of her solicitor. Find out why she wasn't sent to Broadmoor or Rampton. Find out why she refused to offer a defence. And find out what made her commit the murders in the first place. There's a story there somewhere.' She watched the frown on Roz's face deepen and shrugged. 'I know. It's not your sort of thing, but you've brought this on yourself. I've been pressing you for months to produce an outline. Now it's this or nothing. To tell you the truth, I think he's done it on purpose. If you write it, it will sell, if you refuse to write it because it's pure sensationalism, then he's found a good excuse to drop you.'

Roz's reaction surprised her. 'OK,' she said mildly, taking the piece of paper and tucking it into her handbag.

'I thought you'd refuse.'

'Why?'

'Because of the way the tabloids sensationalized what happened to *you*.'

Roz shrugged. 'Maybe it's time someone showed them how to handle human tragedy with dignity.' She wouldn't write it, of course – she had no intention of writing anything any more – but she gave Iris an encouraging smile. 'I've never met a murderess before.'

Roz's application to visit Olive Martin for the purposes of research was passed on by the Prison Governor to the Home Office. It was several weeks before permission was given in a grudging processed letter from a civil servant. While Martin had consented to the visits, she reserved the right at any time to withdraw consent, without reason and without prejudice. It was emphasized that the visits had been authorized only on the understanding that there would be no breaches of the prison regulations, that the Governor's word would be final in all circumstances, and that Ms Leigh would be held liable should she contribute in any way to an undermining of prison discipline.

Roz found it hard to look at Olive. Good manners and the woman's ugliness precluded staring and the monstrous face was so flat, so unresponsive, that her eyes kept sliding off it like butter off a baked potato. Olive, for her part, watched Roz greedily. Attractive looks put no such limitations on staring – quite the reverse, they invite it – and Roz was, in any case, a novelty. Visitors were rare in Olive's life, particularly ones who came without the reforming baggage of missionary zeal.

After the cumbersome business of getting her seated, Roz gestured towards the tape-recorder. 'If you remember, I mentioned in my second letter that I'd like to record our chats. I presumed when the Governor gave permission for it that you'd agreed.' Her voice was pitched too high.

Olive shrugged a kind of acquiescence.

'You've no objections, then?'

A shake of the head.

'Fine. I'm switching on now. Date, Monday, April twelve. Conversation with Olive Martin.' She consulted her all too sketchy list of questions. 'Let's start with some factual details. When were you born?'

No answer.

Roz looked up with an encouraging smile, only to be confronted by the woman's unblinking scrutiny. 'Well,' she said, 'I think I have that detail already. Let's see. Eighth of September, nineteen sixty-four, which makes you twenty-eight. Am I right?' No response. 'And you were born in Southampton General, the first of Gwen and Robert Martin's two daughters. Your sister, Amber, came along two years later on the fifteenth of July, nineteen sixty-six. Were you pleased about that? Or would you rather have had a brother?' Nothing.

Roz did not look up this time. She could feel the weight of the woman's eyes upon her. 'Your parents liked colours, obviously. I wonder what they would have called Amber if she'd been a boy?' She gave a nervous giggle. 'Red? Ginger? Perhaps it was a good thing the baby was another girl.' She listened to herself in disgust. *Goddamnit, why the hell did I agree to this!* Her bladder was hurting.

A fat finger reached out and switched off the tape-recorder. Roz watched it with a horrible fascination. 'There's no need to be so frightened,' said a deep, surprisingly cultured voice. 'Miss Henderson was teasing you. They all know I'm completely harmless. If I wasn't, I'd be in Broadmoor.' A strange rumbling noise vibrated the air. A laugh? Roz wondered. 'Stands to reason, really.' The finger hovered over the switches. 'You see, I do what normal people do when I have objections to something. I express them.' The finger moved to *Record* and gently pushed the button. 'Had Amber been a boy they would have called him Jeremy after my mother's father. Colour didn't come into it. In actual fact, Amber was christened Alison. I called her Amber because, at the age of two, I couldn't get my tongue round the "*l*" or the "*s*". It suited her. She had lovely honey-blonde hair, and as she grew up she always answered to Amber and never to Alison. She was very pretty.'

Roz waited a moment until she was sure she had her voice under control. 'Sorry.'

'That's all right. I'm used to it. Everyone is afraid at first.'

'Does that upset you?'

A flicker of amusement twitched the fatness round her eyes. 'Would it upset you?'

'Yes.'

'Well, then. Have you got a cigarette?'

'Sure.' Roz took an unopened pack from her briefcase and pushed it across the table with a box of matches. 'Help yourself. I don't smoke.'

'You would if you were in here. Everyone smokes in here.' She fumbled her way into the cigarette packet and lit up with a sigh of contentment. 'How old are you?'

'Thirty-six.'

'Married?'

'Divorced.'

'Children?'

Roz shook her head. 'I'm not the maternal type.'

'Is that why you got divorced?'

'Probably. I was more interested in my career. We went our separate ways very amicably.' Absurd, she thought, to bother with pain management in front of Olive but the trouble was that if you told a lie often enough it became a truth, and the hurt only returned occasionally, in those strange, disorientating moments of wakening when she thought she was still at home with a warm body wrapped in her arms, hugging, loving, laughing.

Olive blew a smoke ring into the air. 'I'd have liked

children. I got pregnant once but my mother persuaded me to get rid of it. I wish I hadn't now. I keep wondering what sex it was. I dream about my baby sometimes.' She gazed at the ceiling for a moment, following the wisp of smoke. 'Poor little thing. I was told by a woman in here that they wash them down the sink – you know, when they've vacuumed them out of you.'

Roz watched the big lips suck wetly on the tiny cigarette and thought of foetuses being vacuumed out of wombs. 'I didn't know that.'

'About the sink?'

'No. That you'd had an abortion.'

Olive's face was impassive. 'Do you know anything about me?'

'Not much.'

'Who've you asked?'

'Your solicitor.'

Another wheeze rumbled up through the caverns of her chest. 'I didn't know I had one.'

'Peter Crew,' said Roz with a frown, pulling a letter from her briefcase.

'Oh, him.' Olive's tone was contemptuous. 'He's a creep.' She spoke with undisguised venom.

'He says here he's your solicitor.'

'So? Governments say they care. I haven't heard a word from him in four years. I told him to get stuffed when he came up with his wonderful idea to get me an indefinite stay at Broadmoor. Slimy little sod. He didn't like me. He'd have wet himself with excitement if he could have got me certified.'

'He says' – Roz skimmed through the letter without thinking – 'ah, yes, here it is. "Unfortunately Olive failed to grasp that a plea of diminished responsibility would have ensured her receiving the sort of help in a secure psychiatric unit that would, in all probability, have meant her release into society within, at the most, fifteen years. It has always been obvious to me—" ' She came to an abrupt stop as sweat broke out across her back. *Any problems like, for example, she objects*

8

violently . . . Was she completely out of her mind? She smiled weakly. 'Frankly, the rest is irrelevant.'

' "It has always been obvious to me that Olive is psychologically disturbed, possibly to the point of paranoid schizophrenia or psychopathy." Is that what it says?' Olive stood the glowing butt of her cigarette on the table and took another from the packet. 'I don't say I wasn't tempted. Assuming I could have got the court to accept that I was temporarily insane when I did it, I would almost certainly be a free woman by now. Have you seen my psychological reports?' Roz shook her head. 'Apart from an unremitting compulsion to eat, which is generally considered abnormal – one psychiatrist dubbed it a tendency to severe self-abuse – I am classified "normal".' She blew out the match with a gust of amusement. 'Whatever normal means. You've probably got more hang-ups than I have but I assume you fall into a "normal" psychological profile.'

'I wouldn't know,' said Roz, fascinated. 'I've never been analysed.' *I'm too frightened of what they might find*.

'You get used to it in a place like this. I reckon they do it to keep their hand in and it's probably more fun talking to a mother-hacker than a boring old depressive. I've had five different psychiatrists put me through the hoops. They love labels. It makes the filing system easier when they're trying to sort out what to do with us. I create problems for them. I'm sane but dangerous, so where the hell do they put me? An open prison's out of the question in case I get out and do it again. The public wouldn't like that.'

Roz held up the letter. 'You say you were tempted. Why didn't you go along with it if you thought there was a chance of getting out earlier?'

Olive didn't answer immediately but smoothed the shapeless dress across her thighs. 'We make choices. They're not always right but, once made, we have to live with them. I was very ignorant before I came here. Now I'm streetwise.' She inhaled a lungful of smoke. 'Psychologists, policemen, prison officers, judges, they were all out of the same mould.

Men in authority with complete control of my life. Supposing I'd pleaded diminished responsibility and they'd said this girl can never get better. Lock the door and throw away the key. Twenty-five years amongst sane people was so much more attractive to me than a whole life with mad ones.'

'And what do you think now?'

'You learn, don't you? We get some real nut cases in here before they're transferred on. They're not so bad. Most of them can see the funny side.' She balanced a second dog-end next to her first. 'And I'll tell you something else, they're a damn sight less critical than the sane ones. When you look like me, you appreciate that.' She scrutinized Roz from between sparse blonde eyelashes. 'That's not to say I'd have pleaded differently had I been more *au fait* with the system. I still think it would have been immoral to claim I didn't know what I was doing when I knew perfectly well.'

Roz made no comment. What can you say to a woman who dismembers her mother and sister and then calmly splits hairs over the morality of special pleading?

Olive guessed what she was thinking and gave her wheezy laugh. 'It makes sense to me. By my own standards, I've done nothing wrong. It's only the law, those standards set by society, that I've transgressed.'

There was a certain biblical flourish about that last phrase, and Roz remembered that today was Easter Monday. 'Do you believe in God?'

'No. I'm a pagan. I believe in natural forces. Worshipping the sun makes sense. Worshipping an invisible entity doesn't.'

'What about Jesus Christ? He wasn't invisible.'

'But he wasn't God either.' Olive shrugged. 'He was a prophet, like Billy Graham. Can you swallow the garbage of the Trinity? I mean, either there's one God or there's a mountainful of them. It just depends on how imaginative you feel. I, for one, have no cause to celebrate that Christ is Risen.'

Roz, whose faith was dead, could sympathize with Olive's cynicism. 'So, if I understand you correctly, you're saying there is no absolute right or wrong, only individual conscience and the law.' Olive nodded. 'And your conscience isn't troubling you because you don't think you've done anything wrong.'

Olive looked at her with approval. 'That's it.'

Roz chewed her bottom lip in thought. 'Which means you believe your mother and sister deserved to die.' She frowned. 'Well, I don't understand, then. Why didn't you put up a defence at your trial?'

'I had no defence.'

'Provocation. Mental cruelty. Neglect. They must have done *something* if you felt you were justified in killing them.'

Olive took another cigarette from the pack but didn't answer. 'Well?'

The intense scrutiny again. This time Roz held her gaze. 'Well?' she persisted.

Abruptly, Olive rapped the window pane with the back of her hand. 'I'm ready now, Miss Henderson,' she called out.

Roz looked at her in surprise. 'We've forty minutes yet.'

'I've talked enough.'

'I'm sorry. I've obviously upset you.' She waited. 'It was unintentional.'

Olive still didn't answer but sat impassively until the Officer came in. Then she grasped the edge of the table and, with a shove from behind, heaved herself to her feet. The cigarette, unlit, clung to her lower lip like a string of cotton wool. 'I'll see you next week,' she said, easing crabwise through the door and shambling off down the corridor with Miss Henderson and the metal chair in tow.

Roz sat on for several minutes, watching them through the window. Why had Olive balked at the mention of justification? Roz felt unreasonably cheated – it was one of the few questions she had wanted an answer to – and yet . . . Like the first stirrings of long dormant sap, her curiosity began to reawaken. God knows, there was no sense to it – she and Olive were as different as two women could be – but she had to admit an odd liking for the woman.

She snapped her briefcase closed and never noticed that her pencil was missing.

Iris had left a breathy message on the answerphone. 'Ring me with all the dirt . . . Is she perfectly ghastly? If she's as mad and as fat as her solicitor said, she must be terrifying. I'm agog to hear the gory details. If you don't phone, I shall come round to the flat and make a nuisance of myself . . .'

Roz poured herself a gin and tonic and wondered if Iris's insensitivity was inherited or acquired. She dialled her number. 'I'm phoning because it's the lesser of two evils. If I had to watch you drooling your disgusting prurience all over my carpet, I should be sick.' Mrs Antrobus, her bossy white cat, slithered round her legs, stiff tailed and purring. Roz winked down at her. She and Mrs Antrobus had a relationship of long standing, in which Mrs Antrobus wore the trousers and Roz knew her place. There was no persuading Mrs A. to do anything she didn't want.

'Oh, goody. You liked her, then?'

'What a revolting woman you are.' She took a sip from her glass. 'I'm not sure that *like* is quite the word I would use.'

'How fat is she?'

'Grotesque. And it's sad, not funny.'

'Did she talk?'

'Yes. She has a very pukka accent and she's a bit of an intellectual. Not at all what I expected. Very sane, by the way.'

'I thought the solicitor said she was a psychopath.'

'He did. I'm going to see him tomorrow. I want to know who gave him that idea. According to Olive, five psychiatrists have diagnosed her normal.'

'She might be lying.'

'She's not. I checked with the Governor afterwards.' Roz reached down to scoop Mrs Antrobus against her chest. The cat, purring noisily, licked her nose. It was only cupboard love. She was hungry. 'Still, I wouldn't get too excited about this, if I were you. Olive may refuse to see me again.'

'Why, and what's that awful row?' demanded Iris.

'Mrs Antrobus.'

'Oh God! The mangy cat.' Iris was diverted. 'It sounds as if you've got the builders in. What on earth are you doing to it?'

'Loving it. She's the only thing that makes this hideous flat worth coming back to.'

'You're mad,' said Iris, whose contempt for cats was matched only by her contempt for authors. 'I can't think why you wanted to rent it in the first place. Use the money from the divorce and get something decent. Why might Olive refuse to see you?'

'She's unpredictable. Got very angry with me suddenly and called a halt to the interview.'

She heard Iris's indrawn gasp. 'Roz, you wretch! You haven't blown it, I hope.'

Roz grinned into the receiver. 'I'm not sure. We'll just have to wait and see. Got to go now. Bye-ee.' She hung up smartly on Iris's angry squeaking and went into the kitchen to feed Mrs Antrobus. When the phone rang again, she picked up her gin, moved into her bedroom, and started typing.

Olive took the pencil she had stolen from Roz and stood it carefully alongside the small clay figure of a woman that was propped up at the back of her chest of drawers. Her moist lips worked involuntarily, chewing, sucking, as she studied the figure critically. It was crudely executed, a lump of dried grey clay, unfired and unglazed but, like a fertility symbol from a less sophisticated age, its femininity was powerful. She selected a red marker from a jar and carefully coloured in the slab of hair about the face, then, changing to a green marker, filled in on the torso a rough representation of the silk shirtwaisted dress that Roz had been wearing.

To an observer her actions would have appeared childish. She cradled the figure in her hands like a tiny doll, crooning over it, before replacing it beside the pencil which, too faintly for the human nose, still carried the scent of Rosalind Leigh.

TWO

Peter Crew's office was in the centre of Southampton, in a street where estate agents predominated. It was a sign of the times, thought Roz, as she walked past them, that they were largely empty. Depression had settled on them, as on everything else, like a dark immovable cloud.

Peter Crew was a gangling man of indeterminate age, with faded eyes and a blond toupee parted at the side. His own hair, a yellowish white, hung beneath it like a dirty net curtain. Every so often, he lifted the edge of the hair-piece and poked a finger underneath to scratch his scalp. The inevitable result of so much ill-considered stretching was that the toupee gaped perpetually in a small peak above his nose. It looked, Roz thought, like a large chicken perched on top of his head. She rather sympathized with Olive's contempt for him.

He smiled at her request to tape their conversation, a studied lift of the lips which lacked sincerity. 'As you please.' He folded his hands on his desk. 'So, Miss Leigh, you've already seen my client. How was she?'

'She was surprised to hear she still had a solicitor.'

'I don't follow.'

'According to Olive, she hasn't heard from you in four years. Are you still representing her?'

His face assumed a look of comical dismay but, like his smile, it lacked conviction. 'Good Heavens. Is it as long as that? Surely not. Didn't I write to her last year?'

'You tell me, Mr Crew.'

He fussed to a cabinet in the corner and flicked through the files. 'Here we are. Olive Martin. Dear me, you're right.

14

Four years. Mind you,' he said sharply, 'there's been no communication from her either.' He pulled out the file and brought it across to his desk. 'The law is a costly business, Miss Leigh. We don't send letters for fun, you know.'

Roz lifted an eyebrow. 'Who's paying, then? I assumed she was on Legal Aid.'

He adjusted his yellow hat. 'Her father paid, though, frankly, I'm not sure what the position would be now. He's dead, you know.'

'I didn't know.'

'Heart attack a year ago. It was three days before anyone found him. Messy business. We're still trying to sort out the estate.' He lit a cigarette and then abandoned it on the edge of an overflowing ashtray.

Roz pencilled a doodle on her notepad. 'Does Olive know her father's dead?'

He was surprised. 'Of course she does.'

'Who told her? Obviously, your firm didn't write.'

He eyed her with the sudden suspicion of an unwary rambler coming upon a snake in the grass. 'I telephoned the prison and spoke to the Governor. I thought it would be less upsetting for Olive if the news was given personally.' He became alarmed. 'Are you saying she's never been told?'

'No. I just wondered why, if her father had money to leave, there's been no correspondence with Olive. Who's the beneficiary?'

Mr Crew shook his head. 'I can't reveal that. It's not Olive, naturally.'

'Why naturally?'

He tut-tutted crossly. 'Why do you think, young woman? She murdered his wife and younger daughter and condemned the poor man to live out his last years in the house where it happened. It was completely unsaleable. Have you any idea how tragic his life became? He was a recluse, never went out, never received visitors. It was only because there were milk bottles on the doorstep that anyone realized there was something wrong. As I say, he'd been dead for three days. Of course he wasn't going to leave money to Olive.'

Roz shrugged. 'Then why did he pay her legal bills? That's hardly consistent, is it?'

He ignored the question. 'There would have been difficulties, in any case. Olive would not have been allowed to benefit financially from the murder of her mother and her sister.'

Roz conceded the point. 'Did he leave much?'

'Surprisingly, yes. He made a tidy sum on the stock market.' His eyes held a wistful regret as he scratched vigorously under his toupee. 'Whether through luck or good judgement he sold everything just before Black Monday. The estate is now valued at half a million pounds.'

'My God!' She was silent for a moment. 'Does Olive know?'

'Certainly, if she reads the newspapers. The amount has been published and, because of the murders, it found its way into the tabloids.'

'Has it gone to the beneficiary yet?'

He frowned heavily, his brows jutting. 'I'm afraid I'm not at liberty to discuss that. The terms of the will preclude it.'

Roz shrugged and tapped her teeth with her pencil. 'Black Monday was October eighty-seven. The murders happened on September ninth, eighty-seven. That's odd, don't you think?'

'In what way?'

'I'd expect him to be so shell-shocked that stocks and shares would be the last thing he'd worry about.'

'Conversely,' said Mr Crew reasonably, 'that very fact would demand that he find something to occupy his mind. He was semi-retired after the murders. Perhaps the financial pages were his only remaining interest.' He looked at his watch. 'Time presses. Was there anything else?'

It was on the tip of Roz's tongue to ask why, if Robert Martin had made a killing on the stock exchange, he had chosen to live out his days in an unsaleable house. Surely a man worth half a million could have afforded to move, irrespective of what his property was worth? What, she wondered, was in that house to make Martin sacrifice himself to it? But she sensed Crew's hostility to her and decided that discretion was the better part of valour. This man was one of the few sources of corroborative information open to her and she would need him again, even though his sympathies clearly lay more with the father than the daughter. 'Just one or two more questions this morning.' She smiled pleasantly, a studied use of charm as insincere as his. 'I'm still feeling my way on this, Mr Crew. To tell you the truth, I'm not yet convinced there's a book in it.' And what an understatement that was. She wasn't intending to write anything. Or was she?

He steepled his fingers and tapped them together impatiently. 'If you remember, Miss Leigh, I made that very point in my letter to you.'

She nodded gravely, pandering to his ego. 'And as I told you, I don't want to write Olive's story simply to cover the pages with lurid details of what she did. But one part of your letter implied an angle that might be worth pursuing. You advised her to plead not guilty to murder on the grounds of diminished responsibility. Had that succeeded, you suggested, she would have been found guilty of manslaughter and would, in all probability, have been sentenced to indefinite detention. I think you went on to estimate ten to fifteen years in a secure unit if she had been given psychiatric treatment and had responded favourably to it.'

'That is correct,' he agreed. 'And I think it was a reasonable estimate. Certainly she would have served nothing like the twenty-five year sentence the judge recommended she serve.'

'But she rejected your advice. Do you know why?'

'Yes. She had a morbid fear of being locked up with mad people and she misunderstood the nature of indefinite detention. She was convinced that it meant endless, and, try as we might, we could not persuade her otherwise.'

'In that case, why didn't you lodge a not guilty plea on her behalf? The very fact that she couldn't grasp what you were telling her implies that she wasn't capable of pleading for herself. You must have thought she had a defence or you wouldn't have suggested it.'

He smiled grimly. 'I don't quite understand why, Miss

Leigh, but you seem to have decided that we failed Olive in some way.' He scribbled a name and address on a piece of paper. 'I suggest you talk to this man before you come to any more erroneous conclusions.' He flicked the paper in her direction. 'He's the barrister we briefed for her defence. Graham Deedes. In the event, she outmanoeuvred us and he was never called to defend her.'

'But why? How could she outmanoeuvre you?' She frowned. 'I'm sorry if I sound critical, Mr Crew, and please believe me, you are wrong in assuming I have reached any unfavourable conclusions.' But was that really true? she wondered. 'I am simply a perplexed onlooker asking questions. If this Deedes was in a position to raise serious doubts over her quote *sanity* unquote, then surely he should have insisted that the court hear her defence whether she wanted it or not. Not to put too fine a point on it, if she was bonkers then the system had a duty to recognize the fact, even if she herself thought she was sane.'

He relented a little. 'You're using very emotive language, Miss Leigh – there was never a question of pleading insanity, only diminished responsibility – but I do take your point. I used the word outmanoeuvred advisedly. The simple truth is that a few weeks before the scheduled date of her trial, Olive wrote to the Home Secretary demanding to know whether she had the right to plead guilty or whether, under British law, this right was denied her. She claimed that undue pressure was being brought to bear to force a lengthy trial that would do nothing to help her but only prolong the agony for her father. The trial date was postponed while tests were carried out to discover if she was fit to plead. She was ruled eminently fit and was allowed to plead guilty.'

'Good Lord!' Roz chewed her lower lip. 'Good Lord!' she said again. 'Were they right?'

'Of course.' He noticed the forgotten cigarette with a curl of ash dripping from its end and, with a gesture of annoyance, stubbed it out. 'She knew exactly what the consequences would be. They even told her what sort of sentence to expect.

Nor would prison have come as any surprise to her. She spent four months on remand before the trial. Frankly, even had she agreed to defend herself the result would still have been the same. The evidence for a plea of diminished responsibility was very flimsy. I doubt we could have swung a jury.'

'And yet in your letter you said that, in spite of everything, you are still convinced she's a psychopath. Why?'

He fingered the file on his desk. 'I saw the photographs of Gwen and Amber's bodies, taken before their removal from the kitchen. It was a slaughterhouse running with blood, the most horrifying scene I have ever witnessed. Nothing will ever convince me that a psychologically stable personality could wreak such atrocity on anyone, let alone on a mother and sister.' He rubbed his eyes. 'No, despite what the psychiatrists say – and you must remember, Miss Leigh, that whether or not psychopathy is a diagnosable disease is under constant debate – Olive Martin is a dangerous woman. I advise you to be extremely wary in your dealings with her.'

Roz switched off her tape-recorder and reached for her briefcase. 'I suppose there's no doubt that she did it.'

He stared at her as if she had said something dirty. 'None at all,' he snapped. 'What are you implying?'

'It just occurs to me that a simple explanation for the discrepancy between the psychiatric evidence of Olive's normality and the quite *ab*normal nature of the crime is that she didn't do it but is covering for whoever did.' She stood up and gave a small shrug in face of his tight-lipped expression. 'It was just a thought. I agree it makes little sense, but nothing about this case makes much sense. I mean, if she really *is* a psychopathic murderess she wouldn't have cared tuppence about putting her father through the mill of a trial. Thank you for your time, Mr Crew. I can see myself out.'

He held up a hand to hold her back. 'Have you read her statement, Miss Leigh?'

'Not yet. Your office promised to send it to me.'

He sorted through the file and took out some stapled sheets of paper. 'This is a copy you may keep,' he told her, passing the pages across the desk. 'I urge you to read it before you go any further. It will persuade you, I think, as it persuaded me, of Olive's guilt.'

Roz picked up the papers. 'You really don't like her, do you?'

His eyes hardened. 'I have no feelings for her, one way or the other. I merely question society's rationale in keeping her alive. She kills people. Don't forget that, Miss Leigh. Good day to you.'

It took Roz an hour and a half to drive back to her flat in London and for most of that time Crew's words – *She kills people* – obscured all other thoughts. She took them out of context and wrote them large across the screen of her mind, dwelling on them with a kind of grim satisfaction.

It was later, curled up in an armchair, that she realized the journey home was a complete blank. She had no recollection, even, of leaving Southampton, a city she wasn't familiar with. *She* could have killed someone, crushing them under the wheels of her car, and she wouldn't have been able to remember when or how it happened. She stared out of her sitting-room window at the dismal grey façades opposite, and she wondered quite seriously about the nature of diminished responsibility.

STATEMENT MADE BY OLIVE MARTIN – 9.9.87 –
9.30 P.M.
PRESENT: DS HAWKSLEY, DS WYATT, E.P. CREW
(SOLICITOR)

My name is Olive Martin. I was born on 8th September, 1964. I live at 22 Leven Road, Dawlington, Southampton. I am employed as a clerk in the Department of Health and Social Security in Dawlington High Street. Yesterday was my birthday. I am twenty-three years old. I have always lived at home. My relationship with my mother and sister has never been close. I get on well with my father. I weigh eighteen and a half stone and my mother and sister have always teased me about it. Their nickname for me was Fattie-Hattie, after Hattie Jacques, the actress. I am sensitive to being laughed at for my size.

Nothing was planned for my birthday and that upset me. My mother said I wasn't a child any more and that I must organize my own treats. I decided to show her I was capable of doing something on my own. I arranged to have today off work with the idea of taking the train to London and spending the day sight-seeing. I did not organize the treat for yesterday, my birthday, in case she had planned a surprise for the evening which is what she did for my sister's twenty-first birthday in July. She did not. We all spent the evening quietly watching television. I went to bed feeling very upset. My parents gave me a pale pink jumper for my birthday present. It was very unflattering and I didn't like it. My sister gave me some new slippers which I did like.

I woke up feeling nervous about going to London on my own. I asked Amber, my sister, to phone in sick and come with me. She has been working in *Glitzy*, a fashion boutique in Dawlington, for about a month. My mother got very angry about this and stopped her. We had an argument over breakfast and my father left for work in the middle of it. He is fifty-five and works three days a week, as a book-keeper for a private haulage company. For many years he owned his own garage. He sold it in 1985 because he had no son to take it over.

The argument became very heated after he left, with my mother blaming me for leading Amber astray. She kept calling me Fattie and laughing at me for being too wet to go to London alone. She said I had been a disappointment to her from the day I was born. Her shouting gave me a headache. I was still very upset that she had done nothing for my birthday and I was jealous because she had given Amber a birthday party.

I went to the drawer and took out the rolling pin. I hit her with it to make her be quiet, then I hit her again when she started screaming. I might have stopped then but Amber started screaming because of what I had done. I had to hit her too. I have never liked noise.

I made myself a cup of tea and waited. I thought I had knocked them out. They were both lying on the floor. After an hour I wondered if they were dead. They were very pale and hadn't moved. I know that if you hold a mirror to someone's mouth and there is no mist on it afterwards it means they are dead. I used the mirror from my handbag. I held it to their mouths for a long time but there was no mist. Nothing.

I became frightened and wondered how to hide the bodies. At first, I thought of putting them in the attic, but they were too heavy to carry upstairs. Then I decided the sea would be the best place as it's only two miles from our house, but I can't drive and, anyway, my father had taken the car. It seemed to me that if I could make them smaller I could fit them into suitcases and carry them that way. I have cut chickens into portions many times. I thought it would be easy to do the same thing with Amber and my mother. I used an axe that we kept in the garage and a carving knife from the kitchen drawer.

It wasn't at all like cutting up chickens. I was tired by two o'clock and I had only managed to take off the heads and the legs and three of the arms. There was a lot of blood and my hands kept slipping. I knew my father would be home soon and that I could never finish by then as I still had to carry the pieces to the sea. I realized it would be better to ring the police and admit what I had done. I felt much happier once I had made this decision.

It never occurred to me to leave the house and pretend that someone else had done it. I don't know why except that my mind was set on hiding the bodies. That's all I thought about. I did not enjoy cutting them up. I had to undress them so I could see where the joints were. I did not know I'd mixed the pieces up. I rearranged them out of decency, but there was so much blood that I couldn't tell which body was which. I must have put my mother's head on Amber's body by mistake. I acted alone.

I am sorry for what I have done. I lost my temper and behaved stupidly. I confirm that everything written here is true.

Signed – OLIVE MARTIN

The statement was a photocopy, covering three typed sheets of A4. On the reverse of the last sheet was a photocopied extract from what was presumably the pathologist's report. It was brief, just a concluding paragraph, and there was no indication to show who had written it.

The injuries to the heads are entirely consistent with a blow or blows from a heavy solid object. These were inflicted before death and were not fatal. While there is no forensic evidence to suggest that the rolling pin was the weapon used, there is none to prove it wasn't. Death in both cases was caused by severance of the carotid artery during the decapitation process. Examination of the axe revealed considerable rusting beneath the blood stains. It is highly probable that it was blunt before it was used to dismember the bodies. The extensive bruising around the cuts on Amber Martin's neck and trunk indicate three or four strikes with an axe before the carving knife was used to cut the throat. It is unlikely that she ever regained consciousness. In Mrs Gwen Martin's case, however, the lacerations to her hands and forearms, inflicted before death, are consistent with her regaining conscious-ness and trying to defend herself. Two stabbing incisions below the jawline imply two failed attempts before her throat was successfully cut with the knife. These attacks were carried out with savage ferocity.

Roz read the pages through then put them on the table beside her and stared into the middle distance. She felt very cold. *Olive Martin took an axe* . . . Oh, God! No wonder Mr Crew called her a psychopath. Three or four strikes with a blunted axe and Amber was still alive! Bile rose in her throat, nauseous, bitter, gagging. *She must stop thinking about it.* But she couldn't, of course. The muffled thuds of metal bouncing off soft flesh boomed loudly in her brain. *How dark and shadowy the flat was.* She reached out abruptly and snapped on a table lamp but the light did nothing to dispel the vivid pictures that crowded her imagination, nightmare visions of a madwoman, frenzied by blood-lust. And the bodies . . .

How far had she committed herself to writing this book? Had she signed anything? Had she received an advance. She couldn't remember and a cold fist of panic squeezed her insides. She was living in a twilight world where so little mattered that day followed day with nothing to distinguish their passing. She thrust herself out of her chair and paced about the floor, cursing Iris for bouncing her, cursing herself for her own insanity, and cursing Mr Crew for not sending her the statement when she'd first written to him.

She seized the telephone and dialled Iris's number. 'Have I signed anything on the Olive Martin book? Why? Because I damn well can't write it, that's why. The woman scares the bloody shit out of me and I am not visiting her again.'

'I thought you liked her.' Iris spoke calmly through a mouthful of supper.

Roz ignored this comment. 'I've got her statement here and the pathologist's report, or his conclusions at least. I should have read them first. I'm not doing it. I will not glorify what she did by writing a book about it. My God, Iris, they were alive when she cut their heads off. Her poor wretched mother tried to ward off the axe. It's making me sick just thinking about it.'

'OK.'

'OK what?'

'Don't write it.'

Roz's eyes narrowed suspiciously. 'I thought you'd argue at least.'

'Why? One thing I've learnt in this business is that you can't force people to write. Correction. You can if you're persistent and manipulative enough, but the result is always below par.' Roz heard her take a drink. 'In any case, Jenny Atherton sent me the first ten chapters of her new book this morning. It's all good stuff on the inherent dangers of a poor self-image, with obesity as number one confidence crippler. She's unearthed a positive goldmine of film and television personalities who've all sunk to untold depths since gaining weight and being forced off camera. It's disgustingly tasteless, of course, like all Jenny's books, but it'll sell. I think you should send all your gen – sorry about the pun – to her. Olive would make rather a dramatic conclusion, don't you think, particularly if we can get a photograph of her in her cell.'

'No chance.'

'No chance of getting a photograph? Shame.'

'No chance of my sending anything to Jenny Atherton. Honestly, Iris,' she stormed, losing her temper, 'you really are beneath contempt. You should be working for the gutter press. You believe in exploiting anyone just as long as they bring in the cash. Jenny Atherton is the last person I'd allow near Olive.'

'Can't see why,' said Iris, now chewing heartily on something. 'I mean if you don't want to write about her and you're refusing ever to visit her again because she makes you sick, why cavil at somebody else having a bash?'

'It's the principle.'

25

'Can't see it, old thing. Sounds more like dog in the manger to me. Listen, I can't dally. We've got people in. At least let me tell Jenny that Olive's up for grabs. She can start from scratch. It's not as though you've got very far, is it?'

'I've changed my mind,' Roz snapped. 'I will do it. Good-bye.' She slammed the receiver down.

At the other end of the line, Iris winked at her husband. 'And you accuse me of not caring,' she murmured. 'Now, what could have been more caring than that?'

'Hobnailed boots,' Gerry Fielding suggested acidly.

Roz read Olive's statement again. 'My relationship with my mother and sister was never close.' She reached for her tape-recorder and rewound the tape, flicking to and fro till she found the piece she wanted. 'I called her Amber because, at the age of two, I couldn't get my tongue round the "*l*" or the "*s*". It suited her. She had lovely honey-blonde hair, and as she grew up she always answered to Amber and never to Alison. She was very pretty . . .'

It meant nothing of course, in itself. There was no unwritten law that said psychopaths were incapable of pretending. Rather the reverse, in fact. But there was a definite softening of the voice when she spoke about her sister, a tenderness which from anyone else Roz would have interpreted as love. And why hadn't she mentioned the fight with her mother? Really, that was very odd. It could well have been her justification for what she did that day.

The chaplain, quite unaware that Olive was behind him, started violently as a large hand fell on his shoulder. It wasn't the first time she had crept up on him and he wondered again, as he had wondered before, how she managed to do it. Her normal gait was a painful shuffle which set his teeth on edge every time he heard its approach. He steeled himself and turned with a friendly smile. 'Why, Olive, how nice to see you. What brings you to the chapel?'

26

The bald eyes were amused. 'Did I frighten you?'

'You startled me. I didn't hear you coming.'

'Probably because you weren't listening. You must listen first if you want to hear, Chaplain. Surely they taught you that much at theological college. God talks in a whisper at the best of times.'

It would be easier, he thought sometimes, if he could despise Olive. But he had never been able to. He feared and disliked her but he did not despise her. 'What can I do for you?'

'You had some new diaries delivered this morning. I'd like one.'

'Are you sure, Olive? These are no different from the others. They still have a religious text for every day of the year and last time I gave you one you tore it up.'

She shrugged. 'But I need a diary so I'm prepared to tolerate the little homilies.'

'They're in the vestry.'

'I know.'

She had not come for a diary. That much he could guess. But what did she plan to steal from the chapel while his back was turned? What *was* there to steal except Bibles and prayer books?

A candle, he told the Governor afterwards. Olive Martin took a six-inch candle from the altar. But she, of course, denied it, and though her cell was searched from top to bottom, the candle was never found.

THREE

Graham Deedes was young, harassed, and black. He saw Roz's surprise as she came into his room, and he frowned his irritation. 'I had no idea black barristers were such a rarity, Miss Leigh.'

'Why do you say that?' she asked curiously, sitting down in the chair he indicated.

'You looked surprised.'

'I am, but not by your colour. You're much younger than I expected.'

'Thirty-three,' he said. 'Not so young.'

'No, but when you were briefed to appear for Olive Martin you can only have been twenty-six or twenty-seven. That *is* young for a murder trial.'

'True,' he agreed, 'but I was only the junior. The QC was considerably older.'

'But you did most of the preparation?'

He nodded. 'Such as there was. It was a very unusual case.'

She took her tape-recorder from her bag. 'Have you any objections to being recorded?'

'Not if you intend to talk about Olive Martin.'

'I do.'

He chuckled. 'Then I've no objections, for the simple reason that I can tell you virtually nothing about her. I saw the woman once, on the day she was sentenced, and I never even spoke to her.'

'But I understood you were preparing a diminished responsibility defence. Didn't you meet her in the course of doing that?'

'No, she refused to see me. I did all my work from material her solicitor sent me.' He smiled ruefully. 'Which wasn't much, I have to say. We would, quite literally, have been laughed out of court if we'd had to proceed, so I was quite relieved when the judge ruled her guilty plea admissible.'

'What arguments would you have used if you had been called?'

'We planned two different approaches.' Deedes considered for a moment. 'One, that the balance of her mind was temporarily disturbed – as far as I recall it was the day after her birthday and she was deeply upset because instead of paying her attention the family teased her about being fat.' He raised his eyebrows in query and Roz nodded. 'In addition, I believe, she made a reference in her statement to not liking noise. We did manage to find a doctor who was prepared to give evidence that noise can cause such violent distress in some people that they may act out of character in trying to stop it. There was no psychiatric or medical evidence, however, to prove that Olive was of this type.' He tapped his forefingers together. 'Two, we were going to work backwards from the appalling savagery of the crime and invite the court to draw what we hoped to persuade them was an inescapable inference – that Olive was a psychopath. We hadn't a cat's chance on the balance of her mind argument, but the psychopathy' – he made a see-saw motion with one hand – 'maybe. We found a professor of psychology who was prepared to stick his neck out after seeing the photographs of the bodies.'

'But did he ever *talk* to her?'

He shook his head. 'There wasn't time and she wouldn't have seen him anyway. She was quite determined to plead guilty. I assume Mr Crew told you that she wrote to the Home Office demanding an independent psychiatric report to prove that she was competent to plead?' Roz nodded. 'After that there was really nothing we could do. It was an extraordinary business,' he mused. 'Most defendants fall over themselves to come up with excuses.'

'Mr Crew seems convinced she's a psychopath.'

'I think I'd agree with him.'

'Because of what she did to Amber and her mother? You don't have any other evidence?'

'No. Isn't that enough?'

'Then how do you explain that five psychiatrists have all diagnosed her normal?' Roz looked up. 'She's had several sessions, as far as I can gather, in the prison.'

'Who told you this? Olive?' He looked sceptical.

'Yes, but I spoke to the Governor afterwards and she verified it.'

He shrugged. 'I wouldn't place too much reliance on it. You'd have to see the reports. It depends who wrote them and why they were testing her.'

'Still, it's odd, don't you think?'

'In what way?'

'You'd expect some measurable level of sociopathic behaviour over a period of time if she was a psychopath.'

'Not necessarily. Prison may be the sort of controlled environment that suits her. Or perhaps her particular psychopathy was directed against her family. Something brought it on that day and once rid of them, she settled down.' He shrugged again. 'Who knows? Psychiatry is hardly an exact science.' He was silent for a moment. 'In my experience, well-adjusted people don't hack their mothers and their sisters to death. You do know they were still alive when she set to with the axe?' He smiled grimly. 'She knew it, too. Don't imagine she didn't.'

Roz frowned. 'There is another explanation,' she said slowly, 'but the trouble is, while it fits the facts, it's too absurd to be credible.'

He waited. 'Well?' he asked at last.

'Olive didn't do it.' She saw his amused disbelief and hurried on. 'I'm not saying I go along with it, I'm just saying that it fits the facts.'

'*Your* facts,' he pointed out gently. 'It seems to me you're being a little selective in what you choose to believe.'

'Maybe.' Roz remembered her extremes of mood of the previous evening.

He watched her for a moment. 'She knew a great deal about the murders for someone who wasn't responsible for them.'

'Do you think so?'

'Of course. Don't you?'

'She doesn't say anything about her mother trying to ward off the axe and the carving knife. But that must have been the most frightening part. Why didn't she mention it?'

'Shame. Embarrassment. Traumatic amnesia. You'd be surprised how many murderers blot what they've done from their memories. Sometimes it's years before they come to terms with their guilt. In any case, I doubt the struggle with her mother was as frightening for Olive as you suggest. Gwen Martin was a tiny woman, five feet at the most, I would think. Physically, Olive took after her father, so containing her mother would have been easy for her.' He saw the hesitation in Roz's eyes. 'Let me put a question to *you*. Why would Olive confess to two murders she didn't commit?'

'Because people do.'

'Not when they have their lawyers present, Miss Leigh. I accept that it happened, which is why new rules were introduced governing the taking of evidence, but Olive did not fall into the category of either forced confession or having her confession subsequently tampered with. She had legal representation throughout. So I repeat, why would she confess to something she didn't do?'

'To protect someone else?' She was relieved they weren't in court. He was a bruising cross-examiner.

'Who?'

She shook her head. 'I don't know.'

'There was no one else except her father, and he was at work. The police had him thoroughly checked and his alibi was unbreakable.'

'There was Olive's lover.'

He stared at her.

'She told me she'd had an abortion. Presumably, then, she must have had a lover.'

He found that very entertaining. 'Poor Olive.' He laughed. 'Well, I guess an abortion is as good a way as any of keeping her end up. Especially' – he laughed again – 'if everyone believes her. I shouldn't be too gullible, if I were you.'

She smiled coldly. 'Perhaps it's you who is being gullible by subscribing to the cheap male view that a woman like Olive could not attract a lover.'

Deedes studied her set face and wondered what was driving her. 'You're right, Miss Leigh, it was cheap, and I apologise.' He raised his hands briefly, then dropped them again. 'But this is the first I have heard about an abortion. Let's just say it strikes me as a little unlikely. And somewhat convenient, perhaps? It's not something you can ever really check, is it, not without Olive's permission. If laymen were allowed to browse through other people's medical records some very delicate secrets might be exposed.'

Roz regretted her waspish remark. Deedes was a nicer man than Crew and hadn't deserved it. 'Olive mentioned an abortion. *I* assumed the lover. But perhaps she was raped. Babies can be conceived as easily in hate as in love.'

He shrugged. 'Beware of being used, Miss Leigh. Olive Martin dominated the court the day she appeared in it. I had the impression then, and still have it, that it was *we* who were dancing to *her* tune not she to ours.'

Dawlington was a small eastern suburb of Southampton, once an isolated village, now swallowed up in the great urban expansion of the twentieth century. It maintained an identity of a sort by the busy trunk-roads that gave it tarmac boundaries but, even so, the place was easy to miss. Only a tired peeling shop sign, advertising *Dawlington Newsagents*, alerted Roz to the fact that she had left one suburb and entered another. She drew into the kerb before a left-hand turning and consulted her map. She was, presumably, in the High Street and the road to the left – she squinted at the sign – was Ainsley Street. She ran her finger across the grid. 'Ainsley Street,' she muttered. 'Come on, you bugger, where are you? OK. Leven Road. First right, second left.' With a glance in her driving mirror, she pulled out into the traffic and turned right.

Olive's story, she thought, grew odder by the minute, as she studied number twenty-two, Leven Road, from her parked car. Mr Crew had said the house was unsaleable. She had imagined something out of a Gothic novel, twelve months of dereliction and decay since the death of Robert Martin, a house condemned by the haunting horror in its kitchen. Instead, the reality was a cheerful little semi, freshly painted, with pink, white, and red geraniums nodding in boxes beneath its windows. Who, she wondered, had bought it? Who was brave enough (or ghoulish enough?) to live with the ghosts of that tragic family? She double-checked the address from press cuttings she had put together that morning in the archives basement of the local newspaper. There was no mistake. A black and white photograph of 'The House of Horror' showed this same neat semi, but without its window-boxes.

She climbed out of the car and crossed the road. The house remained stubbornly silent to her ring on the doorbell, so she went next door and tried there. A young woman answered with a sleepy toddler clinging round her neck. 'Yes?'

'Hello,' said Roz, 'I'm sorry to bother you.' She indicated towards her right. 'It's your neighbours I really want to talk to but there's no one in. Have you any idea when they might be back?'

The young woman thrust out a hip to support the child more easily and subjected Roz to a penetrating glare. 'There's nothing to see, you know. You're wasting your time.'

'I'm sorry?'

'They pulled the innards out of the house and revamped the whole of the inside. They've done it up nice. There's nothing to see, no blood stains, no spirits roaming about, nothing.' She pressed the child's head against her shoulder, a casual, proprietary gesture, a statement of tender motherhood at odds with the hostility in her voice. 'You want to know what I think? You should see a psychiatrist. It's the likes of you who're the real sick people of society.' She prepared to close the door.

Roz raised her palms in a gesture of surrender. She smiled

33

sheepishly. 'I haven't come to gawp,' she said. 'My name is Rosalind Leigh and I'm working in co-operation with the late Mr Martin's solicitor.'

The woman eyed her suspiciously. 'Oh, yeah? What's his name?'

'Peter Crew.'

'You could of got it from the paper.'

'I have a letter from him. May I show it to you? It will prove I am who I say I am.'

'Go on then.'

'It's in the car. I'll fetch it.' She retrieved her briefcase hurriedly from the boot, but when she got back, the door was closed. She rang several times and waited for ten minutes on the doorstep, but it was obvious the young woman had no intention of answering. From a room above came the wail of a baby. Roz listened to the mother's soothing tones as she climbed the stairs, then, thoroughly annoyed with herself, she retreated to the car and pondered her next step.

The press cuttings were disappointing. It was names she wanted, names of friends or neighbours, even old school teachers, who could give her background detail. But the local newspaper had, like the nationals, sensationalized the crime's horror without uncovering any details about Olive's life or why she might have done it. There were the usual quotes from 'neighbours' – all anonymous and all wise after the event – but they were so uniformly unenlightening that Roz suspected imaginative journalism at work.

'No, I'm not surprised,' said a neighbour, 'shocked and appalled, yes, but not surprised. She was a strange girl, unfriendly, kept herself to herself. Not like the sister. She was the attractive, outgoing one. We all liked Amber.' 'The parents found her very difficult. She wouldn't mix or make friends. She was shy, I suppose, because of her size but she had a way of looking at you that wasn't normal.'

Beyond the sensationalism, there had been nothing to write about. There was no police investigation to report – Olive had phoned them herself, had confessed to the crime in the presence of her solicitor, and had been charged with murder. Because she had pleaded guilty there had been no salacious details from a lengthy trial, no names of friends or associates to draw on, and her sentencing had rated a single paragraph under the headline: TWENTY-FIVE YEARS FOR BRUTAL MURDERS. A conspiracy of journalistic apathy seemed to surround the whole event. Of the five cardinal Ws of the journalist's creed – Where?, When?, What?, Who?, and Why? – the first four had been amply covered. Everyone knew what had happened, who had done it, where, and when. But no one, it seemed, knew why. Nor, and this was the real puzzle, had anyone actually asked. Could teasing alone really drive a young woman to such a pitch of anger that she would hack her family to pieces?

With a sigh, Roz switched on the radio and fed Pavarotti into the tape-deck. Bad choice, she thought, as 'Nessun Dorma' flooded the car and brought back bitter memories of a summer she would rather forget. Strange how a piece of music could be so evocative, but then the path to separation had been choreographed around the television screen with 'Nessun Dorma' triggering the stops and starts of their rows. She could remember every detail of every World Cup football match. They were the only peaceful periods in a summer of war. How much better, she thought wearily, if she had called a halt then instead of dragging the misery out to its far more terrible conclusion.

A net curtain, in the semi to the right, number 24, twitched behind a Neighbourhood Watch sticker which proclaimed itself loudly against the glass. A case, Roz wondered, of locking the stable door after the horse had bolted? Or was that same net curtain twitching the day Olive wielded her chopper? Two garages filled the gap between the houses, but it was possible the occupants had heard something. '*Olive Martin took an axe and gave her mother forty whacks . . .*' The words circled in her brain as they had done, on and off, for days.

She resumed her contemplation of number 22, but watched the net curtain out of the corner of her eye. It moved again, plucked by prying fingers, and she felt unreasonably irritated by the busybody spying on her. It was an empty, wasted life that had time to stand and stare. What sort of interfering old bitch inhabited there, she wondered? The frustrated spinster who got off on voyeurism? Or the bored and boring wife with nothing better to do than find fault? Then something clicked inside her head, a realignment of thought like the points on a railway line. Just the sort of busybody she wanted, of course, but why had that not occurred to her immediately? Really, she worried about herself. She spent so much time in neutral now, just listening to the footfalls, leading nowhere, that echoed in her memory.

A frail old man opened the door, a small, shrunken person with transparent skin and bowed shoulders. 'Come in, come in,' he said, standing back and ushering her into his corridor. 'I heard what you said to Mrs Blair. She won't talk to you, and I'll tell you something else, it wouldn't help you if she did. They only came four years ago when the first youngster was on the way. Didn't know the family at all and, as far as I know, never spoke to poor old Bob. What shall I say? She's got a nerve. Typical of today's youngsters. Always wanting something for nothing.' He muttered on, leading the way into his living room. 'Resents living in a goldfish bowl but forgets that they got the house for a pittance just because it *was* a goldfish bowl. Ted and Dorothy Clarke virtually gave the place away because they couldn't stand it any longer. What shall I say? Ungrateful girl. Imagine what it's like for those of us who've always lived here. No bargains for us. We have to put up with it, don't we? Sit down. Sit down.'

'Thank you.'

'You're from Mr Crew, you say. They found the child yet?'

He stared into her face with disconcertingly bright blue eyes.

Roz stared back, her mind racing. 'That's not my province,' she said carefully, 'so I'm not sure where they are on that one. I'm conducting a follow-up of Olive's case. You did know that Mr Crew is still representing her?'

'What's to represent?' he asked. His eyes strayed in disappointment. 'Poor little Amber. They should never have made her give it up. I said it would cause trouble.'

Roz sat very still and stared at the worn carpet.

'People don't listen, of course,' he said crossly. 'You give them well-meant advice and they tell you you're interfering. What shall I say? I could see where it would lead.' He fell into a resentful silence.

'You're talking about the child,' said Roz at last.

He looked at her curiously. 'If they'd found him, you'd know.'

It was a boy, then. 'Oh, yes.'

'Bob did his best but there's rules about these things. They'd signed him away, given up their stake, so to speak. You'd think it was different where money's concerned, but there's no contest for the likes of us against the government. What shall I say? They're all thieves.'

Roz made what she could of this speech. Was he talking about Mr Martin's will? Was this child (Amber's child?) the beneficiary? On the pretext of looking for a handkerchief, she opened her bag and surreptitiously switched on her tape-recorder. This conversation, she felt, was going to be tortuous. 'You mean,' she tried tentatively, 'that the government will get the money?'

'Course.'

She nodded wisely. 'Things aren't exactly stacked in our favour.'

'Never are. Damn thieves. Take every last penny off you. And what for? To make sure the skivers go on breeding like rabbits at the expense of the rest of us. Makes you sick. There's a woman in the council houses has five children, and all by different fathers. What shall I say? They're all worthless. Is that the sort of breeding stock we want in this country? Good-for-nothings, with not a brain between them. Where's the sense in encouraging a woman like that? Should have sterilized her and put a stop to it.'

Roz was noncommittal, unwilling to be drawn down a cul-de-sac, even more unwilling to antagonize him. 'I'm sure you're right.'

'Course I'm right, and it'll be the death of the species. Before the dole, she'd have starved to death and her brood with her, and quite right too. What shall I say? It's the survival of the fittest in this world. There's no other species molly-coddles its rotten apples the way we do, and certainly none that pays its rotten apples to produce more rotten apples. Makes you sick. How many children have you got?'

Roz smiled faintly. 'None, I'm afraid. I'm not married.'

'See what I mean?' He cleared his throat noisily. 'Makes you sick. What shall I say? It's your sort, decent sort, should have the children.'

'How many do you have, Mr – er—?' She made a play of consulting her diary, as if looking for his name.

'Hayes. Mr Hayes. Two lads. Fine boys. Grown up now, of course. Only the one granddaughter,' he added morosely. 'It's not right. I keep telling them they've a duty to their class but I could be pissing in the wind – excuse my French – for all the good it does.' His face set into familiar lines of irritation. His obsession was clearly a deep-seated one.

Roz knew she had to take the plunge or one hobby horse would follow another as inexorably as night follows day. 'You're a very perceptive man, Mr Hayes. Why were you so sure that making Amber give up her son would cause trouble?'

'Stands to reason there'd come a time when he was wanted again. It's sod's law, isn't it? The minute you throw something out, that's the minute you find you needed it after all. But it's too late by then. It's gone. My wife was one, forever throwing things away, pots of paint, carpet, and two years later you needed to patch. Me, I hoard. What shall I say? I value everything.'

'So, are you saying Mr Martin wasn't bothered about his grandson before the murders?'

He touched the end of his nose with thumb and forefinger. 'Who's to say? He kept his own counsel, did Bob. It was Gwen who insisted on signing the kid away. Wouldn't have it in the house. Understandable, I suppose, in view of Amber's age.'

'How old was she?'

He frowned. 'I thought Mr Crew knew all this.'

She smiled. 'He does but, as I told you, it's not my province. I'm just interested, that's all. It seems so tragic.'

'It is that. Thirteen,' he said wistfully. 'She was thirteen. Poor little kid. Didn't know anything about anything. Some lout at the school was responsible.' He jerked his head towards the back of his house. 'Parkway Comprehensive.'

'Is that the school Amber and Olive went to?'

'Hah!' His old eyes were amused. 'Gwen wouldn't have stood for that. She sent them to the posh Convent where they learnt their times tables and didn't learn the facts of life.'

'Why didn't Amber have an abortion? Were they Catholics?' She thought again about Olive and foetuses being washed down the sink.

'They didn't know she was pregnant, did they? Thought it was puppy fat.' He cackled suddenly. 'Rushed her off to hospital with suspected appendicitis and out pops a bouncing baby boy. They got away with it, too. Best kept secret I've ever come across. Even the nuns didn't know.'

'But you knew,' she prompted.

'The wife guessed,' he said owlishly. 'It was obvious something untoward had happened, and not appendicitis neither. Gwen was well-nigh hysterical the night it happened and my Jeannie put two and two together. Still, we know how to keep our mouths shut. No reason to make life harder for the kid. It wasn't her fault.'

Roz did some rapid mental arithmetic. Amber was two years younger than Olive which would have made her twenty-six if she were still alive. 'Her son's thirteen,' she said, 'and due to inherit half a million pounds. I wonder why Mr Crew can't find him. There must be records of the adoption.'

'I heard they'd found traces.' The old man clicked his false teeth with disappointment. 'But, there, it was probably just rumour, Brown Australia,' he muttered with disgust, as if that explained everything. 'I ask you.'

Roz allowed this cryptic remark to pass unchallenged. Time enough to puzzle over it later without claiming ignorance yet again. 'Tell me about Olive,' she invited. 'Were you surprised that she did what she did?'

'I hardly knew the girl.' He sucked his teeth. 'And you don't feel surprised when people you know get hacked to death, young lady, you feel bloody sick. It did for my Jeannie. She was never the same afterwards, died a couple of years later.'

'I'm sorry.'

He nodded, but it was clearly an old wound that had healed. 'Used to see the child come and go but she wasn't a great talker. Shy, I suppose.'

'Because she was fat?'

He pursed his lips thoughtfully. 'Maybe. Jeannie said she was teased a lot, but I've known fat girls who've been the life and soul of the party. It was her nature, I think, to look on the black side. Never laughed much. No sense of humour. That sort doesn't make friends easily.'

'And Amber did?'

'Oh, yes. She was very popular.' He glanced back down the passages of time. 'She was a pretty girl.'

'Was Olive jealous of her?'

'Jealous?' Mr Hayes looked surprised. 'I've never thought about it. What shall I say? They always seemed very fond of each other.'

Roz shrugged her bewilderment. 'Then why did Olive kill her? And why mutilate the bodies? It's very odd.'

He scowled suspiciously. 'I thought you were representing her. You should know if anyone does.'

'She won't say.'

He stared out of the window. 'Well, then.'

Well then what? 'Do you know why?'

40

'Jeannie reckoned it was hormones.'

'Hormones?' Roz echoed blankly. 'What sort of hormones?'

'You know.' He looked embarrassed. 'Monthly ones.'

'Ah.' PMT? she wondered. But it was hardly a subject she could pursue with him. He was of a generation where menstruation was never mentioned. 'Did Mr Martin ever say why he thought she did it?'

He shook his head. 'The subject didn't arise. What shall I say? We saw very little of him afterwards. He talked about his will once or twice, and the child – it was all he thought about.' He cleared his throat again. 'He became a recluse, you know. Wouldn't have anyone in the house, not even the Clarkes, and there was a time when Ted and he were close as brothers.' His mouth turned down at the corners. 'It was Ted started it, mind. Took against Bob for some reason and wouldn't go in. And others followed suit, of course, the way they do. Reckon I was his only friend at the end. It was me as realized something was wrong, seeing the milk bottles outside.'

'But why did he stay? He was rich enough to let number twenty-two go for peanuts. You'd have thought he'd go any-where rather than stay with the ghosts of his family.'

Mr Hayes muttered to himself. 'Never understood it myself. Perhaps he wanted his friends about him.'

'You said the Clarkes moved. Where did they go?'

He shook his head. 'No idea. They upped and went one morning without a word to anyone. A removal van took out their furniture three days later and the house stood empty for a year till the Blairs bought it. Never heard a word from them since. No forwarding address. Nothing. What shall I say? We were good friends, the six of us, and I'm the only one left now. Strange business.'

Very strange, thought Roz. 'Can you remember which estate agent sold the house?'

'Peterson's, but you won't learn anything from them. Little Hitlers,' he said, 'all bursting with self-importance. Told me to mind my own business when I went in and asked what was what. It's a free world, I pointed out, no reason why a man shouldn't ask after his friends, but oh, no, they had instructions of confidentiality or some such rubbish. What shall I say? Made out it was me the Clarkes were cutting their ties with. Hah! More likely Bob, I told them, or ghosts. And they said if I spread those sort of rumours, they'd take action. You know who I blame. The estate agents' federation, if there is one, which I doubt . . .' He rambled on, venting his spleen out of loneliness and frustration.

Roz felt sorry for him. 'Do you see much of your sons?' she asked when he drew to a halt.

'Now and then.'

'How old are they?'

'Forties,' he said after a moment's thought.

'What did they think of Olive and Amber?'

He pinched his nose again and waggled it from side to side. 'Never knew them. Left home long before either of the girls reached their teens.'

'They didn't baby-sit or anything like that?'

'My lads? You wouldn't catch them baby-sitting.' His old eyes moistened, and he nodded towards the sideboard where photographs of two young men in uniform crowded the surface. 'Fine boys. Soldiers.' He thrust out his chest. 'Took my advice and joined up. Mind, they're out of jobs now, what with the bloomin' regiment being cut from under them. It makes you sick when you think them and me's served Queen and country for nigh on fifty years between us. Did I tell you I was in the desert during the war?' He looked vacantly about the room. 'There's a photograph somewhere of Churchill and Monty in a jeep. We all got one, us boys who were out there. Worth a bob or two, I should think. Now where is it?' He became agitated.

Roz picked up her briefcase. 'Don't worry about it now, Mr Hayes. Perhaps I could see it next time I come.'

'You coming back?'

'I'd like to, if it's no trouble.' She took a card from her handbag, flicking the switch on the recorder at the same time.

'That's my name and telephone number. Rosalind Leigh. It's a London number but I'll be down here regularly over the next few weeks, so if you feel like a chat' – she smiled encouragingly and stood up – 'give me a ring.'

He regarded her with astonishment. 'A chat. Goodness me. A youngster like you has better things to do with her time.'

Too right, she thought, but I do need information. Her smile, like Mr Crew's, was false. 'I'll be seeing you then, Mr Hayes.'

He pushed himself awkwardly out of his chair and held out a marbled hand. 'It's been a pleasure meeting you, Miss Leigh. What shall I say? It's not often an old man sees charming young ladies out of the blue.'

He spoke with such sincerity that she felt chastened by her own lack of it. Why, oh why, she wondered, was the human condition so damn bloody?

FOUR

██████

R oz found the local convent with the help of a policeman. 'That'll be St Angela's,' he told her. 'Left at the
traffic lights and left again. Large red-brick building
set back from the road. You can't miss it. It's the
only decent piece of architecture still standing round
there.'

It reared in solid Victorian magnificence above its surrounding clutter of cheap concrete obsolescence, a monument to
education in a way that none of the modern prefabricated
schools could ever be. Roz entered the front door with a
sense of familiarity, for this was a schooling she recognized.
Glimpses through classroom doors of desks, blackboards,
shelves of books, attentive girls in neat uniforms. A place
of quiet learning, where parents could dictate the sort of
education their daughters received simply by threatening to
remove the pupils and withhold the fees. And whenever
parents had that power the requirements were always the
same: discipline, structure, results. She peeped through a
window into what was obviously the library. Well, well, no
wonder Gwen had insisted on sending the girls here. Roz
would put money on Parkway Comprehensive being an
unruly bedlam where English, History, Religion and Geogra-
phy were all taught as the single subject of General Studies,
spelling was an anachronism, French an extra-curricular
activity, Latin unheard of, and Science a series of chats about
the greenhouse effect. . . .

'Can I help you?'

She turned with a smile. 'I hope so.'

A smart woman in her late fifties had paused in front of a door marked Secretary. 'Are you a prospective parent?'

'I wish I were. It's a lovely school. No children,' she explained at the woman's look of puzzled enquiry.

'I see. So how can I help you?'

Roz took out one of her cards. 'Rosalind Leigh,' she introduced herself. 'Would it be possible for me to talk to the headmistress?'

'Now?' said the woman in surprise.

'Yes, if she's free. If not, I can make an appointment and come back later.'

The woman took the card and read it closely. 'May I ask what you want to talk about?'

Roz shrugged. 'Just some general information about the school and the sort of girls who come here.'

'Would you be the Rosalind Leigh who wrote *Through the Looking Glass* by any chance?'

Roz nodded. *Through the Looking Glass*, her last book and her best, had sold well and won some excellent reviews. A study of the changing perceptions of female beauty down the ages, she wondered now how she had ever managed to summon the energy to write it. A labour of love, she thought, because the subject had fascinated her.

'I've read it.' The other smiled. 'I agreed with very few of your conclusions but it was extremely thought-provoking none the less. You write lovely prose, but I'm sure you know that.'

Roz laughed. She felt an immediate liking for the woman. 'At least you're honest.'

The other looked at her watch. 'Come into my office. I have some parents to see in half an hour, but I'm happy to give you general information until then. This way.' She opened the secretary's door and ushered Roz through to an adjoining office. 'Sit down, do. Coffee?'

'Please.' Roz took the chair indicated and watched her busy herself with a kettle and some cups. 'Are you the headmistress?'

'I am.'

'They were always nuns in my day.'

'So you're a convent girl. I thought you might be. Milk?'

'Black and no sugar, please.'

She placed a steaming cup on the desk in front of Roz and sat down opposite her. 'In fact I am a nun. Sister Bridget. My order gave up wearing the habit quite some time ago. We found it tended to create an artificial barrier between us and the rest of society.' She chuckled. 'I don't know what it is about religious uniforms, but people try to avoid you if they can. I suppose they feel they have to be on their best behaviour. It's very frustrating. The conversation is often so stilted.'

Roz crossed her legs and relaxed into the chair. She was unaware of it but her eyes betrayed her. They brimmed with all the warmth and humour that, a year ago, had been the outward expression of her personality. Bitterness, it seemed, could only corrode so far. 'It's probably guilt,' she said. 'We have to guard our tongues in case we provoke the sermon we know we deserve.' She sipped the coffee. 'What made you think I was a convent girl?'

'Your book. You get very hot under the collar about established religions. I guessed you were either a lapsed Jew or a lapsed Catholic. The Protestant yoke is easier to discard, being far less oppressive in the first place.'

'In fact I wasn't a lapsed anything when I wrote *Through the Looking Glass*,' said Roz mildly. 'I was a good Catholic still.'

Sister Bridget interpreted the cynicism in her voice. 'But not now.'

'No. God died on me.' She smiled slightly at the look of understanding on the other woman's face. 'You read about it, I suppose. I can't applaud your taste in newspapers.'

'I'm an educator, my dear. We take the tabloids here as well as the broadsheets.' She didn't drop her gaze or show embarrassment, for which Roz was grateful. 'Yes, I read about it and I would have punished God, too. It was very cruel of Him.'

Roz nodded. 'If I remember right,' she said, reverting to

her book, 'religion is confined to only one chapter of my book. Why did you find my conclusions so hard to agree with?'

'Because they are all drawn from a single premiss. As I can't accept the premiss, then I can't agree with the conclusions.'

Roz wrinkled her brow. 'Which premiss?'

'That beauty is only skin deep.'

Roz was surprised. 'And you don't think that's true?'

'No, not as a general rule.'

'I'm speechless. And you a nun!'

'Being a nun has nothing to do with it. I'm streetwise.'

It was an unconscious echo of Olive. 'You really believe that beautiful people are beautiful all the way through? I can't accept that. By the same token ugly people are ugly all the way through.'

'You're putting words into my mouth, my dear.' Sister Bridget was amused. 'I am simply questioning the idea that beauty is a surface quality.' She cradled her coffee cup in her hands. 'It's a comfortable thought, of course – it means we can all feel good about ourselves – but beauty, like wealth, is a moral asset. The wealthy can afford to be law abiding, generous and kind. The very poor cannot. Even kindness is a struggle when you don't know where your next penny is coming from.' She gave a quirky smile. 'Poverty is only uplifting when you can choose it.'

'I wouldn't disagree with that, but I don't see the connection between beauty and wealth.'

'Beauty cushions you against the negative emotions that loneliness and rejection inspire. Beautiful people are prized – they always have been, you made that point yourself – so they have less reason to be spiteful, less reason to be jealous, less reason to covet what they can't have. They tend to be the focus of all those emotions, rarely the instigators of them.' She shrugged. 'You will always have exceptions – most of them you uncovered in your book – but, in my experience, if a person is attractive then that attractiveness runs deep. You can argue which comes first, the inner beauty or the outer, but they do tend to walk together.'

'So if you're rich and beautiful the pearly gates will swing open for you?' She smiled cynically. 'That's a somewhat radical philosophy for a Christian, isn't it? I thought Jesus preached the exact opposite. Something like it's easier for a camel to pass through the eye of a needle than for a rich man to enter the kingdom of heaven.'

Sister Bridget laughed good-humouredly. 'Yours was obviously an excellent convent.' She stirred her coffee absent-mindedly with a biro. 'Yes, He did say that but, if you put it in context, it supports my view, I think, rather than detracts from it. If you remember, a wealthy young man asked Him how he could have eternal life. Jesus said: keep the commandments. The youth answered: I have kept them, since childhood, but what more can I do. If you want to be perfect, said Jesus – and I emphasize the *perfect* – sell all you have and give it to the poor, *then* follow me. The young man went away sorrowing because he had many possessions and could not bring himself to sell them. It was then Jesus made the reference to the camel and the eye of the needle. He was, you see, talking about perfection, not goodness.' She sucked the end of her biro. 'In fairness to the young man, I have always assumed that to sell his possessions would have meant selling houses and businesses with tenants and employees in them, so the moral dilemma would have been a difficult one. But what I think Jesus was saying was this: so far you have been a good man, but to test how good you really are, reduce yourself to abject poverty. Perfection is to follow me and keep the commandments when you are so poor that stealing and lying are a way of life if you want to be sure of waking up the next morning. An impossible goal.' She sipped her coffee. 'I could be wrong, of course.' There was a twinkle in her eye.

'Well, I'm not going to argue the toss with you on that,' said Roz bluntly. 'I suspect I'd be on a hiding to nothing. But I reckon you're on very bumpy ground with your beauty is a moral asset argument. What about the pitfalls of vanity and arrogance? And how do you explain that some of the nicest people I know are, by no stretch of the imagination, beautiful?'

Sister Bridget laughed again, a happy sound. 'You keep twisting my words. I have never said that to be nice you have to be beautiful. I merely dispute your assertion that beautiful people are *not* nice. My observation is that very often they are. At the risk of labouring the point, they can afford to be.'

'Then we're back to my previous question. Does that mean ugly people are very often not nice?'

'It doesn't follow, you know, any more than saying poor people are invariably wicked. It just means the tests are harder.' She cocked her head on one side. 'Take Olive and Amber as a case in point. After all, that's why you've really come to see me. Amber led a charmed life. She was quite the loveliest child I've ever seen and with a nature to match. Everyone adored her. Olive, on the other hand, was universally unpopular. She had few redeeming features. She was greedy, deceitful, and often cruel. I found her very hard to like.'

Roz made no attempt to deny her interest. The conversation had, in any case, been about them from the beginning. 'Then you were being tested as much as she was. Did you fail? Was it impossible to like her?'

'It was very difficult until Amber joined the school. Olive's best quality was that she loved her sister, without reserve and quite unselfishly. It was really rather touching. She fussed over Amber like a mother hen, often ignoring her own interests to promote Amber's. I've never seen such affection between sisters.'

'So why did she kill her?'

'Why indeed? It's time that question was asked.' The older woman drummed her fingers impatiently on the desk. 'I visit her when I can. She won't tell me, and the only explanation I can offer is that her love, which was obsessional, turned to a hate that was equally obsessional. Have you met Olive?'

Roz nodded.

'What did you make of her?'

'She's bright.'

'Yes, she is. She could have gone to university if only the then headmistress had managed to persuade her mother of the advantages. I was a lowly teacher in those days.' She sighed. 'But Mrs Martin was a decided woman, and Olive very much under her thumb. There was nothing we, as a school, could do to make her change her mind. The two girls left together, Olive with three good A-levels and Amber with four rather indifferent O-levels.' She sighed again. 'Poor Olive. She went to work as a cashier in a supermarket while Amber, I believe, tried her hand at hairdressing.'

'Which supermarket was it?'

'Pettit's in the High Street. But the place went out of business years ago. It's an off-licence now.'

'She was working at the local DHSS, wasn't she, at the time of the murders?'

'Yes and doing very well, I believe. Her mother pushed her into it, of course.' Sister Bridget reflected for a moment. 'Funnily enough, I bumped into Olive quite by chance just a week or so before the murders. I was pleased to see her. She looked' – she paused – 'happy. Yes, I think happy is exactly the word for it.'

Roz let the silence drift while she busied herself with her own thoughts. There was so much about this story that didn't make sense. 'Did she get on with her mother?' she asked at last.

'I don't know. I always had the impression she preferred her father. It was Mrs Martin who wore the trousers, of course. If there were choices to be made, it was invariably she who made them. She was very domineering, but I don't recall Olive voicing any antagonism towards her. She was a difficult woman to talk to. Very correct, always. She appeared to watch every word she said in case she gave herself away.' She shook her head. 'But I never did find out what it was that needed hiding.'

There was a knock on the connecting door and a woman popped her head inside. 'Mr and Mrs Barker are waiting, Sister. Are you ready for them?'

'Two minutes, Betty.' She smiled at Roz. 'I'm sorry. I'm not sure I've been very helpful. Olive had one friend while she was here, not a friend as you or I would know it, but a girl with whom she talked rather more than she did with any of the others. Her married name is Wright – Geraldine Wright – and she lives in a village called Wooling about ten miles north of here. If she's willing to talk to you then I'm sure she can tell you more than I have. The name of her house is Oaktrees.'

Roz jotted down the details in her diary. 'Why do I have the feeling you were expecting me?'

'Olive showed me your letter the last time I saw her.'

Roz stood up, gathering her briefcase and handbag together. She regarded the other woman thoughtfully. 'It may be that the only book I can write is a cruel one.'

'I don't think so.'

'No, I don't think so either.' She paused by the door. 'I've enjoyed meeting you.'

'Come and see me again,' said Sister Bridget. 'I'd like to know how you get on.'

Roz nodded. 'I suppose there's no doubt that she did it?'

'I really don't know,' said the other woman slowly. 'I've wondered, of course. The whole thing is so shocking that it *is* hard to accept.' She seemed to come to a conclusion. 'Be very careful, my dear. The only certainty about Olive is that she lies about almost everything.'

Roz jotted down the name of the arresting officer from the press clippings and called in at the police station on her way back to London. 'I'm looking for a DS Hawksley,' she told the young constable behind the front desk. 'He was with this division in nineteen eighty-seven. Is he still here?'

He shook his head. 'Jacked it in, twelve – eighteen months ago.' He leaned his elbows on the counter and eyed her over with an approving glance. 'Will I do instead?'

Her lips curved involuntarily. 'Perhaps you can tell me where he went?'

'Sure. He opened a restaurant in Wenceslas Street. Lives in the flat above it.'

'And how do I find Wenceslas Street?'

'Well, now' – he rubbed his jaw thoughtfully – 'by far the easiest way is to hang around for half an hour till the end of my shift. I'll take you.'

She laughed. 'And what would your girlfriend say to that?'

'A ruddy mouthful. She's got a tongue like a chain-saw.' He winked. 'I won't tell her if you won't.'

'Sorry, sunshine. I'm shackled to a husband who hates policemen only marginally less than he hates toy-boys.' Lies were always easier.

He grinned. 'Turn left out of the station and Wenceslas Street is about a mile down on the left. There's an empty shop on the corner. The Sergeant's restaurant is bang next door to it. It's called the Poacher.' He tapped his pencil on the desk. 'Are you planning to eat there?'

'No,' she said, 'it's purely business. I don't intend to hang around.'

He nodded approval. 'Wise woman. The Sergeant's not much of a cook. He'd have done better to stick with policing.'

She had to pass the restaurant to reach the London road. Rather reluctantly she pulled into its abandoned car park and climbed out of the car. She was tired, she hadn't planned on talking to Hawksley that day, and the young constable's light-hearted flirtation depressed her because it had left her cold.

The Poacher was an attractive red-brick building, set back from the road with the car park in front. Leaded bay windows curved out on either side of a solid oak door and wistaria, heavy with buds, grew in profusion across the whole façade. Like St Angela's Convent it was at odds with its surroundings.

The shops on either side, both apparently empty, their windows a repository for advertising stickers, complemented each other in cheap post-war pragmatism but did nothing for the old faded beauty in their midst. Worse, a thoughtless council had allowed a previous owner to erect a two-storey extension behind the red-brick frontage, and it gloomed above the restaurant's tiled roof in dirty pebble-dashed concrete. An attempt had been made to divert the wistaria across the roof but, starved of sunlight by the jutting property to the right, the probing tendrils showed little enthusiasm for reaching up to veil the dreary elevation.

Roz pushed open the door and went inside. The place was dark and deserted. Empty tables in an empty room, she thought despondently. Like her. Like her life. She was on the point of calling out, but thought better of it. It was all so peaceful and she was in no hurry. She tiptoed across the floor and took a stool at a bar in the corner. A smell of cooking lingered on the air, garlicky, tempting, reminding her that she hadn't eaten all day. She waited a long time, unseen and unheard, a trespasser upon another's silence. She thought about leaving, unobtrusively, as she had come, but it was strangely restful and her head drooped against her hand. Depression, an all too constant companion, folded its arms around her again, and turned her mind, as it often did, to death. She would do it one day. Sleeping pills or the car. The car, always the car. Alone, at night, in the rain. So easy just to turn the wheel and find a peaceful oblivion. It would be justice of a sort. Her head hurt where the hate swelled and throbbed inside it. God, what a mess she had become. If only someone could lance her destructive anger and let the poison go. Was Iris right? Should she see a psychiatrist? Without warning, the terrible unhappiness burst like a flood inside her, threatening to spill out in tears.

'Oh, shit!' she muttered furiously, dashing at her eyes with the palms of her hands. She scrabbled in her bag for her car keys. 'Shit! Shit! And more bloody shit! Where the hell are you?'

A slight movement caught her attention and she lifted her head abruptly. A shadowy stranger leant against the back counter, quietly polishing a glass and watching her.

She blushed furiously and looked away. 'How long have you been there?' she demanded angrily.

'Long enough.'

She retrieved her keys from the inside of her diary and glared at him briefly. 'What's that supposed to mean?'

He shrugged. 'Long enough.'

'Yes, well, you're obviously not open yet, so I'll be on my way.' She pushed herself off the stool.

'Suit yourself,' he said with supreme indifference. 'I was just about to have a glass of wine. You can go or you can join me. I'm easy either way.' He turned his back on her and uncorked a bottle. The colour receded from her cheeks.

'Are you Sergeant Hawksley?'

He lifted the cork to his nose and sniffed it appreciatively. 'I was, once. Now I'm just plain Hal.' He turned round and poured the wine into two glasses. 'Who's asking?'

She opened her bag again. 'I've got a card somewhere.'

'A voice would do just as well.' He pushed one of the glasses towards her.

'Rosalind Leigh,' she said shortly, propping the card against the telephone on the bar.

She stared at him in the semi-darkness, her embarrassment temporarily forgotten. He was hardly a run of the mill restaurateur. If she had any sense, she thought, she would take to her heels now. He hadn't shaved and his dark suit hung in rumpled folds as if he'd slept in it. He had no tie and half the buttons on his shirt were missing, revealing a mass of tight black curls on his chest. A swelling contusion on his upper left cheek was rapidly closing the eye above it, and thick dried blood encrusted both nostrils. He raised his glass with an ironic smile. 'To your good health, Rosalind. Welcome to the Poacher.' There was a lilt to his voice, a touch of Geordie, tempered by long association with the South.

'It might be more sensible to drink to your good health,' she said bluntly. 'You look as though you need it.'

'To us then. May we both get the better of whatever ails us.'

'Which, in your case, would appear to be a steamroller.'

He fingered the spreading bruise. 'Not far off,' he agreed. 'And you? What ails you?'

'Nothing,' she said lightly. 'I'm fine.'

'Sure you are.' His dark eyes rested kindly on her for a moment. 'You're half alive and I'm half dead.' He drained his glass and filled it again. 'What did you want with Sergeant Hawksley?'

She glanced about the room. 'Shouldn't you be opening up?'

'What for?'

She shrugged. 'Customers.'

'Customers,' he echoed thoughtfully. 'Now there's a beautiful word.' He gave a ghost of a chuckle. 'They're an endangered species, or haven't you heard? The last time I saw a customer was three days ago, a skinny little runt with a rucksack on his back who was scratching about in search of a vegetarian omelette and decaffeinated coffee.' He fell silent.

'Depressing.'

'Yes.'

She eased herself on to the stool again. 'It's not your fault,' she said sympathetically. 'It's the recession. Everyone's going under. Your neighbours already have, by the look of it.' She gestured towards the door.

He reached up and flicked a switch at the side of the bar. Muted lamplight glowed around the walls, bringing a sparkle to the glasses on the tables. She looked at him with alarm. The contusion on his cheek was the least of his problems. Bright red blood was seeping from a scab above his ear and running down his neck. He seemed unaware of it. 'Who did you say you were?' His dark eyes searched hers for a moment then moved past her to search the room.

'Rosalind Leigh. I think I should call an ambulance,' she said helplessly. 'You're bleeding.'

She had a strange feeling of being outside herself, quite remote from this extraordinary situation. Who was this man? Not her responsibility, certainly. She was a simple bystander who had stumbled upon him by accident. 'I'll call your wife,' she said.

He gave a lop-sided grin. 'Why not? She always enjoyed a good laugh. Presumably she still does.' He reached for a tea-towel and held it to his head. 'Don't worry, I'm not going to die on you. Head wounds always look worse than they are. You're very beautiful. "From the east to western Ind, No jewel is like Rosalind."'

'It's Roz and I'd rather you didn't quote that,' she said sharply. 'It annoys me.'

He shrugged. '*As You Like It*.'

She sucked in an angry breath. 'I suppose you think that's original.'

'A tender nerve, I see. Who are we talking about?' He looked at her ring finger. 'Husband? Ex-husband? Boyfriend?'

She ignored him. 'Is there anyone else here? Someone in the kitchen? You should have that cut cleaned.' She wrinkled her nose. 'In fact you should have this *place* cleaned. It stinks of fish.' The smell, once noticed, was appalling.

'Are you always this rude?' he asked curiously. He rinsed the tea-towel under a tap and watched the blood run out of it. 'It's me,' he said matter of factly. 'I went for a ride on a ton of mackerel. Not a pleasant experience.' He gripped the edge of the small sink and stood staring into it, head lowered in exhaustion, like a bull before the *coup de grâce* of the matador.

'Are you all right?' Roz watched him with a perplexed frown creasing her forehead. She didn't know what to do. It wasn't her problem, she kept telling herself, but she couldn't just walk away from it. Supposing he passed out? 'Surely there's someone I can call,' she insisted. 'A friend. A neighbour. Where do you live?' But she knew that. In the flat above, the young policeman had said.

'Jesus, woman,' he growled, 'give it a rest, for Christ's sake.'

'I'm only trying to help.'

'Is that what you call it? It sounded more like nagging to me.' He was alert suddenly, listening to something she couldn't hear.

'What's the matter?' she asked, alarmed by his expression.

'Did you lock the door after you?'

She stared at him. 'No. Of course I didn't.'

He dowsed the lights and padded across to the entrance door, almost invisible in the sudden darkness. She heard the sound of bolts being thrust home.

'Look—' she began, getting off her stool.

He loomed up beside her and put an arm around her shoulder and a finger to her lips. 'Quiet, woman.' He held her motionless.

'But—'

'Quiet!'

A car's headlamps swept across the windows, slicing the darkness with white light. The engine throbbed in neutral for a moment or two, then the gears engaged and the vehicle drove away. Roz tried to draw away but Hawksley's arm only gripped her more firmly. 'Not yet,' he whispered.

They stood in silent immobility among the tables, statues at a spectral feast. Roz shook herself free angrily. 'This is absolutely absurd,' she hissed. 'I don't know what on earth is going on but I'm not staying like this for the rest of the night. Who was in that car?'

'Customers,' he said regretfully.

'You're mad.'

He took her hand. 'Come on,' he whispered, 'we'll go upstairs.'

'We will not,' she said, snatching her hand away. 'My God, doesn't anyone think about anything except screwing these days.'

Amused laughter fanned her face. 'Who said anything about screwing?'

'I'm going.'

'I'll see you out.'

She took a deep breath. 'Why do you want to go upstairs?'

'My flat's up there and I need a bath.'

'So what do you want me for?'

He sighed. 'If you remember, Rosalind, it was you who came in here asking for me. I've never met a woman who was so damn prickly.'

'Prickly!' she stuttered. 'My God, that's rich. You stink to high heaven, you've obviously been in a fight, you plunge us into total darkness, moan about not having any customers and then turn them away when they do come, make me sit for five minutes without moving, try to manhandle me upstairs. . . .' She paused for breath. 'I think I'm going to be sick,' she blurted out.

'Oh, great! That's all I need.' He took her hand again. 'Come on. I'm not going to rape you. To tell you the truth I haven't the strength at the moment. What's wrong?'

She stumbled after him. 'I haven't eaten all day.'

'Join the club.' He led her through the darkened kitchen and unlocked a side door, reaching past her to switch on some lights. 'Up the stairs,' he told her, 'and the bathroom's on the right.'

She could hear him double-locking the door behind her as she collapsed on the lavatory seat and pressed her head between her knees, waiting for the waves of nausea to pass.

The light came on. 'Here. Drink this. It's water.' Hawksley squatted on the floor in front of her and looked into her white face. She had skin like creamy alabaster and eyes as dark as sloes. A very cold beauty, he thought. 'Do you want to talk about it?'

'What?'

'Whatever's making you so unhappy.'

She sipped the water. 'I'm not unhappy. I'm hungry.'

He put his hands on his knees and pushed himself upright. 'OK. Let's eat. How does sirloin steak sound?'

She smiled weakly. 'Wonderful.'

'Thank God for that! I've got a freezer full of the flaming stuff. How do you like it?'

'Rare but—'

'But what?'

She pulled a face. 'I think it's the smell that's making me sick.' She put her hands to her mouth. 'I'm sorry but I really think it would be better if you got cleaned up first. Mackerel-flavoured sirloin doesn't appeal over much.'

He sniffed at his sleeve. 'You don't notice it after a while.' He turned the taps on full and emptied bath foam into the running water. 'There's only the one loo, I'm afraid, so if you're going to puke you'd better stay there.' He started to undress.

She stood up hurriedly. 'I'll wait outside.'

He dropped his jacket on to the floor and unbuttoned his shirt. 'Just don't be sick all over my carpets,' he called after her. 'There's a sink in the kitchen. Use that.' He was easing the shirt carefully off his shoulders, unaware that she was still behind him, and she stared in horror at the blackened scabs all over his back.

'What happened to you?'

He pulled the shirt back on. 'Nothing. Scoot. Make yourself a sandwich. There's bread on the side and cheese in the fridge.' He saw her expression. 'It looks worse than it is,' he said prosaically. 'Bruising always does.'

'What happened?'

He held her gaze. 'Let's just say I fell off my bike.'

With a contemptuous smile, Olive extracted the candle from its hiding place. They had given up body searches after a woman haemorrhaged in front of one of the Board of Visitors following a particularly aggressive probing of her vagina for illicit drugs. The Visitor had been a MAN. (Olive always thought of men in capital letters.) No woman would have fallen for it. But MEN, of course, were different. Menstruation disturbed them, particularly if the blood flowed freely enough to stain the woman's clothes.

The candle was soft from the warmth of her body and she

pulled off the end and began to mould it. Her memory was good. She had no doubt of her ability to imbue the tiny figure with a distinct individuality. This one would be a MAN.

Roz, preparing sandwiches in the kitchen, looked towards the bathroom door. The prospect of questioning Hawksley about the Olive Martin case unnerved her suddenly. Crew had become very annoyed when she questioned *him*; and Crew was a civilized man – in so far as he did not look as if he'd spent half an hour in a dark alley having the shit beaten out of him by Arnold Schwarzenegger. She wondered about Hawksley. Would he be annoyed when he learnt that she was delving into a case he had been involved with? The idea was an uncomfortable one.

There was a bottle of champagne in the fridge. On the rather naïve assumption that another injection of alcohol might make Hawksley more amenable, Roz put it on a tray with the sandwiches and a couple of glasses.

'Were you saving the champagne?' she asked brightly – *too brightly?* – placing the tray on the lavatory seat lid and turning round.

He was lying in a welter of foam, black hair slicked back, face cleaned and relaxed, eyes closed. ''Fraid so,' he said.

'Oh.' She was apologetic. 'I'll put it back then.'

He opened one eye. 'I was saving it for my birthday.'

'And when's that?'

'Tonight.'

She gave an involuntary laugh. 'I don't believe you. What's the date?'

'The sixteenth.'

Her eyes danced wickedly. 'I still don't believe you. How old are you?' She was unprepared for his look of amused recognition and couldn't stop the adolescent flush that tinged her pale cheeks. He thought she was flirting with him. *Well – dammit! – maybe she was.* She had grown weary of suffocating under the weight of her own misery.

'Forty. The big four-o.' He pushed himself into a sitting position and beckoned for the bottle. 'Well, well, this is jolly.' His lips twitched humorously. 'I wasn't expecting company or I'd have dressed for the occasion.' He unbound the wire and eased out the cork, losing only a dribble of bubbly into the foam before filling the glasses that she held out to him. He lowered the bottle to the floor and took a glass. 'To life,' he said, clinking hers.

'To life. Happy birthday.'

His eyes watched her briefly, before closing again as he leant his head against the back of the bath. 'Eat a sandwich,' he murmured. 'There's nothing worse than champagne on an empty stomach.'

'I've had three already. Sorry I couldn't wait for the sirloin. You have one.' She put the tray beside the bottle and left him to help himself. 'Do you have a laundry basket or something?' she asked, stirring the heap of stinking clothes with her toe.

'They're not worth saving. I'll chuck 'em out.'

'I can do that.'

He yawned. 'Bin bags. Second cupboard on the left in the kitchen.'

She carried the bundle at arm's length and sealed the lot into three layers of clean white plastic. It took only a few minutes but when she went back he was asleep, his glass clasped in loose fingers against his chest.

She removed it carefully and put it on the floor. What now? she wondered. She might have been his sister, so unaroused was he by her presence. Go or stay? She had an absurd longing to sit quietly and watch him sleep but she was nervous of waking him. He would never understand her need to be at peace, just briefly, with a man.

Her eyes softened. It was a nice face. No amount of battering and bruising could hide the laughter lines, and she knew that if she let it it would grow on her and make her pleased to see it. She turned away abruptly. She had been nurturing her bitterness too long to give it up as easily as this. God had not been punished enough.

She retrieved her handbag from where she'd dropped it beside the lavatory and tiptoed down the stairs. But the door was locked and the key was missing. She felt more foolish than concerned, like the embarrassed eavesdropper trapped inside a room whose only object is to escape without being noticed. He must have put the wretched thing in his pocket. She crept back up to the kitchen to scrabble through the dirty clothes bundle but the pockets were all empty. Perplexed, she stared about the work surfaces, searched the tables in the sitting-room and bedroom. If keys existed, they were well hidden. With a sigh of frustration, she pulled back a curtain to see if there was another way out, a fire escape or a balcony, and found herself gazing on a window full of bars. She tried another window and another. All were barred.

Predictably, anger took over.

Without pausing to consider the wisdom of what she was doing, she stormed into the bathroom and shook him violently. 'You bastard!' she snapped. 'What the hell do you think you're playing at! What are you? Some kind of Bluebeard. I want to get out of here. Now!'

He was hardly awake before he'd smashed the champagne bottle against the tiled wall, caught her by the hair, and thrust the jagged glass against her neck. His bloodshot eyes blazed into hers before a sort of recognition dawned and he let her go, pushing her away from him. 'You stupid bitch,' he snarled. 'Don't you ever do that again.' He rubbed his face vigorously to clear it of sleep.

She was very shaken. 'I want to go.'

'So what's stopping you?'

'You've hidden the key.'

He looked at her for a moment, then started to soap himself. 'It's on the architrave above the door. Turn it twice. It's a double lock.'

'Your windows are all barred.'

'They are indeed.' He splashed water on his face. 'Goodbye, Ms Leigh.'

'Goodbye.' She made a weak gesture of apology. 'I'm sorry. I thought I was a prisoner.'

He pulled out the plug and tugged a towel off the rail. 'You are.'

'But – you said the key—'

'Goodbye, Ms Leigh.' He splayed his hand against the door and pushed it to, forcing her out.

She should not be driving. The thought hammered in her head like a migraine, a despairing reminder that self-preservation was the first of all the human instincts. But he was right. She *was* a prisoner and the yearning to escape was too strong. So easy, she thought, so very, very easy. Successive headlamps grew from tiny distant pinpoints to huge white suns, sweeping through her windscreen with a beautiful and blinding iridescence, drawing her eyes into the heart of their brilliance. The urge to turn the wheel towards the lights was insistent. How painless the transition would be at the moment of blindness and how bright eternity. *So easy . . . so easy . . . so easy. . . .*

FIVE

O live took a cigarette and lit it greedily. 'You're late. I was afraid you wouldn't come.' She sucked down the smoke. 'I've been dying for a bloody fag.' Her hands and shift were filthy with what looked like dried clay.

'Aren't you allowed cigarettes?'

'Only what you can buy with your earnings. I always run out before the end of the week.' She rubbed the backs of her hands vigorously and showered the table with small grey flakes.

'What is that?' Roz asked.

'Clay.' Olive left the cigarette in her mouth and set to work, plucking the smears from her bosom. 'Why do you think they call me the Sculptress?'

Roz was about to say something tactless, but thought better of it. 'What do you make?'

'People.'

'What sort of people? Imaginary people or people you know?'

There was a brief hesitation. 'Both.' She held Roz's gaze. 'I made one of you.'

Roz watched her for a moment. 'Well, I just hope you don't decide to stick pins into it,' she said with a faint smile. 'Judging by the way I feel today, somebody else is at that already.'

A flicker of amusement crossed Olive's face. She abandoned the smears and fixed Roz with her penetrating stare. 'So what's wrong with you.'

Roz had spent a weekend in limbo, analysing and re-analysing until her brain was on fire. 'Nothing. Just a headache, that's all.' And that was true as far as it went. Her situation hadn't altered. She was still a prisoner.

Olive screwed her eyes against the smoke. 'Changed your mind about the book?'

'No.'

'OK. Fire away.'

Roz switched on the tape-recorder. 'Second conversation with Olive Martin. Date: Monday, April nineteen. Tell me about Sergeant Hawksley, Olive, the policeman who arrested you. Did you get to know him well? How did he treat you?'

If the big woman was surprised by the question, she didn't show it, but then she didn't show anything very much. She thought for some moments. 'Was he the dark-haired one? Hal, I think they called him.'

Roz nodded.

'He was all right.'

'Did he bully you?'

'He was all right.' She drew on her cigarette and stared stolidly across the table. 'Have you spoken to him?'

'Yes.'

'Did he tell you he threw up when he saw the bodies?' There was an edge to her voice. Of amusement? Roz wondered. Somehow, amusement didn't quite square.

'No,' she said. 'He didn't mention that.'

'He wasn't the only one.' A short silence. 'I offered to make them a pot of tea but the kettle was in the kitchen.' She transferred her gaze to the ceiling, aware, perhaps, of having said something tasteless. 'Matter of fact, I liked him. He was the only one who talked to me. I might have been deaf and dumb for all the interest the others showed. He gave me a sandwich at the police station. He was all right.'

Roz nodded. 'Tell me what happened.'

Olive took another cigarette and lit it from the old one. 'They arrested me.'

'No. I mean before that.'

'I called the police station, gave my address, and said the bodies were in the kitchen.'

'And before that?'

Olive didn't answer.

Roz tried a different tack. 'The ninth of September, eighty-seven, was a Wednesday. According to your statement you killed and dismembered Amber and your mother in the morning and early afternoon.' She watched the woman closely. 'Did none of the neighbours hear anything, come and investigate?'

There was a tiny movement at the corner of one eye, a tic, hardly noticeable amidst the fat. 'It's a man, isn't it?' said Olive gently.

Roz was puzzled. 'What's a man?'

Sympathy peeped out from between the puffy, bald lids. 'It's one of the few advantages of being in a place like this. No men to make your life a misery. You get the odd bit of bother, of course, husbands and boyfriends playing up on the outside, but you don't get the anguish of a daily relationship.' She pursed her lips in recollection. 'I always envied the nuns, you know. It's so much easier when you don't have to compete.'

Roz played with her pencil. Olive was too canny to discuss a man in her own life, she thought, assuming there had ever been one. *Had she told the truth about her abortion?* 'But less rewarding,' she said.

A rumble issued from the other side of the table. 'Some reward you're getting. You know what my father's favourite expression was? The game is not worth the candle. He used to drive my mother mad with it. But it's true in your case. Whoever it is you're after, he's not doing you any good.'

Roz drew a doodle on her pad, a fat cherub inside a balloon. Was the abortion a fantasy, a perverted link in Olive's mind with Amber's unwanted son? There was a long silence. She pencilled in the cherub's smile and spoke without thinking. 'Not whoever,' she said, 'whatever. It's what I want, not who I want.' She regretted it as soon as she'd said it. 'It's not important.'

Again there was no response and she began to find Olive's

silences oppressive. It was a waiting game, a trap to make her speak. And then what? The toe-curling embarrassment of stammered apologies.

She bent her head. 'Let's go back to the day of the murders,' she suggested.

A meaty hand suddenly covered hers and stroked the fingers affectionately. 'I know about despair. I've felt it often. If you keep it bottled up, it feeds on itself like a cancer.'

There was no insistence in Olive's touch. It was a display of friendship, supportive, undemanding. Roz squeezed the fat, warm fingers in acknowledgement then withdrew her hand. *It's not despair*, she was going to say, *just overwork and tiredness*. 'I'd like to do what you did,' she said in a monotone, 'and kill someone.' There was a long silence. Her own statement had shocked her. 'I shouldn't have said that.'

'Why not? It's the truth.'

'I doubt it. I haven't the guts to kill anyone.'

Olive stared at her. 'That doesn't stop you wanting to,' she said reasonably.

'No. But if you can't summon the guts then I don't think the will is really there.' She smiled distantly. 'I can't even find the guts to kill myself and sometimes I see that as the only sensible option.'

'Why?'

Roz's eyes were over bright. 'I hurt,' she said simply. 'I've been hurting for months.' *But why was she telling Olive all this instead of the nice safe psychiatrist Iris had recommended? Because Olive would understand.*

'Who do you want dead?' The question vibrated in the air between them like a tolled bell.

Roz thought about the wisdom of answering. 'My ex-husband,' she said.

'Because he left you?'

'No.'

'What did he do?'

But Roz shook her head. 'If I tell you, you'll try to persuade me I'm wrong to hate him.' She gave a strange laugh. 'And I need to hate him. Sometimes I think it's the only thing that's keeping me alive.'

'Yes,' said Olive evenly. 'I can understand that.' She breathed on the window and drew a gallows in the mist with her finger. 'You loved him once.' It was a statement, expecting no reply, but Roz felt compelled to answer.

'I can't remember now.'

'You must have done.' The fat woman's voice became a croon. 'You can't hate what you never loved, you can only dislike it and avoid it. Real hate, like real love, consumes you.' With a sweep of her large palm she wiped the gallows from the window. 'I suppose,' she went on, matter of factly, 'you came to see me to find out whether murder is worth it.'

'I don't know,' Roz said honestly. 'Half the time I'm in limbo, the other half I'm obsessed by anger. The only thing I'm sure of is that I'm slowly falling apart.'

Olive shrugged. 'Because it's inside your head. Like I said, it's bad to keep things bottled up. It's a pity you're not a Catholic. You could go to confession and feel better immediately.'

Such a simple solution had never occurred to Roz. 'I was a Catholic, once. I suppose I still am.'

Olive took another cigarette and placed it reverently between her lips like a consecrated wafer. 'Obsessions,' she murmured, reaching for a match, 'are invariably destructive. That, at least, I have learnt.' She spoke sympathetically. 'You need more time before you can talk about it. I understand. You think I'll pick at the scab and make you bleed again.'

Roz nodded.

'You don't trust people. You're right. Trust has a way of rebounding. I know about these things.'

Roz watched her light the cigarette. 'What was your obsession?'

She flicked Roz a strangely intimate look but didn't answer. 'I needn't write this book, you know, not if you don't want me to.'

Olive smoothed her thin blonde hair with the back of her

thumb. 'It'll upset Sister Bridget if we give up now. I know you've seen her.'

'Does that matter?'

Olive shrugged. 'It might upset *you* if we give up now. Does *that* matter?'

She smiled suddenly and her whole face brightened. How very *nice* she looked, thought Roz. 'Maybe, maybe not,' she said. 'I'm not convinced myself that I want to write it.'

'Why not?'

Roz pulled a face. 'I should hate to turn you into a freak side-show.'

'Aren't I that already?'

'In here perhaps. Not outside. They've forgotten all about you outside. It may be better to leave it that way.'

'What would persuade you to write it?'

'If you tell me why.'

The silence grew between them. Ominous. 'Have they found my nephew?' Olive asked at last.

'I don't think so.' Roz frowned. 'How did you know they were looking for him?'

Olive gave a hearty chuckle. 'Cell telegraph. Everyone knows everything in here. There's bugger-all else to do except mind other people's business, and we all have solicitors and we all read the newspapers and everyone talks. I could have guessed anyway. My father left a lot of money. He would always leave it to family if he could.'

'I spoke to one of your neighbours, a Mr Hayes. Do you remember him?' Olive nodded. 'If I understood him right, Amber's child was adopted by some people called Brown who've since emigrated to Australia. I assume that's why Mr Crew's firm is having so much difficulty in tracing him. Big place, common name.' She waited for a moment but Olive didn't say anything. 'Why do you want to know? Does it make a difference to you whether he's found or not?'

'Maybe,' she said heavily.

'Why?'

Olive shook her head.

'Do you want him found?'

The door crashed open, startling them both. 'Time's up, Sculptress. Come on, let's be having you.' The officer's voice boomed about the peaceful room, tearing the fabric of their precarious intimacy. Roz saw her own irritation reflected in Olive's eyes. But the moment was lost.

She gave an involuntary wink. 'It's true what they say, you know. Time does fly when you're enjoying yourself. I'll see you next week.' The huge woman lumbered awkwardly to her feet.

'My father was a very lazy man, which is why he let my mother rule the roost.' She rested a hand against the door jamb to balance herself. 'His other favourite saying, because it annoyed her so much, was: never do today what can always be done tomorrow.' She smiled faintly. 'As a result, of course, he was completely contemptible. The only allegiance he recognized was his allegiance to himself, but it was allegiance without responsibility. He should have studied existentialism.' Her tongue lingered on the word. 'He would have learnt something about man's imperative to choose and act wisely. We are all masters of our fate, Roz, including you.' She nodded briefly then turned away, drawing the prison officer and the metal chair into her laborious, shuffling wake.

Now what, Roz wondered, watching them, was that supposed to mean?

'Mrs Wright?'

'Yes?' The young woman held the front door half open, a restraining hand hooked into her growling dog's collar. She was pretty in a colourless sort of way, pale and fine drawn with large grey eyes and a swinging bob of straw-gold hair.

Roz offered her card. 'I'm writing a book about Olive Martin. Sister Bridget at your old convent school suggested you might be prepared to talk to me. She said you were the closest friend Olive had there.'

Geraldine Wright made a pretence of reading the card then

offered it back again. 'I don't think so, thank you.' She said it in the sort of tone she might have used to a Jehovah's Witness. She prepared to close the door.

Roz held it open with her hand. 'May I ask why not?'

'I'd rather not be involved.'

'I don't need to mention you by name.' She smiled encouragingly. 'Please, Mrs Wright. I won't embarrass you. That's not the way I work. It's information I'm after, not exposure. No one will ever know you were connected with her, not through me or my book at least.' She saw a slight hesitancy in the other woman's eyes. 'Ring Sister Bridget,' she urged. 'I know she'll vouch for me.'

'Oh, I suppose it's all right. But only for half an hour. I have to collect the children at three thirty.' She opened the door wide and pulled the dog away from it. 'Come in. The sitting room's on the left. I'll have to shut Boomer in the kitchen or he won't leave us alone.'

Roz walked through into the sitting room, a pleasant, sunny space with wide patio doors opening out on to a small terrace. Beyond, a neat garden, carefully tended, merged effortlessly into a green field with distant cows. 'It's a lovely view,' she said as Mrs Wright joined her.

'We were lucky to get it,' said the other woman with some pride. 'The house was rather out of our price range, but the previous owner took a bridging loan on another property just before the interest rates went through the roof. He was so keen to be shot of this one we got it for twenty-five thousand less than he was asking. We're very happy here.'

'I'm not surprised,' said Roz warmly. 'It's a beautiful part of the world.'

'Let's sit down.' She lowered herself gracefully into an armchair. 'I'm not ashamed of my friendship with Olive,' she excused herself. 'I just don't like talking about it. People are so persistent. They simply won't accept that I knew nothing about the murders.' She examined her painted fingernails. 'I hadn't seen her, you know, for at least three years before it happened and I certainly haven't seen her since. I really can't think what I can tell you that will be of any use.'

Roz made no attempt to record the conversation. She was afraid of scaring the woman. 'Tell me what she was like at school,' she said, taking out a pencil and notepad. 'Were you in the same form?'

'Yes, we both stayed on to do A-levels.'

'Did you like her?'

'Not much.' Geraldine sighed. 'That does sound unkind, doesn't it? Look, you really won't use my name, will you? I mean, if there's a chance you will, I just won't say any more. I should hate Olive to know how I really felt about her. It would be so hurtful.'

Of course it would, thought Roz, but why would you care? She took some headed notepaper from her briefcase, wrote two sentences on it and signed it. ' "I, Rosalind Leigh, of the above address, agree to treat all information given to me by Mrs Geraldine Wright of Oaktrees, Wooling, Hants, as confidential. I shall not reveal her as the source of any information, either verbally or in writing, now or at any time in the future." There. Will that do?' She forced a smile. 'You can sue me for a fortune if I break my word.'

'Oh dear, she'll guess it's me. I'm the only one she talked to. At school, anyway.' She took the piece of paper. 'I don't know.'

God, what a ditherer! It occurred to Roz then that Olive may well have found the friendship as unrewarding as Geraldine appeared to have done. 'Let me give you an idea of how I'll use what you tell me, then you'll see there's nothing to worry about. You've just said you didn't like her much. That will end up in the book as something like: "Olive was never popular at school." Can you go along with that?'

The woman brightened. 'Oh, yes. That's absolutely true anyway.'

'OK. Why wasn't she popular?'

'She never really fitted in, I suppose.'

'Why not?'

'Oh dear.' Geraldine shrugged irritatingly. 'Because she was fat, perhaps.'

This was going to be like drawing teeth, slow and extremely painful. 'Did she try to make friends or didn't she bother?'

'She didn't really bother. She hardly ever said anything, you know, just used to sit and stare at everyone else while they talked. People didn't like that very much. To tell you the truth, I think we were all rather frightened of her. She was very much taller than the rest of us.'

'Was that the only reason she scared you? Her size?'

Geraldine thought back. 'It was a sort of over-all thing. I don't know how to describe it. She was very quiet. You could be talking to someone and you'd turn round to find her standing right behind you, staring at you.'

'Did she bully people?'

'Only if they were nasty to Amber.'

'And did that happen often?'

'No. Everyone liked Amber.'

'OK.' Roz tapped her pencil against her teeth. 'You say you were the only one Olive spoke to. What sort of things did you talk about?'

Geraldine plucked at her skirt. 'Just things,' she said unhelpfully. 'I can't remember now.'

'The sort of things all girls talk about at school.'

'Well, yes, I suppose so.'

Roz gritted her teeth. 'So you discussed sex, and boys, and clothes, and make-up?'

'Well, yes,' she said again.

'I find that hard to believe, Mrs Wright. Not unless she's changed a great deal in ten years. I've met her, you know. She's not remotely interested in trivia and she doesn't like talking about herself. She wants to know about me and what I do.'

'That's probably because she's in prison and you're her only visitor.'

'I'm not, in actual fact. Also, I am told that most prisoners do the exact opposite when someone visits them. They talk about themselves nineteen to the dozen because it's the only time they get a sympathetic hearing.' She raised a speculative eyebrow. 'I think it's Olive's nature to quiz the person she's talking to. I suspect she's always done it, and that's why none of you liked her very much. You probably thought she was nosy.' Pray God, I'm right, she thought, because this one, who's about as manipulable as putty, will say I am regardless.

'How funny,' said Geraldine. 'Now you mention it, she did ask a lot of questions. She was always wanting to know about my parents, whether they held hands and kissed, and whether I'd ever heard them making love.' She turned her mouth down. 'Yes, I remember now, that's why I didn't like her. She was forever trying to find out how often my parents had sex, and she used to push her face up close when she asked, and stare.' She gave a small shudder. 'I used to hate that. She had such greedy eyes.'

'Did you tell her?'

'About my parents?' Geraldine sniggered. 'Not the truth, certainly. I didn't know myself. Whenever she asked, I always said, yes, they'd had sex the night before, just to get away from her. Everyone did. It became a silly sort of game in the end.'

'Why did she want to know?'

The woman shrugged. 'I always thought it was because she had a dirty mind. There's a woman in the village who's just the same. The first thing she says to anyone is, "Tell me all the gossip," and her eyes light up. I hate that sort of thing. She's the last person to hear what's going on, of course. She puts people's backs up.'

Roz thought for a moment. 'Did Olive's parents kiss and cuddle?'

'Lord, no!'

'You're very certain.'

'Well, of course. They loathed each other. My mother said they only stayed together because he was too lazy to move out and she was too mercenary to let him.'

'So Olive was looking for reassurance?'

'I'm sorry?'

'When she asked you about your parents,' said Roz coolly, 'she was looking for reassurance. The poor kid was trying to find out if hers were the only ones who didn't get on.'

'Oh,' said Geraldine in surprise. 'Do you think so?' She made a pretty little moue with her lips. 'No,' she said, 'I'm sure you're wrong. It was the sex bits she wanted to know about. I told you, her eyes had a greedy look.'

Roz let this pass. 'Did she tell lies?'

'Yes, that was another thing.' Memories chased themselves across her face. 'She was always lying. How odd, I'd forgotten that. In the end, you know, nobody ever believed anything she said.'

'What did she lie about?'

'Everything.'

'What in particular? Herself? Other people? Her parents?'

'Everything.' She saw the impatience in Roz's face. 'Oh dear, it's so hard to explain. She told stories. I mean, she couldn't open her mouth without telling stories. Oh dear, let me see now. All right, she used to talk about boyfriends that didn't exist, and she said the family had been on holiday to France one summer but it turned out they'd stayed at home, and she kept talking about her dog, but everyone knew she didn't have a dog.' She pulled a face. 'And she used to cheat, of course, all the time. It was really annoying that. She'd steal your homework out of your satchel when you weren't looking and crib your ideas.'

'She was bright, though, wasn't she? She got three A-levels.'

'She passed them all but I don't think her grades were anything to shout home about.' It was said with a touch of malice. 'Anyway, if she was so bright, why couldn't she get herself a decent job? My mother said it was embarrassing going to Pettit's and being served by Olive.'

Roz looked away from the colourless face to gaze out over the view from the window. She let some moments pass while common sense battled with the angry reproaches that were clamouring inside her head. After all, she thought, she could be wrong. And yet . . . And yet it seemed so clear to her that Olive must have been a deeply unhappy child. She forced herself to smile. 'Olive was obviously closer to you than anyone else, except, perhaps, her sister. Why do you think that was?'

'Oh, goodness, I haven't a clue. My mother says it's because I reminded her of Amber. I couldn't see it myself, but it's true that people who saw the three of us together always assumed Amber was my sister and not Olive's.' She thought back. 'Mother's probably right. Olive stopped following me around quite so much when Amber joined the school.'

'That must have been a relief.' There was a certain acidity in her tone, mercifully lost on Geraldine.

'I suppose so. Except' – she added this as a wistful after-thought – 'nobody dared tease when Olive was with me.'

Roz watched her for a moment. 'Sister Bridget said Olive was devoted to Amber.'

'She was. But then everyone liked Amber.'

'Why?'

Geraldine shrugged. 'She was nice.'

Roz laughed suddenly. 'To be frank, Amber's beginning to get up my nose. She sounds too damn good to be true. What was so special about her?'

'Oh dear.' She frowned in recollection. 'Mother said it was because she was willing. People put on her, but she never seemed to mind. She smiled a lot, of course.'

Roz drew her cherub doodle on the notepad and thought about the unwanted pregnancy. 'How was she put upon?'

'I suppose she just wanted to please. It was only little things, like lending out her pencils and running errands for the nuns. I needed a clean sports shirt once for a netball match, so I borrowed Amber's. That sort of thing.'

'Without asking?'

Surprisingly, Geraldine blushed. 'You didn't need to, not with Amber. She never minded. It was only Olive who got angry. She was perfectly beastly about that sports shirt.' She looked at the clock. 'I shall have to go. It's getting late.' She stood up. 'I haven't been very helpful, I'm afraid.'

'On the contrary,' said Roz, pushing herself out of her chair, 'you've been extremely helpful. Thank you very much.'

They walked into the hall together.

'Did it never seem odd to you,' Roz asked as Geraldine opened the front door, 'that Olive should kill her sister?'

'Well, yes, of course it did. I was terribly shocked.'

'Shocked enough to wonder if she actually did it? In view of all you've said about their relationship it seems a very unlikely thing for her to do.'

The wide grey eyes clouded with uncertainty. 'How strange. That's just what my mother always said. But if she didn't do it, then why did she say she did?'

'I don't know. Perhaps because she makes a habit of protecting people.' She smiled in a friendly way. 'Would your mother be prepared to talk to me, do you think?'

'Oh Lord, I shouldn't think so. She hates anyone even knowing I was at school with Olive.'

'Will you ask her anyway? And if she agrees, phone me at that number on the card.'

Geraldine shook her head. 'It would be a waste of time. She won't agree.'

'Fair enough.' Roz stepped through the door and on to the gravel. 'What a lovely house this is,' she said with enthusiasm, looking up at the clematis over the porch. 'Where were you living before?'

The other woman grimaced theatrically. 'A nasty modern box on the outskirts of Dawlington.'

Roz laughed. 'So coming here was by way of a culture shock.' She opened the car door. 'Do you ever go back to Dawlington?'

'Oh, yes,' said the other. 'My parents still live there. I see them once a week.'

Roz tossed her bag and briefcase on to the back seat. 'They must be very proud of you.' She held out a hand. 'Thank you for your time, Mrs Wright, and please don't worry, I shall be very careful how I use the information you've given me.' She lowered herself on to the driver's seat and pulled the door to. 'There's just one last thing,' she said through the open window, her dark eyes guileless. 'Can I have your maiden name so I can cross you off the school list Sister Bridget gave me? I don't want to go troubling you again by mistake.'

'Hopwood,' said Geraldine helpfully.

It wasn't difficult to locate Mrs Hopwood. Roz drove to the library in Dawlington and consulted the local telephone directory. There were three Hopwoods with Dawlington addresses. She made a note of these with their numbers, found a telephone box and rang each in turn, claiming to be an old friend of Geraldine's and asking to speak to her. The first two denied any knowledge of such a person, the last, a man's voice, told her that Geraldine had married and was now living in Wooling. He gave her Geraldine's telephone number and told her, rather sweetly, how nice it had been to talk to her again. Roz smiled as she put down the receiver. Geraldine, she thought, took after her father.

This impression was forcibly confirmed when Mrs Hopwood rattled her safety chain into place and opened the front door. She eyed Roz with deep suspicion. 'Yes?' she demanded.

'Mrs Hopwood?'

'Yes.'

Roz had planned a simple cover story but, seeing the hard glint in the woman's eyes, decided to abandon it. Mrs Hopwood was not the type to take kindly to flannel. 'I'm afraid I bamboozled your daughter and your husband into giving away this address,' she said with a slight smile. 'My name's—'

'Rosalind Leigh and you're writing a book about Olive. I know. I've just had Geraldine on the phone. It didn't take her long to put two and two together. I'm sorry but I can't help you. I hardly knew the girl.' But she didn't close the door. Something – curiosity? – kept her there.

'You know her better than I do, Mrs Hopwood.'

'But I haven't chosen to write a book about her, young woman. Nor would I.'

'Not even if you thought she was innocent?'

Mrs Hopwood didn't answer.

'Supposing she didn't do it? You've considered that, haven't you?'

'It's not my affair.' She started to close the door.

'Then whose affair is it, for God's sake?' demanded Roz, suddenly angry. 'Your daughter paints a picture of two sisters, both of whom were so insecure that one told lies and cheated to give herself some status and the other was afraid to say no in case people didn't like her. What the hell was happening to them at home to make them like that? And where were you then? Where was anybody? The only real friend either of them had was the other.' She saw the thin compression of the woman's lips through the gap in the door and she shook her head contemptuously. 'Your daughter misled me, I'm afraid. From something she said I thought you might be a Samaritan.' She smiled coldly. 'I see you're a Pharisee, after all. Goodbye, Mrs Hopwood.'

The other clicked her tongue impatiently. 'You'd better come in, but I'm warning you, I shall insist on a transcript of this interview. I will not have words put into my mouth afterwards simply to fit some sentimental view you have of Olive.'

Roz produced her tape-recorder. 'I'll tape the whole thing. If you have a recorder you can tape it at the same time, or I can send you a copy of mine.'

Mrs Hopwood nodded approval as she unhooked the chain and opened the door. 'We have our own. My husband can set it up while I make a cup of tea. Come in, and wipe your feet, please.'

Ten minutes later they were ready. Mrs Hopwood took

natural control. 'The easiest way is for me to tell you everything I remember. When I've finished you can ask me questions. Agreed?'

'Agreed.'

'I said I hardly knew Olive. That's true. She came here
perhaps five or six times in all, twice to Geraldine's birthday
parties, and on three or four occasions to tea. I didn't take to
her. She was a clumsy girl, slow, impossible to talk to, lacking
in humour, and, frankly, extremely unattractive. This may
sound harsh and unkind but there you are – you can't pretend
feelings that you don't have. I wasn't sorry when her friendship with Geraldine died a natural death.' She paused to
collect her thoughts.

'After that, I really had very little to do with her. She never
came to this house again. I heard stories, of course, from
Geraldine and Geraldine's friends. The impression I formed
was very much along the lines you set out earlier – a sad,
unloved, and unlovely child, who had resorted to boasting
about holidays she hadn't taken and boyfriends she didn't
have to make up for unhappiness at home. The cheating, I
think, was the result of her mother's constant pressure to do
well, as indeed was the compulsive eating. She was always
plump but during her adolescence her eating habits became
pathological. According to Geraldine, she used to steal food
from the school kitchen and cram it, in its entirety, into her
mouth, as if she were afraid someone would take it away from
her before she had finished.

'Now, you would interpret this behaviour, I imagine, as a
symptom of a troubled home background.' She looked enquiringly at Roz, who nodded. 'Yes, well, I think I'd agree with
you. It wasn't natural, and nor was Amber's submissiveness,
although I must stress I never witnessed either girl in action,
so to speak. I am relating only what I was told by Geraldine
and her friends. In any event, it did trouble me, mostly
because I had met Gwen and Robert Martin when I went to
collect Geraldine on the few occasions she was invited to their
house. They were a very strange couple. They hardly spoke.

He lived in a downstairs room at the back of the house and she and the two girls lived at the front. As far as I could make out, virtually all contact between them was conducted through Olive and Amber.' Seeing Roz's expression, she stopped. 'No one's told you this yet?'

Roz shook her head.

'I never did know how many people were aware of it. She kept up appearances, of course, and, frankly, had Geraldine not told me she had seen a bed in Mr Martin's study, I wouldn't have guessed what was going on.' She wrinkled her brow. 'But it's always the way, isn't it? Once you begin to suspect something, then everything you see confirms that suspicion. They were never together, except at the odd parents' evening, and then there would always be a third party with them, usually one of the teachers.' She smiled self-consciously. 'I used to watch them, you know, not out of malice – my husband will confirm that – but just to prove myself wrong.' She shook her head. 'I came to the conclusion that they simply loathed each other. And it wasn't just that they never spoke, they couldn't bring themselves to exchange *anything* – touches, glances – anything. Does that make sense to you?'

'Oh, yes,' said Roz with feeling. 'Hatred has as strong a body language as love.'

'It was she, I think, who was the instigator of it all. I've always assumed he must have had an affair which she found out about, though I must stress I don't know that. He was a nice looking man, very easy to talk to, and, of course, he got out and about with his job. Whereas she, as far as I could see, had no friends at all, a few acquaintances perhaps, but one never came across her socially. She was a very controlled woman, cold and unemotional. Really rather unpleasant. Certainly not the type one could ever grow fond of.' She was silent for a moment. 'Olive was very much her daughter, of course, both in looks and personality, and Amber his. Poor Olive,' she said with genuine compassion. 'She did have very little going for her.'

Mrs Hopwood looked at Roz and sighed heavily. 'You asked me earlier where I was while all this was going on. I was bringing up my own children, my dear, and if you have any yourself you will know it's hard enough to cope with them, let alone interfere with someone else's. I do regret now that I didn't say anything at the time, but, really, what could I have done? In any case, I felt it was the school's responsibility.' She spread her hands. 'But there you are, it's so easy with hindsight, and who could possibly have guessed that Olive would do what she did? I don't suppose anyone realized just how disturbed she was.' She dropped her hands to her lap and looked helplessly at her husband.

Mr Hopwood pondered for a moment. 'Still,' he said slowly, 'there's no point pretending we've ever believed she killed Amber. I went to the police about that, you know, told them I thought it was very unlikely. They said my disquiet was based on out-of-date information.' He sucked his teeth. 'Which of course was true. It was five years or so since we'd had any dealings with the family, and in five years the sisters could well have learned to dislike each other.' He fell silent.

'But if Olive didn't kill Amber,' Roz prompted, 'then who did?'

'Gwen,' he said with surprise, as if it went without saying. He smoothed his white hair. 'We think Olive walked in on her mother battering Amber. That would have been quite enough to send her berserk, assuming she had retained her fondness for the girl.'

'Was Gwen capable of doing such a thing?'

They looked at each other. 'We've always thought so,' said Mr Hopwood. 'She was very hostile towards Amber, probably because Amber was so like her father.'

'What did the police say?' asked Roz.

'I gather Robert Martin had already suggested the same thing. They put it to Olive and she denied it.'

Roz stared at him. 'You're saying Olive's father told the police that he thought his wife had battered his younger daughter to death and that Olive then killed her mother?'

He nodded.

'God!' she breathed. 'His solicitor never said a word about that.' She thought for a moment. 'It implies, you know, that Gwen had battered the child before. No man would make an accusation like that unless he had grounds for it, would he?'

'Perhaps he just shared our disbelief that Olive could kill her sister.'

Roz chewed her thumbnail and stared at the carpet. 'She claimed in her statement that her relationship with her sister had never been close. Now, I might go along with that if I accept that in the years after school they drifted apart, but I can't go along with it if her own father thought they were still so close that Olive would kill to revenge her.' She shook her head. 'I'm damn sure Olive's barrister never got to hear about this. The poor man was trying to conjure a defence out of thin air.' She looked up. 'Why did Robert Martin give up on it? Why did he let her plead guilty? According to her she did it to spare him the anguish of a trial.'

Mr Hopwood shook his head. 'I really couldn't say. We never saw him again. Presumably, he somehow became convinced of her guilt.' He massaged arthritic fingers. 'The problem for all of us is trying to accept that a person we know is capable of doing something so horrible, perhaps because it shows up the fallibility of our judgement. We knew her before it happened. You, I imagine, have met her since. In both cases, we have failed to see the flaw in her character that led her to murder her mother and sister, and we look for excuses. In the end, though, I don't think there are any. It's not as if the police had to beat her confession out of her. As far as I understand it, it was they who insisted she wait till her solicitor was present.'

Roz frowned. 'And yet you're still troubled by it.'

He smiled slightly. 'Only when someone pops up to stir the dregs again. By and large we rarely think about it. There's no getting away from the fact that she signed a confession saying she did it.'

'People are always confessing to crimes they didn't

commit,' countered Roz bluntly. 'Timothy Evans was hanged for his confession, while downstairs Christie went on burying his victims under the floorboards. Sister Bridget said Olive lied about everything, you and your daughter have both cited lies she told. What makes you think she was telling the truth in this one instance?'

They didn't say anything.

'I'm so sorry,' said Roz with an apologetic smile. 'I don't mean to harangue you. I just wish I understood what it was all about. There are so many inconsistencies. I mean why, for example, did Robert Martin stay in the house after the deaths? You'd expect him to move heaven and earth to get out of it.'

'You must talk to the police,' said Mr Hopwood. 'They know more about it than anyone.'

'Yes,' Roz said quietly, 'I must.' She picked up her cup and saucer from the floor and put them on the table. 'Can I ask you three more things? Then I'll leave you in peace. First, is there anyone else you can think of who might be able to help me?'

Mrs Hopwood shook her head. 'I really know very little about her after she left school. You'll have to trace the people she worked with.'

'Fair enough. Second, did you know that Amber had a baby when she was thirteen years old?' She read the astonishment in their faces.

'Good Heavens!' said Mrs Hopwood.

'Quite. Third . . .' She paused for a moment, remembering Graham Deedes' amused reaction. Was it fair to make Olive a figure of fun? 'Third,' she repeated firmly, 'Gwen persuaded Olive to have an abortion. Do you know anything about that?'

Mrs Hopwood looked thoughtful. 'Would that have been at the beginning of eighty-seven?'

Roz, unsure how to answer, nodded.

'I was having problems of my own with a prolonged menopause,' said Mrs Hopwood, matter of factly. 'I bumped into her and Gwen quite by chance at the hospital. It was the last time I saw them. Gwen was very jumpy. She tried to pretend they were there for a gynaecological reason of her own but I couldn't help noticing that it was clearly Olive who had the problem. The poor girl was in tears.' She tut-tutted crossly. 'What a mistake not to let her have it. It explains the murders, of course. They must have happened around the time the baby would have been due. No wonder she was disturbed.'

Roz drove back to Leven Road. This time the door to number 22 stood ajar and a young woman was clipping the low hedge that bordered the front garden. Roz drew her car into the kerb and stepped out. 'Hi,' she said, holding out her hand and shaking the other's firmly. Immediate, friendly contact, she hoped, would stop this woman barring the door to her as her neighbour had done. 'I'm Rosalind Leigh. I came the other day but you were out. I can see your time's precious so I won't stop you working, but can we talk while you're doing it?'

The young woman shrugged as she resumed her clipping. 'If you're selling anything, and that includes religion, then you're wasting your time.'

'I want to talk about your house.'

'Oh, Christ!' said the other in disgust. 'Sometimes I wish we'd never bought the flaming thing. What are you? Psychical bloody research? They're all nutters. They seem to think the kitchen is oozing with ectoplasm or something equally disgusting.'

'No. Far more earthbound. I'm writing a follow-up report on the Olive Martin case.'

'Why?'

'There are some unanswered questions. Like, for example, why did Robert Martin remain here after the murders?'

'And you're expecting me to answer that?' She snorted. 'I never even met him. He was long dead before we moved in. You should talk to old Hayes' – she jerked her head towards the adjoining garages – 'he's the only one who knew the family.'

'I have talked to him. He doesn't know either.' She glanced

towards the open front door but all she could see was an expanse of peach wall and a triangle of russet carpet. 'I gather the house has been gutted and redecorated. Did you do that yourselves or did you buy it after it was done?'

'We did it ourselves. My old man's in the building trade. Or was,' she corrected herself. 'He was made redundant ten, twelve months ago. We were lucky, managed to sell our other house without losing too much, and bought this for a song. Did it without a mortgage, too, so we're not struggling the way some other poor sods are.'

'Has he found another job?' Roz asked sympathetically.

The young woman shook her head. 'Hardly. Building's all he knows and there's precious little of that at the moment. Still, he's trying his best. Can't do more than that, can he?' She lowered the shears. 'I suppose you're wondering if we found anything when we gutted the house.'

Roz nodded. 'Something like that.'

'If we had, we'd have told someone.'

'Of course, but I wouldn't have expected you to find anything incriminating. I was thinking more in terms of impressions. Did the place look loved, for example? Is that why he stayed? Because he loved it?'

The woman shook her head. 'I reckon it was more of a prison. I can't swear to it because I don't know for sure, but my guess is he only used one room and that was the room downstairs at the back, the one that was attached to the kitchen and the cloakroom with its own door into the garden. Maybe he went through to the kitchen to cook, but I doubt it. The connecting door was locked and we never found the key. Plus, there was an ancient Baby Belling still plugged into one of the sockets in that room, which the house clearers couldn't be bothered to take, and my bet is he did all his cooking on that. The garden was nice. I think he lived in the one room and the garden, and never went into the rest of the house at all.'

'Because the door was locked?'

'No, because of the nicotine. The windows were so thick

with it that the glass looked yellow. And the ceiling' – she pulled a face – 'was dark brown. The smell of old tobacco was overpowering. He must have smoked non-stop in there. It was disgusting. But there were no nicotine stains anywhere else in the house. If he ever went beyond the connecting door, then it can't have been for very long.'

Roz nodded. 'He died of a heart attack.'

'I'm not surprised.'

'Would you object to my taking a look inside?'

'There's no point. It's completely different. We knocked out any walls that weren't structural and changed the whole layout downstairs. If you want to know what it looked like when he was here, then I'll draw you a plan. But you don't come in. If I say yes to you, then there's no end to it, is there? Any Tom, Dick, or Harry can demand to put his foot through our door.'

'Point taken. A plan would be more helpful, anyway.' She reached into the car for a notepad and pencil and passed it across.

'It's much nicer now,' said the self-possessed young woman, drawing with swift strokes. 'We've opened up the rooms and put some colour into them. Poor Mrs Martin had no idea at all. I think, you know, she was probably rather boring. There.' She passed the notepad back. 'That's the best I can do.'

'Thank you,' said Roz studying the plan. 'Why do you think Mrs Martin was boring?'

'Because everything – walls, doors, ceilings, *everything* – was painted white. It was like an operating theatre, cold and antiseptic, without a spot of colour. And she didn't have pictures either, because there were no marks on the walls.' She shuddered. 'I don't like houses like that. They never look lived in.'

Roz smiled as she glanced up at the red-brick façade. 'I'm glad it's you who bought it. I should think it feels lived in now. I don't believe in ghosts myself.'

'Put it this way, if you want to see ghosts, you'll see them.

If you don't, you won't.' She tapped the side of her head. 'It's all in the mind. My old dad used to see pink elephants but no one ever thought *his* house was haunted.'

Roz was laughing as she drove away.

SIX

▬

The car park of the Poacher was as deserted as before but this time it was three o'clock in the afternoon, lunchtime was over, and the door was bolted. Roz tapped on the window pane but, getting no response, made her way round to the alley at the back where the kitchen door must be. It stood ajar and from inside came the sound of singing.

'Hello,' she called. 'Sergeant Hawksley?' She put her hand on the door to push it wider and almost lost her balance when it was whipped away from her. 'You did that on purpose!' she snapped. 'I could have broken my arm.'

'Good God, woman,' he said in mock disgust. 'Can't you open your mouth without nagging? I'm beginning to think I did my ex-wife an injustice.' He crossed his arms, a fish slice dangling from one hand. 'What do you want this time?'

He had a peculiar talent for putting her at a disadvantage. She bit back an angry retort. 'I'm sorry,' she said instead. 'It's just that I nearly fell over. Look, are you busy at the moment or can I come in and talk to you?' She examined his face warily for signs of further damage but there were none that hadn't been there before.

'I'm busy.'

'What if I came back in an hour? Could you talk then?'

'Maybe.'

She gave a rueful smile. 'I'll try again at four.'

He watched her walk up the alleyway. 'What are you going to do for an hour?' he called after her.

She turned round. 'I expect I'll sit in the car. I've some notes to work on.'

He swung the fish slice. 'I'm cooking *steak au poivre* with some lightly steamed vegetables and potatoes fried in butter.'

'Bully for you,' she said.

'There's enough for two.'

She smiled. 'Is that an invitation or a refined form of torture?'

'It's an invitation.'

She came back slowly. 'Actually, I'm starving.'

A slight smile warmed his face. 'So what's new?' He took her into the kitchen and pulled out a chair at the table. He eyed her critically as he turned the gas up under some simmering pans. 'You look as if you haven't had a square meal in days.'

'I haven't.' She recalled what the young policeman had said. 'Are you a good cook?'

He turned his back on her without answering, and she regretted the question. Talking to Hawksley was almost as intimidating as talking to Olive. She couldn't speak, it seemed, without treading on a nerve. Except for a muted thank you when he poured her a glass of wine she sat in uncomfortable silence for five minutes, wondering how to open the conversation. She was highly doubtful that he would greet her proposed book on Olive with any enthusiasm.

He placed the steaks on warmed plates, surrounded them with fried whole potatoes, steamed mangetout, and baby carrots, and garnished them with the juices from the pan. 'There,' he said, whisking a plate in front of Roz, apparently unaware of her discomfort, 'that'll put some colour in your cheeks.' He sat down and attacked his own plate. 'Well, come on, woman. What are you waiting for?'

'A knife and fork.'

'Ah!' He pulled open a drawer in the table and slid some cutlery across. 'Now, get stuck in and don't yatter while you're eating. Food should be enjoyed for its own sake.'

She needed no further bidding but set to with a will. 'Fabulous,' she said at last, pushing her empty plate to one side with a sigh of contentment. 'Absolutely fabulous.'

He arched a sardonic eyebrow. 'So what's the verdict? Can I cook or can I cook?'

She laughed. 'You can cook. May I ask you something?'

He filled her empty glass. 'If you must.'

'If I hadn't turned up would you have eaten all that yourself?'

'I might have drawn the line at one steak.' He paused. 'Then again I might not. I've no bookings for tonight and they don't keep. I'd probably have eaten them both.'

She heard the trace of bitterness in his voice. 'How much longer can you stay open without customers?' she asked incautiously.

He ignored the question. 'You said you wanted to talk to me,' he reminded her. 'What about?'

She nodded. Apparently, he had no more desire than she to lick wounds in public. 'Olive Martin,' she told him. 'I'm writing a book about her. I believe you were one of the arresting officers.'

He didn't answer immediately but sat looking at her over the rim of his wine glass. 'Why Olive Martin?'

'She interests me.' It was impossible to gauge his reaction.

'Of course.' He shrugged. 'She did something completely horrific. You'd be very unnatural if you didn't find her interesting. Have you met her?'

She nodded.

'And?'

'I like her.'

'Only because you're naïve.' He stretched his long arms towards the ceiling, cracking the joints in his shoulders. 'You steeled yourself to delve in the sewer, expecting to pull out a monster, and you've landed yourself something comparatively pleasant instead. Olive's not unusual in that. Most criminals are pleasant most of the time. Ask any prison officer. They know better than anyone that the penal system relies almost entirely on the goodwill of the prisoners.' His eyes narrowed. 'But Olive hacked two completely innocent women to death. The fact that she presents a human face to you now doesn't make what she did any less horrific.'

'Have I said it does?'

'You're writing a book about her. Even if you castigate her, she will still be something of a celebrity.' He leaned forward, his tone unfriendly. 'But what about her mother and sister? Where is the justice for them in giving their murderer the thrill and the kudos of being written about?'

Roz dropped her eyes. 'It does worry me,' she admitted. 'No, that's wrong.' She looked up. 'It *did* worry me. I'm a little more sure now of where I'm heading. But I take your point about her victims. It's all too easy to focus on Olive. She's alive and they're dead, and the dead are difficult to recreate. You have to rely on what other people tell you, and just as their perceptions at the time were not always accurate, neither are their memories now.' She sighed. 'I still have reservations – there's no point in pretending I don't – but I need to understand what happened that day before I can make up my mind.' She fingered the stem of her wine glass. 'I think I may very well be naïve but I'd need convincing that that is a bad thing. I could argue, with considerable justification, that anyone delving regularly in sewers must come up jaundiced.'

'What's that supposed to mean?' He was amused.

She looked at him again. 'That what Olive did shocks you but doesn't surprise you. You've known, or known of, other people who've done similar things before.'

'So?'

'So you never established *why* she did it. Whereas I, being naïve' – she held his gaze – 'am surprised as well as shocked and I want to know why.'

He frowned. 'It's all in her statement. I can't remember the exact details now, but she resented not being given a birthday party, I think, and then blew a fuse when her mother got angry with her for persuading the sister to ring in sick the next day. Domestic violence erupts over the most trivial things. Olive's motives were rather more substantial than some I've known.'

Roz bent down to open her briefcase. 'I've a copy of her statement here.' She handed it across and waited while he read it through.

'I can't see your problem,' he said at last. 'She makes it clear as crystal why she did it. She got angry, hit them, and then didn't know how to dispose of the bodies.'

'That's what she says, I agree, but it doesn't mean it's *true*. There's at least one blatant lie in that statement and possibly two.' She tapped her pencil on the table. 'In the first paragraph she says that her relationship with her mother and sister had never been close but that's been flatly contradicted by everyone I've spoken to. They all say she was devoted to Amber.'

He frowned again. 'What's the other lie?'

She leaned over with her pencil and put a line by one of the middle paragraphs. 'She says she held a mirror to their lips to see if there was any mist. According to her, there wasn't, so she proceeded to dismember the bodies.' She turned the pages over. 'But here, according to the pathologist, Mrs Martin put up a struggle to defend herself before her throat was cut. Olive makes no mention of that in her statement.'

He shook his head. 'That doesn't mean a damn thing. Either she decided to put a gloss on the whole affair out of belated shame, or shock simply blotted the less acceptable bits out of her memory.'

'And the lie about not getting on with Amber? How do you explain that away?'

'Do I need to? The confession was completely voluntary. We even made her wait until her solicitor arrived to avoid any hint of police pressure.' He drained his glass. 'And you're not going to try and argue that an innocent woman would confess to a crime like this?'

'It's happened before.'

'Only after days of police interrogation and then, when it comes to the trial, they plead not guilty and deny their statement. Olive did neither.' He looked amused. 'Take it from me, she was so damned relieved to get it all off her chest she couldn't confess fast enough.'

'How? Did she deliver a monologue or did you have to ask questions?'

He clasped his hands behind his neck. 'Unless she's changed a great deal I should imagine you've already discovered that Olive doesn't volunteer information easily.' He cocked his head enquiringly. 'We had to ask questions but she answered them readily enough.' He looked thoughtful. 'For most of the time she sat and stared at us as if she were trying to engrave our faces on her memory. To be honest, I live in terror of her getting out and doing to me what she did to her family.'

'Five minutes ago you described her as comparatively pleasant.'

He rubbed his jaw. 'Comparatively pleasant as far as *you* were concerned,' he corrected her. 'But you were expecting something inhuman, which is why you find it difficult to be objective.'

Roz refused to be drawn again down this blind alley. Instead she took her recorder from her briefcase and put it on the table. 'Can I tape this conversation?'

'I haven't agreed to talk to you yet.' He stood up abruptly and filled a kettle with water. 'You'd do better,' he said after a moment, 'to ring Detective Sergeant Wyatt. He was there when she gave her statement, and he's still on the Force. Coffee?'

'Please.' She watched him select a dark Arabica and spoon the grounds into a cafetière. 'I really would rather talk to you,' she said evenly. 'Policemen are notoriously difficult to pin down. It could take me weeks to get an interview with him. I won't quote you, I won't even name you, if you'd rather I didn't, and you can read the final draft before it goes to print.' She gave a hollow laugh. 'Assuming it ever gets that far. What you say may persuade me not to write it.'

He looked at her, absent-mindedly scratching his chest through his shirt, then made up his mind. 'All right. I'll tell you as much as I can remember but you'll have to double-check everything. It's a long time ago and I can't vouch for my memory. Where do I start?'

'With her telephone call to the police.'

He waited for the kettle to boil, then filled the cafetière and placed it on the table. 'It wasn't a 999 call. She looked up the number in the book and dialled the desk.' He shook his head, remembering. 'It started out as a farce because the sergeant on duty couldn't make head or tail of what she was saying.'

He was shrugging into his jacket at the end of his shift when the desk sergeant came in and handed him a piece of paper with an address on it. 'Do me a favour, Hal, and check this out on your way home. It's Leven Road. You virtually pass it. Some madwoman's been bawling down the phone about chicken legs on her kitchen floor.' He pulled a face. 'Wants a policeman to take them away.' He grinned. 'Presumably she's a vegetarian. You're the cookery expert. Sort it out, there's a good chap.'

Hawksley eyed him suspiciously. 'Is this a wind-up?'

'No. Scout's honour.' He chuckled. 'Look, she's obviously a mental case. They're all over the place, poor sods, since the Government chucked 'em on to the streets. Just do as she asks or we'll have her phoning all night. It'll take you five minutes out of your way.'

Olive Martin, red eyed from weeping, opened the door to him. She smelt strongly of B.O. and her bulky shoulders were hunched in unattractive despair. So much blood was smeared over her baggy T-shirt and trousers that it took on the property of an abstract pattern and his eyes hardly registered it. And why should they? He had no premonition of the horror in store. 'D.S. Hawksley,' he said with an encouraging smile, showing her his card. 'You rang the police station.'

She stepped back, holding the door open. 'They're in the kitchen.' She pointed down the corridor. 'On the floor.'

'OK. We'll go down and have a look. What's your name, love?'

'Olive.'

'Right, Olive, you lead the way. Let's see what's upset you.'

Would it have been better to know what was in there? Probably not. He often thought afterwards that he could never have entered the room at all if he'd been told in advance that he was about to step into a human abattoir. He stared in horror at the butchered bodies, the axe, the blood that ran in rivers across the floor, and his shock was so great that he could hardly breathe for the iron fist that thrust against his diaphragm and squeezed the breath from his lungs. The room reeked of blood. He leant against the door jamb and sucked desperately at the sickly, cloying air, before bolting down the corridor and retching over and over again into the tiny patch of front garden.

Olive sat on the stairs and watched him, her fat moon face as white and pasty as his. 'You should have brought a friend,' she told him miserably. 'It wouldn't have been so bad if there'd been two of you.'

He held a handkerchief to his lips as he used his radio to summon assistance. While he spoke he eyed her warily, registering the blood all over her clothes. Nausea choked him. Je-*sus*! JESUS! How mad was she? *Mad enough to take the axe to him?* 'For God's sake, make it quick,' he shouted into the mouthpiece. 'This is an emergency.' He stayed outside, too frightened to go back in.

She looked at him stolidly. 'I won't hurt you. There's nothing to be afraid of.'

He mopped at his forehead. 'Who are they, Olive?'

'My mother and sister.' Her eyes slid to her hands. 'We had a row.'

His mouth was dry with shock and fear. 'Best not talk about it,' he said.

Tears rolled down her fat cheeks. 'I didn't mean it to happen. We had a row. My mother got so angry with me. Should I give my statement now?'

He shook his head. 'There's no hurry.'

She stared at him without blinking, her tears drying in dirty streaks down her face. 'Will you be able to take them away before my father comes home?' she asked him after a minute or two. 'I think it would be better.'

Bile rose in his throat. 'When do you expect him back?'

'He leaves work at three o'clock. He's part-time.'

Hal glanced at his watch, an automatic gesture. His mind was numb. 'It's twenty to now.'

She was very composed. 'Then perhaps a policeman could go there and explain what's happened. It would be better,' she said again. They heard the wail of approaching sirens. 'Please,' she said urgently.

He nodded. 'I'll arrange it. Where does he work?'

'Carters Haulage. It's in the Docks.'

He was passing the message on as two cars, sirens shrieking, swept round the corner and bore down on number 22. Doors flew open all along the road and curious faces peered out. Hal switched off the radio and looked at her. 'All done,' he said. 'You can stop worrying about your father.'

A large tear slipped down her blotchy face. 'Should I make a pot of tea?'

Hal thought of the kitchen. 'Better not.'

The sirens stilled as policemen erupted from the cars. 'I'm sorry to cause so much bother,' she said into the silence.

She spoke very little after that, but only, thought Hal on reflection, because nobody spoke to her. She was packed into the living room, under the eye of a shocked W.P.C., and sat in bovine immobility watching the comings and goings through the open door. If she was aware of the mounting horror that was gathering about her, she didn't show it. Nor, as time passed and the signs of emotion faded from her face, did she display any further grief or remorse for what she had done. Faced with such complete indifference, the consensus view was that she was mad.

'But she wept in front of you,' interrupted Roz. 'Did *you* think she was mad?'

'I spent two hours in that kitchen with the pathologist, trying to work out the order of events from the blood splashes over the floor, the table, the kitchen units. And then, after the photographs had been taken, we embarked on the grisly jigsaw of deciding which bit belonged to which woman. Of course I thought she was mad. No normal person could have done it.'

Roz chewed her pencil. 'That's begging the question, you know. All you're really saying is that the act itself was one of madness. I asked you if, from your experience of her, you thought Olive was mad.'

'And you're splitting hairs. As far as I could see, the two were inextricably linked. Yes, I thought Olive was mad. That's why we were so careful to make sure her solicitor was there when she made her statement. The idea of her getting off on a technicality and spending twelve months in hospital before some idiot psychiatrist decided she was responding well enough to treatment to be allowed out scared us rigid.'

'So did it surprise you when she was judged fit to plead guilty?'

'Yes,' he admitted, 'it did.'

At around six o'clock attention switched to Olive. Areas of dried blood were lifted carefully from her arms and each fingernail was minutely scraped before she was taken upstairs to bathe herself and change into clean clothes. Everything she had been wearing was packed into individual polythene bags and loaded into a police van. An inspector drew Hal to one side.

'I gather she's already admitted she did it.'

Hal nodded. 'More or less.'

Roz interrupted again. 'Less is right. If what you said earlier is correct, she did not admit anything. She said they'd had a row, that her mother got angry, and she didn't mean it to happen. She didn't say she had killed them.'

Hal agreed. 'I accept that. But the implication was there which is why I told her not to talk about it. I didn't want her claiming afterwards that she hadn't been properly cautioned.' He sipped his coffee. 'By the same token, she didn't deny killing them, which is the first thing an innocent person would have done, especially as she had their blood all over her.'

'But the point is, you assumed her guilt before you knew it for a fact.'

'She was certainly our prime suspect,' he said drily.

The inspector ordered Hal to take Olive down to the station. 'But don't let her say anything until we can get hold of a solicitor. We'll do it by the book. OK?'

Hal nodded again. 'There's a father. He'll be at the nick by now. I sent a car to pick him up from work but I don't know what he's been told.'

'You'd better find out then, and, for Christ's sake, Sergeant, if he doesn't know, then break it to him gently or you'll give the poor sod a heart attack. Find out if he's got a solicitor and if he's willing to have him or her represent his daughter.'

They put a blanket over Olive's head when they took her out to the car. A crowd had gathered, lured by rumours of a hideous crime, and cameramen jostled for a photograph. Boos greeted her appearance and a woman laughed. 'What good's a blanket, boys? You'd need a bloody marquee to cover that fat cow. I'd recognize her legs anywhere. What you done, Olive?'

Roz interrupted again when he jumped the story on to his meeting with Robert Martin at the police station.

'Hang on. Did she say anything in the car?'

He thought for a moment. 'She asked me if I liked her dress. I said I did.'

'Were you being polite?'

'No. It was a vast improvement on the T-shirt and trousers.'

'Because they had blood on them?'

'Probably. No,' he contradicted himself, ruffling his hair, 'because the dress gave her a bit of shape, I suppose, made her look more feminine. Does it matter?'

Roz ignored this. 'Did she say anything else?'

'I think she said something like: "That's good. It's my favourite." '

'But in her statement, she said she was going to London. Why wasn't she wearing the dress when she committed the murders?'

He looked puzzled. 'Because she was going to London in trousers, presumably.'

'No,' said Roz stubbornly. 'If the dress was her favourite, then that's what she would have worn for her trip to town. London was her birthday treat to herself. She probably had dreams of bumping into Mr Right on Waterloo station. It simply wouldn't occur to her to wear anything but her best. You need to be a woman to understand that.'

He was amused. 'But I see hundreds of girls walking around in shapeless trousers and baggy T-shirts, particularly the fat ones. I think they look grotesque but they seem to like it. Presumably they're making a statement about their refusal to pander to conventional standards of beauty. Why should Olive have been any different?'

'Because she wasn't the rebellious type. She lived at home under her mother's thumb, took the job her mother wanted her to take, and was apparently so unused to going out alone for the day that she had to beg her sister to go with her.' She drummed her fingers impatiently on the table. 'I'm right. I know I am. If she wasn't lying about the trip to London then she should have been wearing her dress.'

He was not impressed. 'She was rebellious enough to kill her mother and sister,' he remarked. 'If she could do that, she could certainly go to London in trousers. You're splitting hairs again. Anyway, she might have changed to keep the dress clean.'

'But she definitely intended to go to London? Did you check that?'

'She certainly booked the day off work. We accepted that

London was where she was going because, as far as we could establish, she hadn't mentioned her plans to anyone else.'

'Not even to her father?'

'If she did, he didn't remember it.'

Olive waited in an interview room while Hal spoke to her father. It was a difficult conversation. Whether he had schooled himself to it, or whether it was a natural trick of behaviour, Robert Martin reacted little to anything that was said to him. He was a handsome man but, in the way that a Greek sculpture is handsome, he invited admiration but lacked warmth or attraction. His curiously impassive face had an unlined and ageless quality, and only his hands, knotted with arthritis, gave any indication that he had passed his middle years. Once or twice he smoothed his blond hair with the flat of his hand or touched his fingers to his tie, but for all the expression on his plastic features Hal might have been passing the time of day. It was impossible to gauge from his expression how deeply he was shocked or whether, indeed, he was shocked at all.

'Did you like him?' asked Roz.

'Not much. He reminded me of Olive. I don't know where I am with people who hide their feelings. It makes me uncomfortable.'

Roz could identify with that.

Hal kept detail to a minimum, informing him only that the bodies of his wife and one of his daughters had been discovered that afternoon in the kitchen of his house, and that his other daughter, Olive, had given the police reason to believe she had killed them. .

Robert Martin crossed his legs and folded his hands calmly in his lap. 'Have you charged her with anything?'

'No. We haven't questioned her either.' He watched the

other man closely. 'Frankly, sir, in view of the serious nature of the possible charges we think she should have a solicitor with her.'

'Of course. I'm sure my man, Peter Crew, will come.' Mild enquiry twitched his brows. 'What's the procedure? Should I telephone him?'

Hal was puzzled by the man's composure. He wiped a hand across his face. 'Are you sure you understand what's happened, sir?'

'I believe so. Gwen and Amber are dead and you think Olive murdered them.'

'That's not quite accurate. Olive has implied that she was responsible for their deaths but, until we take a statement from her, I can't say what the charges will be.' He paused for a moment. 'I want you to be quite clear on this, Mr Martin. The Home Office pathologist who examined the scene had no doubts that considerable ferocity was used both before and after death. In due course, I'm afraid to say, we will have to ask you to identify the bodies and you may, when you see them, feel less charitably inclined towards any possible suspect. On that basis, do you have any reservations about your solicitor representing Olive?'

Martin shook his head. 'I would be happier dealing with someone I know.'

'There may be a conflict of interests. Have you considered that?'

'In what way?'

'At the risk of labouring the point, sir,' said Hal coldly, 'your wife and daughter have been brutally murdered. I imagine you will want the perpetrator prosecuted?' He lifted an eyebrow in enquiry and Martin nodded. 'Then you may well want a solicitor yourself to ensure that the prosecution proceeds to your satisfaction, but if your own solicitor is already representing your daughter, he will be unable to assist you because your interests will conflict with your daughter's.'

'Not if she's innocent.' Martin pinched the crease in his trousers, aligning it with the centre of his knee. 'I am really not concerned with what Olive may have implied, Sergeant Hawksley. There is no conflict of interest in my mind. Establishing her innocence and representing me in pressing for a prosecution can be done by the same solicitor. Now, if you could lend me the use of a telephone, I will ring Peter Crew, and afterwards, perhaps you will allow me to talk to my daughter.'

Hal shook his head. 'I'm sorry, sir, but that won't be possible, not until we've taken a statement from her. You will also be required to make a statement. You may be allowed to speak to her afterwards, but at the moment I can't guarantee it.'

'And that,' he said, recalling the incident, 'was the one and only time he showed any emotion. He looked quite upset, but whether because I'd denied him access to Olive or because I'd told him he'd have to make a statement, I don't know.' He considered for a moment. 'It must have been the denial of access. We went through every minute of that man's day and he came out whiter than white. He worked in an open-plan office with five other people and, apart from the odd trip to the lavatory, he was under someone's eye the whole day. There just wasn't time for him to go home.'

'But you did suspect him?'

'Yes.'

Roz looked interested. 'In spite of Olive's confession?'

He nodded. 'He was so damn cold blooded about it all. Even identifying the bodies didn't faze him.'

Roz thought for a moment. 'There was another conflict of interest which you don't seem to have considered.' She chewed her pencil. 'If Robert Martin was the murderer, he could have used his solicitor to manipulate Olive into confessing. Peter Crew makes no secret of his dislike of her, you know. I think he regrets the abolition of capital punishment.'

Hal folded his arms, then smiled in amusement. 'You'll have to be very careful if you intend to make statements like that in your book, Miss Leigh. Solicitors are not required to like their clients, they merely have to represent them. In any case, Robert Martin dropped out of the frame very rapidly. We toyed with the idea that he killed Gwen and Amber before he went to work and Olive then set about disposing the bodies to protect him, but the numbers didn't add up. He had an alibi even for that. There was a neighbour who saw her husband off to work a few minutes before Martin himself left. Amber and Gwen were alive then because she spoke to them on their doorstep. She remembered asking Amber how she was getting on at Glitzy. They waved as Martin drove away.'

'He could have gone round the corner and come back again.'

'He left home at eight-thirty and arrived at work at nine. We tested the drive and it took half an hour.' He shrugged. 'As I said, he was whiter than white.'

'What about lunch? Could he have gone back then?'

'He had a pint and a sandwich in the local pub with two men from the office.'

'OK. Go on.'

There was little more to tell. In spite of Crew's advice to remain silent, Olive agreed to answer police questions, and at nine-thirty, expressing relief to have got the whole thing off her chest, she signed her statement and was formally charged with the murder of her mother and sister.

Following her remand into custody on the morning of the next day, Hal and Geoff Wyatt were given the task of detailing the police case against her. It was a straightforward collating of pathological, forensic, and police evidence, all of which, upon examination, supported the facts given in Olive's statement. Namely that, acting alone, she had, on the morning of the ninth of September, 1987, murdered her mother and sister by cutting their throats with a carving knife.

SEVEN

There was a lengthy silence. Hal splayed his hands on the scrubbed deal table and pushed himself to his feet. 'How about some more coffee?' He watched her industrious pen scribbling across a page of her notebook. 'More coffee?' he repeated.

'Mm. Black, no sugar.' She didn't look up but went on writing.

'Sure, baas. Don't mind me, baas. I'se just de paid help, baas.'

Roz laughed. 'Sorry. Yes, thank you, I'd love some more coffee. Look, if you can just bear with me for a moment, I've a few questions to ask and I'm trying to jot them down while the thing's still fresh.'

He watched her while she wrote. Botticelli's *Venus*, he had thought the first time he saw her, but she was too thin for his liking, hardly more than seven stone and a good five feet six. She made a fabulous clothes'-horse, of course, but there was no softness to hug, no comfort in the tautly strung body. He wondered if her slenderness was a deliberate thing or if she lived on her nerves. The latter, he thought. She was clearly a woman of obsessions if her crusade for Olive was anything to go by. He put a fresh cup of coffee in front of her but stayed standing, cradling his own coffee cup between his hands.

'OK,' she said, sorting out the pages, 'let's start with the kitchen. You say the forensic evidence supported Olive's statement that she acted alone. How?'

He thought back. 'You have to picture that place. It was a slaughter house, and every time she moved she left footprints in the congealing blood. We photographed each one separately and they were all hers, including the bloody prints that her shoes left on the carpet in the hall.' He shrugged. 'There were also bloody palm-prints and fingerprints over most of the surfaces where she had rested her hands. Again all hers. We did raise other fingerprints, admittedly, including about three, I think, which we were never able to match with any of the Martins or their neighbours, but you'd expect that in a kitchen. The gas man, the electricity man, a plumber maybe. There was no blood on them so we inclined to the view that they had been left in the days prior to the murder.'

Roz chewed her pencil. 'And the axe and the knife? I suppose they had only her fingerprints.'

'Actually no. The cutting weapons were so smeared that we couldn't get anything off them at all.' He chuckled at her immediate interest. 'You're chasing red herrings. Wet blood is slippery stuff. It would have been very surprising if we *had* found some perfect prints. The rolling pin had three damn good ones, all hers.'

She made a note. 'I didn't know you could take them off unpolished wood.'

'It was solid glass, two feet long, a massive thing. I suppose if we were surprised by anything it was that the blows she struck with it hadn't killed Gwen and Amber. They were both tiny women. By rights she should have smashed their skulls with it.' He sipped his coffee. 'It leant some credence to her story, in fact, that she only tapped them lightly in the first instance to make them shut up. We were afraid she might use that in her defence to get the charge reduced to manslaughter, the argument being that she slit their throats *only* because she believed they were already dead and she was trying to dismember them in panic. If she could then go on to show that the initial blows with the rolling pin were struck with very little force – well, she might almost have persuaded a jury that the whole thing was a macabre accident. Which is one good reason, by the way, why she never mentioned the fight with her mother. We did push her on that, but she kept insisting that no mist on the mirror meant they were dead.'

He pulled a face. 'So I spent a very unpleasant two days working with the pathologist and the bodies, going step by step through what actually happened. We ended up with enough evidence of the fight Gwen put up to save her life to press a murder charge. Poor woman. Her hands and arms were literally cut to ribbons where she had tried to ward off the blows.'

Roz stared into her coffee for some minutes. 'Olive was very kind to me the other day. I can't imagine her doing something like that.'

'You've never seen her in a rage. You might think differently if you had.'

'Have you seen her in a rage?'

'No,' he admitted.

'Well, I find it difficult even to imagine that. I accept she's put on a lot of weight in the last six years but she's a heavy, stolid type. It's highly strung, impatient people who lose their tempers.' She saw his scepticism and laughed. 'I know, I know, amateur psychology of the worst kind. Just two more questions then I'll leave you in peace. What happened to Gwen and Amber's clothes?'

'She burnt them in one of those square wire incinerators in the garden. We retrieved some scraps from the ashes which matched the descriptions that Martin gave of the clothes the two women had been wearing that morning.'

'Why did she do that?'

'To get rid of them, presumably.'

'You didn't ask her?'

He frowned. 'I'm sure we must have done. I can't remember now.'

'There's nothing in her statement about burning clothes.'

He lowered his head in reflection and pressed a thumb and forefinger to his eyelids. 'We asked her why she took their clothes off,' he murmured, 'and she said they had to be naked or she couldn't see where to make the cuts through the joints. I think Geoff then asked her what she had done with the clothes.' He fell silent.

'And?'

He looked up and rubbed his jaw pensively. 'I don't think she gave an answer. If she did, I can't remember it. I have a feeling the information about the scraps in the incinerator came in the next morning when we made a thorough search of the garden.'

'So you asked her then?'

He shook his head. 'I didn't, though I suppose Geoff may have done. Gwen had a floral nylon overall that had melted over a lump of wool and cotton. We had to peel it apart into its constituent elements but there was enough there that was recognizable. Martin ID'd the bits and so did the neighbour.' He stabbed a finger in the air. 'There were some buttons, too. Martin recognized those straightaway as being from the dress his wife had been wearing.'

'But didn't you wonder why Olive took time out to burn the clothes? She could have put them in the suitcases with the bodies and dumped the whole lot in the sea.'

'The incinerator certainly wasn't burning at five o'clock that night or we'd have noticed it; therefore disposing of the clothes must have been one of the first things she did. She wouldn't have seen it as taking time out because at that stage she probably still thought dismembering two bodies would be comparatively easy. Look, she was trying to get rid of evidence. The only reason she panicked and called us in was because her father was coming home. If it had been just the three women living in that house she could have gone through with her plan, and we'd have had the job of trying to identify some bits and pieces of mutilated flesh found floating in the sea off Southampton. She might even have got away with it.'

'I doubt it. The neighbours weren't stupid. They'd have wondered why Gwen and Amber were missing.'

'True,' he conceded. 'What was the other question?'

'Did Olive's hands and arms have a lot of scratches on them from her fight with Gwen?'

He shook his head. 'None. She had some bruising but no scratches.'

Roz stared at him. 'Didn't that strike you as odd? You said Gwen was fighting for her life.'

'She had nothing to scratch with,' he said almost apologetically. 'Her fingernails were bitten to the quick. It was rather pathetic in a woman of her age. All she could do was grip Olive's wrists to try and keep the knife away. That's what the bruises were. Deep finger-marks. We took photographs of them.'

With an abrupt movement Roz squared her papers and dropped them into her briefcase. 'Not much room for doubt then, is there?' she said, picking up her coffee cup.

'None at all. And it wouldn't have made any difference, you know, if she'd kept her mouth shut or pleaded not guilty. She would still have been convicted. The evidence against her was overwhelming. In the end, even her father had to accept that. I felt quite sorry for him then. He became an old man overnight.'

Roz glanced at the tape, which was still running. 'Was he very fond of her?'

'I don't know. He was the most undemonstrative person I've ever met. I got the impression he wasn't fond of any of them but' – he shrugged – 'he certainly took Olive's guilt very badly.'

She drank her coffee. 'Presumably the post-mortem revealed that Amber had had a baby when she was thirteen?'

He nodded.

'Did you pursue that at all? Try and trace the child?'

'We didn't see the need. It had happened eight years before. It was hardly likely to have any bearing on the case.' He waited, but she didn't say anything. 'So? Will you go on with the book?'

'Oh, yes,' she said.

He looked surprised. 'Why?'

'Because there are more inconsistencies now than there were before.' She held up her fingers and ticked them off point by point. 'Why was she crying so much when she telephoned the police station that the desk sergeant couldn't understand what she was saying? Why wasn't she wearing her best dress for London? Why did she burn the clothes? Why did her father think she was innocent? Why wasn't he shocked by Gwen and Amber's deaths? Why did she say she didn't like Amber? Why didn't she mention the fight with her mother if she intended to plead guilty? Why were the blows from the rolling pin so comparatively light? Why? Why? Why?' She dropped her hands to the table with a wry smile. 'They may very well be red herrings but I can't get rid of a gut feeling that there's something wrong. Ultimately, perhaps, I cannot square your and her solicitor's conviction that Olive was mad with the assessments of five psychiatrists who all say she's normal.'

He studied her for some minutes in silence. 'You accused me of assuming her guilt before I knew it for a fact, but you're doing something rather worse. You're assuming her innocence *in spite of* the facts. Supposing you manage to whip up support for her through this book of yours – and in view of the way the judicial system is reeling at the moment, that's not as unlikely as it should be – have you no qualms about releasing someone like her back into society?'

'None at all, if she's innocent.'

'And if she isn't, but you get her out anyway?'

'Then the law is an ass.'

'All right, if she didn't do it, who did?'

'Someone she cared about.' She finished her coffee and switched off the tape. 'Anything else just doesn't make sense.' She shut the recorder into her briefcase and stood up. 'You've been very kind to give up so much of your time. Thank you, and thank you for the lunch.' She held out a hand.

He took it gravely. 'My pleasure, Miss Leigh.' Her fingers, soft and warm in his, moved nervously when he held them too long, and he thought she seemed suddenly rather afraid of him. It was probably for the best. One way and another, she spelt trouble.

She walked to the door. 'Goodbye, Sergeant Hawksley. I hope the business picks up for you.'

110

He gave a savage smile. 'It will. This is what's known as a temporary blip, I assure you.'

'Good.' She paused. 'There's just one last thing. I understand Robert Martin told you he thought the more likely scenario was that Gwen battered Amber, and Olive then killed Gwen trying to defend her sister. Why did you dismiss that possibility?'

'It didn't hold water. The pathologist established that both throats were cut with the same hand. The size, depth, and angle of the wounds were consistent with one attacker. Gwen wasn't just fighting for herself, you know, she was fighting for Amber, too. Olive is completely ruthless. You would be very foolish to forget that.' He smiled again but the smile didn't reach his eyes. 'If you'll take my advice you'll abandon the whole thing.'

Roz shrugged. 'I tell you what, Sergeant' – she gestured towards the restaurant – 'you mind your business, and I'll mind mine.'

He listened to her heels tapping away down the alley, then reached for the telephone and dialled. 'Geoff,' he snapped into the mouthpiece, 'get down here, will you? We need to talk.' His eyes hardened as he listened to the voice at the other end. 'Like hell it's not your problem. I'm damned if I'll be the fall guy for this one.'

Roz glanced at her watch as she drove away. It was four thirty. If she pushed it she might catch Peter Crew before he went home for the day. She found a parking space in the centre of Southampton and arrived at his office just as he was leaving.

'Mr Crew!' she called, running after him.

He turned with his unconvincing smile, only to frown when he saw who it was. 'I've no time to talk to you now, Miss Leigh. I have an engagement.'

'Let me walk with you,' she urged. 'I won't delay you, I promise.'

He gave a nod of acquiescence and set off again, the hair of his toupee bobbing in time to his steps. 'My car isn't far.'

Roz did not waste time on pleasantries. 'I gather Mr Martin left his money to Amber's illegitimate son. I have been told' – she stretched the truth like a piece of elastic – 'that he was adopted by some people called Brown who have since emigrated to Australia. Can you tell me if you've made any progress in finding him?'

Mr Crew shot her an annoyed glance. 'Now where did you find that out, I wonder?' His voice clipped the words angrily. 'Has someone in my practice been talking?'

'No,' she assured him. 'I had it from an independent source.'

His eyes narrowed. 'I find that hard to believe. May I ask who it was?'

Roz smiled easily. 'Someone who knew Amber at the time the baby was born.'

'How did they know the name?'

'I've no idea.'

'Robert certainly wouldn't have talked,' he muttered. 'There are rules governing the tracing of adopted children, which he was well aware of, but even allowing for that he was passionate on the subject of secrecy. If the child were to be found he didn't want any publicity surrounding the inheritance. The stigma of the murders could follow the boy all his life.' He shook his head crossly. 'I must insist, Miss Leigh, that you keep this information to yourself. It would be gross irresponsibility to publish it. It could jeopardize the lad's future.'

'You really do have quite the wrong impression of me,' said Roz pleasantly. 'I approach my work with immense care, and I do not set out to expose people for the sake of it.'

He turned a corner. 'Well, be warned, young lady. I shan't hesitate to take out an injunction against your book if I think it justified.' A gust of wind lifted the toupee's peak and he pressed it firmly to his head like a hat.

Roz, a step or two behind him, scurried alongside. 'Fair enough,' she said, biting back her laughter. 'So, on that basis, could you answer my question? Have you found him yet? Are you anywhere near finding him?'

He padded on doggedly. 'Without wishing to be offensive, Miss Leigh, I don't see how that information can help you. We have just agreed you won't be publishing it.'

She decided to be straight with him. 'Olive knows all about him, knows her father left him his money, knows you're looking for him.' She lifted her hands at his expression of irritation. 'Not, in the first instance, from me, Mr Crew. She's very astute and what she hadn't guessed for herself she picked up on the prison grapevine. She said her father would always leave money to family if he could so it hardly required much imagination to guess that he would try and trace Amber's child. Anyway, whether or not you've had any success seems to matter to her. I hoped you could tell me something that would set her mind at rest.'

He stopped abruptly. 'Does she want him found?'

'I don't know.'

'Hm. Perhaps she thinks the money will come to her in the absence of the named beneficiary?'

Roz showed her surprise. 'I don't think that's ever occurred to her. It couldn't, anyway, could it? You made that point before.'

Mr Crew set off again. 'Robert did not insist that Olive should be kept in the dark. His only instruction was that we should avoid distressing her unnecessarily. Wrongly, perhaps, I assumed that knowledge of the terms of the will *would* distress her. However, if she is already acquainted with them – well, well, you can leave that with me, Miss Leigh. Was there anything else?'

'Yes. Did Robert Martin ever visit her in prison?'

'No. I'm sorry to say he never spoke to her again after she was charged with the murders.'

Roz caught his arm. 'But he thought she was innocent,' she protested with some indignation, 'and he paid her legal bills. Why wouldn't he see her? That was very cruel, wasn't it?'

There was a sharp gleam in the man's eyes. 'Very cruel,'

he agreed, 'but not on Robert's part. It was Olive who refused to see him. It drove him to his death, which, I think, was her intention all along.'

Roz frowned unhappily. 'You and I have very different views of her, Mr Crew. I've only experienced her kindness.' The frown deepened. 'She did know he wanted to see her, I suppose.'

'Of course. As a prosecution witness he had to apply to the Home Office for special permission to visit her, even though she was his daughter. If you contact them they'll verify it for you.' He moved on again and Roz had to run to keep up with him.

'What about the inconsistencies in her statement, Mr Crew? Did you ask her about them?'

'What inconsistencies?'

'Well, for example, the fact that she doesn't mention the fight with her mother but claims Gwen and Amber were dead before she started to dismember them.'

He cast an impatient glance at his watch. 'She was lying.'

Roz caught at his arm again and forced him to stop. 'You were her solicitor,' she said angrily. 'You had a duty to believe her.'

'Don't be naïve, Miss Leigh. I had a duty to *represent* her.' He shook himself free. 'If solicitors were required to believe everything their clients told them there would be little or no legal representation left.' His lips thinned in distaste. 'In any case I did believe her. She said she killed them and I accepted it. I had to. In spite of every attempt I made to suggest she said nothing, she insisted on making her confession.' His eyes bored into hers. 'Are you telling me now that she denies the murders?'

'No,' Roz admitted, 'but I don't think the version she gave the police is the correct one.'

He studied her for a moment. 'Did you talk to Graham Deedes?' She nodded. 'And?'

'He agrees with you.'

'The police?'

She nodded again. 'One of them. He also agrees with you.'

'And doesn't that tell you anything?'

'Not really. Deedes was briefed by you and never even spoke to her and the police have been wrong before.' She brushed a curl of red hair from her face. 'Unfortunately, I don't have your faith in British justice.'

'Obviously not.' Crew smiled coolly. 'But your scepticism is misplaced this time. Good day to you, Miss Leigh.' He loped away up the wind-swept street, the absurd toupee held in place under his hand, his coat-tails whipping about his long legs. He was a comical figure, but Roz did not feel like laughing. For all his idiotic mannerisms he had a certain dignity.

She telephoned St Angela's Convent from a payphone but it was after five o'clock and whoever answered said Sister Bridget had gone home for the evening. She called Directory Enquiries for the DSS number in Dawlington, but, when she tried it, the office had closed for the night and there was no answer. Back in her car she pencilled in a rough timetable for the following morning, then sat for some time with her notebook propped against the steering-wheel, running over in her mind what Crew had told her. But she couldn't concentrate. Her attention kept wandering to the more attractive lure of Hal Hawksley in the Poacher's kitchen.

He had an unnerving trick of catching her eye when she wasn't expecting it, and the shock to her system every time was cataclysmic. She thought 'going weak at the knees' was something invented by romantic authoresses. But the way things were, if she went back to the Poacher, she'd need a Zimmer frame just to make it through the door! *Was she mad?* The man was some sort of gangster. Whoever heard of a restaurant without customers? People had to eat, even in recessions. With a rueful shake of her head, she fired the engine and set off back to London. *What the hell, anyway!* Sod's law predicated that because thoughts of him filled her mind with erotic fantasies his thoughts of her (if he thought about her at all) would be anything but libidinous.

London, when she reached it, was fittingly clogged and oppressive with Thursday night rush-hour traffic.

An older motherly inmate, elected by the others, paused nervously by the open door. The Sculptress terrified her but, as the girls kept saying, she was the only one Olive would talk to. You remind her of her mother, they all said. The idea alarmed her, but she *was* curious. She watched the huge brooding figure, clumsily rolling a cigarette paper around a meagre sprinkling of tobacco, for several moments before she spoke. 'Hey, Sculptress! Who's the redhead you're seeing?'

Except for a brief flick of her eyes, Olive ignored her.

'Here, have one of mine.' She fished a pack of Silk Cut from her pocket and proffered it. The response was immediate. Like a dog responding to the ringing tap of its dinner plate, Olive shuffled across the floor and took one, secreting it in the folds of her dress somewhere. 'So who's the redhead?' persisted the other.

'An author. She's writing a book about me.'

'Christ!' said the older woman in disgust. 'What she want to write about you for? I'm the one got bloody stitched up.'

Olive stared at her. 'Maybe I did, too.'

'Oh, sure,' the other sniggered, tapping her thigh. 'Now pull the other one. It's got frigging bells on.'

A wheeze of amusement gusted from Olive's lips. 'Well, you know what they say: you can fool some of the people all of the time and all of the people some of the time . . .' She paused invitingly.

'But not all of the people all of the time,' the woman finished obligingly. She wagged her finger. 'You haven't got a prayer.'

Olive's unblinking eyes held hers. 'So who needs prayers?' She tapped the side of her head. 'Find yourself a gullible journalist, then use a bit more of this. Even *you* might get somewhere. She's an opinion-former. You fool her and she fools everyone else.'

'That stinks!' declared the woman incautiously. 'It's only the bloody psychos they're ever interested in. The rest of us poor sods can go hang ourselves for all they care.'

Something rather unpleasant shifted at the back of Olive's tiny eyes. 'Are you calling me a psycho?'

The woman smiled weakly and retreated a step. 'Hey, Sculptress, it was a slip of the tongue.' She held up her hands. 'OK? No harm done.' She was sweating as she walked away.

Behind her, using her bulk to obscure what she was doing from prying eyes, Olive took the clay figure she was working on from her bottom drawer and set her ponderous fingers to moulding the child on its mother's lap. Whether it was intentional or whether she hadn't the skill to do it differently, the mother's crude hands, barely disinterred from the clay, seemed to be smothering the life from the baby's plump, round body.

Olive crooned quietly to herself as she worked. Behind the mother and child, a series of figures, like grey gingerbread men, lined the back of the table. Two or three had lost their heads.

He sat slumped on the steps outside the front door of her block of flats, smelling of beer, his head buried in his hands. Roz stared at him for several seconds, her face blank of expression. 'What are you doing here?'

He had been crying, she saw. 'We need to talk,' he said. 'You never talk to me.'

She didn't bother to answer. Her ex-husband was very drunk. There was nothing they could say that hadn't been said a hundred times before. She was so tired of his messages on her answerphone, tired of the letters, tired of the hatred that knotted inside her when she heard his voice or saw his handwriting.

He plucked at her skirt as she tried to pass, clinging to it like a child. 'Please, Roz. I'm too pissed to go home.'

She took him upstairs out of an absurd sense of past duty. 'But you can't stay,' she told him, pushing him on to the sofa. 'I'll ring Jessica and get her to come and collect you.'

'Sam's sick,' he muttered. 'She won't leave him.'

Roz shrugged unsympathetically. 'Then I'll call a cab.'

'No.' He reached down and jerked the jackplug from its socket. 'I'm staying.

There was a raw edge to his voice which was a warning, if she had chosen to heed it, that he was in no mood to be trifled with. But they had been married too long and had had too many bruising rows for her to allow him to dictate terms. She had only contempt for him now. 'Please yourself,' she said. 'I'll go to a hotel.'

He stumbled to the door and stood with his back to it. 'It wasn't my fault, Roz. It was an accident. For God's sake, will you stop punishing me?'

EIGHT

Roz closed her eyes and saw again the tattered, pale face of her five-year-old daughter, as ugly in death as she had been beautiful in life, her skin ripped and torn by the exploding glass of the windscreen. Could she have accepted it more easily, she wondered as she had wondered so many times before, if Rupert had died too? Could she have forgiven him, dead, as she could not forgive him, alive? 'I never see you,' she said with a tight smile, 'so how can I be punishing you? You're drunk and you're being ridiculous. Neither of which conditions is any way out of the ordinary.' He had an unhealthy and uncared-for look which fuelled her scorn and made her impatient. 'Oh, for God's sake,' she snapped, 'just get out, will you? I don't feel anything for you any more and, to be honest, I don't think I ever did.' But that wasn't true, not really. 'You can't hate what you never loved,' Olive had said.

Tears slithered down his drink-sodden face. 'I weep for her every day, you know.'

'Do you, Rupert? I don't. I haven't the energy.'

'Then you didn't love her as much as I loved her,' he sobbed, his body heaving to control itself.

Roz's lips curled contemptuously. 'Really? Then why your indecent haste to provide her replacement? I worked it out, you know. You must have impregnated your precious Jessica within a week of walking away unscathed from the – *accident*.' She larded the word with sarcasm. 'Is Sam a good replacement, Rupert? Does he wind your hair round his finger the way Alice used to do? Does he laugh like her? Does he wait

119

by the door for you and hug your knees and say: "Mummy, Mummy, Daddy's home"?' Her anger made her voice brittle. 'Does he, Rupert? Is he everything Alice was and more? Or is he nothing like her and that's why you have to weep for her every day?'

'He's a baby, for Christ's sake.' He clenched his fists, her hatred mirrored in his eyes. 'God, you're a fucking bitch, Roz. I never set out to replace her. How could I? Alice was Alice. I couldn't bring her back.'

She turned away to look out of the window. 'No.'

'Then why do you blame Sam? It wasn't his fault either. He doesn't even know he had a half-sister.'

'I don't blame Sam.' She stared at a couple, lit by orange light, on the other side of the road. They held each other tenderly, stroking hair, stroking arms, kissing. How naïve they were. They thought love was kind. 'I resent him.'

She heard him blunder against her coffee table. 'That's just bloody spite,' he slurred.

'Yes,' she said quietly, more to herself than to him, her breath misting the glass, 'but I don't see why you should be happy when I am not? You killed my daughter but you got away with it because the law said you'd suffered enough. I've suffered far more and my only crime was to let my adulterous husband have access to his daughter because I knew she loved him and I didn't want to see her unhappy.'

'If you'd only been more understanding,' he wept, 'it would never have happened. It was your fault, Roz. You're the one who really killed her.' She didn't hear his approach. She was turning back into the room when his fist smashed against her face.

It was a shabby, sordid fight. Where words had failed them – the very predictability of their conversations meant they were always forearmed – they hit and scratched instead in a brutish desire to hurt. It was a curiously passionless exercise, motivated more by feelings of guilt than by hate or revenge, for at the back of both their minds was the knowledge that it was the failure of their marriage, the war they had conducted between themselves, that had led Rupert to accelerate away in frustrated anger with their daughter, unstrapped, upon the back seat. And who could have foreseen the car that would hurtle out of control across a central reservation and, under the force of its impact, toss a helpless five-year-old through shards of broken glass, smashing her fragile skull as she went? An act of God, according to the insurance company. But for Roz, at least, it had been God's final act. He and Alice had perished together.

Rupert was the first to stay his hand, aware, perhaps, that the fight was an unequal one or because, quite simply, he had sobered up. He crawled away to sit huddled in a corner. Roz fingered the tenderness round her mouth and licked blood from her lips, then closed her eyes and sat for several minutes in restful silence, her murderous anger assuaged. They should have done this a long time ago. She felt at peace for the first time in months, as if she had exorcised her own guilt in some way. She should, she knew, have gone out to the car that day and strapped Alice into the seat herself, but instead she had slammed the front door on them both and retreated to the kitchen to nurse her hurt pride with a bottle of gin and an orgy of tearing up photographs. Perhaps, after all, she had needed to be punished too. Her guilt had never been expiated. Her own atonement, a private rending of herself, had brought about her disintegration and not her redemption.

Enough, she saw now, was enough. *'We are all masters of our fate, Roz, including you.'*

She pushed herself gingerly to her feet, located the jackplug and inserted it back into its socket. She glanced at Rupert for a moment, then dialled Jessica. 'It's Roz,' she said. 'Rupert's here and he needs collecting, I'm afraid.' She heard the sigh at the other end of the line. 'It's the last time, Jessica, I promise.' She gave a hint of a laugh. 'We've declared a truce. No more recriminations. OK, half an hour. He'll be waiting for you downstairs.' She replaced the receiver. 'I mean it, Rupert. It's over. It was an accident. Let's stop blaming each other and find some peace at last.'

Iris Fielding's insensitivity was legendary but even she was shocked by the sight of Roz's battered face the next day. 'God, you look awful!' she said bluntly, making straight for the drinks cabinet and pouring herself a brandy. As an after-thought she poured one for Roz. 'Who did it?'

Roz closed the door and limped back to the sofa.

Iris drained her glass. 'Was it Rupert?' She proffered the second glass to Roz who shook her head to the brandy and the question.

'Of course it wasn't Rupert.' She lowered herself carefully on to the sofa, half lying, half sitting, while Mrs Antrobus stalked across the soft fluff of her dressing-gowned chest to butt her chin with an affectionate head. 'Could you feed Mrs A. for me? There's an opened tin in the fridge.'

Iris glowered at Mrs Antrobus. 'Horrible flea-bitten crea-ture. Where were you when your mistress needed you?' But she disappeared into the kitchen and rattled a saucer anyway. 'Are you sure it wasn't Rupert?' she asked again when she re-emerged.

'No. Not his style at all. The fights we have are entirely verbal and infinitely more bruising.'

Iris looked thoughtful. 'You've always told me how sup-portive he's been.'

'I lied.'

Iris looked even more thoughtful. 'So who was it?'

'Some creep I picked up at a wine bar. He was more fanci-able with his clothes on than off, so I told him to get stuffed and he took exception.' She saw a question in Iris's eyes and smiled cynically through her split lip. 'No, he didn't rape me. My virtue is intact. I defended it with my face.'

'Hm. Well, far be it from me to criticize, my love, but wouldn't it have been more sensible to defend your face with your virtue? I'm not a great believer in fighting over lost causes.' She drank Roz's brandy. 'Did you call the police?'

'No.'

'A doctor?'

'No.' She put a hand on the telephone. 'And you're not calling them either.'

Iris shrugged. 'So what have you been doing all morning?'

'Trying to work out how I could get by without calling anyone. At midday, I realized I couldn't. I've used all my aspirin, I've no food in the house, and I'm not going out looking like this.' She raised bruised and suspiciously bright eyes. 'So I thought of the least shockable and the most ego-centric person I know and I telephoned her. You'll have to go out shopping for me, Iris. I need enough to last me a week.'

Iris was amused. 'I would never deny that I'm egocentric but why is that important?'

Roz bared her teeth. 'Because you're so wrapped up in yourself you'll have forgotten all about this by the time you get home. Plus, you're not going to pressure me into doing the right thing and nailing the little bastard. It wouldn't reflect well on your agency if one of your authors was in the habit of bringing home pick-ups from wine bars.' She clenched both hands over the telephone and Iris watched her knuckles whiten under the strain.

'True,' she agreed calmly.

Roz relaxed a little. 'I really couldn't bear it, you know, if this got out, and it will if doctors or the police are involved. You know the bloody press as well as I do. Any excuse, and they'll plaster their front pages all over again with pictures of Alice in the wreckage.' Poor little Alice. Malign providence had put a freelance photographer beside the dual carriageway when she was tossed like a rag doll from Rupert's car. His dramatic shots – published, according to the tabloid editors, as a tragic reminder to other families of the importance of wearing seat belts – had been Alice's most lasting memorial. 'You can imagine the sordid parallels they'll draw. MOTHER DISFIGURED LIKE DAUGHTER. I couldn't survive it a second time.' She fished in her pocket and produced a shopping list. 'I'll write you a cheque when you come back. And whatever you do, don't forget the aspirin. I'm in agony.'

Iris tucked the shopping list into her bag. 'Keys,' she said, holding out her hand. 'You can go to bed while I'm out. I'll let myself back in.'

Roz pointed to her keys on a shelf by the door. 'Thank you,' she said, 'and, Iris—' She didn't finish.

'And, Iris, what?'

She made an attempt at a wry grimace but abandoned it because it was too painful. 'And, Iris, I'm sorry.'

'So am I, old thing.' She gave an airy wave and let herself out of the flat.

For reasons best known to herself, Iris returned a couple of hours later with the shopping and a suitcase. 'Don't look at me like that,' she said severely, administering aspirin in a glass of water. 'I intend to keep an eye on you for a day or two. For entirely mercenary purposes, of course. I like to guard my investments closely. And anyway,' she scratched under Mrs Antrobus's chin, 'someone's got to feed this revolting moggy for you. You'll only start howling if it dies of starvation.'

Roz, depressed and very lonely, was touched.

Detective Sergeant Geoff Wyatt toyed unhappily with his wine glass. His stomach was playing up, he was very tired, it was Saturday, he would rather have been at a Saints' football match, and the sight of Hal tucking into a plateful of rare steak needled him. 'Look,' he said, trying to keep the irritation out of his voice, 'I hear what you're saying but evidence is evidence. What are you expecting me to do? Tamper with it?'

'It's hardly evidence if it was tampered with at the outset,' Hal snapped. 'It was a frame, for Christ's sake.' He pushed his plate away. 'You should have had some,' he said acidly. 'It might have improved your temper.'

Wyatt looked away. 'There's nothing wrong with my temper and I ate before I got here.' He lit a cigarette and glanced towards the door into the restaurant. 'I've never felt comfortable in kitchens, not since seeing those women on Olive's floor. Too many murder weapons and too much bloody meat about the place. Couldn't we go next door?'

'Don't be a fool,' said Hal curtly. 'Damn it, Geoff, you owe me a few one way and another.'

Wyatt sighed. 'How's it going to help you if I get suspended for doing dodgy favours for an ex-copper?'

'I'm not asking for dodgy favours. Just get the pressure taken off. Give me a breathing space.'

'How?'

'You could start by persuading the Inspector to back off.'

'And that's not dodgy?' His mouth turned down. 'Anyway, I've tried. He's not playing. He's new, he's honest, and he doesn't like anyone who bends the rules, particularly policemen.' He tapped ash on the floor. 'You should never have left the Force, Hal. I did warn you. It's very lonely outside.'

Hal rubbed his unshaven face. 'It wouldn't be so bad if my erstwhile colleagues didn't keep treating me like a criminal.'

Wyatt stared at the remains of the steak on Hal's plate. He felt very queasy. 'Well, if it comes to that, you shouldn't have been so damn careless, then they wouldn't have to.'

Hal's eyes narrowed unpleasantly. 'One of these days you're going to wish you hadn't said that.'

With a shrug, Wyatt ground his cigarette against his shoe and tossed the butt into the sink. 'Can't see it, old son. I've been shitting my backside off ever since the Inspector rumbled you. It's made me ill, it really has.' He pushed back his chair and stood up. 'Why the hell did you have to cut corners instead of doing it by the book the way you were supposed to?'

Hal nodded towards the door. 'Out,' he said, 'before I rip your two-faced head off.'

'What about that check you wanted me to run?'

Hal fished in his pocket and removed a piece of paper. 'That's her name and address. See if there's anything on her.'

'Like what?'

Hal shrugged. 'Anything that will give me a lever. This book she's writing is too well timed.' He frowned. 'And I don't believe in coincidence.'

One of the few advantages of being fat was that it was easier to hide things. Another bulge here or there passed unnoticed and the soft cavity between Olive's breasts could accommodate itself to almost anything. In any case, she had noticed very early on that the officers preferred not to search her too diligently on the rare occasions when they thought it necessary. She had assumed at first that they were frightened of her, but she soon came to recognize that it was her fatness that inhibited them. Politically correct thinking within the prison service meant that while they were free to say what they liked about her behind her back they had to guard their tongues in her presence and treat her with a modicum of respect. Thus the helpful legacy of her anguished tears during strip-searches at the beginning, when her huge, repulsive body shook with distress, was a reluctance on the part of the screws now to do anything more than a perfunctory running of their hands down the sides of her shift.

But she had problems. Her small family of wax figures, absurdly cheerful in their painted cottonwool wigs and strips of dark material which she had wound around them like miniature suits, kept softening against the warmth of her skin and losing their shape. With infinite patience, she set her awkward fingers to remoulding them, first removing the pins which skewered the wigs to each of the heads. She wondered idly if the one of Roz's husband looked anything like him.

'What a ghastly place this is,' said Iris, gazing critically about the bleak grey walls of Roz's flat from her place on the vinyl sofa. 'Haven't you ever felt the urge to liven it up a bit?'

'No. I'm just passing through. It's a waiting room.'

'You've been here twelve months. I can't think why you don't use the money from the divorce and buy yourself a house.'

Roz rested her head against the back of her chair. 'I like waiting rooms. You can be idle in them without feeling guilty. There's nothing to do except wait.'

Thoughtfully, Iris put a cigarette between her brilliant red lips. 'What are you waiting for?'

'I don't know.'

She flicked a lighter to the tip of her cigarette while her penetrating eye-lined gaze fixed uncomfortably on Roz. 'One thing does puzzle me,' she said. 'If it wasn't Rupert, then why did he leave another tearful message on my answer-phone, telling me he had behaved badly?'

'Another?' Roz stared at her hands. 'Does that mean he's done it before?'

'With tedious regularity.'

'You've never mentioned it.'

'You've never asked me.'

Roz digested this for some moments in silence, then let out a long sigh. 'I've been realizing recently how dependent I've become on him.' She touched her sore lip. 'His dependence hasn't changed, of course. It's the same as it always was, a constant demand for reassurance. Don't worry, Rupert. It's not your fault, Rupert. Everything will be all right, Rupert.' She spoke the words without emphasis. 'It's why he prefers women. Women are more sympathetic.' She fell silent.

'How does that make you dependent on him?'

Roz gave a slight smile. 'He's never left me alone long enough to let me think straight. I've been angry for months.' She shrugged. 'It's very destructive. You can't concentrate on anything because the anger won't go away. I tear his letters up without reading them, because I know what they'll say, but his handwriting sets my teeth on edge. If I see him or hear him, I start shaking.' She gave a hollow laugh. 'You can become obsessed by hatred, I think. I could have moved a long time ago but, instead, I stay here waiting for Rupert to make me angry. That's how I'm dependent on him. It's a prison of sorts.'

Iris wiped her cigarette end round the rim of an ashtray. Roz was telling her nothing she hadn't worked out for herself a long time ago, but she had never been able to put it into words for the simple reason that Roz had never let her. She wondered what had happened to bring the barbed wire down. Clearly, it was nothing to do with Rupert, however much Roz might like to think it was. 'So how are you going to break out of this prison? Have you decided?'

'Not yet.'

'Perhaps you should do what Olive has done,' said Iris mildly.

'And what's that?'

'Let someone else in.'

Olive waited by her cell door for two hours. One of the officers, wondering why, paused to talk to her. 'Everything all right, Sculptress?'

The fat woman's eyes fixed on her. 'What day is it?' she demanded.

'Monday.'

'That's what I thought.' She sounded angry.

The officer frowned. 'Are you sure there's nothing wrong?'

'There's nothing.'

'Were you expecting a visitor?'

'No. I'm hungry. What's for tea?'

'Pizza.' Reassured, the officer moved on. It made sense. There were few hours in the day when Olive *wasn't* hungry, and the threat of withholding her meals was often the only way to control her. A medical officer had tried to persuade her once of the benefits of dieting. He had come away very shaken and never tried again. Olive craved food in the way others craved heroin.

*

In the end Iris stayed for a week and filled the sterile waiting room of Roz's life with the raucous baggage of hers. She ran up a colossal telephone bill phoning her clients and customers at home and abroad, piled the tables with magazines, dropped ash all over the floor, imported armfuls of flowers which she abandoned in the sink when she couldn't find a vase, left the washing-up in tottering stacks on the kitchen work-tops, and regaled Roz, when she wasn't doing something else, with her seemingly inexhaustible flow of anecdotes.

Roz said her farewells on the following Thursday afternoon with some relief and rather more regret. If nothing else, Iris had shown her that a solitary life was emotionally, mentally, and spiritually deadening. There was, after all, only so much that one mind could encompass, and obsessions grew when ideas went unchallenged.

Olive's destruction of her cell that night took the prison by surprise. It was ten minutes before the duty governor was alerted and another ten before a response was possible. It required eight officers to restrain her. They forced her to the ground and brought their combined weight to bear on her, but as one remarked later: 'It was like trying to contain a bull elephant.'

She had wreaked complete havoc on everything. Even the lavatory bowl had shattered under a mighty blow from her welded metal chair which, bent and buckled, had been discarded amongst the shards of porcelain. The few possessions which had adorned her chest of drawers lay broken across the floor and anything that could be lifted had been hurled in fury against the walls. A poster of Madonna, ripped limb from limb, lay butchered on the floor.

Her rage, even under sedation, continued long into the night from the confines of an unfurnished cell, designed to cool the tempers of ungovernable inmates.

'What the hell's got into her?' demanded the duty governor.

'God knows,' said a shaken officer. 'I've always said she should be in Broadmoor. I don't care what the psychiatrists say, she's completely mad. They've no business to leave her here and expect us to look after her.'

They listened to the muffled bellowings from behind the locked door. 'BI-ITCH! BI-ITCH! BI-ITCH!'

The duty governor frowned. 'Who's she talking about?'

The officer winced. 'One of us, I should think. I wish we could get her transferred. She puts the wind up me, she really does.'

'She'll be fine again tomorrow.'

'Which is why she puts the wind up me. You never know where you are with her.' She tucked her hair back into place. 'You noticed none of her clay figures were touched except the ones she's already mutilated?' She smiled cynically. 'And have you seen that mother and child she's working on? The mother's only smothering her baby, for God's sake. It's obscene. Presumably it's supposed to be Mary and Jesus.' She sighed. 'What do I tell her? No breakfast if she doesn't calm down?'

'It's always worked in the past. Let's hope nothing's changed.'

NINE

The following morning, a week later than planned, Roz was shown through to a clerical supervisor at the Social Security office in Dawlington. He regarded her scabby lip and dark glasses with only mild curiosity and she realized that for him her appearance was nothing unusual. She introduced herself and sat down. 'I telephoned yesterday,' she reminded him.

He nodded. 'Some problem that goes back over six years, you said.' He tapped his forefingers on the desk. 'I should stress we're unlikely to be able to help. We've enough trouble chasing current cases, let alone delving into old records.'

'But you were here six years ago?'

'Seven years in June,' he said without enthusiasm. 'It won't help, I'm afraid. I don't remember you or your circumstances.'

'You wouldn't.' She smiled apologetically. 'I was a little economical with the truth on the telephone. I'm not a consumer. I'm an author. I'm writing a book about Olive Martin. I need to talk to someone who knew her when she worked here and I didn't want a straight refusal down the phone.'

He looked amused, glad perhaps that he was spared an impossible search for lost benefits. 'She was the fat girl down the corridor. I didn't even know what her name was until it appeared in the paper. As far as I remember, I never exchanged more than a dozen words with her. You probably know more about her than I do.' He crossed his arms. 'You should have said what you wanted. You could have saved yourself a drive.'

Roz took out her notebook. 'That doesn't matter. It's names

I need. People who did speak to her. Is there anyone else who's been here as long as you?'

'A few, but no one who was friendly with Olive. A couple of reporters came round at the time of the murders and there wasn't a soul who admitted to passing anything more than the time of day with her.'

Roz felt his distrust. 'And who can blame them?' she said cheerfully. 'Presumably it was the gutter press looking for a juicy headline. I HELD THE HAND OF A MONSTER or something equally tasteless. Only publicity seekers or idiots allow themselves to be used by Wapping to boost their grubby profits.'

'And your book won't make a profit?' There was a dry inflection in his voice.

She smiled. 'A very modest one by newspaper standards.' She pushed her dark glasses to the top of her head, revealing her eyes and the yellow rings around them. 'I'll be honest with you. I was dragooned into this research by an irritable agent demanding copy. I found the subject distasteful and was prepared to abandon it after a token meeting with Olive.' She looked at him, turning her pencil between her fingers. 'Then I discovered that Olive was human and very likeable, so I kept going. And almost everyone I've spoken to has given a similar answer to you. They hardly knew her, they never talked to her, she was just the fat girl down the corridor. Now, I could write my book on that theme alone, how social ostracism led a lonely, unloved girl to turn in a fit of frenzied anger on her teasing family. But I'm not going to because I don't think it's true. I believe there's been a miscarriage of justice. I believe Olive is innocent.'

Surprised, he reassessed her. 'It shocked us rigid when we heard what she'd done,' he admitted.

'Because you thought it out of character?'

'Totally out of character.' He thought back. 'She was a good worker, brighter than most, and she didn't clock-watch like some of them. OK, she was never going to set the world alight, but she was reliable and willing and she didn't make waves or get involved in office politics. She was here about eighteen months and while no one would have claimed her as a bosom friend she made no enemies either. She was one of those people you only think about when you want something done and then you remember them with relief because you know they'll do it. You know the type?'

She nodded. 'Boring but dependable.'

'In a nutshell, yes.'

'Did she tell you anything about her private life?'

He shook his head again. 'It was true what I said at the beginning. Our paths rarely crossed. Any contact we had was work related and even that was minimal. Most of what I've just told you was synthesized from the amazed reactions of the few who did know her.'

'Can you give me their names?'

'I'm not sure I can remember.' He looked doubtful. 'Olive would know them better than I do. Why don't you ask her?'

Because she won't tell me. She won't tell me anything. 'Because,' she said instead, 'I don't want to hurt her.' She saw his look of puzzlement and sighed. 'Supposing doors get slammed in my face and I'm given the cold shoulder by Olive's so-called friends. She's bound to ask me how I got on, and how would I answer her? Sorry, Olive, as far as they're concerned you're dead and buried. I couldn't do that.'

He accepted this. 'All right, there is someone who might be willing to help you but I'm not prepared to give you her name without her permission. She's elderly, retired now, and she may not want to be involved. If you give me five minutes, I'll telephone and see how she feels about talking to you.'

'Was she fond of Olive?'

'As much as anyone was.'

'Then will you tell her that I don't believe Olive murdered her mother and sister and that's why I'm writing the book.' She stood up. 'And please impress on her that it's desperately important I talk to someone who knew her at the time. So far I've only managed to trace one old school friend and a teacher.' She walked to the door. 'I'll wait outside.'

True to his word, he was five minutes. He joined her in the

corridor and gave her a piece of paper with a name and address on it. 'Her name's Lily Gainsborough. She was the cleaner-cum-tea-lady in the good old days before privatized cleaning and automatic coffee machines. She retired three years ago at the age of seventy, lives in sheltered accommodation in Pryde Street.' He gave her directions. 'She's expecting you.' Roz thanked him. 'Give my regards to Olive when you see her,' he said, shaking her hand. 'I had more hair and less flab six years ago, so a description won't be much use, but she might remember my name. Most people do.'

Roz chuckled. His name was Michael Jackson.

'Of course I remember Olive. Called her "Dumpling", didn't I, and she called me "Flower". Get it, dear? Because of my name, Lily. There wasn't an ounce of harm in her. I never believed what they said she done and I wrote and told her so when I heard where they'd sent her. She wrote me back and said I was wrong, it was all her fault and she had to pay the penalty.' Old wise eyes peered short-sightedly at Roz. 'I understood what she meant, even if no one else did. She never did it but it wouldn't have happened if she'd not done what she shouldn't have. More tea, dear?'

'Thank you.' Roz held out her cup and waited while the frail old lady hefted a large stainless steel teapot. A relic from her job on the tea trolley? The tea was thick and charged with tannin, and Roz could hardly bring herself to drink it. She accepted another indigestible scone. 'What did she do that she shouldn't have?'

'Upset her mum, that's what. Took up with one of the O'Brien boys, didn't she?'

'Which one?'

'Ah, well, that I'm not too sure about. I've always thought it was the baby, young Gary – mind, I only saw them together once and those boys are very alike. Could have been any of them.'

'How many are there?'

'Now you're asking.' Lily pursed her mouth into a wrinkled rosebud. 'It's a big family. Can't keep track of them. Their mum must be a grandmother twenty times over and I doubt she's reached sixty yet. Gyppos, dear. Bad apples the lot of them. In and out of prison that regular you'd think they owned the place. The mum included. Taught them to steal soon as they could walk. The kids kept being taken off her, of course, but never for very long. Always found their way home. Young Gary was sent to a boarding school – approved schools, they was called in my day – did quite well by all accounts.' She crumbled a scone on her plate. 'Till he went home, that is. She had him back on the thieving quicker than you can say knife.'

Roz thought for a moment. 'Did Olive tell you she was going out with one of them?'

'Not in so many words.' She tapped her forehead. 'Put two and two together, didn't I? She was that pleased with herself, lost some weight, bought some pretty dresses from that boutique her sister went to work in, dabbed some colour on her face. Made herself look quite bonny, didn't she? Stood to reason there was a man behind it somewhere. Asked her once who it was and she just smiled and said, "No names no pack drill, Flower, because Mummy would have a fit if she ever found out." And then, two or three days later, I came across her with one of the O'Brien boys. Her face gave her away, as sunny as the day is long it was. That was him all right – the one she was soppy over – but he turned away as I passed, and I never did know exactly which O'Brien he was.'

'But what made you think it was an O'Brien anyway?'

'The uniform,' said Lily. 'They all wore the same uniform.'

'They were in the Army?' asked Roz in surprise.

'Leathers, they call them.'

'Oh, I see. You mean they're bikers, they ride motorbikes.'

'That's it. Hell's Angels.'

Roz drew her brows together in a perplexed frown. She had told Hal with absolute conviction that Olive was not the rebellious type. But Hell's Angels, for God's sake! Could a convent girl get more rebellious than that? 'Are you sure about this, Lily?'

'Well, as to being sure, I don't know as I'm sure about anything any more. There was a time when I was sure that governments knew better how to run things than I did. Can't say as I do these days. There was a time when I was sure that if God was in his heaven all would be right with the world. Can't say as I think that now. If God's there, dear, He's blind, deaf, and dumb, far as I'm concerned. But, yes, I am sure my poor Dumpling had fallen for one of the O'Briens. You'd only to look at her to see she was head over heels in love with the lad.' She compressed her lips. 'Bad business. Bad business.'

Roz sipped the bitter tea. 'And you think it was the O'Brien lad who murdered Olive's mother and sister?'

'Must have been, mustn't it? As I said, dear, bad apples.'

'Did you tell the police any of this?' asked Roz curiously.

'I might have done if they'd asked, but I didn't see no point in volunteering the information. If Dumpling wanted them kept out, then that was her affair. And, to tell you the truth, I wasn't that keen to run up against them. Stick together, they do, and my Frank had passed on not many months before. Wouldn't have stood a chance if they'd come looking, would I?'

'Where do they live?'

'The Barrow Estate, back of the High Street. Council likes to keep 'em together, under their eye so to speak. It's a shocking place. Not an honest family there, and they're not all O'Briens neither. Den of thieves, that's what it is.'

Roz took another thoughtful sip from her cup. 'Are you prepared to let me use this information, Lily? You do realize that if there's anything in it it could help Olive.'

'Course I do, dear. Why would I tell you otherwise?'

'The police would become involved. They'd want to talk to you.'

'I know that.'

'In which case your name would be out, and the O'Briens could still come looking for you.'

The old eyes appraised her shrewdly. 'You're only a slip of a thing, dear, but you've survived a beating by the look of it. Reckon I can too. In any case,' she went on stoutly, 'I've spent six years feeling bad about not speaking up, and I was that glad when young Mick phoned and said you was coming, you wouldn't believe. You go ahead, dear, and don't mind about me. It's safer here, anyway, than my old place. They could have set the whole thing alight and I'd have been dead long before anyone'd have thought of phoning for help.'

If Roz had expected to see a chapter of Hell's Angels rampaging about the Barrow Estate she was disappointed. At lunchtime on a Friday it was an unexceptional place, where only the odd dog barked and young women, in ones and twos, pushed babies in prams piled high with shopping for the weekend. Like too many council estates there was a naked and uncared for look about it, a recognition that what it offered was not what its tenants wanted. If individuality was present in these dull uniform walls then it was inside, away from view. But Roz doubted its existence. She had a sense of empty spaces marking time where people waited for somebody else to offer them something better. Like her, she thought. Like her flat.

As she drove away she passed a large school, advertising itself with a tired sign beside the gate. Parkway Comprehensive. Children milled about the tarmac, the sound of their voices loud in the warm air. Roz slowed the car to watch them for a moment. Groups of children played the same games whichever school they went to, but she could see why Gwen had turned her nose up at Parkway and had sent her girls to the convent. Its close proximity to the Barrow Estate would worry even the most liberal of parents, and Gwen certainly wasn't that. But it was ironic, if what Lily and Mr Hayes had said was true, that both Gwen's daughters had succumbed to the attractions of this other world. Was that in spite of or because of their mother? she wondered.

She told herself she needed a tame policeman to give her

the low-down on the O'Briens, and her road led inevitably to the Poacher. Being lunchtime the door to the restaurant was unlocked, but the tables were as empty as ever. She selected one well away from the window and sat down, her dark glasses firmly in place.

'You won't need those,' said Hawksley's amused voice from the kitchen doorway. 'I don't intend to put the lights on.'

She smiled, but did not remove the glasses. 'I'd like to order some lunch.'

'OK.' He held the door wide. 'Come into the kitchen. It's more comfortable in there.'

'No, I'll have it in here.' She stood up. 'At the table in the window. I'd like the door open and' – she looked for amplifiers and found them – 'some loud music, preferably jazz. Let's liven the place up a bit. Nobody wants to eat in a morgue, for God's sake.' She seated herself in the window.

'No,' he said, an odd inflection in his voice. 'If you want lunch, you eat it in here with me. Otherwise, you go somewhere else.'

She studied him thoughtfully. 'This has nothing to do with the recession, has it?'

'What hasn't?'

'Your non-existent customers.'

He gestured towards the kitchen. 'Are you going or staying?'

'Staying,' she said, standing up. What was this all about? she wondered.

'It's really none of your concern, Miss Leigh,' he murmured, reading her mind. 'I suggest you stick to what you know and leave me to deal with my affairs in my own way.' Geoff had phoned through the results of his check the previous Monday. 'She's kosher,' he had said. 'A London-based author. Divorced. Had a daughter who died in a car accident. No previous connections with anyone in the area. Sorry, Hal.'

'OK,' Roz said mildly, 'but you must admit it's very intriguing. I was effectively warned off eating here by a policeman when I went to the station to find out where you were. I've been wondering why ever since. With friends like that you don't really need enemies, do you?'

His smile didn't reach his eyes. 'Then you're very brave to accept my hospitality a second time.' He held the door wide.

She walked past him into the kitchen. 'Just greedy,' she said. 'You're a better cook than I am. In any case, I intend to pay for what I eat unless, of course' – her smile didn't reach her eyes either – 'this isn't a restaurant at all, but a front for something else.'

That amused him. 'You've an overactive imagination.' He pulled out a chair for her.

'Maybe,' she said, sitting down. 'But I've never met a res-taurateur before who barricades himself behind bars, presides over empty tables, has no staff, and looms up in the dark looking like something that's been fed through a mincing machine.' She arched her eyebrows. 'If you didn't cook so well, I'd be even more inclined to think this wasn't a restaurant.'

He leaned forward abruptly and removed her dark glasses, folding them and laying them on the table. 'And what should I deduce from this?' he said, unexpectedly moved by the damage done to her beautiful eyes. 'That you're not a writer because someone's left his handprints all over your face?' He frowned suddenly. 'It wasn't Olive, was it?'

She looked surprised. 'Of course not.'

'Who was it, then?'

She dropped her gaze. 'No one. It's not important.'

He waited for a moment. 'Is it someone you care about?'

'No.' She clasped her hands loosely on the table top. 'Rather the reverse. It's someone I don't care about.' She looked up with a half smile. 'Who beat you up, Sergeant? Someone *you* care about?'

He pulled open a fridge door and examined its contents. 'One of these days your passion for poking your nose into other people's business is going to get you into trouble. What do you fancy? Lamb?'

'I really came to see you for some more information,' she told him over coffee.

Humour creased his eyes. He really was extraordinarily attractive, she thought, wistfully aware that the attraction was all one way. Lunch had been a friendly but distant meal, with a large sign between them saying: so far and no further. 'Go on, then.'

'Do you know the O'Brien family? They live on the Barrow Estate.'

'Everyone knows the O'Briens.' He frowned at her. 'But if there's a connection between them and Olive I'll eat my hat.'

'You're going to have galloping indigestion then,' she said acidly. 'I've been told she was going out with one of the sons at the time of the murders. Probably Gary, the youngest. What's he like? Have you met him?'

He linked his hands behind his head. 'Someone's winding you up,' he murmured. 'Gary is marginally brighter than the rest of them, but I'd guess his educational level is still about fourteen years old. They are the most useless, inadequate bunch I've ever come across. The only thing they know how to do is petty thieving and they don't even do that very well. There's Ma O'Brien and about nine children, mostly boys, all grown up now, and, when they're not in prison, they play box and cox in a three-bedroomed house on the estate.'

'Aren't any of them married?'

'Not for long. Divorce is more prevalent in that family than marriage. The wives usually make other arrangements while their men are inside.' He flexed his laced fingers. 'They produce a lot of babies, though, if the fact that a third generation of O'Briens has started appearing regularly in the juvenile courts is anything to go by.' He shook his head. 'Someone's winding you up,' he said again. 'For all her sins Olive wasn't stupid and she'd have to have been brain-dead to fall for a jerk like Gary O'Brien.'

'Are they really as bad as that?' she asked him curiously. 'Or is this police animosity?'

He smiled. 'I'm not police, remember? But they're that bad,' he assured her. 'Every patch has families like the O'Briens. Sometimes, if you're really unlucky, you get an estateful of them, like the Barrow Estate, when the council decides to lump all its bad apples into one basket and then expects the wretched police to throw a cordon round it.' He gave a humourless laugh. 'It's one of the reasons I left the Force. I got sick to death of being sent out to sweep up society's messes. It's not the police who create these ghettos, it's the councils and the governments, and ultimately society itself.'

'Sounds reasonable to me,' she said. 'In that case why do you despise the O'Briens so much? They sound as if they need help and support rather than condemnation.'

He shrugged. 'I suppose it's because they've already had more help and support than you or I will ever be offered. They take everything society gives them and then demand more. There's no quid pro quo with people like that. They put nothing in to compensate for what they've had out. Society owes them a living and, by God, they make sure society pays, usually in the shape of some poor old woman who has all her savings stolen.' His lips thinned. 'If you'd arrested those worthless shits as often as I have, you'd despise them, too. I don't deny they represent an underclass of society's making, but I resent their unwillingness to try and rise above it.' He saw her frown. 'You look very disapproving. Have I offended your liberal sensibilities?'

'No,' she said with a twinkle in her eye. 'I was just thinking how like Mr Hayes you sound. Remember him? ''What shall I say?'' ' – she mimicked the old man's soft burr – ' ''They should all be strung up from the nearest lamppost and shot.'' ' She smiled when he laughed.

'My sympathies with the criminal classes are a trifle frayed at the moment,' he said after a moment. 'More accurately, my sympathies in general are frayed.'

'Classic symptoms of stress,' she said lightly, watching

him. 'Under pressure we always reserve our compassion for ourselves.'

He didn't answer.

'You said the O'Briens are inadequate,' Roz prompted. 'Perhaps they can't rise above their situation.'

'I believed that once,' he admitted, toying with his empty wine glass, 'when I first joined the police force, but you have to be very naïve to go on believing it. They're professional thieves who simply don't subscribe to the same values as the rest of us hold. It's not a case of *can't*, but more a case of *won't*. Different ball game entirely.' He smiled at her. 'And if you're a policeman who wants to hold on to the few drops of human kindness that remain to you, you get out quick the minute you realize that. Otherwise you end up as unprincipled as the people you're arresting.'

Curiouser and curiouser, thought Roz. So he had little sympathy left for the police either. He gave the impression of a man under siege, isolated and angry within the walls of his castle. But why should his friends in the police have abandoned him? Presumably he had had some. 'Have any of the O'Briens been charged with murder or GBH?'

'No. As I said, they're thieves. Shoplifting, pick-pocketing, house burglaries, cars, that sort of thing. Old Ma acts as a fence whenever she can get her hands on stolen property but they're not violent.'

'I was told they're all Hell's Angels.'

He gave her an amused look. 'You've been given some very duff information. Are you toying with the idea, perhaps, that Gary did the murders and Olive was so besotted with him that she took the rap on his behalf?'

'It doesn't sound very plausible, does it?'

'About as plausible as little green men on Mars. Apart from anything else, Gary is scared of his own shadow. He was challenged once during a burglary – he didn't think anyone was in the house – and he burst into tears. He could no more have cut Gwen's throat while she was struggling with him than you or I could. Or for that matter, than his brothers could. They're skinny little foxes, not ravening wolves. Who on earth have you been talking to? Someone with a sense of humour, obviously.'

She shrugged, suddenly out of patience with him. 'It's not important. Offhand, do you know the O'Briens' address? It would save me having to look it up.'

He grinned. 'You're not planning on going there?'

'Of course I am,' she said, annoyed by his amusement. 'It's the most promising lead I've had. And now that I know they're not axe-wielding Hell's Angels, I'm not so worried about it. So what's their address?'

'I'll come with you.'

'Think again, sunshine,' she said roundly. 'I don't want you queering my pitch. Are you going to give me the address or must I look it up?'

'Number seven, Baytree Avenue. You can't miss it. It's the only house in that road with a satellite dish. Nicked for sure.'

'Thank you.' She reached for her handbag. 'Now, if we can just settle my bill, I'll leave you in peace.'

He unfolded himself from his chair and walked round to draw hers back. 'On the house,' he said.

She stood up and regarded him gravely. 'But I'd like to pay. I didn't come here at lunchtime just to scrounge off you and, anyway' – she smiled – 'how else can I show my appreciation of your cooking? Money always speaks louder than words. I can say it was fabulous, like the last time, but I might just be being polite.'

He raised a hand as if he was going to touch her, then dropped it abruptly. 'I'll see you out,' was all he said.

TEN

Roz drove past the house three times before she could pluck up enough courage to get out and try the door. In the end it was pride that led her up the path. Hal's amusement had goaded her. A tarpaulined motorbike was parked neatly on a patch of grass beside the fence.

The door was opened by a bony little woman with a sharp, scowling face, her thin lips drawn down in a permanently dissatisfied bow. 'Yes?' she snapped.

'Mrs O'Brien?'

"Oo's asking?"

Roz produced a card. 'My name's Rosalind Leigh.' The sound of a television blared out from an inner room.

The woman glanced at the card but didn't take it. 'Well, what do you want? If it's the rent, I put it in the post yesterday.' She folded her arms across her thin chest and dared Roz to dispute this piece of information.

'I'm not from the council, Mrs O'Brien.' It occurred to her that the woman couldn't read. Apart from her telephone number and address, Roz's card had only her name and her profession on it. Author, it stated clearly. She took a flyer. 'I work for a small independent television company,' she said brightly, her mind searching rapidly for some plausible but tempting bait. 'I'm researching the difficulties faced by single parents with large families. We are particularly interested in talking to a mother who has problems keeping her sons out of trouble. Society is very quick to point the finger in these situations and we feel it's time to redress the balance.' She saw the lack of comprehension on the woman's face. 'We'd like to give the mother a chance to give her side of the story,' she explained. 'There seems to be a common pattern of continual harassment and interference from people in authority – social services, the council, the police. Most mothers we've spoken to feel that if they'd been left alone they wouldn't have had the problems.'

A gleam of interest lit the other's eyes. 'That's true enough.'

'Are you willing to take part?'

'Maybe. 'Oo sent you?'

'We've been conducting some research in the local courts,' she said glibly. 'The name O'Brien popped up quite frequently.'

'Not surprised. Will I get paid?'

'Certainly. I'd need to talk to you for about an hour now to get a rough idea of your views. For that you will receive an immediate cash payment of fifty pounds.' Ma would turn her nose up at anything less, she thought. 'Then, if we think your contribution is valuable and if you agree to be filmed, we will pay you at the same hourly rate while the cameras are here.'

Ma O'Brien pursed her meagre lips and proceeded to splatter aitches about the place. 'Han hundred,' she said, 'hand h'I'll do it.'

Roz shook her head. Fifty pounds would clean her out anyway. 'Sorry. It's a standard fee. I'm not authorized to pay any more.' She shrugged. 'Never mind. Thank you for your time, Mrs O'Brien. I've three other families on my list. I'm sure one of them will jump at the chance to get their own back at authority and earn some money while they're doing it.' She turned away. 'Look out for the programme,' she called over her shoulder. 'You'll probably see some of your neighbours on it.'

'Not so 'asty, Mrs. Did I say no? Course I didn't. But I'd be a mug not to try for more hif there was more to be 'ad. Come in. Come in. What d'you say your name was?'

'Rosalind Leigh.' She followed Ma into a sitting room and took a chair while the little woman turned off the television and flicked aimlessly at some non-existent dust on the set.

'This is a nice room,' said Roz, careful to keep the surprise from her voice. A three-piece suite of good quality burgundy leather ringed a pale Chinese rug in pinks and greys.

'All bought and paid for,' snapped Ma.

Roz didn't doubt her for a moment. If the police spent as much time in her house as Hal had implied, then she was hardly likely to furnish it with hot goods. She took out her tape-recorder. 'How do you feel about my recording this conversation? It'll be a useful gauge for the sound man when he comes to set levels for filming, but if the microphone puts you off then I'm quite happy to make notes instead.'

'Get on with you,' she said, perching on the sofa. 'I'm not afraid of microphones. We've got a karaoke next door. You gonna ask questions or what?'

'That's probably easiest, isn't it? Let's start with when you first came to this house.'

'Ah, well, now, they was built twenty year ago, near enough, and we was the first family hin. There was six of us, including my old man, but 'e got nicked shortly after and we never seen 'im again. The old bastard buggered hoff when they let 'im out.'

'So you had four children?'

'Four in the 'ouse, five in care. Bloody hinterference, like you said. Kept taking the poor little nippers hoff me, they did. Makes you sick, it really does. They wanted their ma, not some do-good foster mother who was only in it for the money.' She hugged herself. 'I always got them back, mind. They'd turn up on my doorstep, regular as clockwork, no matter 'ow many times they was taken away. The council's tried everything to break us up, threatened me with a one-roomed flat even.' She sniffed. '"Arassment, like you said. I remember one time . . .'

She required little prompting to tell her story but rambled on with remarkable fluency for nearly three-quarters of an hour. Roz was fascinated. Privately she dismissed at least fifty per cent of what she was hearing, principally because Ma blithely maintained that her boys were and always had been innocent victims of police frames. Even the most gullible of listeners would have found that difficult to swallow. Nevertheless, there was a dogged affection in her voice whenever she referred to her family and Roz wondered if she was really as callous as Lily had painted her. She certainly portrayed herself as a hapless victim of circumstances beyond her control, though whether this was something she genuinely believed or whether she was saying what she thought Roz wanted to hear, Roz couldn't tell. Ma, she decided, was a great deal smarter than she let on.

'Right, Mrs O'Brien, let me see if I've got it right,' she said at last, interrupting the flow. 'You've got two daughters, both of whom are single parents like you, and both of whom have been housed by the council. You have seven sons. Three are currently in prison, one is living with his girlfriend, and the remaining three live here. Your oldest child is Peter, who's thirty-six, and your youngest is Gary, who's twenty-five.' She whistled. 'That was some going. Nine babies in eleven years.'

'Two sets of twins in the middle. Boy and a girl each time. Mind, it was 'ard work.'

Unmitigated drudgery, thought Roz. 'Did you want them?' she asked curiously. 'I can't think of anything worse than having nine children.'

'Never 'ad much say in it, dear. There weren't no abortion in my day.'

'Didn't you use contraceptives?'

To her surprise, the old woman blushed. 'Couldn't get the 'ang of them,' she snapped. 'The old man tried a rubber once but didn't like it and wouldn't do it again. Old bugger. No skin off 'is nose if I kept falling.'

It was on the tip of Roz's tongue to ask why Ma couldn't get the hang of contraceptives when the penny dropped. If she couldn't read and she was too embarrassed to ask how to use them, they'd have been useless to her. Good God, she thought, a little education would have saved the country a fortune where this family was concerned. 'That's men for you,' she said lightly. 'I noticed a motorbike outside. Does that belong to one of the boys?'

'Bought and paid for,' came the belligerent refrain. 'It's

Gary's. Motorbike mad, 'e is. There was a time when three of the boys 'ad bikes, now it's just Gary. They was all working for one of them messenger companies till the bloody coppers went round and got them sacked. Victimization, pure and simple. 'Ow's a man to work hif the police keep waving 'is record under the boss's noses. Course, they lost the bikes. They was buying them on the never-never and they couldn't keep up the payments.'

Roz made sympathetic noises. 'When was that? Recently?'

'Year of the gales. I remember the electricity was off when the boys came 'ome to say they'd been given the push. We'd got one blooming candle.' She firmed her lips. 'Bloody awful night, that was. Depressing.'

Roz kept her expression as neutral as she could. Was Lily right, after all, and Hal wrong? 'The nineteen eight-seven gales,' she said. 'The first ones.'

'That's it. Mind, it 'appened again two years later. No electricity for a week the second time, hand you get no compensation for the 'ardship neither. I tried and the buggers told me hif I didn't pay what I owed they'd cut me hoff for good and all.'

'Did the police give a reason for getting your boys the sack?' asked Roz.

'Hah!' Ma sniffed. 'They never give reasons for nothing. It was victimization, like I said.'

'Did they work for the messenger company long?'

Old eyes regarded her suspiciously. 'You're mighty interested all of a sudden.'

Roz smiled ingenuously. 'Only because this was an occasion when three of your family were trying to go straight and build careers for themselves. It would make good television if we could show that they were denied that opportunity because of police harassment. Presumably it was a local firm they were working for?'

'Southampton.' Ma's mouth became an inverted horse-shoe. 'Bloody silly name it 'ad too. Called theirselves Wells-Fargo. Still, the boss was a ruddy cowboy so maybe it wasn't so silly after all.'

Roz suppressed a smile. 'Is it still in business?'

'Last I 'eard, it was. That's it. You've 'ad your 'our.'

'Thank you, Mrs O'Brien.' She patted the tape-recorder. 'If the producers like what they hear I might need to come back and talk to your sons. Would that be acceptable, do you think?'

'Don't see why not. Can't see them sneezing at fifty quid apiece.' Ma held out her hand.

Dutifully, Roz took two twenty-pound notes and a ten from her wallet and laid them on the wrinkled palm. Then she started to gather her things together. 'I hear Dawlington's quite famous,' she remarked chattily.

'Oh yeah?'

'I was told Olive Martin murdered her mother and sister about half a mile down the road.'

'Oh, 'er,' said Ma dismissively, standing up. 'Strange girl. Knew 'er quite well at one time. Used to clean for the mother when she and 'er sister were nippers. She took a real fancy to Gary. Used to pretend 'e was 'er doll whenever I took 'im halong with me. There was only three years between them but she was nearly twice as big as my skinny little runt. Strange girl.'

Roz busied herself with sorting out her briefcase. 'It must have been a shock hearing about the murders then. If you knew the family, that is.'

'Can't say I gave it much thought. I was only there six month. Never liked 'er. She only took me on for a bit of snobbery, then got rid of me the minute she found hout my old man was in the nick.'

'What was Olive like as a child. Was she violent to your Gary?'

Ma cackled. 'Used to dress 'im up in 'er sister's frocks. God, 'e looked a sight. Like I said, she treated 'im like a doll.'

Roz snapped the locks on her briefcase and stood up. 'Were you surprised she became a murderess?'

'No more surprised by that than by anything else. There's nowt so queer as folk.' She escorted Roz to the front door and stood, arms akimbo, waiting for her to leave.

'It might make an interesting introduction to the programme,' Roz mused, 'the fact that Gary was a doll-substitute for a notorious murderess. Does he remember her?'

Ma cackled again. 'Course 'e remembers 'er. Carried messages between 'er and 'er fancy man, didn't 'e, when she was workin' for the Social.'

Roz made a beeline for the nearest telephone. Ma O'Brien either wouldn't or couldn't elaborate on her tantalizing statement and had closed the door abruptly when pressed for information on Gary's whereabouts. Roz dialled Directory Enquiries and asked for Wells-Fargo in Southampton, then used her last fifty pence to call the number she was given. A bored female voice on the other end gave her the company's address and some directions on how to find it. 'We close in forty minutes,' was the woman's parting shot.

By dint of parking on a double yellow line and shrugging off the prospect of a parking ticket Roz made it to the Wells-Fargo office with ten minutes to spare. It was a dingy place, approached through a doorway between two shops and up a flight of uncarpeted stairs. Two anaemic Busy Lizzies and an ancient Pirelli calendar were the only spots of colour against the yellowed walls. The bored female voice resolved itself into a bored-looking middle-aged woman who was counting the seconds to the start of her weekend.

'We don't often see customers,' she remarked, filing her nails. 'I mean if they can bring their package here they might just as well deliver it themselves.' It was an accusation, as if she felt Roz were wasting company time. She abandoned her nails and held out a hand. 'What is it and where's it for?'

'I'm not a customer,' said Roz. 'I'm an author and I'm hoping you can give me some information for a book I'm writing.' Stirrings of interest animated the other's face so Roz pulled forward a chair and sat down. 'How long have you been working here?'

'Too long. What sort of book?'

Roz watched her closely. 'Do you remember Olive Martin? She murdered her mother and sister in Dawlington six years ago.' She saw immediate recognition in the woman's eyes. 'I'm writing a book about her.'

The woman returned to her nails but didn't say anything.

'Did you know her?'

'God, no.'

'Did you know *of* her? Before the murders, that is. I've been told one of your messengers delivered letters to her.' It was true enough. The only trouble was that she didn't know if Gary was working for Wells-Fargo when he did it.

A door to an inner office opened and a man fussed out. He looked at Roz. 'Did this lady want to see me, Marnie?' His fingers ran involuntarily up and down his tie, playing it like a clarinet.

The nail file vanished from sight. 'No, Mr Wheelan. She's an old friend of mine. Popped in to see if I've time for a drink before I go home.' She stared hard at Roz, her eyes demanding support. There was a curious intimacy in her expression as if she and Roz already shared a secret.

Roz smiled amiably and glanced at her watch. 'It's nearly six now,' she said. 'Half an hour won't delay you too much, will it?'

The man made shooing motions with his hands. 'You two get on then. I'll lock up tonight.' He paused in the doorway, his forehead wrinkling anxiously. 'You didn't forget to send someone to Hasler's, did you?'

'No, Mr Wheelan. Eddy went two hours ago.'

'Good, good. Have a nice weekend. What about Prestwick's?'

'All done, Mr Wheelan. There's nothing outstanding.' Marnie raised her eyes to heaven as he closed the door behind him. 'He drives me mad,' she muttered. 'Fuss, fuss, fuss, all the time. Come on, quick, before he changes his mind. Friday evenings are always the worst.' She scurried across to the door and started down the stairs. 'He hates weekends, that's his trouble, thinks the business is going to fold because we have two consecutive days without orders. He's paranoid. Had me working Saturday mornings last year till he realized we were simply sitting around twiddling our thumbs because none of the offices we deal with open on a Saturday.' She pushed through the bottom door and stepped out on to the pavement. 'Look, we can forget about that drink. I'd like to get home in reasonable time for once.' She looked at Roz, measuring the other's reaction.

Roz shrugged. 'Fine. I'll go and talk to Mr Wheelan about Olive Martin. He doesn't seem to be in any hurry.'

Marnie tapped her foot impatiently. 'You'll get me sacked.'

'*You* talk to me then.'

There was a long pause while the other woman considered her options. 'I'll tell you what I know, as long as you keep it to yourself,' she said at last. 'Is that a deal? It's not going to help you one little bit, so you won't need to use it.'

'Suits me,' said Roz.

'We'll talk as we walk. The station's this way. If we hurry I might be able to catch the six thirty.'

Roz caught her arm to hold her back. 'My car's over there,' she said. 'I'll drive you instead.' She took Marnie across the road and unlocked the passenger door. 'OK,' she said, getting in the other side and starting the engine. 'Fire away.'

'I did know of her, or at least I knew of *an* Olive Martin. I can't swear it's the same one because I never saw her, but the description sounded right when I read about her in the newspaper. I've always assumed it was the same person.'

'Who gave you her description?' asked Roz, turning into the main road.

'There's no point asking questions,' snapped Marnie. 'It'll just take longer. Let me tell the story my way.' She collected her thoughts. 'I said back there that we hardly ever see customers. Sometimes office managers come in to suss out what sort of operation we run, but normally it's all done by telephone. Somebody wants something delivered, they phone us and we dispatch a rider, simple as that. Well, one lunchtime, when Wheelan was out getting his sandwiches, this man came into the office. He had a letter that he wanted delivered that afternoon to a Miss Olive Martin. He was prepared to pay over the odds if the dispatch rider would hang around outside where she worked and give it to her quietly as she was leaving. He was absolutely adamant that it wasn't to be taken inside and said he was sure I understood why.'

Roz forgot herself. 'And did you?'

'I assumed they were having an affair and that neither of them wanted people asking questions. Anyway, he gave me a twenty-quid note for the one letter, and we're talking six years ago, remember, plus a very good description of Olive Martin, right down to the clothes she was wearing that day. Well, I thought it was a one-off and as that old bastard Wheelan pays peanuts at the best of times, I pocketed the cash and didn't bother to record the transaction. Instead, I got one of our riders who lived in Dawlington to do it freelance, as it were, on his way home. He got ten for doing virtually nothing and I kept the other ten.' She motioned with her hand. 'You take the next right at the traffic lights and then right at the roundabout.'

Roz put on her indicator. 'Was that Gary O'Brien?'

Marnie nodded. 'I suppose the little sod's been talking.'

'Something like that,' said Roz, avoiding a direct answer. 'Did Gary ever meet this man?'

'No, only Olive. It turned out he'd known her before – she used to look after him when he was a child or something – so he had no trouble recognizing her and didn't bungle the job by trying to give the letter to the wrong woman. Which, considering what an oaf he was, I thought he might do. Pull in here.' She glanced at her watch as Roz drew to a halt. 'That's grand. OK, well, the upshot of the whole thing going so smoothly was that Olive's bloke started to use us quite regularly. All in all we must have delivered about ten letters in the six months before the murders. I think he realized we were doing it on the side because he always came in at lunchtime after Wheelan had gone out. I reckon he used to wait until he saw the old fool leave.' She shrugged. 'It stopped with the murders and I've never seen him since. And that's all I can tell you except that Gary got really nervous after Olive was arrested and said we should keep our mouths shut about what we knew or the police would be down on us like a ton of bricks. Well, I wasn't keen to say anything anyway, not because of the police but because of Wheelan. He'd have burst a blood vessel if he'd found out we'd been running a bit of private enterprise behind his back.'

'But didn't the police turn up anyway about a month later to warn Wheelan against the O'Brien brothers?'

Marnie looked surprised. 'Who told you that?'

'Gary's mother.'

'First I've heard of it. As far as I know they just got bored. Gary wasn't so bad because he loved his motorbike but the other two were the most work-shy creeps I've ever come across. In the end they were skiving off so often that Wheelan sacked the lot. It's about the only decision he's ever made that I agreed with. God, they were unreliable.' She checked her watch again. 'To tell you the truth it amazed me that Gary delivered Olive's letters so conscientiously. I did wonder if he had a bit of a yen for her himself.' She opened the car door. 'I'll have to go.'

'Hang on,' said Roz sharply. 'Who was this man?'

'No idea. We dealt in cash and he never gave his name.'

'What did he look like?'

'I'll miss my train.'

Roz leant across and pulled the door to. 'You've got ten minutes and if you don't give me a decent description I'll go straight back to your office and spill the beans to Wheelan.'

Marnie shrugged petulantly. 'He was fifty-odd, old enough to be her father if the age they gave for her in the paper was right. Quite good-looking in a smarmy sort of way, very clean cut and conservative. He had a posh accent. He smoked. He always wore a suit and tie. He was about six foot and he had blond hair. He never said very much, just sort of waited for me to speak, never smiled, never got excited. I remember his eyes because they didn't go with his hair. They were very dark brown. And that's it,' she said firmly. 'I don't know any more about him and I don't know anything at all about her.'

'Would you recognize him from a photograph?'

'Probably. Do you know him then?'

Roz drummed her fingers on the steering-wheel. 'It doesn't make any sense but it sounds exactly like her father.'

ELEVEN

The officer on the gate checked Roz's name against his list the following Monday, then picked up the telephone. 'The Governor wants to see you,' he said, dialling a number.

'What for?'

'I wouldn't know, miss.' He spoke into the telephone. 'Miss Leigh's here for Martin. There's a note that she's to see the Governor first. Yes. Will do.' He pointed with his pencil. 'Straight through the first set of gates and you'll be met the other side.'

It was horribly reminiscent of being hauled before the head-mistress at school, thought Roz, waiting nervously in the secretary's office. She was trying to remember if she'd broken any rule. *Bring nothing in and take nothing out. Don't pass messages*. But she had done that, of course, when she spoke to Crew about the will. The slimy little toad must have ratted on her!

'You can go in now,' the secretary told her.

The Governor gestured towards a chair. 'Sit down, Miss Leigh.'

Roz lowered herself into the easy chair, hoping she looked less guilty than she felt. 'I wasn't expecting to see you.'

'No.' She studied Roz for a moment or two, then seemed to reach a decision. 'There's no point beating about the bush. Olive has had her privileges suspended and we think you may be the indirect cause of the suspension. According to the log-book you didn't come in last week, and I'm told Olive was very upset about it. Three days later she destroyed her

156

cell and had to be sedated.' She saw Roz's surprise. 'She's been very volatile ever since and, under the circumstances, I am not happy about letting you back in. I think it's something I need to discuss with the Home Office.'

God! Poor old Olive! Why on earth didn't I have the sense to phone? Roz folded her hands in her lap and collected her thoughts rapidly. 'If it was three days before she did anything, what makes you think it was because of my not turning up? Did she say it was?'

'No, but we're stumped for any other explanation and I'm not prepared to risk your safety.'

Roz mulled this over for a moment or two. 'Let's assume for a moment you're right – though I should emphasize that I don't think you are – then if I don't show up again won't that distress her even more?' She leaned forward. 'Either way it would be more sensible to let me talk to her. If it *was* to do with my non-appearance then I can reassure her and calm her down; if it *wasn't*, then I see no reason why I should be punished with Home Office delays and wasted journeys when I haven't contributed to Olive's disturbance.'

The Governor gave a slight smile. 'You're very confident.'

'I've no reason not to be.'

It was the Governor's turn to reflect. She studied Roz in silence for some time. 'Let's be clear,' she said finally, 'about what sort of woman Olive really is.' She tapped her pencil on the desk. 'I told you when you first came here that there was no psychiatric evidence of psychopathy. That was true. It means that when Olive butchered her mother and sister she was completely sane. She knew exactly what she was doing, she understood the consequences of her act, and she was prepared to go ahead with it, despite those consequences. It also means – and this is peculiarly relevant to you – that she cannot be cured because there is nothing to cure. Under similar circumstances – unhappiness, low self-image, betrayal, in other words whatever triggers her anger – she would do the same thing again with the same disregard for the consequences because, in simple terms, having weighed them up, she would consider the consequences worth the action. I would add, and again this is peculiarly relevant to you, that the consequences are far less daunting to her now than they would have been six years ago. On the whole Olive enjoys being in prison. She has security, she has respect, and she has people to talk to. Outside, she would have none of them. And she knows it.'

It *was* like being up before her old headmistress. The confident voice of authority. 'So what you're saying is that she would have no qualms about taking a swipe at me because an additional sentence would only mean a longer stay here? And she would welcome that?'

'In effect, yes.'

'You're wrong,' said Roz bluntly. 'Not about her sanity. I agree with you, she's as sane as you or I. But you're wrong about her being a danger to me. I'm writing a book about her and she wants that book written. If it *is* me she's angry with, and I stress again that I don't think it is, then her interpretation of my non-appearance last week may be that I've lost interest, and it would be very poor psychology to let her go on thinking it.' She composed her arguments. 'You have a notice at the gate, presumably all prisons do. It's a declaration of policy. If I remember right, it includes something about helping prison inmates to lead law-abiding lives both inside prison and outside. If that has any meaning at all, and isn't simply a piece of decorative wallpaper to appease the reformers, then how can you justify provoking further punishable outbursts from Olive by denying her visits which the Home Office has already approved?' She fell silent, worried about saying too much. However reasonable the woman might be, she could not afford to have her authority challenged. Few people could.

'Why does Olive want this book written?' asked the Governor mildly. 'She hasn't sought public notoriety before and you're not the first author to show an interest in her. We had several applications in the early days. She refused them all.'

'I don't know,' said Roz honestly. 'Perhaps it has something to do with her father's death. She claimed that one of her reasons for pleading guilty was to avoid putting him through the mill of a trial.' She shrugged. 'Presumably she felt a book would have been just as devastating to him, so waited till he died.'

The Governor was more cynical. 'Alternatively, while he was alive, her father was in a position to contest what she said; dead, he cannot. However, that is no concern of mine. My concern is with the ordered running of my prison.' She tapped her fingers impatiently on her desk. She had no desire at all to be drawn into a three-cornered dispute between herself, the Home Office, and Roz, but time-consuming correspondence with civil servants would pale into insignificance beside the murder of a civilian inside her prison. She had hoped to persuade Roz to abort the visit herself. She was surprised and, if the truth be told, rather intrigued by her own failure. *What was Rosalind Leigh getting right in her relationship with Olive that the rest of them were getting wrong?* 'You may talk to her for half an hour,' she said abruptly, 'in the Legal Visits room, which is larger than the one you are used to. There will be two male officers present throughout the interview. Should either you or Olive breach any regulation of this prison, your visits will cease immediately and I will personally ensure that they will never resume. Is that understood, Miss Leigh?'

'Yes.'

The other nodded. 'I'm curious, you know. Are you raising her expectations by telling her your book will get her released?'

'No. Apart from anything else, she won't talk to me about the murders.' Roz reached for her briefcase.

'Then why are you so confident you're safe with her?'

'Because as far as I can make out I'm the only outsider she's met who's not frightened of her.'

Privately, she retracted that statement as Olive was ushered into the Legal Visits room by two large male officers who then retreated to the door behind Olive's back and stationed themselves on either side of it. The woman's look of dislike was chilling, and Roz recalled Hal saying to her that she might think differently about Olive if she ever saw her in a rage.

'Hi.' She held Olive's gaze. 'The Governor has allowed me to see you, but we're on trial, both of us. If we misbehave today my visits will be stopped. Do you understand?'

BITCH, Olive mouthed, unseen by the officers. FUCKING BITCH. But was she referring to Roz or the Governor? Roz couldn't tell.

'I'm sorry I didn't make it last Monday.' She touched her lip where the ugly scab still showed. 'I got thrashed by my miserable husband.' She forced a smile. 'I couldn't go out for a week, Olive, not even for you. I do have some pride, you know.'

Olive examined her stolidly for a second or two then dropped her eyes to the cigarette packet on the table. She plucked greedily at a cigarette and popped it between her fat lips. 'I've been on the block,' she said, flaring a match to the tip. 'The bastards wouldn't let me smoke. And they've been starving me.' She threw a baleful glance behind her. 'Bastards! Did you kill him?'

Roz followed her gaze. Every word she and Olive said would be reported back. 'Of course not.'

Olive smoothed the limp, greasy hair from her forehead with the hand that held the cigarette. A streak of nicotine staining along her parting showed she had done it many times before. 'I didn't think you would,' she said contemptuously. 'It's not as easy as it looks on the telly. You've heard what I did?'

'Yes.'

'So why have they let you see me?'

'Because I told the Governor that whatever you had done was nothing to do with me. Which it wasn't, was it?' She pressed one of Olive's feet with hers under the table. 'Presumably somebody else upset you?'

'Bloody Chaplain,' said Olive morosely. A bald eyelid

drooped in a wink. 'Told me that God would do the rock'n'roll in heaven if I got down on my knees and said: "Alleluiah, I repent." Stupid sod. He's always trying to make religion relevant to modern criminals with low IQs. We can't cope with "There will be much rejoicing in heaven over one sinner that repenteth", so we get God will do the fucking rock'n'roll instead.' She listened with some satisfaction to the snorts of amusement behind her, then her eyes narrowed. I TRUSTED YOU, she mouthed at Roz.

Roz nodded. 'I assumed it was something like that.' She watched Olive's meaty fingers play with the tiny cigarette. 'But it was rude of me not to phone the prison and ask them to pass on a message. I had the mother and father of all headaches most of last week. You'll have to put it down to that.'

'I know you did.'

Roz frowned. 'How?'

With a flick of her fingers Olive squeezed the glowing head from the cigarette and dropped it into an ashtray on the table. 'Elementary, my dear Watson. Your ex gave you two black eyes if all that yellow round them isn't some weird sort of make-up. And headaches usually accompany black eyes.' But she was bored with the subject and fished an envelope abruptly from her pocket. She held it above her head. 'Mr Allenby, sir. Are you going to let me show this to the lady?'

'What is it?' asked one of the men, stepping forward.

'Letter from my solicitor.'

He took it from her raised hand, ignoring the two-fingered salute she gave him, and skimmed through it. 'I've no objections,' he said, placing it on the table and returning to his place by the door.

Olive prodded it towards Roz. 'Read it. He says the chances of tracing my nephew are virtually nil.' She reached for another cigarette, her eyes watching Roz closely. There was a strange awareness in them as if she knew something that Roz didn't, and Roz found it disturbing. Olive, it seemed, now held the initiative in this unnatural glasshouse relationship of theirs but why and when she had taken it, Roz couldn't begin to fathom. It was she, wasn't it, who had engineered this meeting against the odds?

Surprisingly, Crew had handwritten his letter in a neat, sloping script, and Roz could only assume he had composed it out of office hours and decided not to waste company time and money by having it typed. She found that oddly offensive.

Dear Olive,

I understand from Miss Rosalind Leigh that you are acquainted with some of the terms of your late father's will, principally those concerning Amber's illegitimate son. The bulk of the estate has been left in trust to the child although other provisions have been made in the event of failure on our part to trace him. Thus far, my people have met with little success and it is fair to say that we are increasingly pessimistic about our chances. We have established that your nephew emigrated to Australia with his family some twelve years ago when he was little more than a baby but, following their move from a rented flat in Sydney where they remained for the first six months, the trail goes cold. Unfortunately the child's adopted surname is a common one and we have no guarantee that he and his family remained in Australia. Nor can we rule out the possibility that the family decided to add to their name or change it entirely. Carefully worded advertisements in several Australian newspapers have produced no response.

Your father was most insistent that we should be circumspect in how we traced the child. His view, which I endorsed wholeheartedly, was that great damage could be done if there was any publicity associated with the bequest. He was very conscious of the shock his grandson might suffer if he learnt through an incontinent media campaign of his tragic association with the Martin family. For this reason, we have kept and will continue to keep your nephew's name a closely guarded secret. We are pressing on with our enquiries but, as your father stipulated a limited period for searches, the likelihood is that I, as executor, will be obliged to adopt the alternative provisions specified. These are a range of donations to hospitals and charities which care entirely for the needs and welfare of children.

Although your father never instructed me to keep the terms of his will from you, he was very concerned that you should not be distressed by them. It was for this reason that I thought it wiser to keep you in ignorance of his intentions. Had I known that you were already in possession of some of the facts, I should have corresponded sooner.

Trusting you are in good health,

Yours sincerely,

Peter Crew

Roz refolded the letter and pushed it back to Olive. 'You said last time that it mattered to you if your nephew was found, but you didn't enlarge on it.' She glanced towards the two officers, but they were showing little interest in anything except the floor. She leaned forward and lowered her voice. 'Are you going to talk to me about it now?'

Olive jammed her cigarette angrily into the ashtray. She made no attempt to keep her voice down. 'My father was a terrible MAN.' Even in speech the word carried capital letters. 'I couldn't see it at the time but I've had years to think about it and I can see it now.' She nodded towards the letter. 'His conscience was troubling him. That's why he wrote that will. It was his way of feeling good about himself after the appalling damage he'd done. Why else would he leave his money to Amber's baby when he never cared shit for Amber herself?'

Roz looked at her curiously. 'Are you saying your father did the murders?' she murmured.

Olive snorted. 'I'm saying, why use Amber's baby to white-wash himself?'

'What had he done that needed whitewashing?'

But Olive didn't answer.

Roz waited a moment, then tried a different tack. 'You said your father would always leave money to family if he could. Does that mean there's other family he could have left it to? Or did you hope he'd leave it to you?'

Olive shook her head. 'There's no one. Both my parents were only children. And he couldn't leave it to me, could me?' She slammed her fist on the table, her voice rising furiously. 'Otherwise everyone would kill their fucking families!' The great ugly face leered at Roz. YOU WANTED TO, mouthed the sausage lips.

'Keep the volume down, Sculptress,' said Mr Allenby mildly, 'or the visit finishes now.'

Roz pressed a finger and thumb to her eyelids where she could feel her headache coming back. *Olive Martin took an axe* – she tried to thrust the thought away, but it wouldn't go – *and gave her mother forty whacks*. 'I don't understand why the will makes you so angry,' she said, forcing her voice to sound steady. 'If family was important to him who else is there except his grandson?'

Olive stared at the table, her jaw jutting aggressively. 'It's the principle,' she muttered. 'Dad's dead. What does it matter now what people think?'

Roz recalled something Mrs Hopwood had said. *'I've always assumed he must have had an affair . . .'* She took a shot in the dark. 'Do you have a half-brother or sister somewhere? Is that what you're trying to tell me?'

Olive found this amusing. 'Hardly. He'd have to have had a mistress for that and he didn't like women.' She gave a sardonic laugh. 'He did like MEN though.' Again the strange emphasis on the word.

Roz was very taken aback. 'Are you saying he was a homosexual?'

'I'm saying,' said Olive with exaggerated patience, 'that the only person I ever saw make Dad's face light up was our next-door neighbour, Mr Clarke. Dad used to get quite skittish whenever he was around.' She lit another cigarette. 'I thought it was rather sweet at the time, but only because I was too bloody thick to recognize a couple of queens when I saw them. Now I just think it was sick. It's no wonder my mother hated the Clarkes.'

'They moved after the murders,' said Roz thoughtfully. 'Vanished one morning without leaving a forwarding address. No one knows what happened to them or where they went.'

'Doesn't surprise me. I expect *she* was behind it.'

'Mrs Clarke?'

'She never liked him coming round to our house. He used to hop across the fence at the back and he and Dad would shut themselves in Dad's room and not come out for hours. I should think it must have worried her sick after the murders when Dad was all alone in the house.'

Images, gleaned from things people had said, chased themselves across Roz's mind. Robert Martin's vanity and his Peter Pan looks; he and Ted Clarke being as close as brothers; the room at the back with the bed in it; Gwen's keeping up appearances; her frigid flinching from her husband; the secret that needed hiding. It all made sense, she thought, but did it affect anything if Olive hadn't known it at the time?

'Was Mr Clarke his only lover, do you think?'

'How would I know? Probably not,' she went on, contradicting herself immediately. 'He had his own back door in that room he used. He could have been out after rent-boys every night for all any of us would have known about it. I hate him.' She looked as if she were about to erupt again but Roz's look of alarm gave her pause. 'I hated him,' she repeated, before lapsing into silence.

'Because he killed Gwen and Amber?' asked Roz for the second time.

But Olive was dismissive: 'He was at work all day. Everyone knows that.'

Olive Martin took an axe . . . Are you raising her expectations by telling her your book will get her out? 'Did your lover kill them?' She felt she was being clumsy, asking the wrong questions, in the wrong way, at the wrong time.

Olive sniggered. 'What makes you think I had a lover?'

'Someone made you pregnant.'

'Oh, that.' She was scornful. 'I lied about the abortion. I wanted the girls here to think I was attractive once.' She spoke loudly as if intent on the officers hearing everything.

A cold fist of certainty squeezed at Roz's heart. Deedes had warned her of this four weeks ago. 'Then who was the man who sent you letters via Gary O'Brien?' she asked. 'Wasn't he your lover?'

Olive's eyes glittered like snakes' eyes. 'He was Amber's lover.'

Roz stared at her. 'But why would he send letters to you?'

'Because Amber was too frightened to receive them herself. She was a coward.' There was a brief pause. 'Like my father.'

'What was she frightened of?'

'My mother.'

'What was your father frightened of?'

'My mother.'

'And were you frightened of your mother?'

'No.'

'Who was Amber's lover?'

'I don't know. She never told me.'

'What was in his letters?'

'Love, I expect. Everyone loved Amber.'

'Including you?'

'Oh, yes.'

'And your mother. Did she love Amber?'

'Of course.'

'That's not what Mrs Hopwood says.'

Olive shrugged. 'What would she know about it? She hardly knew us. She was always fussing over her precious Geraldine.' A sly smile crept about her mouth, making her ugly. 'What does anybody know about it now except me?'

Roz could feel the scales peeling from her eyes in slow and terrible disillusionment. 'Is that why you waited till your father died before you would talk to anyone? So that there'd be no one left to contradict you?'

Olive stared at her with undisguised dislike then, with a careless gesture – hidden from the officers' eyes but all too visible to Roz – she removed a tiny clay doll from her pocket and turned the long pin that was piercing the doll's head. Red hair. Green dress. It required little imagination on Roz's part to endow the clay with a personality. She gave a hollow laugh. 'I'm a sceptic, Olive. It's like religion. It only works if you believe in it.'

'I believe in it.'

'Then more fool you.' She stood up abruptly and walked to the door, nodding to Mr Allenby to let her out. What had induced her to believe the woman innocent in the first place? And why, for Christ's sake, had she picked on a bloody murderess to fill the void that Alice had left in her heart?

She stopped at a payphone and dialled St Angela's Convent. It was Sister Bridget herself who answered. 'How may I help?' asked her comfortable lilting voice.

Roz smiled weakly into the receiver. 'You could say: "Come on down, Roz, I'll give you an hour to listen to your woes." '

Sister Bridget's light chuckle lost none of its warmth by transmission down the wire. 'Come on down, dear. I've a whole evening free and I like nothing better than listening. Are the woes so bad?'

'Yes. I think Olive did it.'

'Not so bad. You're no worse off than when you started. I live in the house next to the school. It's called Donegal. Totally inappropriate, of course, but rather charming. Join me as soon as you can. We'll have supper together.'

There was a strained note in Roz's voice. 'Do you believe in black magic, Sister?'

'Should I?'

'Olive is sticking pins into a clay image of me.'

'Good Lord!'

'And I've got a headache.'

'I'm not surprised. If I had just had my faith in someone shattered, I would have a headache, too. What an absurd creature she is! Presumably it's her way of trying to regain some semblance of control. Prison is soul destroying in that respect.' She tut-tutted in annoyance. 'Really quite absurd, and I've always had such a high esteem for Olive's intellect. I'll expect you when I see you, my dear.'

Roz listened to the click at the other end, then cradled the receiver against her chest. *Thank God for Sister Bridget* . . . She put the receiver back with two hands that trembled. *Oh, Jesus, Jesus, Jesus! THANK GOD FOR SISTER BRIDGET* . . .

Supper was a simple affair of soup, scrambled eggs on toast, fresh fruit and cheese, with Roz's contribution of a light sparkling wine. They ate in the dining room, looking out over the tiny walled garden where climbing plants tumbled their vigorous new growth in glossy green cascades. It took Roz two hours to run through all her notes and give Sister Bridget a complete account of everything she had discovered.

Sister Bridget, rather more rosy-cheeked than usual, sat in contemplative silence for a long time after Roz had finished. If she noticed the bruises on the other woman's face, she did not remark on them. 'You know, my dear,' she said at last, 'if I'm surprised by anything it is your sudden certainty that Olive is guilty. I can see nothing in what she said to make you overturn your previous conviction that she was innocent.' She raised mildly enquiring eyebrows.

'It was the sly way she smiled when she talked about being the only one who knew anything,' said Roz tiredly. 'There was something so unpleasantly knowing about it. Does that make sense?'

'Not really. The Olive I see has a permanently sly look. I wish she could be as open with me as she seems to have been with you, but I'm afraid she will always regard me as the guardian of her morals. It makes it harder for her to be honest.' She paused for a moment. 'Are you sure you're not simply reacting to her hostility towards you? It's so much easier to believe well of people who like us, and Olive made no secret of her liking for you on the two previous occasions you went to see her.'

'Probably.' Roz sighed. 'But that just means I'm as naïve as everyone keeps accusing me of being.' *Most criminals are pleasant most of the time*, Hal had said.

'I think you probably are naïve,' agreed Sister Bridget, 'which is why you've ferreted out information that none of the cynical professionals thought worth bothering with. Naïvety has its uses, just like everything else.'

'Not when it encourages you to believe lies, it doesn't,' said Roz with feeling. 'I was so sure she had told me the truth about the abortion, and if anything set me questioning her guilt it was that. A secret lover floating around, a rapist even' – she shrugged – 'either would have made a hell of a difference to her case. If he didn't do the murders himself, he might well have provoked them in some way. She cut that ground from under me when she told me the abortion was a lie.'

Sister Bridget looked at her closely for a moment. 'But when did she lie? When she told you about the abortion or, today, when she denied it?'

'Not today,' said Roz decisively. 'Her denial had a ring of truth which her admission never had.'

'I wonder. Don't forget, you were inclined to believe her the first time. Since when, everyone, except Geraldine's mother, has poured cold water on the idea. Subconsciously, you've been slowly conditioned to reject the idea that Olive could have had a sexual relationship with a man. That's made you very quick to accept that what she told you today was the truth.'

'Only because it makes more sense.'

Sister Bridget chuckled. 'It makes more sense to believe that Olive's confession was true but you've highlighted too many inconsistencies to take it at face value. She tells lies, you know that. The trick is to sort out fact from fiction.'

'But why does she lie?' asked Roz in sudden exasperation. 'What good does it do her?'

'If we knew that, we'd have the answer to everything. She lied as a child to shore up the image she wanted to project and to shield herself and Amber from her mother's angry disappointment. She was afraid of rejection. It's why most of us lie, after all. Perhaps she keeps on with it for the same reasons.'

'But her mother and Amber are dead,' Roz pointed out, 'and isn't her image diminished by denying she had a lover?'

Sister Bridget sipped her wine. She didn't respond directly. 'She may, of course, have done it to get her own back. I suppose you've considered that. I can't help feeling she's adopted you as a surrogate Amber or a surrogate Gwen.'

'And look what happened to them.' Roz winced. 'Getting her own back for what, anyway?'

'For missing a visit. You said that upset her.'

'I had good reason.'

'I'm sure you did.' The kind eyes rested on the bruises. 'That's not to say Olive believed you or, if she did, that a week of resentment could be cast off so easily. She may, quite simply, have wanted to spite you in the only way she could, by hurting you. And she's succeeded. You *are* hurt.'

'Yes,' Roz admitted, 'I am. I believed in her. But I'm the one who's feeling rejected, not Olive.'

'Of course. Which is exactly what she wanted to achieve.'

'Even if it means I walk away and abandon her for good?'

'Spite is rarely sensible, Roz.' She shook her head. 'Poor Olive. She must be quite desperate at the moment if she's resorting to clay dolls and outbursts of anger. I wonder what's brought it on. She's been very tetchy with me, too, these last few months.'

'Her father's death,' said Roz. 'There's nothing else.'

Sister Bridget sighed. 'What a tragic life his was. One does wonder what he did to deserve it.' She fell silent. 'I am disinclined to believe,' she went on after a moment, 'that this man who sent the letters was Amber's lover. I think I told you that I bumped into Olive shortly before the murders. I was surprised to see how nice she looked. She was still very big, of course, but she had taken such trouble with her appearance that she looked quite pretty. A different girl entirely from the one who'd been at St Angela's. Such transformations never come about in a vacuum. There's always a reason for them and, in my experience, the reason is usually a man. Then, you know, there is Amber's character to consider. She was never as bright as her sister and she lacked Olive's independence and maturity. I would be very surprised if, at the age of twenty-one, she had been able to sustain an affair with anybody for as long as six months.'

'But you said yourself, men can bring about amazing transformations. Perhaps she changed under his influence.'

'I can't deny that, but if he was Amber's lover, then I can point to a very definite lie that Olive has told you. She would know exactly what was in the letters, either because Amber would have told her or because she would have found a way to open them. She always pried into things that weren't her concern. It sounds so churlish to say it now, but we all had to be very careful of our personal possessions while Olive was at St Angela's. Address books and diaries, in particular, drew her like magnets.'

'Marnie at Wells-Fargo thought Gary O'Brien had a yen for Olive. Perhaps *he* was the man she was dressing up for.'

'Perhaps.'

They sat in silence for some time watching twilight fall. Sister Bridget's cat, a threadbare tabby of advanced years, had curled in a ball on Roz's lap, and she stroked it mechanically in time to its purrs with the same careless affection that she bestowed on Mrs Antrobus. 'I wish,' she murmured, 'there was some independent way of finding out whether or not she had the abortion, but I'd never be allowed within spitting distance of her medical records. Not without her permission, and probably not even then.'

'And supposing it turns out that she didn't have an abortion? Would that tell you anything? It doesn't mean she didn't have a man in her life.'

'No,' agreed Roz, 'but by the same token if she *did* have an abortion then there can be no doubt there *was* a man. I'd be so much more confident about pressing ahead if I knew a lover existed.'

Sister Bridget's perceptive eyes remained on her too long for comfort. 'And so much more confident about dropping the whole thing if you can be convinced he didn't. I think, my dear, you should have more faith in your ability to judge people. Instinct is as good a guide as written evidence.'

'But my instinct at the moment tells me she's guilty as hell.'

'Oh, I don't think so.' Her companion's light laughter rang about the room. 'If it did you wouldn't have driven all these miles to talk to me. You could have sought out your friendly policeman. He would have approved your change of heart.' Her eyes danced. 'I, on the other hand, am the one person you know who could be relied on to fight Olive's corner.'

Roz smiled. 'Does that mean you now think she didn't do it?'

Sister Bridget stared out of the window. 'No,' she said frankly. 'I'm still in two minds.'

'Thanks,' said Roz with heavy irony, 'and you expect me to have faith. That's a bit two-faced, isn't it?'

'Very. But you were chosen, Roz, and I wasn't.'

Roz arrived back at her flat around midnight. The telephone was ringing as she let herself in but after three or four bells the answerphone took over. Iris, she thought. No one else would call at such an unearthly hour, not even Rupert. She had no intention of speaking to her but, out of curiosity, she flicked the switch on the machine to hear Iris leave her message.

'I wonder where you are,' slurred Hal's voice, slack with

drink and tiredness. 'I've been calling for hours. I'm drunk as a skunk, woman, and it's your fault. You're too bloody thin, but what the hell!' He gave a baritone chuckle. 'I'm drowning in shit here, Roz. Me and Olive both. Mad, bad and dangerous to know.' He sighed. *'From East to western Ind, no jewel is like Rosalind.* Who are you, anyway? Nemesis? You lied, you know. You said you'd leave me in peace.' There was the sound of a crash. 'Je-*sus!*' he roared into the telephone. 'I've dropped the bloody bottle.' The line was cut abruptly.

Roz wondered if her grin looked as idiotic as it felt. She switched the answerphone back to automatic and went to bed. She fell asleep almost immediately.

The phone rang again at nine o'clock the next morning. 'Roz?' asked his sober, guarded voice.

'Speaking.'

'It's Hal Hawksley.'

'Hi,' she said cheerfully. 'I didn't know you knew my number.'

'You gave me your card, remember.'

'Oh, yes. What can I do for you?'

'I tried you yesterday, left a message on your answerphone.'

She smiled into the receiver. 'Sorry,' she told him, 'the tape's on the blink. All I got was my ear-drums pierced by high-pitched crackling. Has something happened?'

His relief was audible. 'No.' There was a brief pause. 'I just wondered how you got on with the O'Briens.'

'I saw Ma. It cost me fifty quid but it was worth it. Are you busy today or can I come and chew your ear off again? I need a couple of favours: a photograph of Olive's father and access to her medical records.'

He was happy talking details. 'No chance on the latter,' he told her. 'Olive can demand to see them but you'd have more chance breaking into Parkhurst than breaking into NHS files. I might be able to get hold of a photograph of him, though, if

I can persuade Geoff Wyatt to take a photocopy of the one on file.'

'What about pictures of Gwen and Amber? Could he get photocopies of them too?'

'Depends how strong your stomach is. The only ones I remember are the post-mortem shots. You'll have to get on to Martin's executors if you want pictures of them alive.'

'OK, but I'd still like to see the post-mortem ones if that's possible. I won't try to publish them without the proper authority,' she promised.

'You'd have a job. Police photocopies are usually the worst you'll ever see. If your publisher can make a decent negative out of them, he probably deserves a medal. I'll see what I can do. What time will you get here?'

'Early afternoon? There's someone I need to see first. Could you get me a copy of Olive as well?'

'Probably.' He was silent for a moment. 'High-pitched crackling. Are you sure that's all you heard?'

TWELVE

Peterson's Estate Agency in Dawlington High Street maintained a brave front, with glossy photographs turning enticingly in the window and bright lights inviting the punters in. But, like the estate agents in Southampton centre, the recession had taken its toll here, too, and one neat young man presided over four desks in the despondent knowledge that another day would pass without a single house sale. He jerked to his feet with robotic cheerfulness as the door opened, his teeth glittering in a salesman's smile.

Roz shook her head to avoid raising false hopes. 'I'm sorry,' she said apologetically. 'I haven't come to buy anything.'

He gave an easy laugh. 'Ah, well. Selling perhaps?'

'Not that either.'

'Very wise.' He pulled out a chair for her. 'It's still a buyer's market. You only sell at the moment if you're desperate to move.' He resumed his chair on the other side of the desk. 'How can I help?'

Roz gave him a card. 'I'm trying to trace some people called Clarke who sold their house through this agency three or four years ago and moved out of the area. None of their neighbours knows where they went. I was hoping you might be able to tell me.'

He pulled a face. 'Before my time, I'm afraid. What was the address of the house?'

'Number twenty, Leven Road.'

'I could look it up, I suppose. The file will be out the back if it hasn't been binned.' He looked at the empty desks. 'Unfortunately there's no one to cover for me at the moment so I won't be able to do it until this evening. Unless—' He glanced at Roz's card again. 'I see you live in London. Have you ever thought about buying a second property on the south coast, Mrs Leigh? We have a lot of authors down here. They like to escape to the peace and quiet of the country.'

Her mouth twitched. 'Miss Leigh. And I don't even own a first property. I live in rented accommodation.'

He spun his chair and pulled out a drawer in the filing cabinet behind him. 'Then let me suggest a mutually beneficial arrangement.' His fingers ran nimbly through the files, select-ing a succession of printed pages. 'You read these while I search out that information for you. If a customer comes into the shop, offer them a seat and call for me. Ditto, if the phone rings.' He nodded to a back door. 'I'll leave that open. Just call "Matt" and I'll hear you. Fair?'

'I'm happy if you are,' she said, 'but I'm not planning on buying anything.'

'That's fine.' He walked across to the door. 'Mind you, there's one property there that would fit you like a glove. It's called Bayview, but don't be put off by the name. I shan't be long.'

Roz fingered through the pages reluctantly as if just touch-ing them might induce her to part with her money. He had the soft insidiousness of an insurance salesman. Anyway, she told herself with some amusement, she couldn't possibly live in a house called Bayview. It conjured up too many images of net-curtained guest-houses with beak-nosed landladies in nylon overalls and lacklustre signs saying VACANCIES propped against the downstairs windows.

She came to it finally at the bottom of the pile and the reality, of course, was very different. A small whitewashed coastguard's cottage, the last of a group of four, perched on a cliff near Swanage on the Isle of Purbeck. Two up, two down. Unpretentious. Charming. Beside the sea. She looked at the price.

'Well?' asked Matt, returning a few minutes later with a folder under one arm. 'What do you think?'

'Assuming I could afford it, which I can't, I think I'd freeze to death in the winter from winds lashing in off the sea and be driven mad in the summer by streams of tourists wandering along the coastal path. According to your blurb it passes only a matter of yards from the fence. And that's ignoring the fact that I'd be rubbing shoulders with the inhabitants of the other three cottages, day in, day out, plus the frightening prospect of knowing that sooner or later the cliff will slip and take my very expensive cottage with it.'

He chuckled good-humouredly. 'I knew you'd like it. I'd have bought it myself if it wasn't too far to travel each day. The cottage at the other end has a retired couple in it in their seventies and the two in the middle are weekend cottages. They are situated in the middle of a small headland, well away from the cliff edges, and, frankly, the bricks will crumble long before the foundations do. As for the wind and the tourists, well, it's to the east of Swanage so it's sheltered from the prevailing winds, and the sort of tourists who walk that coastal path are not the sort to disturb your peace, simply because there is no public access beside these cottages. The nearest one is four miles away and you don't get noisy children or drunken lager louts tackling that sort of hike for the fun of it. Which leaves' – his boyish face split into a carefree smile – 'the problem of cost.'

Roz giggled. 'Don't tell me. The owners are so desperate to get rid of it they're prepared to give it away.'

'As a matter of fact, yes. Liquidity problems with their business and this is only a weekend retreat. They'll take a twenty-thousand reduction if someone can come up with cash. Can you?'

Roz closed her eyes and thought of her fifty per cent share of the proceeds of divorce, sitting on deposit. Yes, she thought, I can. 'This is absurd,' she said impatiently. 'I didn't come in to buy anything. I'll hate it. It'll be far too small. And why on earth have you got it on your books? It's miles away.'

'We have a reciprocal arrangement with our other branches.' He had hooked his fish. Now he let her swim a little. 'Let's see what this file can tell us.' He drew it forward and opened it. 'Twenty, Leven Road. Owners: Mr and Mrs Clarke. Instructions: quick sale wanted; carpets and curtains included in asking price. Bought by Mr and Mrs Blair. Completion date: twenty-fifth Feb., eighty-nine.' He looked surprised 'They didn't pay very much for it.'

'It was vacant for a year,' said Roz, 'which would probably explain the low price. Does it give a forwarding address for the Clarkes?'

He read on: 'It says here: "Vendors have asked Peterson's not to divulge any information about their new whereabouts." I wonder why.'

'They fell out with their neighbours,' said Roz, economical as ever with the truth. 'But they must have given a forwarding address,' she remarked reasonably, 'or they wouldn't have asked for it to be withheld.'

He turned over several pages then carefully closed the file, leaving his finger to mark a place. 'We're talking professional ethics here, Miss Leigh. I am employed by Peterson's, and Peterson's were asked to respect the Clarkes' confidence. It would be very wrong to abuse a client's trust.'

Roz thought for a moment. 'Is there anything from Peterson's in writing saying they agreed to honour the Clarkes' request?'

'No.'

'Then I don't see that you're bound by anything. Confidences cannot be inherited. If they could, they would no longer be confidences.'

He smiled. 'That's a very fine distinction.'

'Yes.' She picked up the details of Bayview. 'Supposing I said I wanted to view this cottage at three o'clock this afternoon? Could you arrange it for me, using that telephone over there' – she nodded to the furthest desk – 'while I stay here looking through these other house details?'

'I could, but I'd take it very badly if you failed to keep the appointment.'

'My word's my bond,' she assured him. 'If I say I'm going to do something I always do it.'

He stood up, letting the file fall open on the desk. 'Then I'll phone our Swanage branch,' he told her. 'You will have to collect the key from them.'

'Thank you.' She waited until his back was turned, then swung the file round and jotted down the Clarkes' address on her pad. Salisbury, she noted.

A few minutes later Matt resumed his seat and gave her a map of Swanage with Peterson's estate agency marked with a cross. 'Mr Richards is expecting you at three o'clock.' With a lazy flick of his hand he closed the Clarkes' file. 'I trust you will find your dealings with him as mutually satisfactory as you have found your dealings with me.'

Roz laughed. 'And I hope I don't, or I shall be considerably poorer by this evening.'

Roz approached the Poacher by the alleyway at the back and knocked on the kitchen door. 'You're early,' said Hal, opening it.

'I know, but I have to be in Swanage by three and if I don't leave fairly soon I won't make it. Have you any customers?'

He gave her a withering smile. 'I haven't even bothered to open up.'

She chose to ignore the sarcasm. 'Then come with me,' she said. 'Forget this place for a few hours.'

He didn't exactly jump at the invitation. 'What's in Swanage?'

She handed him the details of Bayview. 'A "des. res." overlooking the sea. I've committed myself to looking at it and I could do with some moral support or I might end up buying the wretched thing.'

'Then don't go.'

'I have to. It's by way of a quid pro quo,' she said obliquely. 'Come with me,' she urged, 'and say no whenever I look like saying yes. I'm a sucker for a soft sell and I've always wanted to live on a cliff by the sea and own a dog and go beachcombing.'

179

He looked at the price. 'Can you afford it?' he asked curiously.

'Just about.'

'Rich lady,' he said. 'Writing is obviously very profitable.'

'Hardly. That was by way of a pay-off.'

'Pay-off for what?' he asked, his eyes veiled.

'It's not important.'

'Nothing ever is in your life.'

She shrugged. 'So you don't want to come? Ah, well, it was only a thought. I'll go on my own.' She looked lonely suddenly.

He glanced behind him towards the restaurant, then abruptly reached his jacket off the back of the door. 'I'll come,' he told her, 'but I'm damned if I'll say no. It sounds like paradise, and the second best piece of advice my mother ever gave me was never get between a woman and what she wants.' He pulled the door to and locked it.

'And what was the best piece of advice?'

He dropped a casual arm across her shoulders – *could she really be as lonely as she looked? The thought saddened him* – and walked her up the alleyway. 'That happiness is no laughing matter.'

She gave a throaty chuckle. 'What's that supposed to mean?'

'It means, woman, that the pursuit of happiness deserves weighty consideration. It's the be-all and end-all of existence. Where is the sense in living if you're not enjoying it?'

'Earning Brownie points for the great hereafter, suffering being good for the soul and all that.'

'If you say so,' he said cheerfully. 'Shall we go in my car? It'll give you a chance to test out your theory.' He led her to an ancient Ford Cortina estate and unlocked the passenger door, pulling it half-open on screaming hinges.

'What theory?' she asked, squeezing inelegantly through the gap.

He shut the door. 'You'll soon find out,' he murmured.

*

They arrived with half an hour to spare. Hal drew into a parking space on the sea front and rubbed his hands. 'Let's have some fish and chips. We passed a kiosk about a hundred yards back and I'm ravenous. It's the fresh air that does it.'

Roz's head, tortoise-like, emerged from the collar of her jacket, slowly easing its frozen jaw and skewering him with gimlet eyes. 'Has this heap of junk got an MOT?' she grated.

'Of course it's got an MOT.' He slapped the steering-wheel. 'She's sound as a bell, just lacks a window or two. You get used to it after a while.'

'A window or two!' she spluttered. 'As far as I can see it hasn't got any windows at all except for the front one. I think I've caught pneumonia.'

'There's no pleasing some women. You wouldn't be whingeing like this if I'd whisked you down to the seaside on a beautiful sunny day in an open-topped cabriolet. You're being snotty-nosed just because it's a Cortina.' He gave an evil chuckle. 'And what about suffering being good for the soul? It's done bugger all for yours, my girl.'

She thrust the screeching door open as far as it would go and crawled out. 'For your information, Hawksley, it is *not* a beautiful sunny day' – she giggled – 'in fact it will probably turn out to be the coldest May day this century. And *had* this been a convertible, we could have stopped to put the top up. In any case, why aren't there any windows?'

He tucked her into the crook of his arm and set off towards the fish and chip kiosk. 'Someone smashed them,' he said matter of factly. 'I haven't bothered to replace them because there's a good chance it will happen again.'

She rubbed the end of her nose to restore the circulation. 'I suppose you're in hock to loan sharks.'

'And if I am?'

She thought of her money on deposit, untouched, going nowhere. 'I might be able to broker you out of your difficulties,' she suggested tentatively.

He frowned. 'Is this charity, Roz, or an offer to negotiate?'

'It's not charity,' she assured him. 'My accountant would have a fit if I offered charity.'

He dropped his arm abruptly. 'Why would you want to negotiate on my behalf? You don't know a damn thing about me.' He sounded angry.

She shrugged. 'I know you're in deep shit, Hawksley. I'm offering to help you out of it. Is that so terrible?' She walked on.

Hal, a step or two behind, cursed himself roundly. What sort of fool lowered his defences just because a woman looked lonely? But loneliness, of course, was the one thing guaranteed to strike a chord. There must have been times when he hadn't been lonely but he was damned, at the moment, if he could remember them.

Roz's delight in the cottage, masked by an unconvincing smile of bored indifference, announced itself loudly as she stared wide-eyed at the views from the windows, noted the double-glazing, admitted grudgingly that, yes, she had always liked open fireplaces, and, yes, she was quite surprised by the size of the rooms. She *had* expected them to be smaller. She poked for several minutes round the patioed garden, said it was a pity there wasn't a greenhouse, then, rather belatedly, obscured her enthusiasm behind a pair of dark glasses to examine a small rose-covered outhouse which was used by the present owners as a third bedroom, but which might, she supposed, at a pinch, serve as a sort of study–library.

Hal and Mr Richards sat on cast-iron chairs in front of the french windows, talking idly about very little and watching her. Mr Richards, thoroughly intimidated by Hal's brusque one-word answers, scented a sale but contained his excitement rather better than Roz.

He stood up when Roz had finished her inspection and, with a disarming smile, offered her his chair. 'I should perhaps have mentioned, Miss Leigh, that the present owners will consider selling the furniture with the house assuming, of course, a satisfactory price can be arranged. I understand none of it is more than four years old and the wear and tear has been minimal with weekend occupation only.' He glanced at his watch. 'Why don't I give you fifteen minutes to talk it over? I'll go for a stroll along the cliff path.' He vanished tactfully through the french windows and a moment later they heard the front door close.

Roz took off her glasses and looked at Hal. Her eyes were childlike in their enthusiasm. 'What do you think? Furniture, too. Isn't it fabulous?'

His lips twitched involuntarily. *Could this be acting?* It was damn good if it was. 'It depends what you want it for.'

'To live in,' she said. 'It would be so easy to work here.' She looked towards the sea. 'I've always loved the sound of waves.' She turned to him. 'What do you think? Should I buy it?'

He was curious. 'Will my opinion make a difference?'

'Probably.'

'Why?'

'Because common sense tells me it would be a mad thing to do. It's miles from everyone I know, and it's expensive for what it is, a pokey little two up, two down. There must be better ways of investing my money.' She studied his set face and wondered why her earlier offer to help had made him so hostile. He was a strange man, she thought. So very approachable as long as she steered clear of talking about the Poacher.

He looked past her towards the cliff-top where Mr Richards was just visible, sitting on a rock and having a quiet smoke. 'Buy it,' he said. 'You can afford it.' His dark face broke into a smile. 'Live dangerously. Do what you've always wanted to do. How did John Masefield put it? "I must down to the seas again, for the call of the running tide/Is a wild call and a clear call that may not be denied." So, live on your cliff by the sea and go beachcombing with your dog. As I said, it sounds like paradise.'

She smiled back, her dark eyes full of humour. 'But the trouble with paradise was that it was boring, which is why, when the one-eyed trouser-snake appeared, Eve was so damn keen to bite into the apple of knowledge.' He was a different man when he laughed. She caught a glimpse of the Hal Hawksley, hail-fellow-well-met, boon companion, who could, were his tables ever full, preside with confident conviviality among them. She threw caution to the winds. 'I wish you'd let me help you. I'd be lonely here. And where's the sense in paying a fortune to be lonely on a cliff?'

His eyes veiled abruptly. 'You really are free with your money, aren't you? Exactly what are you suggesting? A buy-out? A partnership? What?'

God, he was prickly! And he had accused her of it once. 'Does it matter? I'm offering to bail you out of whatever mess you're in.'

His eyes narrowed. 'The only certain thing you know about me, Roz, is that my restaurant is failing. Why would an intelligent woman want to throw good money after bad?'

Why indeed? She would never be able to explain it to her accountant whose idea of sensible living was minimum risk-taking, clean balance sheets, and tax advantageous pension plans. How would she even begin? 'There's this man, Charles, who reduces me to jelly every time I see him. But he's a damn good cook and he loves his restaurant and there's no logical reason why it should be going down the pan. I keep trying to lend him money but he throws it back in my face every time.' Charles would have her certified. She swung her bag on to her shoulder. 'Forget I mentioned it,' she said. 'It's obviously a sore nerve, though I can't imagine why.'

She started to get up but he caught her wrist in a grip of iron and held her in her seat. 'Is this another set-up, Roz?'

She stared at him. 'You're hurting me.' He released her abruptly. 'What are you talking about?' she asked, massaging her wrist.

'You came back.' He rubbed his face vigorously with both hands as if he were in pain. 'Why the hell do you keep coming back?'

She was incensed. 'Because you phoned,' she said. 'I wouldn't have come if you hadn't phoned. God, you're arrogant. They come two a penny like you in London, you know.'

His eyes narrowed dangerously. 'Then offer your money to them,' he said, 'and stop patronizing me.'

Tight-lipped, they took their leave of Mr Richards with false promises of phoning the next day, and drove off up the narrow coast road towards Wareham. Hal, all too conscious of the darkening clouds and the reduction in speed that wet tarmac would enforce on him, concentrated on his driving. Roz, crushed by his hostility which, like a tropical storm, had blown out of nowhere, withdrew into hurt silence. Hal had been gratuitously cruel, and knew it, but he was gripped by his own certainty that this trip had been engineered to get him out of the Poacher. And *God* was Roz good. She had every damn thing: looks, humour, intellect, and just enough vulnerability to appeal to his stupid chivalry. But *he* had phoned *her*. Fool, *Hawksley!* She would have come back, anyway. Someone had to offer him the stinking money. *Sh-i-it!* He slammed his fist against the steering-wheel. 'Why did you want me to come with you?' he demanded into the silence.

'You're a free agent,' she pointed out caustically. 'You didn't have to come.'

It started to rain as they reached Wareham, slanting stair-rods that drove in through the open windows.

'Oh, great!' announced Roz, clutching her jacket about her throat. 'The perfect end to a perfect day. I'll be soaked. I should have come on my own in my own car. I could hardly have had less fun, could I?'

'Why didn't you then? Why drag me out on a wild-goose chase?'

'Believe it or not,' she said icily, 'I was trying to do you a favour. I thought it would be good for you to escape for a couple of hours. I was wrong. You're even more touchy away from the place than you are in it.' He took a corner too fast and threw her against the door, grazing her leather jacket against the buckled chromium window strip. 'For God's sake,' she snapped crossly. 'This jacket cost me a fortune.'

He pulled into the kerb with a screech of rubber. 'OK,' he snarled, 'let's see what we can do to protect it.' He reached across her to take a book of road maps out of the dashboard pocket.

'What good will that do?'

'It will tell me where the nearest station is.' He thumbed through the pages. 'There's one in Wareham and the line goes to Southampton. You can take a taxi back to your car at the other end.' He fished out his wallet. 'That should be enough to pay your way.' He dropped a twenty-pound note into her lap then swung the car on to the road again. 'It's off to the right at the next roundabout.'

'You're a real sweetheart, Hawksley. Didn't your mother teach you any manners along with her little aphorisms about women and life?'

'Don't push your luck,' he growled. 'I'm on a very short fuse at the moment and it doesn't take much to rile me. I spent five years of marriage being criticized for every damn thing I did. I'm not about to repeat the experience.' He drew up in front of the station. 'Go home,' he told her, wiping a weary hand across his damp face. 'I'm doing you a favour.'

She put the twenty-pound note on the dashboard and reached for her handbag. 'Yes,' she agreed mildly, 'I think you probably are. If your wife stuck it out for five years, she must have been a saint.' She pushed the door open on its screaming hinges and eased round it, then bent down to look through the window, thrusting her middle finger into the air. 'Go screw yourself, Sergeant. Presumably it's the only thing that gives you any pleasure. Let's face it, no one else could ever be good enough.'

'Got it in one, Miss Leigh.' He nodded a curt farewell, then spun the wheel in a U-turn. As he drove away the twenty-pound note whipped like a bitter recrimination from the window and fell with the rain into the gutter.

*

Hal was cold and wet by the time he reached Dawlington, and his already evil temper was not improved to find her car still parked at the end of the alleyway where she had left it. He glanced past it, between the buildings, and saw that the back door of the Poacher stood ajar, the wood in splinters where a crowbar had been used to wrench it free of its frame. OH, *Jesus!* She *had* set him up. He knew a moment of total desolation – he was not as immune as he thought himself – before the need to act took over.

He was too angry for common sense, too angry to take even elementary precautions. He ran on light feet, thrust the door wide and weighed in with flailing fists, punching, kicking, gouging, oblivious to the blows that landed on his arms and shoulders, intent only on causing maximum damage to the bastards who were destroying him.

Roz, arriving thirty minutes later with Hal's sodden twenty-pound note clutched in one hand and a blistering letter of denunciation in the other, stared in disbelief at what she saw. The kitchen looked like a scene from Beirut in the aftermath of war. Deserted and destroyed. The table, up-ended, leant drunkenly against the oven, two of its legs wrenched free. Chairs, in pieces, lay amongst shards of broken crockery and jagged glass. And the fridge, tilted forward and balanced precariously on its open door, had poured its contents across the quarry tiling in streams of milk and congealed stock. She held a trembling hand to her lips. Here and there, splashes of bright red blood had tinged the spreading milk pink.

She looked wildly up the alleyway, but there was no one in sight. *What to do?* 'Hal!' she called, but her voice was little more than a whisper. 'Hal!' This time it rose out of control and, in the silence that followed, she thought she heard a sound from the other side of the swing doors into the restaurant. She stuffed the letter and the money into her pockets and reached inside the door for one of the table legs. 'I've called the police,' she shouted, croaky with fear. 'They're on their way.'

The door swung open and Hal emerged with a bottle of wine. He nodded at the table leg. 'What are you planning to do with that?'

She let her arm fall. 'Have you gone mad? Did you do all this?'

'Am I likely to have done it?'

'Olive did.' She stared about her. 'This is just what Olive did. Lost her temper and destroyed her room. She had all her privileges taken away.'

'You're babbling.' He found a couple of glasses in an intact wall cupboard and filled them from the bottle. 'Here.' His dark eyes watched her closely. '*Have* you called the police?'

'No.' Her teeth chattered against the wine glass. 'I thought if you were a burglar you'd run away. Your hand's bleeding.'

'I know.' He took the table leg away from her and put it on top of the oven, then pulled forward the only intact chair from behind the back door and pressed her into it. 'What were you going to do if the burglar ran out this way?'

'Hit him, I suppose.' Her fear was beginning to subside. 'Is this what you thought I'd set you up for?'

'Yes.'

'God!' She didn't know what else to say. She watched while he found a broom and started to sweep the mess towards one corner. 'Shouldn't you leave that?'

'What for?'

'The police.'

He eyed her curiously. 'You said you hadn't called them.'

She digested this in silence for several seconds, then put her glass on the floor beside her. 'This is all a bit heavy for me.' She took the twenty-pound note from her pocket, but left the letter where it was. 'I only came back to give you this.' She held it out as she stood up. 'I'm sorry,' she said with an apologetic smile.

'What for?'

'Making you angry. I seem to have a knack for making people angry at the moment.' He moved towards her to take the money, but stopped abruptly at her look of alarm.

'Goddamnit, woman, do you think *I* did this?'

But he was speaking to thin air. Roz had taken to her heels down the alleyway and the twenty-pound note, once again, fluttered to the ground.

THIRTEEN

oz's sleep that night was intermittent, fitful dozing between turbulent dreams. Olive with an axe, hacking kitchen tables to pieces. *I didn't think you would . . . it's not as easy as it looks on the telly.* . . . Hal's fingers on her wrist, but his face the gleeful face of her brother as he gave her Chinese burns as a child. *Goddamnit, woman, do you think I did this* . . . Olive hanging from the gallows, her face the slimy grey of wet clay. *Have you no qualms about releasing someone like her back into society* . . . A priest with the eyes of Sister Bridget. *It's a pity you're not a Catholic . . . You could go to confession and feel better immediately . . . You keep offering me money . . . The law is an ass . . . Have you called the police . . .*

She woke in the morning to the sound of the phone ringing in her sitting room. Her head was splitting. She snatched up the receiver to shut off the noise. 'Who is it?'

'Well, that's a nice welcome, I must say,' remarked Iris. 'What's eating you?'

'Nothing. What do you want?'

'Shall I phone off,' said Iris sweetly, 'and call you back again in half an hour when you've remembered that I'm your friend and not some piece of dog's dirt that you've just scraped off your shoe?'

'Sorry. You woke me. I didn't sleep very well.'

'M'm, well, I've just had your editor on the phone pressing me for a date – and I don't mean an invitation to dinner. He wants a rough idea of when the book will be ready.'

Roz made a face into the receiver. 'I haven't started writing it yet.'

'Then you'd better get a move on, my darling, because I've told him it will be finished by Christmas.'

'Oh, Iris, for Heaven's sake. That's only six months away and I'm no further forward than the last time I spoke to you. Olive clams up every time we get to the murders. In fact I—'

'Seven months,' Iris cut in. 'Go and grill that dodgy policeman again. He sounds absolutely frightful and I'll bet you anything you like he framed her. They all do it. It boosts their quotas. The buzz word is productivity, darling, something that is temporarily absent from your vocabulary.'

Mrs Clarke listened to Roz's introductory speech about her book on Olive with an expression of complete horror. 'How did you find us?' she asked in a quavering voice. For no particular reason, Roz had pictured her in her fifties or early sixties. She was unprepared for this old woman, closer in age to Mr Hayes than to the age Robert and Gwen Martin would have been if they were still alive.

'It wasn't difficult,' she hedged.

'I've been so afraid.'

It was an odd reaction but Roz let it pass. 'Can I come in? I won't take up much of your time, I promise.'

'I couldn't possibly speak to you. I'm alone. Edward is shopping.'

'Please, Mrs Clarke,' she begged, her voice catching under the strain of her tiredness. It had taken two and a half hours to drive to Salisbury and locate their house. 'I've come such a long way to see you.'

The woman smiled suddenly and held the door wide. 'Come in. Come in. Edward made some cakes specially. He'll be so thrilled you found us.'

With a puzzled frown, Roz stepped inside. 'Thank you.'

'You remember Pussy, of course' – she waved at an ancient cat curled beneath a radiator – 'or was she after your time? I forget things, you know. We'll sit in the lounge. Edward,' she called, 'Mary's here.'

There was no response. 'Edward's gone shopping,' said Roz.

'Oh, yes.' She looked at Roz in confusion. 'Do I know you?'

'I'm a friend of Olive's.'

'I'm a friend of Olive's,' mimicked the old lady. 'I'm a friend of Olive's.' She lowered herself on to the sofa. 'Sit down. Edward's made some cakes specially. I remember Olive. We were at school together. She had long pigtails which the boys used to pull. Such wicked boys. I wonder what happened to them.' She looked at Roz again. 'Do I know you?'

Roz sat awkwardly in an armchair, weighing the ethics of questioning a vulnerable old woman with senile dementia. 'I'm a friend of Olive Martin,' she prompted. 'Gwen and Robert's daughter.' She studied the vacant blue eyes but there was no reaction. She was relieved. Ethics became irrelevant when asking questions was a nonsense. She smiled encouragingly. 'Tell me about Salisbury. Do you like living here?'

Their conversation was an exhausting one, filled with silences, chanting repetition, and strange inconsequential references that left Roz struggling to follow the thread. Twice, she had to divert Mrs Clarke from a sudden realization that she was a stranger, fearing that if she left she would find it impossible to get back in to talk to Edward. With part of her mind she wondered how he coped. Could you go on loving an empty shell when your love was neither reciprocated nor appreciated? Could there ever be enough flashes of lucidity to make the loneliness of caring worthwhile?

Her eye was drawn again and again to the wedding photograph above the mantelpiece. They had married comparatively late, she thought, judging by their ages. He looked to be in his forties, with most of his hair already missing. She looked a little older. But they stood shoulder to shoulder, laughing together out of the frame, two happy, healthy people, with not a care in the world, unaware – and how could they be? – that she carried the seeds of dementia. It was cruel to make a comparison but Roz couldn't help herself. Beside the celluloid woman, so alive, so vivid, so substantial, the real Mrs Clarke was a colourless, trembling shadow. Was this, Roz wondered, why Edward and Robert Martin had become lovers? She found the whole experience immensely depressing and when, at last, the sound of a key grated in the lock, it came like the welcome patter of rain on drought-hardened earth.

'Mary's come to see us,' said Mrs Clarke brightly as her husband entered the room. 'We've been waiting for cakes.'

Roz stood up and handed Mr Clarke one of her cards. 'I did tell her who I was,' she said quietly, 'but it seemed kinder to be Mary.'

He was old, like his wife, and entirely bald, but he still carried himself erect with shoulders squared. He towered above the woman on the sofa who shrank away from him in sudden fear, muttering to herself. Roz wondered if he ever lost his temper with her.

'I really don't leave her alone very often,' he answered defensively, as if she had accused him of it, 'but the shopping has to be done. Everyone's so busy and it's not fair to keep asking the neighbours.' He ran a hand across his bald head and read the card. 'I thought you were Social Services,' he said, this time accusing *her*. 'Author? We don't want an author. What good would an author be to us?'

'I was hoping you could help me.'

'I don't know the first thing about writing. Who gave you my name?'

'Olive did,' said Mrs Clarke. 'She's a friend of Olive's.'

He was shocked. 'Oh, no!' he said. 'No, no, no! You'll have to leave. I'm not having that dragged up again. It's an outrage. How did you get hold of this address?'

'No, no, no!' chanted his wife. 'It's an outrage. No, no, no!'

Roz held her breath and counted to ten, not sure if her sanity or her control would slip first. 'How on earth do you cope?' The words tumbled out as involuntarily as Mrs Clarke's did. 'I'm sorry.' She saw the strain in his face. 'That was unforgivably rude.'

'It's not so bad when we're alone. I just switch off.' He sighed. 'Why have you come? I thought we'd put all that behind us. There's nothing I can do for Olive. Robert tried to help her at the time but it was all thrown back in his face. Why has she sent you here?'

'It's an outrage,' muttered the old woman.

'She hasn't. I'm here off my own bat. Look,' she said, glancing at Mrs Clarke, 'is there somewhere we can talk privately?'

'There's nothing to talk about.'

'But there is,' she said. 'You were a friend of Robert's. You must have known the family better than anyone. I'm writing a book' – she remembered belatedly that her explanations had been given to Mrs Clarke – 'and I can't do it if no one will tell me about Gwen and Robert.'

She had shocked him again. 'Gutter journalism,' he spat. 'I won't have anything to do with it. Leave now, or I shall call the police.'

Mrs Clarke gave a whimper of fear. 'Not the police. No, no, no. I'm afraid of the police.' She peered at the stranger. 'I'm afraid of the police.'

With reason, thought Roz, wondering if the shock of the murders had brought on the dementia. Was that why they had moved away? She picked up her briefcase and handbag. 'I'm no gutter journalist, Mr Clarke. I'm trying to help Olive.'

'She's beyond help. We all are.' He glanced at his wife. 'Olive destroyed everything.'

'I disagree.'

'Please go.'

The thin reedy voice of the old woman broke in on them. 'I never saw Gwen and Amber that day,' she cried plaintively. 'I lied. I lied, Edward.'

He closed his eyes. 'Oh, God,' he murmured, 'what did I ever do to deserve this?' His voice vibrated with repressed dislike.

'Which day?' Roz pressed.

But the moment of lucidity, if that is what it was, had passed. 'We've been waiting for cakes.'

Irritation and something else – relief? – passed across his face. 'She's senile,' he told Roz. 'Her mind's gone. You can't rely on anything she says. I'll show you out.'

Roz didn't move. 'Which day, Mrs Clarke?' she asked gently.

'The day the police came. I said I saw them but I didn't.' She furrowed her brow in perplexity. 'Do I know you?'

Mr Clarke seized Roz roughly by the arm and manhandled her towards the front door. 'Get out of my house!' he stormed. 'Haven't we suffered enough at the hands of that family?' He thrust her into the street and slammed the door.

Roz rubbed her arm reflectively. Edward Clarke, in spite of his age, was a good deal stronger than he looked.

She turned the problem in her mind throughout the long drive home. She was caught in the same dilemma that Olive kept posing her, the dilemma of belief. Was Mrs Clarke telling the truth? Had she lied to the police that day or was her senile recollection faulty? And if she had lied, did it make a difference?

Roz pictured herself in the Poacher's kitchen, listening to Hal talking about Robert Martin's alibi. 'We did wonder if he might have killed Gwen and Amber before he went to work and Olive then attempted to dispose of the bodies to protect him, but the numbers didn't add up. He had an alibi even for that. There was a neighbour who saw her husband off to work a few minutes before Martin himself left. Amber and Gwen were alive then because she spoke to them on their doorstep. She remembered asking Amber how she was getting on at Glitzy. They waved as Martin drove away.'

Mrs Clarke, thought Roz, it had to be. But how remiss of her not to question that statement before? Was it likely that Gwen and Amber would wave goodbye to Robert when so little love was lost between husband and wife? A sentence from Olive's statement pierced her thoughts like a sharp knife. *We had an argument over breakfast and my father left for work in the middle of it.*

So Mrs Clarke had been telling lies. But why? Why give Robert an alibi when, according to Olive, she saw him as a threat?

'There was a neighbour who saw her husband off to work a few minutes before Martin himself left . . .'

God, but she'd been blind. The alibi was Edward's.

She phoned Iris in a fever of excitement from a pay phone. 'I've cracked it, old thing. I know who did it and it wasn't Olive.'

'There you are, you see. Always trust your agent's instincts. I've had a fiver on you with Gerry. He'll be sick as a parrot about losing. So who did do it?'

'The neighbour, Edward Clarke. He was Robert Martin's lover. I think he killed Gwen and Amber out of jealousy.' Breathlessly, she rattled off her story. 'Mind you, I've still got to find a way of proving it.'

There was a lengthy silence at the other end.

'Are you still there?'

'Yes, I was just mourning my five pounds. I know you're excited, darling, but you'll have to sober up and give it a little more thought. If this Edward chopped up Gwen and Amber before Robert went to work, wouldn't Robert have stumbled across the bits in the kitchen?'

'Perhaps they did it together?'

'Then why didn't they kill Olive as well? Not to mention the small matter of why on earth Olive would want to shield her father's homosexual lover. It would make much more sense if Mrs Clarke lied to give Robert an alibi.'

'Why?'

'They were having a raging affair,' declared Iris. 'Mrs C. guessed Robert had done his wife in to give himself a free hand with her and lied through her teeth to protect him. You don't know for sure he was a homosexual. The schoolfriend's mother didn't think he was. Is Mrs C. attractive?'

'Not now. She was once.'

'There you are, then.'

'Why did Robert kill Amber?'

'Because she was there,' said Iris simply. 'I expect she woke up when she heard the fight and came downstairs. Robert would have had no option but to kill her as well. Then he skedaddled and left poor old Olive, who slept through it all, to face the music.'

Somewhat reluctantly, Roz went to see Olive.

'I wasn't expecting you, not after—' Olive left the rest of the sentence unsaid. 'Well, you know.' She smiled shyly.

They were back in their old room, unsupervised. The Governor's qualms, it seemed, had been laid to rest along with Olive's hostility. Really, thought Roz, the prison system never ceased to surprise her. She had foreseen enormous problems, particularly as it was a Wednesday and not her normal day, but there had been none. Access to Olive was once more unrestricted. She pushed forward the cigarette packet. 'You seem to be *persona grata* again,' she said.

Olive accepted a cigarette. 'With you, too?'

Roz arched an eyebrow. 'I felt better after my headache had gone.' She saw distress on the fat face. 'I'm teasing,' she said gently. 'And it was my fault anyway. I should have phoned. Have you had all your privileges restored?'

'Yes. They're pretty decent really, once you calm down.'

'Good.' Roz switched on her tape-recorder. 'I've been to see your next-door neighbours, the Clarkes.'

Olive studied her through the flame of the match, then tipped it thoughtfully towards her cigarette. 'And?'

'Mrs Clarke lied about seeing your mother and sister on the morning of the murders.'

'How do you know?'

'She told me.'

Olive wedged the cigarette firmly between her lips and drew in a lungful of smoke. 'Mrs Clarke's been senile for years,' she said bluntly. 'She had a thing about germs, used to rush about every morning scrubbing the furniture with Domestos and hoovering like mad. People who didn't know them thought she was the char. She always called me Mary which was her mother's name. I should imagine she's completely loopy by now.'

Roz shook her head in frustration. 'She is, but I'll swear she was lucid when she admitted lying. She's frightened of her husband, though.'

Olive looked surprised. 'She was never frightened of him before. If anything, he was more frightened of her. What did he say when she told you she'd lied?'

'He was furious. Ordered me out of the house.' She made a wry face. 'We got off to a bad start. He thought I was from the Social Services, spying on him.'

A wheeze of amusement eddied up through Olive's throat. 'Poor Mr Clarke.'

'You said your father liked him. Did *you*?'

She shrugged indifference. 'I didn't know him well enough to like him or dislike him. I suppose I felt sorry for him because of his wife. He had to retire early to look after her.'

Roz mulled this over. 'But he was still working at the time of the murders?'

'He carried on a small accountancy business from home. Other people's tax returns mostly.' She tapped ash on to the floor. 'Mrs Clarke set fire to their living room once. He was afraid to leave her alone after that. She was very demanding but my mother said most of it was an act to keep him tied to her apron strings.'

'Was that true, do you think?'

'I expect so.' She stood the cigarette on its end, as was her habit, and took another. 'My mother was usually right.'

'Did they have children?'

Olive shook her head. 'I don't think so. I never saw any.' She pursed her lips. '*He* was the child. It was quite funny sometimes watching him scurrying about, doing what he was told, saying sorry when he got it wrong. Amber called him Puddleglum because he was wet and miserable.' She chuckled. 'I'd forgotten that until this minute. It suited him at the time. Does it still?'

Roz thought of his grip on her arms. 'He didn't strike me as being particularly wet,' she said. 'Miserable, yes.'

Olive studied her with her curiously penetrating gaze. 'Why have you come back?' she asked gently. 'You didn't intend to on Monday.'

'What makes you say that?'

'I saw it in your face. You thought I was guilty.'

'Yes.'

Olive nodded. 'It upset me. I hadn't realized what a difference it made to have someone believe I didn't do it. Politicians call it the feel-good factor.' Roz saw dampness on the pale lashes. 'You get used to being viewed as a monster. Sometimes I believe it myself.' She placed one of her disproportionate hands between her huge breasts. 'I thought my heart would burst when you left. Silly, isn't it?' Tears welled in her eyes. 'I can't remember being so upset about anything before.'

Roz waited a moment but Olive didn't go on. 'Sister Bridget knocked some sense into me,' she said.

A glow, like a rising candle flame, lit the fat woman's face. 'Sister Bridget?' she echoed in amazement. 'Does she think I didn't do it? I never guessed. I thought she came out of Christian duty.'

Oh hell, thought Roz, what does a lie matter? 'Of course she thinks you didn't do it. Why else would she keep pushing me so hard?' She watched the tremulous pleasure bring a sort of beauty to the awful ugliness that was Olive, and she thought, I've burnt my boats. I can never again ask her if she's guilty or if she's telling me the truth because, if I do, her poor heart *will* burst.

'I didn't do it,' said Olive, reading her expression.

Roz leaned forward. 'Then who did?'

'I don't know now. I thought I did at the time.' She stood her second cigarette beside the first and watched it die. 'At the time it all made sense,' she murmured, her mind groping into the past.

'Who did you think it was?' asked Roz after a while. 'Someone you loved?'

But Olive shook her head. 'I couldn't bear to be laughed at. In so many ways it's easier to be feared. At least it means people respect you.' She looked at Roz. 'I'm really quite happy here. Can you understand that?'

'Yes,' said Roz slowly, remembering what the Governor had said. 'Oddly enough, I can.'

'If you hadn't sought me out, I could have survived. I'm institutionalized. Existence without effort. I really don't know that I could cope on the outside.' She smoothed her hands down her massive thighs. 'People will laugh, Roz.'

It was a question more than a statement and Roz didn't have an answer, or not the reassuring answer that Olive wanted. People *would* laugh, she thought. There was an intrinsic absurdity about this grotesque woman loving so deeply that she would brand herself a murderess to protect her lover.

'I'm not giving up now,' she said firmly. 'A battery hen is born to exist. You were born to live.' She levelled her pen at Olive. 'And if you don't know the difference between existence and living then read the Declaration of Independence. Living means Liberty and the Pursuit of Happiness. You deny yourself both by staying here.'

'Where would I go? What would I do?' She wrung her hands. 'In all my life I've never lived on my own. I couldn't bear it, not now, not with everyone knowing.'

'Knowing what?'

Olive shook her head.

'Why can't you tell me?'

'Because,' said Olive heavily, 'you wouldn't believe me. No one ever does when I tell the truth.' She rapped on the glass to attract a prison officer's attention. 'You must find out for yourself. It's the only way you'll ever really know.'

'And if I can't?'

'I'm no worse off than I was before. I can live with myself, and that's all that really matters.'

Yes, thought Roz, at the end of the day it probably was. 'Just tell me one thing, Olive. Have you lied to me?'

'Yes.'

'Why?'

The door opened and Olive heaved herself upright with the customary shove from behind. 'Sometimes, it's safer.'

The telephone was ringing as she opened the door to the flat. 'Hi,' she said, thrusting it under her chin and taking off her jacket. 'Rosalind Leigh.' *Pray God it wasn't Rupert.*

'It's Hal. I've been ringing all day. Where the hell have you been?' He sounded worried.

'Chasing clues.' She leant her back against the wall for support. 'What's it to you, anyway?'

'I'm not psychotic, Roz.'

'You damn well behaved like it yesterday.'

'Just because I didn't call the police?'

'Among other things. It's what normal people do when their property's been smashed up. Unless they've done it themselves, of course.'

'What other things?'

'You were bloody rude. I was only trying to help.'

He laughed softly. 'I keep seeing you standing by my door with that table leg. You're a hell of a gutsy lady. Shit scared, but gutsy. I've got those photographs for you. Do you still want them?'

'Yes.'

'Are you brave enough to collect them or do you want me to post them?'

'It's not bravery that's required, Hawksley, it's thick bloody skin. I'm tired of being needled.' She smiled to herself at the pun. 'Which reminds me, was it Mrs Clarke who said Gwen and Amber were alive after Robert went to work?'

There was a slight pause while he tried to see a connection. He couldn't. 'Yes, if she was the one in the attached semi.'

'She was lying. She says now that she didn't see them, which means Robert Martin's alibi is worthless. He could have done it before he went to work.'

'Why would she give Robert Martin an alibi?'

'I don't know. I'm trying to work it out. I thought at first she was alibiing her own husband, but that doesn't hold water. Apart from anything else, Olive tells me he was already retired so he wouldn't have gone to work anyway. Can you remember checking Mrs Clarke's statement?'

'Was Clarke the accountant? Yes?' He thought for a moment. 'OK, he ran most of his business from home but he also looked after the books of several small firms in the area. That week he was doing the accounts of a central heating contractor in Portswood. He was there all day. We checked. He didn't get home until after we had the place barricaded. I remember the fuss he made about having to park his car at the other end of the road. Elderly man, bald, with glasses. That the one?'

'Yes,' she said, 'but what he and Robert did during the day is irrelevant if Gwen and Amber were dead before either of the men left for work.'

'How reliable is Mrs Clarke?'

'Not very,' she admitted. 'What was the earliest estimate of death according to your pathologist?'

He was unusually evasive. 'I can't remember now.'

'Try,' she pressed him. 'You suspected Robert enough to check his alibi so he can't have been ruled out immediately on the forensic evidence.'

'I can't remember,' he said again. 'But if Robert did it, then why didn't he kill Olive as well? And why didn't she try and stop him? There must have been a hell of a row going on. She couldn't possibly have avoided hearing something. It's not that big a house.'

'Perhaps she wasn't there.'

The Chaplain made his weekly visit to Olive's room. 'That's good,' he said, watching her bring curl to the mother's hair with the point of a matchstick. 'Is it Mary and Jesus?'

She looked at him with amusement. 'The mother is suffocating her baby,' she said baldly. 'Is it likely to be Mary and Jesus?'

He shrugged. 'I've seen many stranger things that pass for religious art. Who is it?'

'It's Woman,' said Olive. 'Eve with all her faces.'

He was interested. 'But you haven't given her a face.'

Olive twisted the sculpture on its base and he saw that what he had taken to be curls at the side of the mother's hair was in fact a crude delineation of eyes, nose and mouth. She twisted it the other way and the same rough representation stared out from that side as well. 'Two-faced,' said Olive, 'and quite unable to look you in the eye.' She picked up a pencil and shoved it between the mother's thighs. 'But it doesn't matter. Not to MAN.' She leered unpleasantly. 'MAN doesn't look at the mantelpiece when he's poking the fire.'

Hal had mended the back door and the kitchen table, which stood in its customary place once more in the middle of the room. The floor was scrubbed clean, wall units repaired, fridge upright, even some chairs had been imported from the restaurant and placed neatly about the table. Hal himself looked completely exhausted.

'Have you had any sleep at all?' she asked him.

'Not much. I've been working round the clock.'

'Well, you've performed miracles.' She gazed about her. 'So who's coming to dinner? The Queen? She could eat it off the floor.'

To her surprise he caught her hand and lifted it to his lips, turning it to kiss the palm. It was an unexpectedly delicate gesture from such a hard man. 'Thank you.'

She was at a loss. 'What for?' she asked helplessly.

He released her hand with a smile. 'Saying the right things.' For a moment she thought he was going to elaborate, but all he said was: 'The photographs are on the table.'

Olive's was a mug-shot, stark and brutally unflattering. Gwen and Amber's shocked her as he had said they would.

They were the stuff of nightmares and she understood for the first time why everyone had said Olive was a psychopath. She turned them over and concentrated on the head and shoulders' shot of Robert Martin. Olive was there in the eyes and mouth, and she had a fleeting impression of what might lie beneath the layers of lard if Olive could ever summon the will-power to shed it. Her father was a very handsome man.

'What are you going to do with them?'

She told him about the man who sent letters to Olive. 'The description fits her father,' she said. 'The woman at Wells-Fargo said she'd recognize him from a photograph.'

'Why on earth should her father have sent her secret letters?'

'To set her up as a scapegoat for the murders.'

He was sceptical. 'You're plucking at straws. What about the ones of Gwen and Amber?'

'I don't know yet. I'm tempted to show them to Olive to shock her out of her apathy.'

He raised an eyebrow. 'I'd think twice about that if I were you. She's an unknown quantity, and you may not know her as well as you think you do. She could very easily turn nasty if you present her with her own handiwork.'

She smiled briefly. 'I know her better than I know you.' She tucked the photographs into her handbag and stepped out into the alleyway. 'The odd thing is you're very alike, you and Olive. You demand trust but you don't give it.'

He wiped a weary hand around his two-day growth of stubble. 'Trust is a two-edged sword, Roz. It can make you extremely vulnerable. I wish you'd remember that from time to time.'

FOURTEEN

Marnie studied the photograph of Robert Martin for several seconds then shook her head. 'No,' she said, 'that wasn't him. He wasn't so good looking and he had different hair, thicker, not swept back, more to the side. Anyway, I told you, he had dark brown eyes, almost black. These eyes are light. Is this her father?'

Roz nodded.

Marnie handed the photograph back. 'My mother always said, never trust a man whose earlobes are lower than his mouth. It's the sign of a criminal. Look at his.'

Roz looked. She hadn't noticed it before because of the way his hair swept over them, but Martin's ears were almost unnaturally out of symmetry with the rest of his face. 'Did your mother know any criminals?'

Marnie snorted. 'Of course she didn't. It's just an old wives' tale.' She cocked her head to look at the picture again. 'Anyway, if there was something in it he'd be a Category A by now.'

'He's dead.'

'Perhaps he passed the gene on to his daughter. She's Category A all right.' She got busy with her nail file. 'Where did you get it, as a matter of interest?'

'The photograph? Why do you ask?'

Marnie tapped the top right-hand corner with her file. 'I know where it was taken.'

Roz looked where she was pointing. In the background beyond Martin's head was part of a lampshade with a pattern of inverted *y*s round its base. 'In his house, presumably.'

'Doubt it. Look at the sign round the shade. There's only one place anywhere near here has shades like that.'

The *y*s were lambdas, Roz realized, the international symbol of homosexuality. 'Where?'

'It's a pub near the waterfront. Goes in for drag acts.' Marnie giggled. 'It's a gay knocking-shop.'

'What's it called?'

Marnie giggled again. 'The White Cock.'

The landlord recognized the photograph immediately. 'Mark Agnew,' he told her. 'Used to come here a lot. But I haven't seen him in the last twelve months. What happened to him?'

'He died.'

The landlord pulled a long face. 'I shall have to go straight,' he said with weary gallows humour. 'What with AIDS and the recession I've hardly any customers left.'

Roz smiled sympathetically. 'If it's any consolation I don't think he died of AIDS.'

'Well, it is some consolation, lovey. He put himself about a bit, did Mark.'

Mrs O'Brien regarded her with deep displeasure. Time and her naturally suspicious nature had persuaded her that Roz was nothing to do with television but had come to worm information out of her about her sons. 'You've got a flaming cheek, I must say.'

'Oh,' said Roz with obvious disappointment, 'have you changed your mind about the programme?' Lies, she thought, worked if you kept repeating them.

'Programme, my arse. You're a bloody snooper. What you after? That's what I want to know.'

Roz took Mr Crew's letter out of her briefcase and handed it to the woman. 'I explained it as well as I could last time, but these are the terms of my contract with the television company. If you read it, you'll see that it sets out quite clearly the aims and objectives of the programme they want to make.'

She pointed to Crew's signature. 'That's the director. He listened to the tape we made and liked what he heard. He'll be disappointed if you back out now.'

Ma O'Brien, presented with written evidence, was impressed. She frowned intelligently at the unintelligible words. 'Well,' she said, 'a contract makes a difference. You should of shown me this last time.' She folded it, preparatory to putting it in her pocket.

Roz smiled. 'Unfortunately,' she said, whisking it from Ma's fingers, 'this is the only copy I have and I need it for tax and legal purposes. If it's lost, none of us will get paid. May I come in?'

Ma compressed her lips. 'No reason not to, I suppose.' But suspicion died hard. 'I'm not hanswering hanything fishy, mind.'

'Of course not.' She walked into the sitting room. 'Is any of your family at home? I'd like to include them if possible. The more rounded the picture the better.'

Ma gave it some thought. '*Mike!*' she yelled suddenly. 'Get yourself down. There's a lady wants to talk to you. *Nipper!* In 'ere.'

Roz, who was only interested in talking to Gary, saw fifty-pound notes flying out the window by the bucket-load. She smiled with resignation as two skinny young men joined their mother on the sofa. 'Hi,' she said brightly, 'my name's Rosalind Leigh and I represent a television company which is putting together a programme on social deprivation . . .'

'I told them,' said Ma, cutting her short. 'No need for the sales pitch. Fifty quid per 'ead. That's right, isn't it?'

'As long as I get my money's worth. I'll need another good hour of chat and I'm only really prepared to pay fifty apiece if I can talk to your eldest son, Peter, and your youngest son, Gary. That way I get the broadest viewpoint possible. I want to know what difference it made to your older children being fostered out.'

'Well, you've got Gary,' said Ma, prodding the unprepossessing figure on her left, 'young Nipper 'ere. Pete's in the nick so you'll 'ave to make do with Mike. 'E's number three and spent as much time being fostered as Pete did.'

'Right, let's get on then.' She unfolded her list of carefully prepared questions and switched on her tape-recorder. The two 'boys', she noticed, had perfectly proportioned ears.

She spent the first half-hour talking to Mike, encouraging him to reminisce about his childhood in foster homes, his education (or, more accurately, lack of it through persistent truanting) and his early troubles with the police. He was a taciturn man, lacking even elementary social skills, who found it hard to articulate his thoughts. He made a poor impression and Roz, containing her impatience behind a forced smile, wondered if he could possibly have turned out any worse if Social Services had left him in the care of his mother. Somehow she doubted it. Ma, for all her sins and his, loved him, and to be loved was the cornerstone of confidence.

She turned with some relief to Gary, who had been listening to the conversation with a lively interest. 'I gather you didn't leave home till you were twelve,' she said, consulting her notes, 'when you were sent to a boarding school. Why was that?'

He grinned. 'Truanting, nicking, same as my brothers, only Parkway said I was worse and got me sent off to Chapman 'Ouse. It was OK. I learnt a bit. Got two CSEs before I jacked it in.'

She thought the truth was probably the exact opposite, and that Parkway had said he was a cut above his brothers and worth putting some extra effort into. 'That's good. Did the CSEs make it easier to find a job?'

She might have been talking about a trip to the moon for all the relevance a job seemed to have in his life. 'I never tried. We were doing all right.'

She remembered something Hal had said. 'They simply don't subscribe to the same values that the rest of us hold.' 'You didn't want a job?' she asked curiously.

He shook his head. 'Did *you*, when you left school?'

'Yes,' she said, surprised by the question. 'I couldn't wait to leave home.'

He shrugged, as perplexed by her ambition as she was perplexed by his lack of it. 'We've always stuck together,' he said. 'The dole goes a lot further if it's pooled. You didn't get on with your parents then?'

'Not enough to want to live with them.'

'Ah, well,' he said sympathetically, 'that would explain it then.'

Absurdly, Roz found herself envying him. 'Your mother told me you worked as a motorbike courier at one point. Did you enjoy that?'

'So-so. It was all right at the beginning but there's no fun driving a bike in town and it was all town work. It wouldn't 'ave been so bad if the bastard who ran it 'ad paid us enough to cover the cost of the bikes.' He shook his head. ''E was a mean sod. We 'ad 'em took off us after six months and that was it. No bikes, no work.'

Roz had now heard three different versions of how the O'Brien boys had lost their jobs at Wells-Fargo. Were any of them true, she wondered, or was it that they were all true, but seen from different perspectives? Truth, she thought, was not the absolute she had once believed it to be. 'Your mother told me,' she said with a look of innocent amusement, 'that you had a brush with a murderess while you were doing that job.'

'You mean Olive Martin?' Whatever qualms he had had on the matter at the time of the murders had obviously disappeared. 'Funny business, that. I used to deliver letters to her on a Friday evening from some bloke she was keen on, then – wham! – she did her folks in. Bloody shocked me to tell you the truth. 'Ad no idea she was a nutter.'

'But she must have been to hack her mother and sister to pieces.'

'Yeah.' He looked thoughtful. 'Never did understand it. She was all right. I knew 'er as a kid. She was all right then, as well. It was the bloody mother who was the cow and the stuck-up sister. Christ, she was a 'orrible little swine.'

Roz hid her surprise. *Everyone loved Amber*. How often had she heard that said? 'Maybe Olive had had enough and just snapped one day. It happens.'

'Oh,' he said with a dismissive shrug, 'that's not the bit I don't understand. It's why she didn't just go off with 'er fancy man instead. I mean, even if 'e was married, 'e could've set her up in a flat somewhere. 'E wasn't short of a bob or two judging by what 'e paid to have the letters delivered. Twenty quid a throw. 'E must have been bloody rolling in it.'

She chewed her pencil. 'Maybe she didn't do it,' she mused. 'Maybe the police got the wrong person. Let's face it, it wouldn't be the first time.'

Ma compressed her lips. 'They're all corrupt,' she said. 'Nick anyone for anythink these days. You don't want to be Irish in this country. You've no 'ope if you're Irish.'

'Still,' said Roz, looking at Gary, 'if Olive didn't do it, who did?'

'I'm not saying it wasn't 'er,' he said sharply. 'She went guilty so she must of done it. All I'm saying is she didn't *need* to do it.'

Roz gave a careless shrug. 'Just lost her temper and didn't think. You'll probably find the sister provoked her. You said she was horrible.'

Surprisingly, it was Mike who spoke. 'Street angel, 'ouse devil,' he said. 'Like our Tracey.'

Roz smiled at him. 'What does that mean?'

Ma elucidated. 'A bitch to your family, a perfect darling to everybody else. But our Tracey's nothing like Amber Martin. I always said that child would come a cropper and I was right. You can't face two ways all your life and expect to get away with it.'

Roz showed her curiosity. 'You really did know the family quite well then. I thought you only worked there a short while.'

'So I did, but Amber took a fancy to one of the boys later' –

she paused – 'though I'm blowed if I can remember at the moment which one. Was it you, Nipper?'

He shook his head.

'Chris,' said Mike.

'That's right,' agreed Ma, 'took a real shine to 'im and 'im to 'er. She'd sit in this room, pleased as punch with herself, making sheep's eyes at 'im and she can't 'ave been more than twelve or thirteen. 'E was – what? – fifteen, sixteen but, of course, any attention at that age is flattering and she was a pretty girl, I'll say that for 'er, *and* looked older than she was. Anyway, we saw the real Amber then. She treated Chris like a king and the rest of us like something the cat'd brought in. She had a tongue on 'er like I've never heard. Bitch, bitch, bitch, all the time.' She looked thoroughly indignant. 'Can't think 'ow I kept my 'ands off 'er but I did, for Chris's sake. Besotted, 'e was, poor lad. 'Er mother didn't know, of course. Put a stop to it straight away the minute she found out.'

Roz hoped her expression was less revealing than it felt. Did that make Chris O'Brien the father of Amber's illegitimate child? It made sense. Mr Hayes had referred to a lad from Parkway Comprehensive being responsible, and if Gwen had put a stop to the relationship then she would have known who to blame when a baby appeared. It would also explain the secrecy surrounding Robert Martin's efforts to trace his grandchild. Presumably the O'Briens had no idea that Chris had fathered a son nor that the son, if he could be found, was worth half a million pounds.

'It's fascinating,' she murmured, searching desperately for something to say. 'I've never met anyone so closely associated with a murder. Was Chris upset when Amber was killed?'

'No,' said Ma with an unfeeling chuckle. ''E 'adn't seen 'er in years. Gary was more upset for Olive, weren't you, love?'

He was watching Roz closely. 'Not really,' he said bluntly. 'I was jumpy about being roped in on it. I mean, I'd seen quite a bit of 'er one way and another. Reckoned the cops'd be rounding up everyone she knew and grilling them.' He shook his head. ''Er bloke got off lightly. 'E'd've been 'auled in and no mistake if she'd named a few names to try and get off.'

'Did you ever meet him?'

'No.' His face became suddenly sly and he stared at Roz with an expression that said he saw right through her. 'I know where he took her for sex, though.' He gave a conspiratorial smile. 'What's it worth to you?'

She stared back. 'How do you know?'

'The silly sod used self-sticking envelopes. They're a doddle to open. I read one of the letters.'

'Did he sign it? Do you know his name?'

Gary shook his head. 'Something beginning with P. "All my love, P", was how it finished.'

Roz didn't bother with further pretence. 'Another fifty pounds,' she said, 'on top of the hundred and fifty I've already agreed to. But that's it. I'll be cleaned out.'

'OK.' He held out his hand in unconscious mimicry of his mother. 'Money up front.'

She took out her wallet and emptied it. 'Two hundred pounds.' She counted it on to his palm.

'I knew you wasn't from the television,' said Ma in disgust. 'I bloody knew it.'

'Well?' Roz demanded of Gary.

'It was on for Sunday at the Belvedere Hotel in Farraday Street. "All my love, P." That's the Farraday Street in Southampton, in case you didn't know.'

The route to Southampton took Roz along Dawlington High Street. She had passed Glitzy boutique before the name registered, and nearly caused a pile-up by standing on her brakes in the middle of the road. With a cheerful wave to the furious man behind her, who was mouthing imprecations against women drivers, she drew into a side street and found a parking space.

Glitzy was something of a misnomer, she thought, as she pushed open the door. She had expected designer wear or, at the very least, clothes from the more expensive end of the market. But then, she was used to London boutiques. Glitzy catered very definitely for the cheaper end of the market, wisely recognizing that their customers would be predominantly teenage girls without the wherewithal or the transport to go shopping in the more stylish parts of Southampton.

Roz sought out the manager, a woman in her thirties with a splendid hairdo backcombed into a blonde beehive on top of her head. Roz handed her one of her cards and ran through her spiel about her book on Olive Martin. 'I'm trying to find someone who knew the sister, Amber,' she said, 'and I'm told she worked here during the month before she was murdered. Were you here then? Or do you know anyone who was?'

'No, love, sorry. Staff turns over very quickly in a place like this, young girls normally, doing a short stint till something better comes up. I don't even know who was manager then. You'll have to get on to the owners. I can give you their address,' she finished helpfully.

'Thank you. It's worth a shot, I suppose.'

The woman took her over to the cash desk and sorted through a card index. 'Funny, I remember those murders, but I never put two and two together. You know, that the sister had worked here.'

'She wasn't here very long and I'm not sure it was even reported. The press was more interested in Olive than in Amber.'

'Yeah.' She took out a card. 'Amber. It's not that common a name, is it?'

'I suppose not. It was a nickname, anyway. Her real name was Alison.'

The woman nodded. 'I've been here three years and for three years I've been pressing to have the staff toilet redecorated. The recession's their excuse for not doing it, same as it's their excuse for any wretched thing, from cuts in wages to cheap imported stock that's not even stitched properly. Anyway, the toilet's tiled and that's an expensive job, apparently, chipping off the old ones to put up new.' Roz smiled politely. 'Don't worry, love, it's to the point and I'm getting there. The reason I want new tiles is that someone took a chisel or something similar to the old ones. They scratched graffiti into the surface and then filled in the scratches with some sort of indelible ink. I've tried everything to get it out, bleach, oven cleaner, paint remover, you name it, love, I've tried it.' She shook her head. 'It can't be shifted. And why? Because whoever did it gouged so deep they cut right through the ceramic, and the china clay underneath just goes on absorbing dirt and stains. Every time I look at it, it gives me the shivers. Pure hate, that's what it was done with.'

'What does the graffiti say?'

'I'll show you. It's at the back.' She negotiated a couple of doors, then pushed open another and stood aside to let Roz pass. 'There. It sucks, doesn't it? And, you know, I've always wondered who Amber was. But it must be the sister, mustn't it? Like I say, Amber's not that common a name.'

It was the same two words, repeated ten or eleven times across the tiles, a violent inversion of the hearts and arrows that more usually adorned lavatory walls. **HATES AMBER . . . HATES AMBER . . . HATES AMBER**.

'I wonder who did it?' murmured Roz.

'Someone very sick, I should think. They certainly didn't want her to know, seeing how they've left their name off the front.'

'It depends how you read it,' said Roz thoughtfully. 'If it were set out neatly for you in a circle it would say Amber hates Amber hates Amber ad infinitum.'

The Belvedere was a typical back-street hotel, two substantial semis knocked together and entered via a flight of steps and a pillared front door. The place had an air of neglect as if its customers – sales reps for the main part – had deserted it. Roz rang the bell at the reception desk and waited.

A woman in her fifties emerged from a room at the back, all smiles. 'Good afternoon, madam. Welcome to the Belvedere.' She pulled the registration book towards her. 'Is it a room you're after?'

What terrible things recessions were, thought Roz. How long could people maintain this sad veneer of confident optimism when the reality was empty order books? 'I'm sorry,' she said. 'I'm afraid it isn't.' She handed over one of her cards. 'I'm a freelance journalist and I think someone I'm writing about may have stayed here. I was hoping you could identify her photograph for me.'

The woman tapped a finger on the book then pushed it away. 'Will what you write be published?'

Roz nodded.

'And will the Belvedere be mentioned if whoever it is did stay here?'

'Not if you'd rather it wasn't.'

'My dear, how little you know about the hotel trade. Any publicity would be welcome at the moment.'

Roz laughed as she placed the photograph of Olive on the desk. 'If she came it would have been during the summer of eighty-seven. Were you here then?'

'We were.' The woman spoke with regret. 'We bought in eighty-six when the economy was booming.' She took a pair of glasses from her pocket and popped them on her nose, leaning forward to examine the photograph. 'Oh, yes, I remember her very well. Big girl. She and her husband came most Sundays during that summer. Used to book the room for the day and go home in the evening.' She sighed. 'It was a wonderful arrangement. We were always able to let the room again for the Sunday night. Double pay for one twenty-four-hour period.' She heaved another sigh. 'Chance'd be a fine thing now. I wish we could sell, I really do, but what with so many of the small hotels going bankrupt we wouldn't even get what we paid for it. Soldier on, that's all we can do.'

Roz brought her back to Olive by tapping the photograph. 'What did she and her husband call themselves?'

The woman was amused. 'The usual, I should think. Smith or Brown.'

'Did they sign in?'

'Oh, yes. We're very particular about our register.'

'Could I take a look?'

'Don't see why not.' She opened a cupboard under the desk and sorted out the register for 1987. 'Now, let me see. Ah, here we are. Mr and Mrs Lewis. Well, well, they were more imaginative than most.' She twisted the book so that Roz could look at it.

She gazed at the neat script and thought: Got you, you bastard. 'This is the man's handwriting.' She knew already.

'Oh, yes,' said the woman. 'He always signed. She was a lot younger than he was and very shy, particularly at the beginning. She gained in confidence as time passed, they always do, but she never put herself forward. Who is she?'

Roz wondered if the woman would be so keen to help once she knew, but there was no point in keeping it from her. She would learn all the details the minute the book appeared. 'Her name's Olive Martin.'

'Never heard of her.'

'She's serving a life sentence for murdering her mother and sister.'

'Good lord! Is she the one who—' She made chopping motions with her hands. Roz nodded. 'Good Lord!'

'Do you still want the Belvedere mentioned?'

'Do I heck!' She beamed broadly. 'Of course I do! A murderess in our hotel. Fancy! We'll have a plaque put up in the bedroom. What are you writing exactly? A book? A magazine article? We'll provide photographs of the hotel and the room she stayed in. Well, well, I must say. How exciting! If only I'd known.'

Roz laughed. It was a cold-bloodedly ghoulish display of pleasure at another's misfortune but she couldn't find it in her heart to criticize. Only a fool would look a gift horse in the mouth. 'Before you get too excited,' she warned, 'the book probably won't be published for another year and it will be an exoneration of Olive, not a further condemnation. You see, I believe she's innocent.'

'Better and better. We'll have the book on sale in the foyer. I knew our luck had to turn eventually.' She beamed at Roz. 'Tell Olive she can stay here free of charge for as long as she likes the minute she gets out of prison. We always look after our regulars. Now, my dear, anything else I can help you with?'

'Do you have a photocopying machine?'

'We do. Every mod. con. here, you know.'

'Then may I have a copy of this entry in the register? And perhaps you could also give me a description of Mr Lewis.'

She pursed her lips. 'He wasn't very memorable. Early fifties. Blond, always wore a dark suit, a smoker. Any good?'

'Maybe. Did his hair look natural? Can you remember?'

The woman chuckled. 'There now, I'd forgotten. It never occurred to me till I took them in some tea one day and surprised him adjusting his wig in the mirror. I laughed afterwards, I can tell you. But it was a good one. I wouldn't have guessed just by looking at him. You know him then?'

Roz nodded. 'Would you recognize him from a photograph?'

'I'll try. I can usually remember a face when I see it.'

'Visitor for you, Sculptress.' The officer was in the room before Olive had time to hide what she was doing. 'Come on. Get a move on.'

Olive swept her wax figures into one hand and crushed them together in her palm. 'Who is it?'

'The nun.' She looked at Olive's closed fist. 'What have you got there?'

'Just plasticine.' She uncurled her fingers. The wax figures, carefully painted and clothed in coloured scraps, had merged into a multi-coloured mash, unidentifiable now as the altar candle they had sprung from.

'Well, leave it there. The nun's come to talk to you, not watch you play with plasticine.'

Hal was asleep at the kitchen table, body rigidly upright, arms resting on the table, head nodding towards his chest. Roz watched him for a moment through the window, then tapped lightly on the glass. His eyes, red-rimmed with exhaustion, snapped open to look at her and she was shocked by the extent of his relief when he saw who it was.

He let her in. 'I hoped you wouldn't come back,' he said, his face drawn with fatigue.

'What are you so frightened of?' she asked.

He looked at her with something like despair. 'Go home,' he said, 'this is none of your business.' He went to the sink and ran the cold-water tap, dowsing his head and gasping as the icy stream hit the back of his neck.

From the floor above came a sudden violent hammering.

Roz leapt a foot in the air. '*Oh, my God!* What was that?'

He reached out and gripped her arm, pushing her towards the door. 'Go home,' he ordered. 'Now! I don't want to have to force you, Roz.'

But she stood her ground. 'What's going on? What was that noise?'

'So help me,' he said grimly, 'I will do you some damage if you don't leave now.' But in outright contradiction to the words, he suddenly put his hands on either side of her face and kissed her. 'Oh, God!' he groaned, smoothing the tumbled hair from her eyes. 'I do not want you involved, Roz. *I do not want you involved.*'

She was about to say something when over his shoulder she saw the door into the restaurant swing open. 'Too late,' she said, turning him round. 'We've got company.'

Hal, horribly unprepared, showed his teeth in a wolfish grin. 'I've been expecting you,' he drawled. With a proprietary arm he eased Roz behind him and prepared to defend what was his.

There were four of them, large anonymous men in ski-masks. They said nothing, just weighed in indiscriminately with baseball bats, using Hal as a human target. It happened so fast that Roz was a spectator to their grisly sport almost before she realized it. She, it seemed, was too insignificant to concern them.

Her first angry impulse was to catch out at a flailing arm but the battering she had had at the hands of Rupert two weeks before persuaded her to use her brain instead. With trembling fingers she opened her handbag and removed the three-inch hatpin she had taken to carrying with her, thrusting it upwards into the buttock of the man nearest her. It drove in up to its ornate jade head and a soft groan issued from his mouth as he stood, completely paralysed with shock, the baseball bat slipping to the floor from his slackening fingers. No one noticed, except her.

With an exclamation of triumph she dived on it and brought it up in a swinging arc to smash against the man's balls. He sat on the floor and started to scream.

'I've got one, Hal,' she panted. 'I've got a bat.'

'Then use it, for Christ's sake,' he bellowed, going down under a rain of blows.

'Oh God!' Legs, she thought. She knelt on one knee, swiped at the nearest pair of trousers and crowed with triumph when she made contact. She took another swipe only to have her head jerked up as a hand seized her by the hair and started to pull it out by the roots. Shock and pain flooded her eyes with stinging tears.

Hal, on his hands and knees on the floor, his head protected by his shoulders, was only vaguely aware that the rapidity of the blows beating against his back had lessened. His brain was concentrated on the high-pitched screaming which he thought was coming from Roz. His anger was colossal, triggering such a surge of adrenalin that he exploded to his feet in an all-consuming fury and threw himself at the first man he saw, bearing him back against the gleaming ovens where a saucepan of fish stock bubbled gently. Oblivious to the blow which crashed with the force of a bus between his shoulder blades he bent his victim in an arc over the rings, grabbed the saucepan and upended the boiling liquid over the masked head.

He swung round to face the fourth man and fended off another blow with his forearm before smashing the cast-iron base of the saucepan into the side of an unprotected jaw. The eyes behind the mask registered the briefest glimmer of surprise before rolling helplessly into their sockets. The man was unconscious before he hit the floor.

Exhausted, Hal looked about for Roz. It was a moment or two before he found her, so disorientated was he by the noise of screaming which seemed to be filling the kitchen from every side. He shook his head to clear the fog and looked towards the door. He saw her almost immediately, her neck trapped in the hooked arm of the only man left with any fight in him. Her eyes were closed and her head lolled alarmingly to one side. 'If you make a move,' the man told Hal between jerky breaths, 'I'll break her neck.'

A hatred, so primeval that he couldn't control it, erupted like hot lava in Hal's brain. His actions were instinctive. He lowered his head and charged.

FIFTEEN

Roz swam up to a strange twilight world between oblivion and consciousness. She knew she was there in the room but she felt apart from it as if she were watching what was going on from behind thickened glass. Sound was muted. She had a vague memory of fingers clamping round her throat. And afterwards? She wasn't sure. It had, she thought, been very peaceful.

Hal's face loomed over her. 'Are you all right?' he asked from a great distance.

'Fine,' she murmured happily.

He smacked her on the cheek with the flat of his hand. 'That's my girl,' he told her, his voice muffled by cotton wool. 'Come on, now. Snap out of it. I need some help.'

She glared at him. 'I'll be up in a minute,' she said with dignity.

He hauled her to her feet. 'Now,' he said firmly, 'or we'll be back where we started.' He thrust a baseball bat into her hand. 'I am going to tie them up but you've got to protect my back while I'm doing it. I don't want one of these bastards surprising me.' He looked into her dazed eyes. 'Come on, Roz,' he said savagely, shaking her. 'Pull yourself together and show a bit of character.'

She took a deep breath. 'Has anyone ever told you what a complete and utter turd you are? I nearly died.'

'You fainted,' he said unemotionally, but his eyes were twinkling. 'Hit anything that moves,' he instructed her, 'except the one with his head under the tap. He's in enough agony already.'

Reality came rushing in on wings of sound. Moans and groans and running water. There *was* a man with his head under the tap. She caught a movement out of the corner of her eye and swung the baseball bat in terrified reaction, ramming home the hatpin that its unfortunate recipient was gingerly plucking from his bottom. His screams of reawakened agony were pitiful.

'Oh God!' she cried. 'I've done something awful.' Tears sprang into her eyes.

Hal finished trussing her putative killer, who had been knocked cold by his frenzied charge, and moved on to the other unconscious figure, winding twine expertly about the wrists and ankles. 'What's he yelling for anyway?' he demanded, tethering his victim to the table for good measure.

'He's got a pin in his bottom,' said Roz, her teeth chattering uncontrollably.

Hal approached the man warily. 'What sort of pin?'

'My mother's hatpin.' She gagged. 'I think I'm going to be sick.'

He saw the green ornamental head protruding from the man's Levis and felt a tiny twinge of sympathy. It didn't last. He left it there while he bound the man's wrists and ankles and tethered him, like his friend, to the table. It was almost as an afterthought that he gripped the jade and yanked the hatpin, grinning, from the quivering buttock. 'You arsehole,' he murmured cheerfully, tucking the pin into the front of his jumper.

'I feel ill,' said Roz.

'Sit down, then.' He took a chair and pressed her into it before moving to the back door and flinging it open. 'Out,' he ordered the man at the sink. 'Get yourself to hospital as fast as you can. If your friends have an ounce of decency they'll keep your name to themselves. If they haven't' – he shrugged – 'you've got about half an hour to get yourself admitted before the police come looking for you.'

The man needed no persuading. He launched himself into the fresh air of the alleyway and took to his heels.

With a groan of exhaustion, Hal shut the door and slithered to the floor. 'I need a rest. Do me a favour, sweetheart, and take off their masks. Let's see what we've got.'

Roz's head was aching intolerably where the roots of her hair had been loosened. She looked at him with burning eyes in a pasty white face. 'For your information, Hawksley,' she said icily, 'I'm just about out on my feet. It may have escaped your notice, but if it hadn't been for me you wouldn't have *got* anything.'

He gave a mighty yawn and winced as pain seared around his chest and back. Fractured ribs, he thought tiredly. 'I'll tell you this for free, Roz. As far as I'm concerned you are the most wonderful woman God ever made and I'll marry you if you'll have me.' He smiled sweetly. 'But at the moment I'm bushed. Be kind. Get off your high horse and take their ski-masks off.'

' "Words, words, mere words",' she murmured, but she did as he asked. The side of his face was already thickening where a baseball bat had split the skin. What the hell sort of state must his back be in? Covered in weals, probably, like the last time. 'Do you know any of them?' She studied the slack features of the unconscious man by the door. She had a fleeting impression she knew him, but his head moved and the impression vanished.

'No.' He'd seen her frown of brief recognition. 'Do you?'

'I thought I did,' she said slowly. 'Just for a moment.' She shook her head. 'No. He probably reminded me of someone on the telly.'

Hal pushed himself to his feet and padded over to the sink, his stiffening body protesting at every step. He filled a bowl with water and sloshed it into the gaping mouth, watching the eyes flicker open. They were instantly alert, wary, guarded, all of which told Hal he wasn't likely to get anywhere by asking questions.

With a shrug of resignation, he looked at Roz. 'I need a favour.'

She nodded.

'There's a phonebox about two hundred yards down the main road. Take your car to it, dial 999, tell them the Poacher's been broken into, and then go home. Don't give your name. I'll call you the minute I can.'

'I'd rather stay.'

'I know.' His face softened. She was wearing her lonely look again. He reached out and ran the back of a finger down the line of her cheek. 'Trust me. I *will* call.'

She took a deep breath. 'How long do you want?'

He'd make it up to her one day, he thought. 'Fifteen minutes before you phone.'

She retrieved her handbag from the floor, cramming the contents inside and zippering it closed. 'Fifteen minutes,' she echoed, pulling the door open and stepping outside. She stared at him for a long moment then shut the door and walked away.

Hal waited until her footsteps faded. 'This,' he said gently, reaching for the hatpin, 'is going to be extremely painful.' He grasped the man's hair and forced him down until his face was flat against the floor. 'And I haven't got time for games.' He placed the weight of one knee across the man's shoulders then prised a finger straight in one of the bound fists and pushed the point of the hatpin between the flesh and the nail. He felt the finger flinch. 'You've got five seconds to tell me what the hell is going on before I push it home. One. Two. Three. Four. Five.' He breathed deeply through his nose, closed his eyes and shoved.

The man screamed.

Hal caught 'Foreclosures. You're costing money on the foreclosures' before a ton weight descended on the back of his head.

Sister Bridget, as imperturbable as ever, ushered Roz into her sitting room and sat her in a chair with a glass of brandy. Clearly Roz had been in another fight. Her clothes were filthy and dishevelled, her hair was a mess, and splotchy red marks on her neck and face looked very like the imprint of fingers.

Someone, it seemed, was using her as a target for his spleen, though why she chose to put up with it Sister Bridget couldn't begin to imagine. Roz was as far removed from Dickens' Nancy as anyone could be, and had quite enough independence of spirit to reject the degrading life that a Bill Sykes offered.

She waited placidly while wave after wave of giggles spluttered from Roz's mouth.

'Do you want to tell me about it?' she asked at last, when Roz had composed herself enough to dab at her eyes.

Roz blew her nose. 'I don't think I can,' she said. 'It wasn't at all funny.' Laughter welled in her eyes again and she held the handkerchief to her mouth. 'I'm sorry to be a nuisance but I was afraid I'd have an accident if I tried to drive home. I think it's what's known as an adrenalin high.'

Privately, Sister Bridget decided it was a product of delayed shock, the natural healing process of mind over traumatized body. 'I'm pleased to have you here. Tell me how you're progressing on the Olive front. I saw her today but she wasn't very communicative.'

Grateful for something to take her mind off the Poacher, Roz told her. 'She did have a lover. I've found the hotel they used.' She peered at the brandy glass. 'It was the Belvedere in Farraday Street. They went there on Sundays during the summer of eighty-seven.' She took a sip from the glass then placed it hurriedly on the table beside her and slumped back into the chair, pressing shaking fingers to her temples. 'I'm terribly sorry,' she said, 'but I don't feel at all well. I've got the mother and father of all headaches.'

'I should imagine you have,' said Sister Bridget, rather more tartly than she had intended.

Roz massaged her aching temples. 'This ape tried to pull my hair out,' she murmured. 'I think that's what's done it.' She pressed an experimental hand to the back of her head and winced. 'There's some codeine in my handbag. You couldn't find them for me, could you? I think my head is about to explode.' She giggled hysterically. 'Olive must be sticking pins into me again.'

Tut-tutting with motherly concern, Sister Bridget administered three with a glass of water. 'I'm sorry, my dear,' she said severely, 'but I'm really very shocked. I can't forgive any man who treats a woman like a chattel and, harsh though it may sound, I find it almost as difficult to forgive the woman. Better to live without a man at all than to live with one who is only interested in the degradation of the spirit.'

Roz squinted through one half-closed eyelid, unable to take the glare of light from the window. How indignant the other woman looked, puffing her chest like a pouter pigeon. Hysteria nudged about her diaphragm again. 'You're very harsh all of a sudden. I doubt Olive saw it as degradation. Rather the reverse, I should think.'

'I'm not talking about Olive, my dear, I'm talking about you. This ape you referred to. He isn't worth it. Surely you can see that?'

Roz shook with helpless laughter. 'I'm so sorry,' she said at last. 'You must think me incredibly rude. The trouble is I've been on an emotional rollercoaster for months.' She dabbed at her eyes and blew her nose. 'You must blame Olive for this. She's been a godsend. She's made me feel useful again.'

She saw the polite bewilderment on the other's face and sighed inwardly. Really, she thought, it was so much easier to tell lies. They were one dimensional and uncomplicated. *'I'm fine . . . Everything's fine . . . I like waiting rooms . . . Rupert's been very supportive over Alice . . . We went our separate ways amicably . . .'* It was the tangled web of truth, woven deep into the fragile stuff of character, that made life difficult. She wasn't even sure now what was true and what wasn't. Had she really hated Rupert that much? She couldn't imagine where she had found the energy. All she could really remember was how stifling the last twelve months had been.

'I'm completely infatuated,' she went on wildly as if that explained anything, 'but I've no idea if what I feel is genuine or just pie in the sky hoping.' She shook her head. 'I suppose one never really knows.'

'Oh, my dear,' said Sister Bridget, 'do be careful. Infatuation is a very poor substitute for love. It withers as easily as it flourishes. Love – *real* love – takes time to grow, and how can it do that in an atmosphere of brutality?'

'That's hardly his fault. I could have run away, I suppose, but I'm glad I didn't. I'm sure they'd have killed him if he'd been alone.'

Sister Bridget sighed. 'We seem to be talking at cross purposes. Do I gather the ape is not the man you're infatuated with?'

With streaming eyes, Roz wondered if there was any truth in the phrase *to die laughing*.

'You're very brave,' said Sister Bridget. 'I'd have assumed he was up to no good and run a mile.'

'Perhaps he is. I'm a very poor judge of character, you know.'

Sister Bridget laughed to herself. 'Well, it all sounds very exciting,' she said with a twinge of envy, taking Roz's dress from the tumble-drier and laying it on the ironing board. 'The only man who ever showed any interest in me was a bank clerk who lived three doors away from my parents. He was skin and bone, poor chap, with an enormous Adam's apple that crawled about his throat like a large pink beetle. I simply couldn't bear him. The Church was far more attractive.' She wet her finger and tapped it against the iron.

Roz, wrapped in an old flannelette nightie, smiled. 'And is it still?'

'Not always. But I wouldn't be human if I didn't have regrets.'

'Have you ever been in love?'

'Good Heavens, yes. More often than you have, I expect. Purely platonically, of course. I meet some very attractive fathers in my job.'

Roz chuckled. 'What sort of fathers? The cassocked variety or the ones in trousers?'

Sister Bridget's eyes danced wickedly. 'All I will say, as long as you promise not to quote me, is that I've always found cassocks a little off-putting and, with all the divorces there are these days, I spend more time talking to single men than, frankly, is good for a nun.'

'If things ever work out,' said Roz wistfully, 'and I have another daughter, I'll put her in your school so fast you won't know what hit you.'

'I shall look forward to it.'

'No. I don't believe in miracles. I did once.'

'I'll pray for you,' said Sister Bridget. 'It's time I had something to get my teeth into. I prayed for Olive and look what God sent me.'

'Now you're going to make me cry.'

She woke in the morning with brilliant sunlight bathing her face through a gap in Sister Bridget's spare-room curtains. It was too bright to look at so she cuddled down into the warmth of the duvet and listened instead. Ripples of birdsong swelled in glorious chorus from tiny feathered throats in the garden, and somewhere a radio murmured the news, but too low for her to make out the words. The smell of grilled bacon drifted tantalizingly from the kitchen downstairs, urging her to get up. She tingled with half-remembered vitality and wondered why she had allowed herself to stumble for so long through the blind fog of her depression. Life, she thought, was fabulous and the desire to live it too insistent to be ignored.

She waved goodbye to Sister Bridget, pointed the car towards the Poacher and switched on her stereo, feeding in Pavarotti. It was a very deliberate laying of a ghost. The rich voice surged in the speakers and she listened to it without regret.

The restaurant was deserted, no answer front or back to her knocking. She drove to the payphone she had used the night before and dialled the number, letting it ring for a long time in case Hal was asleep. When he didn't reply, she replaced the receiver and returned to her car. She wasn't concerned – frankly, Hal could look after himself rather better than any other man she had known – and she had more urgent fish to fry. From the dashboard pocket she took an expensive automatic camera with a powerful zoom lens – a legacy of the divorce – and checked it for film. Then, switching on the ignition, she drew out into the traffic.

She had to wait two hours, crouched uncomfortably on the back seat of her car, but she was well rewarded for her patience. When Olive's Svengali finally emerged from his front door he paused for a second or two and presented her with a perfect shot of his face. Magnified by the zoom lens, the dark eyes bored straight through her as she took the picture before they turned away to glance down between the avenue of trees to check for oncoming traffic. She felt the hairs pricking on the back of her neck. He couldn't possibly have seen her – the car was facing away from him with the camera lens propped on her handbag in the back window – but she shivered none the less. The photographs of Gwen and Amber's mutilated bodies, lying on the seat beside her, were a terrible reminder that she was stalking a psychopath.

She arrived back at her flat, hot and tired from the sweltering heat of unheralded summer. The wintry feel of three days before had melted into brilliant blue skies with a promise of more heat to come. She opened the windows of the flat and let in the roar of London traffic. More noticeable than usual, it made her think with a brief wistfulness of the peace and beauty of Bayview.

She checked her answerphone for messages while she poured a glass of water, only to find the tape as she had left it, blank. She dialled the Poacher and listened, this time with mounting anxiety, to the vain ringing at the other end. Where on earth was he? She chewed the knuckle of her thumb in frustration then phoned Iris.

'How would Gerry react if you asked him nicely to put on his solicitor's hat' – Gerald Fielding was a partner in a top London legal practice – 'ring Dawlington police station and make some discreet enquiries before everything winds down for the weekend?'

Iris was never one to beat about the bush. 'Why?' she demanded. 'And what's in it for me?'

'My peace of mind. I'm too twitched at the moment to write anything.'

'Hmm. Why?'

'I'm worried about my shady policeman.'

'*Your* shady policeman?' asked Iris suspiciously.

'That's right.'

Iris heard the amusement in her friend's voice. 'Oh, my God,' she said crossly, 'you haven't gone and fallen for him? He's supposed to be a source.'

'He is – of endless erotic fantasy.'

Iris groaned. 'How can you write objectively about corrupt policemen if you've got the hots for one of them?'

'Who says he's corrupt?'

'He must be, if Olive's innocent. I thought you said he took her confession.'

'*It's a pity you're not a Catholic. You could go to confession and feel better immediately . . .*'

'Are you still there?' demanded Iris.

'Yes. Will Gerry do it?'

'Why can't you make the call yourself?'

'Because I'm involved and they might recognize my voice. I made them a 999 call.'

Iris groaned again. 'What on earth have you been up to?'

'Nothing criminal, at least I don't think so.' She heard the grunt of horror at the other end. 'Look, all Gerry has to do is ask a few innocent questions.'

'Will he have to lie?'

'A white lie or two.'

'He'll have a fit. You know Gerry. Breaks out in a muck sweat at the mere mention of falsehoods.' She sighed loudly. 'What a pest you are. You realize I shall have to bribe him with promises of good behaviour. My life won't be worth living.'

'You're an angel. Now, these are the only details Gerry needs to know. He's trying to contact his client, Hal Hawksley of the Poacher, Wenceslas Street, Dawlington. He has reason to believe the Poacher has been broken into and wonders if the police know where Hal can be contacted. OK?'

'No, it's not OK, but I'll see what I can do. Will you be in this evening?'

'Yes, twiddling my thumbs.'

'Well, try twiddling them round your keyboard,' said Iris acidly. 'I'm fed up with being the only one who does any meaningful work in this lopsided relationship of ours.'

She had had the film developed at a one-hour booth in her local High Street while she did some shopping. Now she spread the prints over her coffee table and studied them. She put the ones of Svengali, the two close-ups of his face and some full-length shots of his back as he walked away, to one side and smiled at the rest. She had forgotten taking them. Deliberately, she thought. They were of Rupert and Alice playing in the garden on Alice's birthday, a week before the accident. They had declared a truce that day, she remembered, for Alice's sake. And they had kept it, up to a point, although as usual the responsibility for refusing to be drawn had been Roz's. As long as she could keep her cool and smile while Rupert let slip his poisoned darts about Jessica, Jessica's flat, and Jessica's job, everything was hunky-dory. Alice's joy in having her parents back together again shone from the photographs.

Roz pushed them tenderly to one side and rummaged through her carrier bag of shopping, removing some cellophane, a paintbrush, and three tubes of acrylic paint. Then, munching into a pork pie, she set to work.

Every now and then she paused to smile at her daughter. She should have had the film developed before, she told Mrs Antrobus, who had curled contentedly into her lap. The rag doll of the newspapers had never been Alice. *This* was Alice.

'He's legged it,' said Iris baldly down the wire two hours later, 'and Gerry has been threatened with all sorts of nasties if he doesn't reveal his client's whereabouts the minute he knows them. There's a warrant out for the wretched man's arrest. Where on earth do you find these ghastly creatures? You should take up with a nice one, like Gerry,' she said severely, 'who wouldn't dream of beating up women or involving them in criminal activities.'

'I know,' agreed Roz mildly, 'but the nice ones are already taken. Did they mention what the charge is against Hal?'

'*Charges*, more like. Arson, resisting arrest, GBH, absconding from the scene of a crime. You name it, he's done it. If he gets in touch with you, don't bother to let me know. Gerry's already behaving like the man who knew the identity of Jack the Ripper but kept it quiet. He'll have a heart attack if he thinks I know where he is.'

'Mum's the word,' Roz promised.

There was a moment's silence. 'You might do better to hang up if he calls. There's a man in hospital with appalling facial burns, apparently, a policeman with a dislocated jaw, and when they arrived to arrest him he was trying to set fire to his restaurant. He sounds horribly dangerous to me.'

'I think you're probably right,' said Roz slowly, wondering what on earth had happened after she left. 'He's got a lovely arse, too. *Aren't* I the lucky one?'

'Cow!'

Roz laughed. 'Thank Gerry for me. I appreciate his niceness even if you don't.'

*

She went to sleep on the sofa in case she missed the phone when it rang. It occurred to her that he might not want to trust himself to an answer machine.

But the telephone remained stubbornly silent all weekend.

SIXTEEN

On Monday morning, with the black dog of depression on her shoulder again, Roz went to the Belvedere Hotel and placed the photograph on the desk. 'Is this Mr Lewis?' she asked the proprietress.

The amiable woman popped on her glasses and took a good look. She shook her head apologetically. 'No, dear, I'm sorry. He doesn't ring a bell at all.'

'Try now.' She smoothed the cellophane across the photograph.

'Good heavens. How extraordinary. Yes, that's Mr Lewis all right.'

Marnie agreed. 'That's him. Dirty bugger.' She screwed up her eyes. 'It doesn't flatter him, does it? What would a young girl see in that?'

'I don't know. Uncritical affection perhaps.'

'Who is he?'

'A psychopath,' said Roz.

The other whistled. 'You want to be careful then.'

'Yes.'

Marnie tapped her carmined nails on the desk. 'Sure you don't want to tell me who he is in case you end up in bits on your kitchen floor?' She flicked Roz a speculative glance. There might, she thought, be some money in this somewhere.

Roz caught the glint in the other's eye. 'No thanks,' she said shortly. 'This is one piece of information I intend to keep to myself. I don't fancy my chances if he learns I'm close.'

'I won't blab,' said Marnie with a pout of injured innocence.

'You can't if I don't put temptation your way.' Roz tucked the photograph into her handbag. 'It would be irresponsible, anyway. You're a prime witness. He could just as easily come after *you* and chop *you* into little pieces.' She smiled coldly. 'I should hate to have that on my conscience.'

Roz returned to her car and sat for some minutes staring out of the window. If ever she had needed a tame ex-policeman to guide her through the maze of legal procedure, she thought, it was now. She was an amateur who could all too easily make mistakes and muck up the chances of a future prosecution. And where would that leave Olive? Languishing in prison, presumably. The verdict against her could only be overturned rapidly if someone else was convicted. On its own the seed of reasonable doubt would take years of germination before the Home Office would feel pressured enough to take notice. How long had the Birmingham Six had to wait for justice? The responsibility to get it right was frightening.

But, loath though she was to admit it, what weighed rather more heavily with her was the knowledge that she hadn't the courage to write the book while Olive's psychopathic lover remained at liberty. Try as she might, she could not get the pictures of Gwen and Amber out of her mind.

She slammed her fists against the steering-wheel. Where are you, Hawksley? *You bastard!* I was always there for you.

Graham Deedes, Olive's one-time barrister, walked into his chambers after a long day in court and frowned in irritation to find Roz parked on a seat outside his door. He looked pointedly at his watch. 'I'm in a hurry, Miss Leigh.'

She sighed, unfolding herself from the hard chair. 'Five minutes,' she begged. 'I've been waiting two hours.'

'No, I'm sorry. We have people coming to dinner and I

promised my wife I wouldn't be late.' He opened his door and went inside. 'Ring and make an appointment. I'm in court for the next three days but I may be able to fit you in towards the end of the week.' He prepared to shut her out.

She stood up and leaned her shoulder on the door jamb, holding the door open with one hand. 'Olive did have a lover,' she told him. 'I know who he is and I've had his photograph identified by two witnesses, one of whom is the owner of the hotel that he and Olive used throughout the summer before the murders. I have a witness who bears out Olive's claim to have had an abortion. The date she gave me implies that Olive's baby, had it lived, would have been born around the time of the murders. I have learned that two people, Robert Martin and the father of a friend of Olive's, quite independently of each other, told the police that Olive was incapable of murdering her sister. The scenario they both offered was that Gwen killed Amber – she didn't like Amber, apparently – and Olive killed Gwen. I admit the forensic evidence doesn't support that case but it proves that serious doubts existed even at the time which I don't think were brought to your attention.' She saw the impatience in his face and hurried on. 'For all sorts of reasons, principally because it was her birthday, I do not believe that Olive was in the house on the night before the murders and I *do* believe that Gwen and Amber were killed much earlier than the time Olive claims to have done it. I think Olive returned home some time during the morning or afternoon of the ninth, found the carnage in the kitchen, knew her lover was responsible, and was so overcome with shock and remorse that she confessed to the crime herself. I think she was very unsure of herself, very distressed, and didn't know how to cope when the main prop in her life, her mother, was so suddenly taken from her.'

He took some papers out of his desk and tucked them into his briefcase. He heard so many imaginative defences that he was more polite than interested. 'I assume you're suggesting that Olive and her lover spent her birthday night together in a hotel somewhere.' Roz nodded. 'Have you any proof of that?'

'No. They weren't registered at the hotel they usually used but that's not surprising. It was a special occasion. They may even have come up to London.'

'In that case why should she assume her lover was responsible? They would have gone back together. Even if he'd dropped her at a distance from her house he wouldn't have had time to do what was done.'

'He would if he'd walked out,' said Roz, 'and left her alone in the hotel.'

'Why would he do that?'

'Because she told him that but for her sister's earlier illegitimate baby and her mother's horror of it happening again he would by now be a proud father.'

Deedes looked at his watch. 'What illegitimate baby?'

'The one Amber had when she was thirteen. There's no dispute about that. The child is mentioned in Robert Martin's will. Gwen managed to hush it up but, as she couldn't hope to do the same thing with Olive, she persuaded her to abort.'

He clicked his tongue impatiently. 'This is all highly fanciful, Miss Leigh. As far as I can see, you've absolutely nothing to support these allegations and you can't go into print accusing somebody else of the murders without either some very strong evidence or enough capital behind you to pay a fortune in libel damages.' He looked at his watch again, torn between going and staying. 'Let's suppose for a moment your hypothesis is right. So, where was Olive's father while Gwen and Amber were being butchered in his kitchen? If I remember correctly he was in the house that night and left for work as usual the following morning. Are you suggesting he didn't know what had happened?'

'Yes, that's exactly what I'm suggesting.'

Deedes's pleasant face scowled in perplexity. 'That's absurd.'

'Not if he was never there. The only people who said he *was* were Olive, Robert himself, and the next-door neighbour, and she only mentioned him in the context of claiming that Gwen and Amber were still alive at eight thirty.'

He shook his head in complete bewilderment. 'So everybody's lying? That's too ridiculous. Why should the neighbour lie?'

Roz sighed. 'I know it's hard to swallow. I've had a lot of time to think about it, so it's easier for me. Robert Martin was a closet homosexual. I've found the gay pub that he used for his pick-ups. He was well known there as Mark Agnew. The landlord recognized his picture immediately. If he was with a lover the night of the murders and went straight to work from there, he wouldn't have known anything about what had happened in the kitchen until he was told by the police.' She raised a cynical eyebrow. 'And he never had to reveal where he really was because Olive, who assumed he must have been in the house, claimed in her statement that she didn't attack her mother until after her father had left.'

'Hang on, hang on,' barked Deedes, as if he were haranguing a difficult witness, 'you can't have it both ways. A minute ago you were suggesting that Olive's lover dashed off in the middle of the night to have it out with Gwen.' He ran a smooth hand over his hair, collecting his thoughts. 'But, as Robert's body wasn't lying in the kitchen when Olive got back, she must have known he hadn't been there. Why claim in her statement he was?'

'Because he should have been. Look, it really doesn't matter what time her lover left her – the middle of the night, early morning – it's irrelevant as far as she was concerned. She didn't have a car, she was probably quite upset about being abandoned, plus she'd taken the day off work, presumably to spend it with her man, so the chances were she didn't get home till after lunch. She must have assumed her lover waited until Robert left for work before going in to tackle Gwen and Amber, so it was quite natural for her to include her father in her statement. He lived and slept downstairs in a back room but it doesn't appear to have occurred to any of them, except possibly Gwen, that he was slipping out at night for casual gay sex.'

He glanced at his watch for a third time. 'It's no good. I shall have to go.' He reached for his coat and folded it over his arm. 'You haven't explained why the neighbour lied.' He ushered her through the door and closed it behind them.

She spoke over her shoulder as she started down the stairs. 'Because I suspect that when the police told her Gwen and Amber had been murdered she jumped to the immediate conclusion that Robert had done it after a row over her husband.' She shrugged at his snort of disbelief. 'She knew all about the strained relationships in that house, knew that her husband spent hours shut up with Robert in the back room, knew jolly well, I should think, that Robert was a homosexual and by inference that her husband was one as well. She must have been beside herself until she heard that Olive had confessed to the murders. The scandal, if Robert had done it for love of Edward, would have been devastating, so, in a rather pathetic attempt to keep him out of it, she said that Gwen and Amber were alive after Edward left for work.' She led him across the hallway. 'Luckily for her the statement was never questioned because it tied in very neatly with what Olive said.'

They pushed through the main doors and walked down the front steps to the pavement. 'Too neatly?' he murmured. 'Olive's version is so simple. Yours is so complicated.'

'The truth always is,' she said with feeling. 'But in actual fact, all three of them only described what was, in effect, a normal Wednesday morning. Not so much neatness, then, as inevitability.'

'I go this way,' he said, pointing up towards Holborn Tube station.

'That's all right. I'll come with you.' She had to walk briskly to keep up with him.

'I don't understand why you're telling me all this, Miss Leigh. The person you should have gone to is Olive's solicitor, Mr Crew.'

She avoided a direct answer. 'You think I've got a case, then?'

He smiled good-humouredly, his teeth very white in his dark face. 'No, you're a long way off that. You may have the *beginnings* of a case. Take it to Mr Crew.'

'You're the barrister,' she persisted doggedly. 'If you were fighting Olive's corner, what would you need to convince a court she's innocent?'

'Proof that she could not have been in the house during the period of time that the murders happened.'

'Or the real murderer?'

'Or the real murderer,' he agreed, 'but I can't see you producing him very easily.'

'Why not?'

'Because there's no evidence against him. Your argument, presumably, is that Olive obscured all the evidence in order to take the blame on herself. She did it very successfully. Everything confirmed her as the guilty party.' He slowed down as they approached the Underground. 'So, unless your hypothetical murderer confesses voluntarily and persuades the police that he knew things that only the murderer could know, there's no way you can overturn Olive's conviction.' He smiled apologetically. 'And I can't see him doing that now, for the simple reason that he didn't do it at the time.'

She telephoned the prison from Holborn Tube station and asked them to tell Olive she wouldn't be in that evening. She had a feeling that things were about to blow up in her face, and the feeling centred on Olive.

It was late by the time she let herself in through the main door of her block. Unusually, the hall was in total darkness. She pressed the time switch to light the stairs and first-floor landing, and sighed when nothing happened. Another power cut, she thought. She could have predicted it. Black was in tune with her mood. She sorted out the key to her flat, by touch, and groped her way up the stairs, trying to remember if she had any candles left over from the last time. With luck there was one in her kitchen drawer, otherwise this was going to be a long and tedious night.

She was fumbling blindly across her door with both hands,

searching for the lock, when something rose up from the floor at her feet and brushed against her.

'*Aa-agh!*' she screamed, beating at it furiously.

Next second she was lifted bodily off the floor while a great palm clamped itself across her mouth. 'Ssh,' hissed Hal in her ear, shaking with laughter. 'It's me.' He kissed her on the nose. '*Ow!*' he roared, letting her go and bending over to clutch himself.

'Serves you right,' she said, scrabbling on the floor for her keys. 'You're lucky I didn't have my hatpin. Ah, got them.' She renewed her search for the lock and found it. 'There.' She tried the lights inside the door but the blackness remained impenetrable. 'Come on,' she said, catching his jacket and pulling him inside. 'I think there's a candle in the kitchen.'

'Everything all right?' called a quavering female voice from the floor upstairs.

'Yes, thank you,' Roz called back. 'I trod on something. How long has the power been off?'

'Half an hour. I've telephoned. There's a fuse gone in a box somewhere. Three hours they said. I told them I wouldn't pay my bill if it was any longer. We should take a stand. Don't you agree?'

'Absolutely,' said Roz, wondering who she was talking to. Mrs Barrett, perhaps. She knew their names from their mail but she rarely saw anyone. ''Bye now.' She closed her door. 'I'll try and find the candle,' she whispered.

'Why are we whispering?' Hal whispered back.

She giggled. 'Because one always does in the dark.'

He stumbled into something. 'This is ridiculous. The street lights aren't out, are they? Your curtains must be closed.'

'Probably.' She pulled open the kitchen drawer. 'I left early this morning.' She felt around the clutter of cotton reels and screwdrivers. 'I think I've found it. Have you any matches?'

'No,' he said patiently, 'otherwise I'd have lit one by now. Do you keep snakes by any chance?'

'Don't be silly. I have a cat.' *But where was Mrs Antrobus?* Her cries should have risen in joyful greeting when the key scraped in the lock. Roz made her way back to the door and groped for her briefcase where she kept the matches that she took in to the prison. She snapped the locks and poked amongst her papers. 'If you can find the sofa,' she told him, 'the curtains are behind it. There's a cord on the left-hand side.'

'I've found something,' he said, 'but it certainly isn't a sofa.'

'What is it?'

'I don't know,' he said cautiously, 'but whatever it is it's rather unpleasant. It's wet and slimy and it's wound itself round my neck. Are you sure you don't keep snakes?'

She gave a nervous laugh. 'Don't be an idiot.' Her fingers knocked against the matchbox and she snatched at it with relief. She struck a match and held it up. Hal was standing in the middle of the room, his head and shoulders swathed in the damp shirt she had washed that morning and hung on a coathanger from the lampshade. She shook with laughter. 'You knew it wasn't a snake,' she said, holding the candle to the spluttering match flame.

He found the cord and swished the curtains back to let in the orange glow from the street lamps outside. With that and the candlelight, the room sprang alive out of the pitch darkness. He gazed about him. Towels, clothes, carrier bags, and photographs lay in clutters on chairs and tables, a duvet sprawled half on and half off the sofa, dirty cups, and empty bags of crisps jostled happily about the floor. 'Well, this is nice,' he said, lifting his foot and prising off the remains of a half-eaten pork pie. 'I can't remember when I felt so much at home.'

'I wasn't expecting you,' she said, taking the pork pie with dignity and dropping it into a waste-paper basket. 'Or at least I thought you'd have the decency to warn me of your arrival with a phone-call first.'

He reached down to stroke the soft ball of white fur that was stretching luxuriously in its warm nest on the duvet. Mrs Antrobus licked his hand in approval before embarking on a comprehensive grooming. 'Do you always sleep on the sofa?' he asked Roz.

'There's no telephone in the bedroom.'

He nodded gravely but didn't say anything.

She moved over to him, the candle tilted to stop the hot wax burning her fingers. 'Oh, God, I'm so pleased to see you. You wouldn't believe. Where did you go? I've been worried sick.'

He lowered his weary forehead and pressed it against her sweet-smelling hair. 'Round and about,' he said, resting his wrists on her shoulders and running the softest of fingers down the lines of her neck.

'There's a warrant out for your arrest,' she said weakly.

'I know.' His lips brushed against her cheek, but so gently that their touch was almost unbearable.

'I'm going to set fire to something,' she groaned.

He reached down to pinch out the candle. 'You already have.' He cupped his strong hands about her bottom and drew her against his erection. 'The question is,' he murmured into the arch of her neck, 'should I have a cold shower before it spreads out of control?'

'Is that a serious question?' *Could* he stop now? *She* couldn't.

'No, a polite one.'

'I'm in agony.'

'You're supposed to be,' he said, his eyes glinting in the orange light. 'Damn it, woman, I've been in agony for weeks.'

Mrs Antrobus, ejected from the duvet, stalked indignantly into the kitchen.

Later, the lights came on, drowning the tiny flame of the candle which, rekindled, had started to splutter in its saucer on the table.

He stroked the hair from Roz's face. 'You are quite the most beautiful woman I've ever seen,' he said.

She smiled wickedly. 'And I thought I was too thin?'

His dark eyes softened 'I knew you were lying about that blasted answerphone.' He ran his hands over her silky arms, gripping them suddenly with urgent fingers. She was completely addictive. He plucked her up and sat her astride his lap. 'I've been dreaming about this.'

'Were they nice dreams?'

'Not a patch on the real thing.'

'Enough,' she said even later, sliding away from him and pulling on her clothes. 'What are you planning to do about this arrest warrant?'

He ignored the question and stirred the photographs on her coffee table. 'Is this your husband?'

'Ex-husband.' She threw him his trousers.

He pulled them on with a sigh, then isolated a close-up of Alice. 'And this must be your daughter,' he said evenly. 'She looks just like you.'

'Looked,' Roz corrected him. 'She's dead.'

She waited for the apology and the change of subject, but Hal smiled and touched a finger to the laughing face. 'She's beautiful.'

'Yes.'

'What was her name?'

'Alice.'

He examined the picture closely. 'I remember falling in love with a little girl just like her when I was six. I was very insecure and I used to ask her every day how much she loved me. She always answered in the same way. She would hold her hands out, like this' – he spread his palms apart, like a fisherman demonstrating the length of a fish – 'and say: this much.'

'Yes,' said Roz, remembering, 'Alice always measured love with her hands. I'd forgotten.'

She tried to take the photograph away, but he moved it out of her reach and tilted it to the light. 'There's a very determined glint in her eyes.'

'She liked her own way.'

'Sensible woman. Did she always get it?'

'Most times. She had very decided views. I remember once . . .' But she fell silent and didn't go on.

Hal shrugged into his shirt and started to button it. 'Like mother, like daughter. I bet she had you wound round her little finger before she could walk. I'd have enjoyed seeing someone get the better of you.'

Roz held a handkerchief to her streaming eyes. 'I'm sorry.'

'What for?'

'Being embarrassing.'

He pulled her against his shoulder and rested his cheek against her hair. What a terrible indictment of Western society it was, that a mother should be afraid to shed tears for her dead daughter in case she embarrassed someone.

'Thank you.' She saw the question in his eyes. 'For listening,' she explained.

'It was no hardship, Roz.' He could sense how insecure she was. 'Are you going to agonize over this all night and wake up tomorrow morning wishing you hadn't told me about Alice?'

He was far too perceptive. She looked away. 'I hate feeling vulnerable.'

'Yes.' He understood that. 'Come here.' He patted his lap. 'Let me tell you about my vulnerabilities. You've been trying to prise them out of me for weeks. Now it's your turn to have a good laugh at my expense.'

'I won't laugh.'

'Ah!' he murmured. 'So that's what this is all about. You're a cut above me. I'll laugh at yours, but you won't laugh at mine.'

She put her arms about him. 'You're so like Olive.'

'I wish you'd stop comparing me with the madwoman of Dawlington.'

'It's a compliment. She's a very nice person. Like you.'

'I'm not nice, Roz.' He held her face between his hands. 'I'm being prosecuted under the Health and Hygiene regulations.

The Environmental Health Inspector's report describes my kitchen as the worst he's ever seen. Ninety-five per cent of the raw meat in the fridge was so rotten it was crawling with maggots. The dry foods should have been in sealed containers, but weren't, and rat droppings were found in all of them. There were open bags of rubbish in the larder. The vegetables had deteriorated so far they had to be discarded, and a live rat was discovered under the cooker.' He arched a weary eyebrow. 'I've lost all my customers because of it, my case comes up in six weeks, and I haven't a leg to stand on.'

SEVENTEEN

Roz didn't speak for some moments. She had invented a number of scenarios to account for what was happening at the Poacher, but never this. It would certainly explain his lack of customers. Who, in their right mind, would eat in a restaurant where the meat had been found crawling with maggots? She had. Twice. But she hadn't known about the maggots. It would have been more honest of Hal to tell her at the outset, she thought, her stomach protesting mildly over what might have gone into it. She felt his gaze upon her and quelled the treacherous stirrings firmly.

'I don't understand,' she said carefully. 'Is this a genuine prosecution? I mean, you appear to have been tried and judged already. How did your customers know what the Inspector found if the case hasn't been to court? And who are the men in ski-masks?' She gave a puzzled frown. 'I can't believe you'd be such a bloody fool, anyway, as to flout the hygiene regulations. Not to the extent of having an entire fridgeful of rotten meat and live rats running around the floor.' She laughed suddenly with relief and smacked a slender palm against his chest. 'You creep, Hawksley! It's a load of old flannel. You're trying to wind me up.'

He shook his head. 'I wish I were.'

She studied him thoughtfully for a moment then pushed herself off his lap and walked through to the kitchen. He heard the sound of a cork being drawn from a bottle and the clink of glasses. She took longer than she should have, and he recalled how his wife had always done the same thing – disappeared into the kitchen whenever she was hurt or disappointed. He had thought Roz different.

247

She reappeared finally with a tray. 'OK,' she said firmly, 'I've had a think.'

He didn't say anything.

'I do not believe you'd keep a dirty kitchen,' she told him. 'You're too much of an enthusiast. The Poacher is the fulfilment of a dream, not a financial investment to be milked for all its worth.' She poured him a glass of wine. 'And you accused me a week ago of setting you up again, which would imply you'd been set up before.' She filled the second glass for herself. 'Ergo, the rat and the rotten meat were planted. Am I right?'

'Right.' He sniffed the wine. 'But I would say that, wouldn't I?'

A very sore nerve, she thought. No wonder he didn't trust anyone. She perched on the edge of the sofa. 'Plus,' she went on, ignoring the comment, 'you've been beaten up twice to my knowledge, had your car windows smashed and the Poacher broken into.' She sipped her wine. 'So what do they want from you?'

He eased the still-bruised muscles in his back. 'Presumably they want me out, and fast. But I haven't a clue why or who's behind it. Six weeks ago I was a contented chef, presiding over a healthy little business without a care in the world. Then I came home from the markets at ten o'clock one morning to find my assistant being berated by the Environmental Health Inspector, my kitchen stinking to high heaven of corruption, and me on the wrong end of a prosecution.' He ruffled his hair. 'The restaurant was closed for three days while I cleaned it. My staff never came back after the closure. My customers, predominantly policemen and their families – which, incidentally, is how the news of the Inspector's visit got out – deserted in droves because they reckoned I'd been cutting corners to line my pockets, and the local restaurateurs are accusing me of giving the whole trade a bad name through my lack of professionalism. I've been effectively isolated.'

Roz shook her head. 'Why on earth didn't you report that break-in last Tuesday?'

He sighed. 'What good would it have done me? I couldn't tie it in to the Health Inspector's visit. I decided to work with some live bait instead.' He saw her bewilderment. 'I caught two of them at it, wrecking the place. I think it was a chance thing. They discovered the restaurant was empty and took their opportunity.' He laughed suddenly. 'I was so angry with you that I had them both upstairs, gagged and handcuffed to my window bars, before they even knew what had hit them. But they were a tough pair,' he said with genuine admiration. 'They weren't going to talk.' He shrugged. 'So I sat it out and waited for someone to come looking for them.'

No wonder he had been frightened. 'Why did you decide it was chance that brought them and not me?' she asked curiously. 'I'd have thought it was me every time.'

The laughter lines rayed out around his eyes. 'You didn't see yourself with that table leg. You were so terrified when the kitchen door opened, so relieved when you saw it was me, and so twitched when I told you I hadn't called the police. No one, but no one, is that good.' He took a mouthful of wine and savoured it for a moment. 'I'm in a catch twenty-two. The police don't believe me. They think I'm guilty, but trying to use clout or cunning to wriggle out of the prosecution. Even Geoff Wyatt, who was my partner and who knows me better than anyone, claims to have had the runs since he saw the Inspector's photographs. They all ate there regularly, partly because I gave them discounts and partly out of a genuine desire to see an ex-copper succeed.' He wiped a weary hand across his mouth. 'Now, I'm *persona non grata* and I can't really blame them. They feel they've been conned.'

'Why would you need to con them?'

'The recession.' He sighed. 'Businesses are going down like ninepins. There's no reason mine should have been immune. What's the first thing a restaurateur's likely to do when he's running out of money? Hang on to dodgy food and serve it up in a curry.'

There was a twisted logic to it. 'Won't your staff speak up for you?'

He smiled grimly. 'The two waitresses have agreed to, but the only one whose word might carry weight is my assistant chef, and he was last heard of heading for France.' He stretched his arms towards the ceiling, and winced as pain seared round his ribs. 'It wouldn't do me any good anyway. He must have been bought. Someone had to let whoever framed me into the kitchen and he had the only other key.' His eyes hardened. 'I should have throttled him when I had the chance but I was so damn shell-shocked I didn't put two and two together fast enough. By the time I had, he'd gone.'

Roz chewed her thumb in thought. 'Didn't that man tell you anything after I left? I assumed you were going to use my hatpin on him.'

Her candour brought a smile to his bleak face. 'I did, but he didn't make much sense. "You're costing money on the foreclosures." That's all he said.' He arched an eyebrow. 'Can you make anything of it?'

'Not unless the bank's about to pull the rug from underneath your feet.'

He shook his head. 'I borrowed the absolute minimum. There's no immediate pressure.' He drummed his fingers on the floor. 'Logically, he should have been referring to the businesses on either side of me. They've both gone bankrupt and in each case the lenders have foreclosed.'

'Well, that's it then,' said Roz excitedly. 'Someone wants all three properties. Didn't you ask him who it was and why?'

He rubbed the back of his head in tender recollection. 'I was clobbered before I had the chance. There was obviously a fifth man who went upstairs during the brawl to release Tweedledum and Tweedledee from the window bars. For all I know, it was that hammering we heard. Anyway, by the time I came to, a chip pan was in flames on the stove, the police had arrived in force, and my next-door neighbour was rabbiting on about how he'd had to call an ambulance because I'd tried to boil a customer in fish stock.' He grinned sheepishly. 'It was a blasted nightmare. So I hit the nearest copper and legged it through the restaurant. It was the only thing I could think of.' He looked at her. 'In any case the idea that someone was trying to get hold of the Poacher was the first thing I thought of. I checked out both the adjoining properties five weeks ago and there's no common factor between them. One was bought privately by a small retail chain and the other was sold at auction to an investment company.'

'They could be fronts. Did you go to Companies' House?'

'What do you think I've been doing for the last three days?' He gritted his teeth angrily. 'I've checked every damn register I can think of and I've got sweet FA to show for it. I don't know what the hell's going on except that the court case will be the last nail in the Poacher's coffin and presumably, at that point, someone will make me an offer to buy the place. Rather like you kept doing the other day.'

She let his anger slide past her. She understood it now. 'By which time it will be too late.'

'Precisely.'

They sat in silence for several minutes.

'Why were you beaten up the first time I saw you?' Roz asked at last. 'That must have followed on the Inspector's visit.'

He nodded. 'It was three or four days after I re-opened. They grabbed me off the doorstep when I unlocked the door. Same MO as you witnessed – men in ski-masks with baseball bats – but that time they shoved me in the back of a fish lorry, drove me ten miles into the New Forest, slapped me about a bit, then dumped me by the side of the road with no money and no cards. It took me all afternoon to walk home, because nobody fancied giving me a lift, and at the end of it' – he flicked her a sideways glance – 'I found Botticelli's *Venus* loitering palely among my tables. I really thought my luck had changed until Venus opened her mouth and turned into a Fury.' He ducked to avoid her hand. 'God, woman' – he grinned – 'I was out on my feet and you tore more strips off me than the bastards in the fish lorry. Rape, for Christ's sake! I could hardly put one foot in front of the other.'

'It's your own fault for having bars on your windows. Why do you, as a matter of interest?'

'They were there when I bought it. The chap before me

had a wife who sleepwalked. I've been glad of them these last few weeks.'

She reverted to her former question. 'But it doesn't explain why, you know. I mean if the idea of the Inspector's visit was to get you to jack it in quickly, then they should have clobbered you the day you re-opened, not four days later. And if they were happy to wait until the court case, then why clobber you at all?'

'I know,' he admitted. 'It made me very suspicious of you. I kept thinking you must be connected with it somehow but I had you checked and you seemed genuine enough.'

'Thanks,' she said drily.

'You'd have done the same.' A frown carved a deep furrow between his brows. 'You must admit it's damned odd the way everything blew up around the time you appeared.'

In all fairness, Roz could see it was. 'But you got stitched up,' she pointed out, 'before you or I had ever heard of each other. It must be coincidence.' She topped up his glass. 'And, anyway, the only common factor between you and me five weeks ago was Olive and you're not suggesting she's behind it. She's hardly confident enough to run a bath on her own, let alone mastermind a conspiracy to defraud you of the Poacher.'

He shrugged impatiently. 'I know. I've been over it a thousand times. None of it makes sense. The only thing I'm sure of is that it's about the neatest operation I've ever come across. I've had the ground cut from under me. I'm the fall guy and I can't even begin to get a fix on who's done it.' He scratched his stubble with weary resignation. 'So, Miss Leigh, how do you feel now about a failed restaurateur with convictions for health violation, GBH, arson, and resisting arrest? Because, barring miracles, that's what I'll be in three weeks.'

Her eyes gleamed above her wine glass. 'Horny.'

He gave an involuntary chuckle. It was the same gleam in the pictured eyes of Alice. 'You look just like your daughter.' He stirred the photographs again. 'You should have them all around the room to remind yourself of how beautiful she was.

I would if she'd been mine.' He heard Roz's indrawn breath and glanced at her. 'Sorry. That was insensitive.'

'Don't be an oaf,' she said. 'I've just remembered where I've seen that man before. I knew I knew him. It's one of Mr Hayes's sons. You know, the old man who lived next door to the Martins. He had photographs of the family on his sideboard.' She clapped her hands. 'Is that a miracle, Hawksley, or is it a miracle? Sister Bridget's prayers must be working.'

She sat at her kitchen table and watched Hal work his magic on the meagre contents of her fridge. He had sloughed off his frustration like a used-up skin and was humming contentedly to himself as he interleaved bacon between thin slices of chicken breast and sprinkled them with parsley. 'You're not planning to stick my hatpin into Mr Hayes, are you?' she asked him. 'I'm sure he hasn't a clue what his beastly son's been up to. He's a dear old thing.'

Hal was amused. 'I shouldn't think so.' He covered the dish with silver foil and put it in the oven. 'But I'm damned if I can see at the moment how the jigsaw fits together. Why did Hayes Junior suddenly up the pressure on me if all he had to do was sit tight and wait for my prosecution?'

'Have him arrested and find out,' said Roz reasonably. 'If it was me, I'd have driven straight down, demanded an address off his father, and sent in the fuzz.'

'And you'd have got precisely nowhere.' He thought for a moment. 'You said you made a tape of your conversation with the old man. I'd like to listen to it. I can't believe it's coincidence. There has to be a stronger link. Why did they all get so twitched suddenly and start wielding baseball bats? It doesn't make sense.'

'You can listen to it now.' She brought her briefcase in from the hallway, located the tape, and set the recorder running on the table. 'We were talking about Amber's illegitimate son,' she explained as the old man's voice quavered out. 'He knew all about him, even down to the child's adopted name and what country he's in. Robert Martin's entire estate is his if they can find him.'

Hal listened with rapt attention. 'Brown?' he queried at the end. 'And living in Australia? How do you know he's right?'

'Because Olive's shitty solicitor threatened me with injunctions when I let on I knew.' She frowned. 'Mind you, I've no idea how Mr Hayes found out. Crew won't even give Olive the child's name. He's paranoid about keeping it secret.'

Hal removed a saucepan of rice from the cooker and drained it. 'How much did Robert Martin leave?'

'Half a million.'

'Christ!' He gave a low whistle. 'Christ!' he said again. 'And it's all on deposit waiting for the child's appearance?'

'Presumably.'

'Who's the executor?'

'The solicitor, Peter Crew.'

Hal spooned the rice into a bowl. 'So what did he say when you tackled him about it? Did he admit they were on the child's track?'

'No. He just kept threatening me with injunctions.' She shrugged. 'But he wrote to Olive and told her the chances were minimal. There's a time limit, apparently, and if the child doesn't turn up the money goes to charity.' She frowned. 'He wrote that letter himself in long hand. I thought he was saving money but, you know, it's far more likely that he didn't want his secretary reading it. She would know if he was telling lies.'

'And meanwhile,' Hal said slowly, 'he is administering the estate and has access to the sort of capital that would be needed to buy up bankrupt businesses.' He stared past her head, his eyes narrowed. 'Plus, he's a solicitor, so probably has inside information on development plans and proposals.' He looked at Roz. 'It would amount to indefinite free credit, as long as no one turned up to claim Robert's money. When did you first go and see Crew?'

She was ahead of him. 'The day before you were beaten up.' Her eyes gleamed excitedly. 'And he was very suspicious of me, kept accusing me of jumping to unfavourable conclusions about his handling of Olive's case. I've got it all on tape.' She scrabbled through her cassettes. 'He said Olive couldn't inherit because she would not be allowed to benefit from Gwen and Amber's death. But, you know, if Olive were innocent' – she pounced triumphantly on the tape – 'it would be a whole new ball game. She could get leave to appeal against the will. And I remember saying to him at the end of the interview that one explanation for the discrepancies between the abnormality of the crime and the normality of Olive's psychiatric tests was that she didn't do it. God, it fits, doesn't it? First he learns that Amber's son is likely to surface and then I turn up, aggressively taking Olive's side. The Poacher must be awfully important to him.'

Hal took the chicken from the oven and put it on the table with the rice. 'You do realize your dear old man must be in it up to his neck? Crew would never have given him chapter and verse on Amber's child unless Hayes has some kind of hold on him.'

She stared at him for a long moment, then removed the Svengali photographs from her briefcase. 'Perhaps he knows Crew is using Robert's money. Or perhaps,' she said slowly, 'he knows who really murdered Gwen and Amber. Either or both could ruin Crew.' She fanned the pictures across the table. 'He was Olive's lover,' she said simply, 'and if I could find out so easily then so could anyone else. Including the police. You let her down, Hal, all of you. It's a betrayal of justice to assume someone's guilt before it's proved.'

Watery blue eyes regarded Roz with undisguised pleasure. 'Well, well. You came back. Come in. Come in.' He peered past her, frowning at Hal in half-recognition. 'Surely we've met before. What shall I say? I never forget a face. Now when could that have been?'

Hal shook the old man's hand. 'Six years ago,' he said pleasantly. 'I was on the Olive Martin case. Sergeant

Hawksley.' The hand fluttered weakly in his, like a tiny bird, but only from old age and decrepitude, Hal thought.

Mr Hayes nodded vigorously. 'I remember now. Unhappy circumstances.' He fussed ahead of them into the sitting room. 'Sit down. Sit down. Any news?' He took a firm chair and sat bolt upright his head cocked enquiringly to one side. On the sideboard behind him his violent son smiled disarmingly into the camera.

Roz took her notebook from her handbag and switched on her recorder again. They had reached a mutual decision that Roz should ask the questions. For, as Hal had pointed out: 'If he knows anything, he's more likely to let it slip while talking to a – what shall I say? – charming young lady about Olive.'

'In fact,' she said in a gossipy voice which grated on Hal but clearly appealed to Mr Hayes, 'there's quite a bit of news one way and another. Where would you like me to begin? With Olive? Or with Amber's baby?' She gave him an approving look. 'You were quite right about them finding traces, you know, in spite of there being thousands of Browns in Australia.'

'Ah,' he said, rubbing his hands, 'I knew they were close. That mean the lad will get the money? What shall I say? It's what Bob wanted. Fair upset him, it did, to think the government would get it all.'

'He made alternative provisions, you know, in case the boy wasn't found. It'll go to various children's charities.'

The old man's mouth compressed into a split of disgust. 'And we all know what sort of children they'll be. The worthless sort. The sort as are never going to make anything of theirselves but live off the rest of us till they drop. And you know who I blame. The social workers. They're namby-pamby when it comes to telling a woman she's had more children than's good for her.'

'Quite,' Roz interrupted hurriedly, reining in the inevitable hobby horse. She tapped her pencil on her notepad. 'Do you remember telling me that your wife thought Olive committed the murders because of hormones?'

He pursed his lips at the abrupt change of subject. 'Maybe.'

'Did your wife say that because she knew Olive had had an abortion the previous Christmas?'

'Maybe.'

'Do you know who the father was, Mr Hayes?'

He shook his head. 'Someone she met through work, we were told. Silly girl. Only did it to cock a snook at Amber.' He fingered his ancient mouth. 'Or that's what I reckoned anyway. Amber had a lot of boyfriends.'

So much for Mr Hayes and Crew in a conspiracy of silence, thought Roz. 'When did you find out about it?'

'Gwen told my Jeannie. She was that upset. Thought Olive was going to up and get married and abandon them all. It would have done for Gwen, that would. She couldn't have coped on her own.'

'Coped with what?'

'Everything,' he said vaguely.

'Housework, you mean?'

'Housework, cooking, bills, shopping. Everything. Olive did everything.'

'What did Gwen do?'

He didn't answer immediately, but seemed to be weighing something in his mind. He glanced across at Hal. 'You lot never did ask many questions. I might have said something if you had.'

Hal eased himself in his chair. 'At the time it was clear cut,' he said carefully. 'But Miss Leigh has unearthed a number of discrepancies which do tend to throw a different light on the affair. What would you have told us, had you been asked?'

Mr Hayes sucked at his false teeth. 'Well, for one thing, Gwen Martin drank too much. She had troubles, I can't deny that, kept up a good front, I can't deny that either, but she was a bad mother. She married beneath herself and it made her bitter. Felt life had dealt her a bad hand and she took it out on Bob and the girls. My Jeannie always said if it hadn't been for Olive the family would have fallen apart years before. It made us sick, of course, what she did, but everyone turns eventually and she was badly put upon one way and another. She shouldn't have killed them, though. Can't forgive that.'

'No,' said Roz thoughtfully. 'So what did Gwen do all day while the other three were out at work?'

The marbled hands fluttered a contradiction. 'Amber was at home more often than not. Work-shy, that one. Never stayed anywhere very long. Used to drive her mother mad listening to pop records at full blast and inviting boys up to her bedroom. She was a pretty girl but my Jeannie said she was difficult. Couldn't see it myself.' He smiled reminiscently. 'She was always charming to me. I had a soft spot for little Amber. But she got on with men, I think, better than she got on with women.' He peered at Roz. 'You asked me about Gwen. What shall I say, Miss Leigh? She kept up appearances. If you knocked on the door she was always smartly dressed, always held herself well, always spoke with icy correctness, but as often as not she was drunk as a lord. Strange woman. Never did know why she took to the bottle, unless it was the business of Amber's baby. She was a lot worse afterwards.'

Roz drew her cherub doodle. 'Robert Martin was an active homosexual but didn't want anyone to know,' she said bluntly. 'Perhaps that's what she found difficult to cope with.'

Mr Hayes sniffed. 'She drove him to it,' he said. 'There was nothing wrong with Bob that a loving wife wouldn't have put right. The two girls were his all right, so there was nothing untoward in the locker at the beginning, if you get my meaning. It was her turned him off women. She was frigid.'

Roz let that pass. Mr Hayes was too set in his views to see that what he said was nonsense and, in any case, there was probably some truth in the idea that Gwen was frigid. Roz found it difficult to believe that Robert Martin could ever have got as far as the altar with a woman who had a normal sexual drive. Her very normality would have been a threat to him. 'But if she was mourning Amber's baby,' she said in feigned puzzlement, 'I don't understand why she didn't try and get him back or at least establish contact with him? Presumably she knew who had adopted him or she wouldn't have been able to tell your Jeannie his name.'

He tut-tutted impatiently. 'It wasn't Jeannie told me the name, it was my son, Stewart, six, seven weeks back. Knew I'd be interested, seeing as how me and Bob were pals.' He wagged a finger at her. 'You don't know much about adoption, that's for sure. Once you sign 'em away, that's it. You're not given a dossier. Gwen never knew who'd got him.'

Roz smiled easily. 'Does your son work for Mr Crew, then? I've not come across him. I thought he took after you and became a soldier.'

'Blooming Army didn't want him any more, did they?' he muttered crossly. 'Cutbacks there, like everywhere else. What shall I say? So much for loyalty to Queen and country. Course he doesn't work for Mr Crew. He's running a small security firm with his brother, but there's precious little work.' He flexed his arthritic fingers in annoyance. 'Trained soldiers and the best they can get is nightwatchmen jobs. Their wives aren't happy, not by a long chalk.'

Roz gritted her teeth behind another ingenuous smile. 'So how did he know the child's name?'

Archly, Mr Hayes tapped the side of his nose. 'No names no pack drill, young lady. Always best.'

Hal leaned forward aggressively and held up a hand. 'One moment, please, Miss Leigh.' He drew his brows together in a ferocious scowl. 'You do realize, Mr Hayes, that if your son doesn't work for Mr Crew then, strictly speaking, he's committed an offence by being in receipt of confidential information. The legal profession is bound by the same codes as the medical profession and if someone in Mr Crew's practice is talking to outsiders, then both he and the police would want to know about it.'

'Bah!' the old man snorted contemptuously. 'You never change, you lot. What shall I say? Quick as lightning to bang up the innocent while the bloody thieves wander around, free as birds, nicking anything they feel like nicking. You should do what you're being paid for, Sergeant, and not go round threatening old men. It was Mr Crew himself gave out that information. He told my lad and my lad told me. How's he supposed to know it's confidential if the blooming solicitor's telling everyone? Stands to reason he'd pass it on, seeing as how I was the only friend Bob had at the end.' He glared suspiciously from Hal to Roz. 'What you bring a policeman for, anyway?'

'Because there's some doubt of Olive's guilt,' said Roż glibly, wondering if being economical with the truth constituted deliberate impersonation of a police officer. 'This gentleman is holding a watching brief while I talk to people.'

'I see,' said Mr Hayes. But it was obvious he didn't.

'I'm nearly finished.' She smiled brightly. 'I found the Clarkes, by the way. Had a chat with them a week or so ago. Poor Mrs Clarke is completely senile now.'

The watery eyes looked amused. 'That doesn't surprise me. She was pretty far gone when I knew her. I sometimes thought my Jeannie was the only sensible woman in the road.'

'I gather Mr Clarke had to stay at home to look after her?' She raised her eyebrows in enquiry. 'But he spent more time with Robert than he spent with her. How friendly were they, Mr Hayes? Do you know?'

It was obvious he understood the point of her question. He chose – out of delicacy? – not to answer it. 'Good friends,' he muttered, 'and who can blame them? Bob's wife was a dipso and Ted's was the silliest creature I've ever met. Cleaned the house from top to bottom every day.' He gave a grunt of contempt. 'Hygiene mad, she was. Used to walk around in nothing but an overall, no undies in case she spread germs, swabbing everything with disinfectant.' He chuckled suddenly. 'Remember once she scrubbed the dining table with neat Domestos to sterilize it. Hah! Ted was hopping mad. He'd just paid for the thing to be french polished after Dorothy's last effort with boiling water. And now she's completely senile, you say. Not surprised. Not surprised at all.'

Roz sat with her pencil poised above her notepad. 'And can you say,' she asked after a moment, 'if Ted and Bob were lovers?'

'No. It weren't none of my business.'

'OK.' She gathered her things together. 'Thank you, Mr

Hayes. I don't know if there's anything Mr Hawksley wants to ask you.' She looked at Hal.

He stood up. 'Only the name of your son's security firm, Mr Hayes.'

The old man eyed him suspiciously. 'What you want that for?'

'Just so I can put a quiet word in the right ear about the leak of privileged information.' He smiled coldly. 'Otherwise I shall have to report it and then there'll be an official complaint.' He shrugged. 'Don't worry. You have my word I won't make an issue out of it, not unless I have to.'

'The word of a policeman, eh? That's not something I'd want to rely on. Certainly not.'

Hal buttoned his jacket. 'It'll have to go through official channels then, and it'll be an inspector coming to see you next time.'

'What shall I say? Blooming blackmail, that's all this is. STC Security, Bell Street, Southampton. There now. Let's see if your word's worth something.'

Hal looked past him towards the photograph of his son. 'Thank you, Mr Hayes,' he said pleasantly. 'You've been very helpful.'

EIGHTEEN

Roz walked back to the car deep in thought. 'What's up?' Hal asked her.

'Just something he said.' She put her bag on the roof and stared into the middle distance, trying to pick up an elusive thread. 'It's no good. I'll have to go back through my notes.' She unlocked the door. 'So what do we do now? Go to the police?' She released Hal's door and he climbed in beside her.

'No. We'd be there all day answering questions and there's no guarantee they'd act at the end of it.' He thought for a moment. 'And it's no good tackling Crew either. If we're going to nail him we'll have to do it through Stewart Hayes and his security firm.'

Roz winced. 'We? Listen, Hawksley, I've already had my hair pulled out once by that gorilla. I'm not sure I fancy it a second time.' She meant it, too.

Hal put his hand on her shoulder and gave it a reassuring squeeze. 'If it's any consolation, I don't think I fancy it much either.' He could smell the scent of soap on her face and with a sigh he moved away. 'But we've got to get it settled one way or another,' he said coolly. 'I can't stand much more of this.'

Her insecurities resurfaced. 'Much more of what?'

'Sitting around in confined spaces with you,' he growled. 'It requires too much blasted self-control. Come on. Let's grasp the nettle. I'll phone Geoff Wyatt and see if I can persuade him to hold my hand while I offer the Poacher for sale.'

'Wouldn't it be easier just to have Hayes arrested?'

'What for?'

'Breaking and entering.'

'On what evidence?'

'Me,' she said. 'I can identify him.'

'He'll have an alibi by now.' He flicked a strand of hair from her cheek with a gesture of casual affection. 'We need to tempt Crew into the open.'

It was Roz's turn to sigh. In the cold light of morning, she was having doubts. 'It's all guesswork, Hal. Crew could be squeaky clean as far as the Poacher's concerned. Mr Hayes likes to give the impression he knows more than he does. It makes him feel important.'

'But it's the only scenario that makes sense.' He stroked his jaw and smiled at her with a confidence he didn't really feel. 'My nose is twitching. It's always a good sign.'

'Of what?'

'That I'm on the right track.'

'You'll lose the Poacher if you're wrong.'

'I'll lose it anyway.' He drummed his fingers on the dashboard. 'Come on,' he said abruptly. 'Let's go. Head for the city centre. Bell Street runs parallel with the main shopping area. We'll stop at the first telephone we see. And keep your eyes peeled for an electrical goods shop.'

She fired the engine and pulled out into the road. 'Why?'

'You'll find out.'

He dialled Dawlington police station and asked to be put through to Geoff Wyatt. 'It's Hal.' He let the angry recriminations run for a moment, then broke in. 'Save your breath. I'm trying to sort it now, but I need your help. What do you have on STC Security in Bell Street? No, I'll wait.' He propped the receiver under his chin and took out a notepad. 'OK. Hayes. Ex-Army. Clean as a whistle. You're sure? Right. Can you meet me there in half an hour?' More squeaks. 'For old time's sake, that's why. No, you bastard, I don't give a monkey's toss if you still feel sick. At the very least, you owe me for Sally. Half an hour.' He hung up.

Roz examined her fingernails with studied uninterest. 'Who's Sally?' she asked.

'My ex.'

'Why does he owe you for her?'

'He married her.'

'God!' She hadn't expected that.

He smiled at her startled expression. 'He did me a favour but doesn't know it. He thinks it's why I left the Force. His guilt is huge and extremely useful at times like this.'

'That's cruel.'

He lifted an eyebrow. 'It hurt at the time.'

'Sorry,' she said regretfully. 'I keep forgetting we both have pasts.'

He pulled her against him. 'The marriage was long dead, and Geoff didn't set out to poach Sally. He's a decent sort. He held her hand out of friendship, and ended up with more than he bargained for. And that's genuine gratitude talking, Roz, not bitterness.' He kissed her nose. 'Poor bastard. He had no idea what he was signing on for.'

'Olive's revenge,' she said slowly.

He frowned as he dialled Directory Enquiries. 'I don't follow.'

Roz gave a hollow laugh. 'She makes clay figures in her room and then sticks pins into them. She did one of me when she was angry with me. I had a migraine for a week.'

'When was that? Yes,' he said into the phone, 'STC Security, Southampton, please.'

'A couple of weeks ago.'

'Someone beat you up a couple of weeks ago,' he pointed out. 'That's why you had a migraine.' He wrote a number on his pad and hung up.

'My ex-husband,' she agreed. 'I told Olive I wanted to kill him and he turned up out of the blue. I could have killed him, too, if I'd had a knife, or been better prepared. I was angry enough.' She shrugged. 'And then there's you and Crew and the Poacher, and Wyatt taking your wife, and her father dying. All people she blames for what's happened to her.'

He looked surprised. 'You don't really believe that, do you?'

She laughed. 'No, of course I don't.' But she did. Only she knew how much her head had hurt when Olive turned the pin.

'STC Security,' said a woman's bright voice at the other end of the wire.

Hal looked at Roz as he spoke. 'Good morning. I'd like to discuss security arrangements for my restaurant with Mr Stewart Hayes.'

'I'm not sure he's available to talk at the moment, sir.'

'He will be for me. Try his number and tell him that Hal Hawksley of the Poacher is on the line.'

'One moment, please.'

Several moments passed before she came back to him. 'Mr Hayes will talk to you now, Mr Hawksley.'

A bluff, friendly voice swelled down the wire. 'Good morning, Mr Hawksley. How may I help you?'

'You can't, Mr Hayes, but I can help you. You have a window of opportunity which will stay open for the length of time it takes me to reach your office. Roughly half an hour.'

'I don't understand.'

'I'm prepared to sell the Poacher, but at my price, and today. That's the only offer you'll ever get.'

There was a short silence. 'I'm not in the market for buying restaurants, Mr Hawksley.'

'But Mr Crew is, so I suggest you consult with him before you allow the window to close.'

There was another silence. 'I don't know any Mr Crew.'

Hal ignored this. 'Tell him the Olive Martin case is about to blow wide open.' He gave Roz a broad wink. 'She is already taking legal advice from another solicitor and is expected to lodge an appeal against the terms of her father's will within seven days on the grounds that she is innocent. Crew buys the Poacher today, at my price, or he doesn't buy it at all. You have half an hour, Mr Hayes.' He hung up.

Geoff was waiting on the pavement when they arrived. 'You didn't mention you were bringing company,' he said suspiciously, bending down to look through the open passenger window.

Hal introduced them. 'Sergeant Wyatt, Miss Rosalind Leigh.'

'Jesus, Hal,' he said in disgust. 'What on earth do you want to bring her for?'

'I fancy her.'

Geoff shook his head in exasperation. 'You're mad.'

Hal opened the door and got out. 'I trust you're referring to my motives in bringing her here. If I thought you were impugning my choice, I'd bop you on the nose.' He looked across the roof at Roz who had got out on the other side and was locking her door. 'I think you should stay in the car.'

'Why?'

'You might get your hair pulled.'

'So might you.'

'It's my battle.'

'And mine, if I'm really thinking of making this relationship permanent. Anyway, you need me. I'm the one with the Tampax.'

'They won't work.'

Roz chuckled at the expression on Geoff's face. 'They will. Trust me.'

Hal tipped a finger at Wyatt. 'Now you know why I brought her.'

'You're both bloody mad.' Geoff dropped his cigarette butt on to the pavement and ground it out beneath his heel. 'So what do you want me for? By rights I should be arresting you.' He eyed Roz curiously. 'I suppose he's told you everything.'

'I shouldn't think so,' she said cheerfully, walking round the back of the car. 'I only learnt half an hour ago that his ex-wife's name was Sally and you married her. So, on that basis, there must be an awful lot more still to come.'

'I was referring,' he said sourly, 'to the numerous prosecutions he's about to face when this little farce is over and I take him down the nick.'

'Oh, them.' She gave a dismissive wave. 'Bits of paper, that's all they are.'

Geoff, not altogether happy with his new marital arrangements, watched her amused exchange of glances with Hal and wondered why other people, infinitely less deserving than he, had all the luck. He listened to Hal's instructions for him with a hand pressed to his queasy stomach.

Roz had expected something seedy and run-down like the Wells-Fargo office: instead they walked into a clean, brightly painted reception with an efficient-looking receptionist behind an efficient-looking desk. Someone, she thought, had spent a great deal of money on STC Security. But who? And where had it come from?

Hal favoured the receptionist with his most charming smile. 'Hal Hawksley. Mr Hayes is expecting me.'

'Oh, yes.' She smiled in return. 'He said to show you straight in.' She leaned forward and pointed down the corridor. 'Third door on the left. Perhaps your friends would like to take a seat out here?' She indicated some chairs in the corner.

'Thank you, miss,' said Geoff. 'Don't mind if I do.' He hefted one as he passed and took it with him down the corridor.

'No,' she called, 'I didn't mean take one away.'

He beamed back at her as Hal and Roz disappeared through the third door without knocking and he stationed himself on the chair in the middle of the closed doorway. 'Very comfortable, I must say.' He lit a cigarette and watched, with some amusement, as she picked up the phone and put through a flustered call.

On the other side of the door, Stewart Hayes replaced the receiver. 'I gather from Lisa that you have a minder, Mr Hawksley. Would he be a policeman by any chance?'

'He would.'

'Ah.' He clasped his hands on his desk, apparently unconcerned. 'Sit down, please.' He smiled at Roz and gestured towards a chair.

Fascinated by him, she took it. This was not the man who had tried to strangle her. He was younger, better looking, bluff and friendly like his voice. The brother, she thought, recalling the photographs on the sideboard. He had his father's smile, with all its sincerity, his father's old-world charm, and under different circumstances she would have found him easy to like. Only his eyes, pale and carefully guarded, implied he had something to hide. Hal remained standing.

The smile embraced them both. 'OK, now perhaps you'd like to explain what you said over the telephone. I'll be honest with you' – his tone suggested he was about to be the exact opposite – 'I don't understand why I've been given half an hour to buy a restaurant *from* someone I've never met *for* someone I've never heard of, and all because a self-confessed murderess wants to contest her father's will.'

Hal glanced about the well-appointed office. 'Expensive,' he said. 'You and your brother are doing well.' He fastened speculative eyes on Hayes. 'Your father thinks you're on the breadline.'

Hayes gave a slight frown but didn't say anything.

'So how much does Crew pay for the baseball-bat treatment? It's risky so it won't come cheap.'

The pale eyes showed faint amusement. 'You've lost me, I'm afraid.'

'Your brother was very easy to identify, Hayes. Photographs of him litter your father's sideboard. But then Crew obviously never warned you about the loose cannon on board. Or perhaps you should have warned him. Does he know your father lived next door to Olive Martin?' He saw the other's incomprehension and nodded to Roz. 'This lady is writing a book about her. Crew was Olive's solicitor, I was her arresting officer, and your father was her neighbour. Miss Leigh has visited us all and she recognized your brother from his snapshot. It is a much smaller world than you ever imagined.'

There was a tiny shift in the pale eyes, a flicker of annoyance. 'Mistaken identity. You'll never prove anything. It's your word against his and he was in Sheffield all last week.'

Hal shrugged well-feigned indifference. 'The window is closing. I came with a genuine offer.' He placed his hands on the desk and leaned forward aggressively. 'I think it runs something like this. Crew has been using Robert Martin's money to buy up bankrupt businesses cheap while he waits for the market to recover, but time's running out on him. Amber's child is not as dead and buried as he thought, and Olive is about to become a *cause célèbre* when Miss Leigh proves her innocent. Either she or her nephew, whoever gets in first, will demand a reckoning of Robert Martin's executor, namely Crew. But the recession has dragged on rather longer than he thought it would and he's in danger of being caught with his hands in the till. He needs to shift some property to make up the shortfall in his books.' He raised an eyebrow. 'What plans are there for the corner of Wenceslas Street, I wonder? A supermarket? Flats? Offices? He needs the Poacher to clinch the deal. I'm offering it to him. Today.'

Hayes wasn't so easily intimidated. 'The way I hear it, Hawksley, your restaurant is about to close anyway. When it does, it will become a liability to you. At which point it will not be you who dictates terms, but whoever is willing to take it off your hands.'

Hal grinned and backed off. 'I'd say that rather depends on who goes down the chute first. Crew faces total extinction if his misappropriation of the Martin money comes to light before my bank decides to foreclose on the Poacher. Crew's taking a hell of a risk if he's backing me to lose.' He nodded to the telephone. 'He can save himself by clinching a deal on the Poacher today. Talk to him.'

Hayes pondered for a moment, then transferred his gaze to Roz. 'I presume you have a tape-recorder in your handbag, Miss Leigh. Would you oblige me by letting me have a look?'

Roz glanced up at Hal, and he nodded. She placed the bag with a bad grace on the desk in front of her.

'Thank you,' said Hayes politely. He opened it and removed the tape-recorder, making a cursory examination of the remaining contents of the handbag before snapping the recorder open and removing the cassette. He pulled the tape from between the rollers and cut it into pieces with a pair of scissors, then he stood up. 'You first, Hawksley. Let's just make sure there are no other little surprises.' He ran expert hands over Hal, then did the same with Roz. 'Good.' He gestured towards the door. 'Tell your minder to move his chair back to Reception and wait there.'

He resumed his seat and waited while Hal relayed the message. After three minutes he used the telephone to establish that Wyatt was out of earshot.

'Now,' he said thoughtfully, 'there seem to be various courses open to me. One is to take you up on your offer.' He picked up a ruler and flexed it between his hands. 'I'm not inclined to do that. You could have put the Poacher on the market at any time in the last six weeks but you didn't, and this sudden urge of yours to sell makes me nervous.' He paused for a moment. 'Two, I can leave things to follow their natural course. The law is a joke and a slow joke at that, and there's only a fifty-fifty chance that Peter Crew's manipulations of Robert Martin's estate will surface before you sink.' He bent the ruler as far as it would go without breaking, then released it abruptly. 'I'm not inclined to do that either. Fifty-fifty is too close to call.' The pale eyes hardened. 'Three, and in many ways this is the most attractive, I can wish an unfortunate accident on the pair of you, thereby killing two birds with one stone.' He flicked a glance at Roz. 'Your death, Miss Leigh, would put Olive and this book you're writing, temporarily at least, on a back burner, and yours, Hawksley, would ensure the Poacher coming on the market. A neat solution, don't you think?'

'Very neat,' agreed Hal. 'But you're not going to do that either. There's still the child in Australia, after all.'

Hayes gave a faint laugh. An echo of his father.

'So what are you going to do?'

'Give you what you came for.'

Hal frowned. 'Which is?'

'Proof that you were framed.' He pulled open a drawer in his desk and removed a transparent polythene folder. Holding it by its top corners he shook the contents – a page of headed notepaper, showing creases where it had once been crumpled – on to his desk. The printed address was a house in one of the more expensive parts of Southampton and written across the page in Crew's handwriting were a series of short notes:

Re: Poacher	Cost £s
Pre-culture bad meat, rat excrement etc	1,000
Key b/door + guaranteed exit/France	1,000
Advance for set-up	5,000
If E H prosecution successful	5,000
Poacher foreclosure	80,000?
SUB-TOTAL	92,000
Site offer	750,000
Less Poacher	92,000
Less 1 Wenceslas St	60,000
Less Newby's	73,000
TOTAL	525,000

'It's genuine,' said Hayes, seeing Hal's scepticism. 'Crew's home address, Crew's handwriting' – he tapped the side of the note with his ruler – 'and his fingerprints. It's enough to get you off the hook but whether it's enough to convict Crew I don't know. That's your problem, not mine.'

'Where did you get it?'

But Hayes merely smiled and shook his head. 'I'm an ex-soldier. I like fall-back positions. Let's just say it came into my possession and, realizing its importance, I passed it on to you.'

Hal wondered if Crew knew the sort of man he had hired. Had this been intended for later blackmail? 'I don't get it,' he said frankly. 'Crew is bound to implicate you. So will I. So will Miss Leigh. One way or another you and your brother will get done. Why make it easy for us?'

Hayes didn't answer directly. 'I'm cutting my losses, Hawksley, and giving you your restaurant back. Be grateful.'

'Like hell, I'll be grateful,' said Hal angrily. His eyes narrowed suspiciously. 'Who's behind this foreclosure racket? You or Crew?'

'There's no racket. Foreclosures are a fact of life at the moment,' said the other. 'Anyone with a little capital can acquire property cheaply. Mr Crew was part of a small perfectly legal syndicate. Unfortunately, he used money that didn't belong to him.'

'So you run the syndicate?'

Hayes didn't answer.

'No racket, my arse,' said Hal explosively. 'The Poacher was never going to come on the market yet you still bought up the properties on either side.'

Hayes flexed the ruler again. 'You'd have sold eventually. Restaurants are appallingly vulnerable.' He gave a slight smile. 'Consider what would have happened if Crew had kept his nerve and sat it out till after your prosecution.' His eyes hardened. 'Consider what would have happened if my brother had told me about the approach Crew made to him. You and I would never have had this conversation for the simple reason that you would not have known who to have it with.'

The flesh crept on Hal's neck. 'The hygiene scam was going to happen anyway?'

The ruler, bent beyond endurance, snapped abruptly. Hayes smiled. 'Restaurants are appallingly vulnerable,' he said again. 'I repeat. Be grateful. If you are, the Poacher will flourish.'

'Which is another way of saying we must keep our mouths shut about your involvement.'

'Of course.' He looked almost surprised, as if the question went without asking. 'Because next time, the fire won't be confined to a chip pan, and you' – his pale eyes rested on Roz – 'and your lady friend won't be so lucky. My brother's pride was hurt. He's itching to have another go at the pair of you.' He pointed to the piece of notepaper. 'You can do what you like with Crew. I don't admire men without principle. He's a lawyer. He had a duty to a dead man's estate and he abused it.'

Hal, rather shaken, picked up the page by its corner and tucked it into Roz's handbag. 'You're no better, Hayes. You abused Crew's confidence when you told your father about Amber's child. But for that we'd never have put Crew in the frame.' He waited while Roz stood up and walked to the door. 'And I'll make damn sure he knows that when the police arrest him.'

Hayes was amused. 'Crew won't talk.'

'What's to stop him?'

He drew the broken ruler across his throat. 'The same thing that will stop you, Hawksley. Fear.' The pale eyes raked Roz from head to toe. 'But in Crew's case, it's his grandchildren he loves.'

Geoff followed them out on to the pavement. 'OK,' he ordered, 'give. What the hell's going on here?'

Hal looked at Roz's pale face. 'We need a drink.'

'Oh, no, you don't,' said Geoff aggressively. 'I've paid my dues, Hal, now you pay yours.'

Hal gripped him fiercely above the elbow, digging his

fingers into the soft flesh. 'Keep your voice down, you cretin,' he muttered. 'There's a man in there who would take out your liver, eat it in front of you, and then start on your kidneys. And he'd smile while he was doing it. Where's the nearest pub?'

Not until they were settled in a tight corner of the saloon, with empty tables all around them, was Hal prepared to speak. He delivered the story in clipped, staccato sentences, emphasizing Crew's role but referring to the intruders at the Poacher only as hired thugs. He finished by removing the note from Roz's handbag and laying it carefully on the table between them. 'I want this bastard screwed, Geoff. Don't even think about letting him worm his way out of it.'

Wyatt was sceptical. 'It's not much, is it?'

'It'll do.'

Wyatt slipped the page into his notebook and tucked it into his jacket pocket. 'So where does STC Security fit in?'

'It doesn't. Hayes got hold of that note for me. That's the extent of his firm's involvement.'

'Ten minutes ago he was going to eat my liver.'

'I was thirsty.'

Wyatt shrugged. 'You're giving me precious little to work with. I can't even guarantee you'll win the Environmental Health prosecution. Crew's bound to deny having anything to do with it.'

There was a silence.

'He's right,' said Roz abruptly, removing a packet of Tampax from her bag.

Hal grasped the hand holding the box and pressed it firmly to the table. 'No, Roz,' he said softly. 'Believe it or not, I care more about you than I do about the Poacher or about abstract justice.'

She nodded. 'I know, Hawksley,' Her eyes smiled into his. 'The trouble is, I care about *you*, too. Which means we're in a bit of a fix. You want to save me and I want to save the Poacher, and the two would seem to be mutually exclusive.'

She started to ease her hands from under his. 'So one of us must win this argument, and it's going to be me because this has nothing to do with abstract justice and everything to do with my peace of mind. I shall feel much happier with Stewart Hayes behind bars.' She shook her head as his hands moved to smother hers again. 'I won't be responsible for you losing your restaurant, Hal. You've gone through hell for it, and you can't give it up now.'

But Hal was no Rupert to be browbeaten or cajoled into doing what Roz wanted. 'No,' he said again. 'We're not playing intellectual games here. What Hayes said was *real*. And he's not threatening to kill you, Roz. He's threatening to maim you.' He lifted one hand to her face. 'Men like him don't kill because they don't need to. They cripple or they disfigure, because a live, broken victim is a more potent encouragement to others than a dead one.'

'But if he's convicted—' she began.

'You're being naïve again,' he cut in gently, smoothing the hair from her face. 'Even if he is convicted, which I doubt – ex-Army, first offence, hearsay evidence, Crew denying everything – he won't go to jail for any length of time. The worst that will happen will be twelve months for conspiracy to defraud, of which he'll serve six. More likely he will be given a suspended sentence. It wasn't Stewart who broke into the Poacher with a baseball bat, remember, it was his brother, and you will have to stand up in court and say that.' His eyes were insistent. 'I'm a realist, Roz. We'll go for Crew and raise enough doubts to get the Health charges lifted. After that' – he shrugged – 'I'll gamble that Hayes can be trusted to leave the Poacher alone.'

She was silent for a moment or two. 'Would you act differently if you'd never met me and I wasn't involved? And don't lie to me, Hal, please.'

He nodded. 'Yes,' he admitted. 'I would act differently. But you *are* involved, so the question doesn't arise.'

'OK.' She relaxed her hands under his and smiled. 'Thank you. I feel much happier now.'

'You agree.' Relieved, he lessened his pressure slightly and she seized the opportunity to snatch the Tampax box out of his grasp.

'No,' she said, 'I don't.' She opened the box, removed some truncated cardboard tubes and upended it to disgorge a miniature voice-activated dictaphone. 'With luck' – she turned to Geoff Wyatt – 'this will have enough on it to convict Hayes. It was at full volume, sitting on his desk, so it should have caught him.'

She rewound the tape for a second or two and then pressed 'play'. Hal's voice was muffled by distance: '. . . *another way of saying we must keep our mouths shut about your involvement with the Poacher?'*

Hayes's, clear as a bell. *'Of course. Because next time, the fire won't be confined to the chip pan, and you and your lady friend won't be so lucky. My brother's pride was hurt. He's itching to have another go at the pair of you.'*

Roz switched it off and pushed it across the table towards Wyatt. 'Will it do any good?'

'If there's more like that, it will certainly help with Hal's prosecution, as long as you're prepared to give evidence to support it.'

'I am.'

He cast a glance at his friend, saw the tension on the other's face and turned back to Roz. 'But Hal's right in everything he's said, assuming I've understood the gist correctly. We *are* talking abstract justice here.' He picked up the dictaphone. 'At the end of the day – whatever sentence this man gets – if he still wants to revenge himself on you, he will. And there's nothing the police will be able to do to protect you. So? Are you sure you want me to take this?'

'I'm sure.'

Wyatt looked at Hal again and gave a helpless shrug. 'Sorry, old man. I did my best, but it looks like you've caught a tigress this time.'

Hal gave his baritone chuckle. 'Don't say it, Geoff, because I already know.'

But Wyatt said it anyway. 'You lucky, bloody sod.'

Olive sat hunched over her table, working on a new sculpture. Eve and her faces and her baby had collapsed under the weight of a fist, leaving the pencil pointing heavenward like an accusing finger. The Chaplain regarded the new piece thoughtfully. A bulky shape, roughly human and lying on its back, seemed to be struggling from its clay base. Strange, he thought, how Olive, with so little skill, made these figures work. 'What are you sculpting now?'

'MAN.'

He could, he thought, have predicted that. He watched the fingers roll a thick sausage of clay and plant it upright on the base at the figure's head. 'Adam?' he suggested. He had the feeling she was playing a game with him. There had been a surge of sudden activity when he entered her room, as if she had been waiting for him to break hours of stillness.

'Cain.' She selected another pencil and laid it across the top of the clay sausage, parallel with the recumbent man, pressing it down till it was held firmly. 'Faustus. Don Giovanni. Does it matter?'

'Yes, it does,' he said sharply. 'Not all men sell their souls to the devil, any more than all women are two-faced.'

Olive smiled to herself and cut a piece of string from a ball on the table. She made a loop in one end and fastened the other round the tip of the pencil so that the string hung down over the figure's head. With infinite care, she tightened the loop about a matchstick. 'Well?' she demanded.

The Chaplain frowned. 'I don't know. The gallows?'

She set the matchstick swinging. 'Or the sword of Damocles. It amounts to the same thing when Lucifer owns your soul.'

He perched on the edge of the table and offered her a cigarette. 'It's not Man in general, is it?' he said, flicking his lighter. 'It's someone specific. Am I right?'

'Maybe.'

'Who?'

She fished a letter from her pocket and handed it to him. He spread the single page on the table and read it. It was a standard letter, personalized on a word processor, and very brief.

Dear Miss Martin,

Please be advised that unforeseen circumstances have obliged Mr Peter Crew to take extended leave from this practice. During his absence his clients' affairs will be covered by his partners. Please be assured of our continued assistance.

Yours etc.

The Chaplain looked up. 'I don't understand.'

Olive inhaled deeply then blew a stream of smoke towards the matchstick. It spiraled wildly before slipping from the noose and striking the clay forehead. 'My solicitor's been arrested.'

Startled, he looked at the clay figure. He didn't bother to ask if she was sure. He knew the efficiency of the cell telegraph as well as she did. 'What for?'

'Wickedness.' She stubbed her cigarette into the clay. 'MAN was born to it. Even you, Chaplain.' She peeped at him to watch his reaction.

He chuckled. 'You're probably right. But I do my best to fight it, you know.'

She took another of his cigarettes. 'I shall miss you,' she said unexpectedly.

'When?'

'When they let me out.'

He looked at her with a puzzled smile. 'That's a long way off. We've years yet.'

But she shook her head and mashed the clay into a ball with the dog end in the middle. 'You never asked me who Eve was.'

The game again, he thought. 'I didn't need to, Olive. I knew.'

She smiled scornfully to herself. 'Yes, you would.' She examined him out of the corner of her eye. 'Did you work it out for yourself?' she asked. 'Or did God tell you? Look, my son, Olive strikes her reflection in the clay. Now help her to come to terms with her own duplicity. Well, don't worry, either way I shall remember what you did for me when I get out.'

What did she want from him? Encouragement that she *would* get out, or rescuing from her lies? He sighed inwardly. Really, it would all be so much easier if he liked her, but he didn't. And *that* was his wickedness.

NINETEEN

Olive regarded Roz with deep suspicion. Contentment had brought a glow to the other woman's usually pale cheeks. 'You look different,' she said in an accusing tone as if what she saw displeased her.

Roz shook her head. 'No. Everything's the same.' Lies *were* safer sometimes. She was afraid Olive would regard her moving in with the police officer who arrested her as a betrayal. 'Did you get my message last Monday night?'

Olive was at her most unattractive, unwashed hair hanging limply about her colourless face, a smear of tomato ketchup ground into the front of her shift, the smell of her sweat almost unbearable in the small room. She vibrated with irritation, her forehead set in a permanent scowl, ready, it seemed to Roz, to reject anything that was said to her. She didn't answer.

'Is something wrong?' Roz asked evenly.

'I don't want to see you any more.'

Roz turned her pencil in her fingers. 'Why not?'

'I don't have to give a reason.'

'It would be polite,' said Roz in the same even tone. 'I've invested a great deal of time, energy, and affection in you. I thought we were friends.'

Olive's lip curled. 'Friends,' she hissed scathingly. 'We're not friends. You're Miss Wonderful making money out of doing her Lady Muck bit and I'm the poor sap who's being exploited.' She splayed her hands across the table top and tried to get up. 'I don't want you to write your book.'

'Because you'd rather be treated with awe in here than

laughed at outside.' Roz shook her head. 'You're a fool, Olive. And a coward as well. I thought you had more guts.'

Olive pursed her fat lips as she struggled to rise. 'I'm not listening,' she said childishly. 'You're trying to make me change my mind.'

'Of course I am.' She rested her cheek against one raised hand. 'I shall write the book whether you want me to or not. I'm not afraid of you, you see. You can instruct a solicitor to take out an injunction to stop me, but he won't succeed because I shall argue that you're innocent, and a court will uphold my right to publish in the interests of natural justice.'

Olive slumped back on to her chair. 'I'll write to a Civil Liberties group. They'll support me.'

'Not when they find out I'm trying to get you released, they won't. They'll support *me*.'

'The Court of Human Rights, then. I'll say what you're doing is an invasion of my privacy.'

'Go ahead. You'll make me a fortune. Everyone will buy the book to find out what the fuss is all about. And if it's argued in a court, whichever one it is, I shall make damn sure this time that the evidence is heard.'

'What evidence?'

'The evidence that proves you didn't do it.'

Olive slammed a meaty fist on to the table. 'I did do it.'

'No, you didn't.'

'I *did*!' roared the fat woman.

'You did not,' said Roz, her eyes flashing with anger. 'When will you face up to the fact that your mother is dead, you silly woman.' She banged the table in her turn. 'She's not there for you any more, Olive, and she never will be, however long you hide in here.'

Two fat tears rolled down Olive's cheeks. 'I don't like you.'

Roz continued brutally. 'You came home, saw what your precious lover had done, and went into shock. And God knows, I don't blame you.' She took the mortuary photographs of Gwen and Amber from her bag and slapped them on the table in front of Olive. 'You adored your mother, didn't you? You always adore the people who need you.'

Olive's anger was enormous. 'That's *crap*, bloody fucking *crap!*'

Roz shook her head. 'I needed you. That's how I know.'

Olive's lip trembled. 'You wanted to know how it felt to kill someone, that's all you needed me for.'

'No.' Roz reached across and took a large, soft hand in hers. 'I needed someone to love. You're very easy to love, Olive.'

The woman tore the hand away and clamped it across her face. 'No one loves me,' she whispered. 'No one's ever loved me.'

'You're wrong,' said Roz firmly. 'I love you. Sister Bridget loves you. And we are not going to abandon you the minute you get out. You must trust us.' She closed her mind on the insidious voice that murmured warnings against a long-term commitment she could never keep and against well-meant lies that could so easily rebound on her. 'Tell me about Amber,' she went on gently. 'Tell me why your mother needed you.'

A sigh of surrender shuddered through the huge frame. 'She wanted her own way all the time, and if she didn't get it she made life hell for everyone. She told lies about things people did to her, spread awful stories, even hurt people sometimes. She poured boiling water down my mother's arm once to punish her, so we used to give in just to make life easy. She was as nice as pie as long as everyone did what she wanted.' She licked the tears from her lips. 'She never took responsibility, you see, but it got worse after the baby was born. Mum said she stopped maturing.'

'To compensate herself?'

'No, to excuse herself.' She twined her fingers in the front of her dress. 'Children get away with behaving badly so Amber went on behaving like a child. She was never told off for getting pregnant. We were too afraid of how she would react.' She wiped her nose with the back of her hand. 'Mum had made up her mind to take her to a psychiatrist. She thought Amber had schizophrenia.' She sighed heavily. 'Then they were killed and it didn't matter any more.'

Roz passed her a Kleenex and waited while she blew her nose. 'Why did she never behave badly at school?'

'She did,' said Olive flatly, 'if people teased her or took her things without asking. I used to have to get quite angry to stop them doing it, but most of the time I made sure no one got on her bad side. She was a lovely person as long as she wasn't crossed. Really,' she insisted, 'a lovely person.'

'The two faces of Eve.'

'Mum certainly thought so.' She took the cigarette packet out of Roz's open briefcase and stripped away the cellophane. 'I used to keep her with me when she wasn't in class. She didn't mind that. The older girls treated her like a pet and that made her feel special. She had no friends of her own age.' She pulled some cigarettes on to the table and selected one.

'How did she hold down a job? You weren't there to protect her then.'

'She didn't. She never lasted anywhere longer than a month. Most of the time she stayed at home with Mum. She made Mum's life a misery.'

'What about Glitzy?'

Olive struck a match and lit the cigarette. 'The same. She'd only done three weeks and she was already talking about leaving. There was some trouble with the other girls. Amber got one of them sacked or something. I can't remember now. Anyway, that's when Mum said enough was enough, and she'd have to see a psychiatrist.'

Roz sat in thoughtful silence for some moments. 'I know who your lover was,' she said abruptly. 'I know that you spent Sundays at the Belvedere in Farraday Street and that you signed in as Mr and Mrs Lewis. I've had his photograph identified by the owner of the Belvedere and by the receptionist at Wells-Fargo. I think he abandoned you in a hotel the night of your birthday when you told him you had aborted his baby, and that he went straight to Leven Road to have it out with Amber and your mother whom he regarded as jointly responsible for the murder of the son or daughter he had always wanted. I think your father was out of the house that night and that the whole thing got out of hand. I think you came home a long time afterwards, discovered the bodies, and went to pieces because you thought it was all your fault.' She took one of Olive's hands in hers again and squeezed it tightly.

Olive closed her eyes and wept quietly, her soft skin caressing Roz's fingers. 'No,' she said at last, releasing the hand. 'It didn't happen like that. I wish it had. At least I'd know then why I did what I did.' Her eyes were curiously unfocused as if they were turned inwards upon herself. 'We didn't plan anything for my birthday,' she said. 'We couldn't. It wasn't a Sunday and Sundays were the only days we could ever be together. That was when his sister-in-law came over to give him some time away from his wife. They both thought he spent the day at the British Legion.' She smiled but there was no humour in it. 'Poor Edward. He was so afraid they'd find out and turn him off without a penny. It was her house and her money and it made him miserable. Puddleglum was such a good name for him, especially when he wore his silly wig. He looked just like a marshwiggle out of Narnia, tall and skinny and hairy.' She sighed. 'It was supposed to be a disguise, you know, in case anyone saw him. To me, it just looked funny. I liked him much better bald.' She sighed again. 'The Silver Chair was Amber's and my favourite book when we were children.'

Roz had guessed. 'And you signed in as Mr and Mrs Lewis because it was C. S. Lewis who wrote it. Were you afraid of Mrs Clarke finding out, or your parents?'

'We were afraid of everyone but mostly of Amber. Jealousy was a disease with her.'

'Did she know about your abortion?'

Olive shook her head. 'Only my mother knew. I never told Edward and I certainly didn't tell Amber. *She* was the only one who was allowed to have sex in our house. She did, too. All the time. Mum had to force her to take the pill every night so she didn't get pregnant again.' She pulled a long face. 'Mum was furious when I fell. We both knew Amber would go mad.'

'Is that why you had the abortion?'

'Probably. It seemed the only sensible solution at the time. I regret it now.'

'You'll have other chances.'

'I doubt it.'

'So what did happen that night?' asked Roz after a moment or two.

Olive stared at her unblinkingly through the smoke from her cigarette. 'Amber found the birthday present Edward had given me. It was well hidden but she used to pry into everything.' Her mouth twisted. 'I was always having to put things back that she'd taken. People thought I was the snooper.' She encircled her wrist with finger and thumb. 'It was an identity bracelet with a tiny silver-chair charm on it. He'd had the tag inscribed: U.R.N.A.R.N.I.A. Do you get it? You are Narnia, Narnia being heaven.' She smiled self-consciously. 'I thought it was wonderful.'

'He was very fond of you.' It was a statement, not a question.

'I made him feel young again.' Tears squeezed from between the bald lids. 'We really didn't harm anyone, just conducted a quiet little affair now and then on Sundays which gave us both something to look forward to.' The tears flowed down her cheeks. 'I wish I hadn't done it now but it was nice to feel special. I never had before and I was so jealous of Amber. She had a lot of boyfriends. She used to take them upstairs. Mum was too frightened of her to say anything.' She sobbed loudly. 'They always laughed at me. I hate being laughed at.'

What a dreadful household it must have been, thought Roz, with each one desperately seeking love but never finding it. Would they have recognized it, anyway, if they had? She waited until Olive had composed herself a little. 'Did your mother know it was Edward?'

'No. I told her it was someone at work. We were very careful. Edward was my father's best friend. It would have devastated everyone if they'd known what we were doing.' She fell silent. 'Well, of course, it did devastate them in the end.'

'They found out.'

The sad head nodded. 'Amber guessed the minute she found the bracelet. I should have known she would. Silver chair, Narnia. The bracelet had to be from Puddleglum.' She sucked in a lungful of smoke.

Roz watched her for a moment. 'What did she do?' she asked when Olive didn't go on.

'What she always did when she was angry. Started a fight. She kept pulling my hair, I remember that. And screaming. Mum and Dad had to tear us apart. I ended up in a tug of war with my father gripping my wrists and tugging one way while Amber tugged my hair the other. All hell broke loose then. She kept yelling that I was having an affair with Mr Clarke.' She stared wretchedly at the table. 'My mother looked as if she was going to be sick – nobody likes the idea of old men getting excited about young girls – I used to see it in the eyes of the woman at the Belvedere.' She turned the cigarette in her fingers. 'But now, you know, I think it was because Mum knew that Edward and my father were doing it as well. That's what really made her sick. Makes *me* sick now.'

'Why didn't you deny it?'

Olive puffed unhappily on her cigarette. 'There was no point. She knew Amber was telling the truth. I suppose it's a kind of instinctive thing. You learn a fact and lots of other little bits and pieces, which didn't make sense at the time, suddenly slot into place. Anyway, all three of them started screeching at me then, my mother in shock, my father in fury.' She shrugged. 'I'd never seen Dad so angry. Mum let out about the abortion and he kept slapping my face and calling me a slut. And Amber kept screaming that he was jealous because he loved Edward, too, and it was so awful' – her eyes welled – 'that I left.' There was a rather comical expression on her face. 'And when I came back the next day there was blood everywhere and Mum and Amber were dead.'

'You stayed out all night?'

Olive nodded. 'And most of the morning.'

'But that's good,' said Roz leaning forward. 'We can prove that. Where did you go?'

'I walked to the beach.' She stared at her hands. 'I was going to kill myself. I wish I had now. I just sat there all night and thought about it instead.'

'Did anyone see you?'

'No. I didn't want to be seen. When it got light I hid behind a dinghy every time I heard someone coming.'

'What time did you get back?'

'About noon. I hadn't had anything to eat and I was hungry.'

'Did you speak to anyone?'

Olive sighed wearily. 'Nobody saw me. If they had I wouldn't be here.'

'How did you get into the house? Did you have a key?'

'Yes.'

'Why?' demanded Roz sharply. 'You said you left. I assumed you just walked out as you were.'

Olive's eyes widened. 'I knew you wouldn't believe me,' she howled. 'No one believes me when I tell the truth.' She started to cry again.

'I do believe you,' said Roz firmly. 'I just want to get it straight.'

'I went to my room first and got my things. I only went out because they were all making so much noise.' She screwed her face in distress. 'My father was weeping. It was horrible.'

'OK. Go on. You're back at the house.'

'I let myself in and went down to the kitchen to get some food. I stepped in all the blood before I even knew it was there.' She looked at the photograph of her mother and the ready tears sprang into her eyes afresh. 'I really don't like to think about it too much. It makes me sick when I think about it.' Her lower lip wobbled violently.

'OK,' said Roz easily, 'let's concentrate on something else. What made you stay? Why didn't you run out into the road and call for help?'

Olive mopped at her eyes. 'I couldn't move,' she said simply. 'I wanted to, but I couldn't. I just stood there thinking how ashamed my mother would be when people saw her without her clothes on.' Her lip kept wobbling like some grotesque toddler's. 'I felt so ill. I wanted to sit down but there wasn't a chair.' She held her hand to her mouth and swallowed convulsively. 'And then Mrs Clarke started banging on the kitchen window. She kept screaming that God would never forgive my wickedness, and there was dribble coming out of her mouth.' A shudder ran through the big shoulders. 'I knew I had to shut her up because she was making it all so much worse. So I picked up the rolling pin and ran across to the back door.' She sighed. 'But I fell over and she wasn't there any more anyway.'

'Is that when you called the police?'

'No.' The wet face worked horribly. 'I can't remember it all now. I went mad for a bit because I had their blood all over me and I kept scraping my hands to clean them. But everything I touched was bloody.' Her eyes widened at the memory. 'I've always been so clumsy and the floor was slippery. I kept stumbling over them and disturbing them and then I had to touch them to put them back again and there was more blood on me.' The sorrowful eyes flooded again. 'And I thought, this is all my fault. If I'd never been born this would never have happened. I sat down for a long time because I felt sick.'

Roz looked at the bowed head in bewilderment. 'But why didn't you tell the police all this?'

She raised drowned blue eyes to Roz's. 'I was going to, but nobody would talk to me. They all thought I'd done it, you see. And all the time I was thinking how it was all going to come out, about Edward and me, and Edward and my father, and the abortion, and Amber, and her baby, and I thought how much less embarrassing it would be for everyone if I said I did it.'

Roz kept her voice deliberately steady. 'Who did you think had done it?'

Olive looked miserable. 'I didn't think about that for ages.' She hunched her shoulders as if defending herself. 'And then I knew my father had done it and they'd find me guilty whatever happened because he was the only one who could save me.' She plucked at her lips. 'And after that, it was quite a relief just to say what everyone wanted me to say. I didn't want to go home, you see, not with Mum dead, and Edward next door and everyone knowing. I couldn't possibly have gone home.'

'How did you know your father had done it?'

A whimper of pure pain, like a wounded animal's, crooned from Olive's mouth. 'Because Mr Crew was so beastly to me.' Sorrow poured in floods down her cheeks. 'He used to come to our house sometimes and he'd pat me on the shoulder and say: "How's Olive?" But in the police station' – she buried her face in her hands – 'he held a handkerchief to his mouth to stop himself being sick and stood on the other side of the room and said: "Don't say anything to me or the police, or I won't be able to help you." I knew then.'

Roz frowned. 'How? I don't understand.'

'Because Dad was the only person who knew I wasn't there, but he never said a word to Mr Crew before, or to the police afterwards. Dad must have done it or he'd have tried to save me. He let me go to prison because he was a coward.' She sobbed loudly. 'And then he died and left his money to Amber's child when he could have left a letter, saying I was innocent.' She beat her hands against her knees. 'What did it matter once he was dead?'

Roz took the cigarette from Olive's fingers and stood it on the table. 'Why didn't you tell the police you thought it was your father who had done it? Sergeant Hawksley would have listened to you. He already suspected your father.'

The fat woman stared at the table. 'I don't want to tell you.'

'You must, Olive.'

'You'll laugh.'

'Tell me.'

'I was hungry.'

Roz shook her head in perplexity. 'I don't understand.'

'The sergeant brought me a sandwich and said I could have a proper dinner when we'd finished the statement.' Her eyes welled again. 'I hadn't eaten all day and I was so hungry,' she wailed. 'It was quicker when I said what they wanted me to say and then I got my dinner.' She wrung her hands. 'People will laugh, won't they?'

Roz wondered why it had never occurred to her that Olive's insatiable craving for food might have been a contributory factor in her confession. Mrs Hopwood had described her as a compulsive eater and stress would have piled on the agonies of the wretched girl's hunger. 'No,' she said firmly, 'no one will laugh. But why did you insist on pleading guilty at your trial? You could have made a fight of it then. You'd had time to think and get over the shock.'

Olive wiped her eyes. 'It was too late. I'd confessed. I had nothing to fight with except diminished responsibility and I wasn't going to let Mr Crew call me a psychopath. I hate Mr Crew.'

'But if you'd told someone the truth they might have believed you. You've told me and I've believed you.'

Olive shook her head. 'I've told you nothing,' she said simply. 'Everything you know you've found out for yourself. That's why you believe it.' Her eyes flooded again. 'I did try at the beginning, when I first came to prison. I told the Chaplain but he doesn't like me and thought I was telling lies. I'd confessed, you see, and only the guilty confess. The psychiatrists were the most frightening. I thought if I denied the crime and didn't show any remorse, they'd say I was sociopathic and send me to Broadmoor.'

Roz looked at the bent head with compassion. Olive had never really stood a chance. And who was to blame at the end of the day? Mr Crew? Robert Martin? The police? Poor Gwen even, whose dependence on her daughter had mapped Olive's life. Michael Jackson had said it all: 'She was one of those people you only think about when you want something done and then you remember them with relief because you know they'll do it.' It had never been Amber who set out to please, she thought, only Olive, and as a result she had grown completely dependent herself. With no one to tell her what to do she had taken the line of least resistance.

'You'll be hearing this officially in the next few days but I'm damned if you should have to wait for it. Mr Crew is on bail at the moment, charged with embezzlement of your father's money and conspiracy to defraud. He may also be charged with conspiracy to murder.' There was a long pause before Olive looked up.

The strange awareness was back in her eyes, a look of triumphant confirmation that made the hair prickle on the back of Roz's neck. She thought of Sister Bridget's simple assertion of *her* truth: *You were chosen, Roz, and I wasn't*. And Olive's truth? What was Olive's truth?

'I know already.' Idly Olive removed a pin from the front of her dress. 'Prison grapevine,' she explained. 'Mr Crew hired the Hayes brothers to do over Sergeant Hawksley's restaurant. You were there, and you and the Sergeant got beaten up. I'm sorry about that but I'm not sorry about anything else. I never liked Mr Hayes much. He always ignored me and talked to Amber.' She stuck the pin into the tabletop. Bits of dried clay and wax still clung to the head.

Roz arched an eyebrow at the pin. 'It's superstitious rubbish, Olive.'

'You said it works if you believe in it.'

Roz shrugged. 'I was joking.'

'*The Encyclopaedia Britannica* doesn't joke.' Olive chanted in a sing-song voice: 'Page 96, volume 25, general heading: Occultism.' She clapped her hands excitedly like an over-boisterous child and raised her voice to a shout. ' "*Witchcraft worked in Salem because the persons involved believed in it.*" ' She saw the frown of alarm on Roz's face. 'It's all nonsense,' she said calmly. 'Will Mr Crew be convicted?'

'I don't know. He's claiming that your father gave him the go-ahead, as executor, to invest the money while the searches were made for your nephew, and the bugger is' – she smiled grimly – 'if the property market takes off again, which it probably will, his investments look very healthy.' Of the other charges, only the conspiracy to defraud Hal of the Poacher had any chance of sticking, purely because Stewart Hayes's brother, a far weaker character than Stewart, had collapsed under police questioning. 'He's denying everything, but the police seem fairly optimistic they can pin assault charges on both him and the Hayes boys. I'd give anything to get him for negligence where your case was concerned. Was he one of the people you tried to tell the truth to?'

'No,' said Olive regretfully. 'There was no point. He'd been Dad's solicitor for years. He'd never have believed Dad had done it.'

Roz started to gather her bits and pieces together. 'Your father didn't kill your mother and sister, Olive. He thought *you* did. Gwen and Amber were alive when he went to work the next morning. As far as he was concerned, your statement was completely true.'

'But he knew I wasn't there.'

Roz shook her head. 'I'll never be able to prove it but I don't suppose he even realized you'd gone. He slept downstairs, remember, and I'll bet a pound to a penny you slipped out quietly to avoid attracting attention to yourself. If you'd only agreed to see him, you'd have sorted it out.' She stood up. 'It's water under the bridge, but you shouldn't have punished him, Olive. He was no more guilty than you are. He loved you. He just wasn't very good at showing it. I suspect his only fault was to take too little notice of the clothes women wore.'

Olive shook her head. 'I don't understand.'

'He told the police your mother owned a nylon overall.'

'Why would he do that?'

Roz sighed. 'I suppose because he didn't want to admit he never looked at her. He wasn't a bad man, Olive. He couldn't help his sexuality any more than you or I can help ours. The tragedy for you all was that none of you could talk about it.' She took the pin from the tabletop and wiped the head clean. 'And I don't believe for one moment that he would ever have blamed you for what happened. Only himself. That's why he went on living in the house. It was his atonement.'

A large tear rolled down Olive's cheek. 'He always said the game wasn't worth the candle.' She held out her hand for the pin. 'If I'd love him less I'd have hated him less, and it wouldn't be too late now, would it?'

TWENTY

Hal was dozing in the car outside, arms crossed, an old cap pulled over his eyes to block out the sun. He raised his head and surveyed Roz lazily from under the brim as she tugged open the driver's door. 'Well?'

She dumped her briefcase on the back seat and slipped in behind the wheel. 'She shot my version down in flames.' She gunned the engine into life and reversed out of the parking slot.

Hal eyed her thoughtfully. 'So where are we going?'

'To tear strips off Edward,' she told him. 'He's had nothing like the punishment he deserves.'

'Is that wise? I thought he was a psychopath.' Hal pulled the cap over his eyes again and settled down for another snooze. 'Still, I'm sure you know what you're doing.' His faith in Roz was unshakeable. She had more bottle than most of the men he knew.

'I do.' She inserted the tape she had just made into the deck and rewound it. 'But you don't, Sergeant, so cock an ear to this. I'm inclined to think it's you I should be tearing strips off. The wretched child – because let's face it, that's all she really is, even now – was starving, and you promised her a ''proper dinner'' when she'd finished her statement. No wonder she couldn't confess fast enough. If she'd told you she *hadn't* done it you'd have kept her waiting for her food.' She turned the volume up full blast.

*

It took several rings of the doorbell before Edward Clarke finally opened the door to them on the burglar chain. He gestured angrily for them to go away. 'You have no business here,' he hissed at Roz. 'I shall call the police if you persist in harassing us.'

Hal moved into his line of sight, smiling pleasantly. 'Detective Sergeant Hawksley, Mr Clarke. Dawlington CID. The Olive Martin case. I'm sure you remember me.'

A look of dejected recognition crossed Edward's face. 'I thought we'd done with all that.'

'I'm afraid not. May we come in?'

The man hesitated briefly and Roz wondered if he was going to call Hal's bluff and demand identification. Apparently not. The ingrained British respect for authority ran deep with him. He rattled the chain and opened the door, his shoulders slumped in weary defeat. 'I knew Olive would talk eventually,' he said. 'She wouldn't be human if she didn't.' He showed them into the sitting room. 'But on my word I knew nothing about the murders. If I'd had any idea what she was like, do you really think I'd have befriended her?'

Roz took the chair she had sat in before and surreptitiously switched on the tape-recorder in her handbag. Hal walked to the window and looked out. Mrs Clarke was sitting on the small patio at the back of the house, her face, vacant of expression, turned towards the sun. 'You and Olive were rather more than friends,' he said without hostility, turning back into the room.

'We didn't harm anyone,' said Mr Clarke, unconsciously echoing Olive. Roz wondered how old he was. Seventy? He looked more, worn out by care of his wife perhaps. The rough wig she had painted on cellophane over his photograph had been a revelation. It was quite true that hair made a man look younger. He squeezed his hands between his knees as if unsure what to do with them. 'Or should I say we did not set out with the intention to harm anyone. What Olive did was incomprehensible to me.'

'But you felt no responsibility for it?'

He stared at the carpet, unable to look at either of them. 'I assumed she had always been unstable,' he said.

'Why?'

'Her sister was. I thought it was a genetic thing.'

'So she behaved oddly before the murders?'

'No,' he admitted. 'As I say, I wouldn't have pursued' – he paused – 'the – relationship – if I had known the kind of person she was.'

Hal changed tack. 'What exactly was your relationship with Olive's father?'

He clamped his knees tighter about his hands. 'Friendly.'

'How friendly?'

Mr Clarke sighed. 'Does it matter now? It was a long time ago and Robert is dead.' His eyes drifted towards the window.

'It matters,' said Hal brusquely.

'We were very friendly.'

'Did you have a sexual relationship?'

'Briefly.' His hands struggled from between his knees and he buried his face in them. 'It sounds so sordid now, but it really wasn't. You have to understand how lonely I was. God knows it's not her fault, but my wife has never been much in the way of a companion. We married late, no children, and her mind has never been strong. I became her nurse and keeper before we'd been married five years, imprisoned in my own house with someone I could barely communicate with.' He swallowed painfully. 'Robert's friendship was all I had and he, as you obviously know, was homosexual. His marriage was as much a prison as mine, though for different reasons.' He pressed the bridge of his nose with a finger and thumb. 'The sexual nature of the relationship was simply a by-product of our dependence on each other. It mattered a great deal to Robert and very much less to me, though I admit that at the time – a period of three or four months only – I genuinely believed myself to be a homosexual.'

'Then you fell in love with Olive?'

'Yes,' said Mr Clarke simply. 'She was very like her father, of course, intelligent, sensitive, really quite charming when she wanted to be, and extraordinarily sympathetic. She made so few demands, unlike my wife.' He sighed. 'It seems strange to say it, in view of what happened later, but she was a very comfortable person to be with.'

'Did Olive know about your relationship with her father?'

'Not from me. She was very naïve in many respects.'

'And Robert didn't know about you and Olive.'

'No.'

'You were playing with fire, Mr Clarke.'

'I didn't plan it, Sergeant. It happened. All I can say in my defence is that I ceased being' – he sought for the right word – 'intimate with Robert the minute I recognized my feelings for Olive. We did not stop being friends, however. That would have been cruel.'

'Bullshit!' said Hal with calculated anger. 'You didn't want to be found out. My guess is you were shafting both of them at the same time and loving every exciting minute of it. And you have the bloody gall to say you don't feel responsible!'

'Why should I?' Clarke said with a flash of spirit. 'My name was never mentioned by either of them. Do you imagine it wouldn't have been if I had unwittingly precipitated the tragedy?'

Roz smiled contemptuously. 'Did you never wonder why Robert Martin wouldn't speak to you after the murders?'

'I assumed he was too distressed.'

'I think you feel a little more than simple distress when you discover that your lover has seduced your daughter,' she said ironically. 'Of course you precipitated it, Mr Clarke, and you knew it. But, by God, you weren't going to say anything. You'd rather see the entire Martin family destroy itself than prejudice your own position.'

'Was that so unreasonable?' he protested. 'They were free to name me. They didn't. How would it have helped if I had spoken out? Gwen and Amber would still have been dead. Olive would still have gone to prison.' He turned to Hal. 'I regret intensely my involvement with the family but I really can't be held responsible if my connection with them led to tragedy. There was nothing illegal about what I did.'

Hal looked out of the window again. 'Tell us why you

moved, Mr Clarke. Was it your decision or your wife's?'

He clamped his hands between his knees again. 'It was a joint decision. Life there became unbearable for both of us. We saw ghosts everywhere. A change of environment seemed the only sensible course.'

'Why were you so keen to keep your forwarding address secret?'

Clarke raised haunted eyes. 'To avoid the past catching up with me. I've lived in constant dread of this.' He looked at Roz. 'It's almost a relief to have it out in the open at last. You probably won't believe that.'

She gave a tight smile. 'The police took a statement from your wife on the day of the murders, saying that she saw Gwen and Amber on the doorstep that morning after you and Robert left for work. But when I came here the other day, she said she had lied about it.'

'I can only repeat what I said to you then,' he answered wearily. 'Dorothy's senile. You can't put any reliance on anything she says. She doesn't even know what day it is most of the time.'

'Was she telling the truth five years ago?'

He nodded. 'In so far as saying they were alive when I left for work, yes, she was. Amber was at the window, watching. I saw her myself. She ducked behind the curtain when I waved at her. I remember thinking how odd that was.' He paused. 'As to whether Dorothy saw Robert leave,' he resumed after a moment, 'I don't know. She said she did and I've always understood that Robert had a cast-iron alibi.'

'Has your wife ever mentioned seeing the bodies, Mr Clarke?' asked Hal casually.

'Good God, no.' He sounded genuinely shocked.

'I just wondered why she saw ghosts. She wasn't particularly friendly with Gwen or Amber, was she? Rather the reverse, I'd have thought, in view of the amount of time you spent at the Martins' house.'

'Everyone in that road saw ghosts,' he said bleakly. 'We all knew what Olive had done to those wretched women. It would have required a very dull imagination not to see ghosts.'

'Can you remember what your wife was wearing the morning of the murders?'

He stared at Hal, surprised by the sudden switch. 'Why do you ask?'

'We've had a report that a woman was seen walking down past the Martins' garage.' The lie rolled glibly off his tongue. 'From the description it was too small for Olive but whoever it was was dressed in what looked like a smart black suit. We'd like to trace her. Could it have been your wife?'

The man's relief was palpable. 'No. She never had a black suit.'

'Was she wearing anything black that morning?'

'No. She wore a floral overall.'

'You're very certain.'

'She always wore it, every morning, to do the housework. She used to get dressed after she'd finished. Except Sundays. She didn't do housework on Sundays.'

Hal nodded. 'The same overall every morning? What happened when it got dirty?'

Clarke frowned, puzzled by the line of questioning. 'She had another one, a plain blue one. But she was definitely wearing the floral one on the day of the murders.'

'Which one was she wearing the day after the murders?'

He licked his lips nervously. 'I can't remember.'

'It was the blue one, wasn't it? And she went on wearing the blue one, I suspect, until you or she bought a spare.'

'I can't remember.'

Hal smiled unpleasantly. 'Does she still have her floral overall, Mr Clarke?'

'No,' he whispered. 'It's a long time since she did any housework.'

'What happened to it?'

'I can't remember. We threw out a lot of things before we moved.'

'How did you find the time to do that?' asked Roz. 'Mr

Hayes said you upped and left one morning and a removal company turned up three days later to pack your stuff for you.'

'Perhaps I sorted through everything when it came here,' he said rather wildly. 'I can't remember the precise order of things so long afterwards.'

Hal scratched his jaw. 'Did you know,' he murmured evenly, 'that your wife identified some charred remains of a floral overall, found in the incinerator in the Martins' garden, as being part of the clothing that Gwen was wearing the day she was murdered?'

Colour drained from Clarke's face, leaving it an unhealthy grey. 'No, I didn't.' The words were barely audible.

'And those remains were carefully photographed and carefully stored, ready to be produced at a future date if there was ever any dispute over their ownership. Mr Hayes, I'm sure, will be able to tell us whether it was your wife's overall or Gwen's.'

Clarke raised his hands in helpless surrender. 'She told me she'd thrown it away,' he pleaded, 'because the iron had scorched a hole through the front. I believed her. She often did things like that.'

Hal hardly seemed to hear him but went on in the same unemotional voice. 'I very much hope, Mr Clarke, that we will find a way of proving that you knew all along that it was your wife who killed Gwen and Amber. I should like to see you tried and convicted of allowing an innocent girl to go to prison for a crime you knew she hadn't committed, particularly a girl whom you used and abused so shamelessly.'

They could never prove it, of course, but he drew considerable satisfaction from the fear that set Clarke's face working convulsively.

'How could I know? I wondered' – his voice rose – 'of course I wondered, but Olive confessed.' His eyes strayed beseechingly to Roz. 'Why did Olive confess?'

'Because she was in deep shock, because she was frightened, because she didn't know what else to do, because her mother was dead, and because she had been brought up to keep secrets. She thought her father would save her, but he didn't, because he thought she had done it. *You* could have saved her, but you didn't, because you were afraid of what people would say. The woman at Wells-Fargo could have saved her, but she didn't, because she didn't want to be involved. Her solicitor could have saved her if he had been a kinder man.' She flicked a glance at Hal. 'The police could have saved her if they'd questioned, just once, the value of confession evidence. But it was six years ago, and six years ago, confessions' – she made a ring with her thumb and forefinger – 'were A-OK. But I don't blame them, Mr Clarke. I blame you. For everything. You played at being a homosexual because you were bored with your wife and then you seduced your lover's daughter to prove you weren't the pervert you thought he was.' She stared at him with disdain. 'And that's how I'm going to portray you in the book that will get Olive out of prison. I really despise people like you.'

'You'll destroy me.'

'Yes.'

'Is that what Olive wants? My destruction?'

'I don't know what Olive wants. I only know what I want, which is to get her released. If it means your destruction, then so be it.'

He sat for some moments in silence, his fingers plucking shakily at the creases in his trousers. Then, as if reaching a sudden decision, he looked at Roz. 'I would have spoken if Olive hadn't confessed. But she did, and I assumed like everyone else that she was telling the truth. Presumably you have no desire to prolong her stay in prison? Her release in advance of your book's publication would improve your sales considerably, wouldn't it?'

'Maybe. What are you suggesting?'

His eyes narrowed. 'If I give you the evidence now that will hasten her release, will you in return promise not to divulge my real name or address in the book? You could refer to me by the name Olive called me, Mr Lewis. Do you agree?'

She smiled faintly. What an unbelievable shit he was. He could never hold her to it, of course, but he didn't seem to realize that. And the police would release his name, anyway, if only as Mrs Clarke's husband. 'I agree. As long as it gets Olive out.'

He stood up, taking some keys out of his pocket, and walked over to an ornate Chinese box on the sideboard. He unlocked it and raised the lid, removing something wrapped in tissue paper and handing it to Hal. 'I found it when we moved,' he said. 'She'd hidden it at the bottom of one of her drawers. I swear I never knew how she got it, but I've always been afraid that Amber must have taunted her with it. She talks about Amber a lot.' He washed his hands in mimicry of Pontius Pilate. 'She calls her the Devil.'

Hal peeled away the tissue paper and looked at what was revealed. A silver bracelet with a tiny silver-chair charm and a tag on which U.R.N.A.R.N.I.A. was barely discernible through a welter of deep angry scratches.

It was almost Christmas before the scales of justice had tipped enough in Olive's favour to allow her to leave the confines of her prison. There would always be doubters, of course, people who would call her the Sculptress till the day she died. After six years the evidence in support of her story was desperately thin. A silver bracelet where it shouldn't have been. Tiny fragments of a burnt floral overall, identified by a senile woman's bitter husband. And, finally, the painstaking reappraisal of the photographic evidence, using sophisticated computer enhancement, which had revealed a smaller, daintier shoe print in the blood beneath a huge ribbed rubber sole mark left by Olive's trainer.

No one would ever know what really happened that day because the truth was locked inside a brain that no longer functioned, and Edward Clarke could not, or would not, shed any light from statements his wife had made in the past. He maintained his complete ignorance of the whole affair, saying that any qualms he might have had had been put to rest by Olive's confession and that the onus for mistakes must lie with her and with the police. The most probable scenario, and the one generally accepted, was that Amber waited until Edward and Robert had left for work and then invited Mrs Clarke into the house to taunt her with the bracelet and the abortion. What happened then was a matter for guesswork but Roz, at least, believed that Mrs Clarke had set about the murders in cold blood and with a clear mind. There was something very calculating about the way she must have donned gloves to perform her butchery and her careful stepping around the blood to avoid leaving too many traces. But most calculating of all was the clever burning of her blood-stained overall amidst Gwen and Amber's clothes and her cool identification of the pieces afterwards as being the overall worn by Gwen that morning. Roz even wondered sometimes if the intention all along had been to implicate Olive. There was no telling now why Mrs Clarke had drawn attention to herself outside the kitchen window, but Roz couldn't help feeling that, had she not done so, Olive might have had enough presence of mind to phone the police immediately before she ran amok in the kitchen and obliterated the evidence that might have exonerated her.

There were to be no disciplinary charges against the police team involved. The chief constable issued a press release, pointing to the recent tightening of police procedure, particularly in relation to confession evidence, but he stressed that as far as Olive's case was concerned the police had taken all available steps to ensure her rights were fully protected. In the circumstances it had been reasonable to assume that her confession was genuine. He took the opportunity to reiterate forcefully the duty imperative on the public never to disturb evidence at the scene of a crime.

Peter Crew's association with the case, particularly in view of his subsequent mishandling of Robert Martin's estate, had attracted considerable and unwelcome interest. At worst he was accused of deliberately engineering Olive's conviction in order to gain access to unlimited funds, and, at best, of bullying an emotionally disturbed young woman at a time when he had a responsibility to safeguard her interests. He denied both accusations strenuously, arguing that he could not have foreseen Robert Martin's success on the stock exchange nor his early death; and claiming that because Olive's story had been remarkably consistent with the forensic evidence he, in the absence of any denials on her part, had, like the police, accepted it as a true statement of fact. He had advised her to say nothing and could not be held liable for her confession. Meanwhile, he remained at liberty on bail, facing the sort of charges that for most of his clients would have resulted in a remand to prison, bullishly declaring his innocence on all counts.

Roz, when she heard what he was saying, was angry enough to waylay him in the street with a local journalist in tow. 'We could argue about liability for ever, Mr Crew, but just explain this to me. If Olive's statement was as consistent with the forensic evidence as you maintain, then why did she claim there was no mist on the mirror at a time when Gwen and Amber were still alive?' She caught his arm as he tried to walk away. 'Why didn't she mention that the axe was too blunt to cut off Amber's head? Why didn't she say she had struck her four times before resorting to the carving knife? Why didn't she describe her fight with her mother and the stabbing incisions she'd made in her mother's throat before cutting it? Why didn't she mention burning the clothes? In fact, try quoting me one detail from Olive's statement that does accord fully with the forensic evidence.'

He shook her off angrily. 'She said she used the axe and the carving knife,' he snapped.

'Neither of which had her fingerprints on them. The forensic evidence did not support her statement.'

'She had their blood all over her.'

'All over is right, Mr Crew. But where does it say in her statement that she rolled in it?'

He tried to walk away but found the journalist blocking his path. 'Footprints,' he said. 'At the time, there were only her footprints.'

'Yes,' said Roz. 'And on that one piece of evidence, which was at odds with all the rest, you made up your mind she was a psychopath and prepared a defence on the grounds of diminished responsibility. Why did you never brief Graham Deedes on the lifelines her poor father was trying to throw her? Why didn't you question your own judgement when she was pronounced fit to plead guilty? Why the hell didn't you treat her like a human being, Mr Crew, instead of a monster?'

He stared at her with dislike. 'Because, Miss Leigh,' he said, 'she *is* a monster. Worse, she's a clever monster. Doesn't it worry you that this wretched woman you've set up to take Olive's place is the only one who's not mentally fit to fight the accusation? And doesn't it worry you that Olive waited till her father died before she would talk to anyone? Mark my words, *he* was the one she intended to smear with her guilt – because he was easy. He was dead. But you gave her Mrs Clarke instead.' He thrust his face angrily into hers. 'The evidence you've unearthed raises doubts, but no more. Computer-enhanced photography is as open to interpretation as the nature of psychopathy.' He shook his head. 'Olive will get out because of it, of course. The law has become very flabby in the last few years. But I was there when she told her story and, as I made clear to you at the start, Olive Martin is a dangerous woman. She's after her father's money. You've been led by the nose, Miss Leigh.'

'She's not half as dangerous as you, Mr Crew. At least she's never paid to have people's businesses destroyed and their lives threatened. You're a cheap crook.'

Crew shrugged. 'If that appears in print, Miss Leigh, I shall sue you for defamation, and it will cost you considerably more in legal fees than it will cost me. I suggest you remember that.'

The journalist watched him walk away. 'He's doing a Robert Maxwell on you.'

'That's the law for you,' said Roz in disgust. 'It's nothing but a big stick if you know how to use it or you're rich enough to employ someone else to use it for you.'

'You don't think he's right about Olive, do you?'

'Of course not,' said Roz angrily, sensing his doubt. 'But at least you know now what she was up against. This country is mad if it assumes that the presence of a solicitor during an interview will automatically protect a prisoner's rights. They are just as fallible, just as lazy, and just as crooked as the rest of us. It cost the Law Society millions last year to compensate clients for their solicitors' misdeeds.'

The book was scheduled to come out within a month of Olive's release. Roz had finished it in record time amidst the peace and seclusion of Bayview, which she bought on impulse when she discovered it was impossible to work above the continuous noise of people enjoying their food in the restaurant downstairs. The Poacher had been relaunched in a whirl of somewhat exaggerated publicity featuring Hal as the heroic underdog fighting the evil of organized crime. His association with the Olive Martin case, particularly his latter efforts to help in securing her release, had only added to the hype. He applauded Roz's decision to buy Bayview. Making love against the back-drop of the ocean was a vast improvement on the metal bars at the Poacher.

And she was safer there.

Hal had discovered within himself a capacity for caring that he hadn't known existed. It went deeper than love, encompassing every emotion from admiration to lust, and, while he would never have described himself as an obsessive man, the stress of worrying about Stewart Hayes, free on bail, slowly became intolerable to him. He was prompted finally to make Hayes a surprise visit at home one day. He found him playing in the garden with his ten-year-old daughter and it was there that he made Hayes an offer Hayes couldn't refuse. A life for a life, a maiming for a maiming, should anything happen to Roz. Hayes recognized such compelling purpose in the dark eyes, perhaps because it's what he would have done himself, that he agreed to an indefinite truce. His love for his daughter, it seemed, was matched only by Hal's love for Roz.

Iris, claiming almost more credit for the book than Roz – 'if it hadn't been for me it would never have been written' – was busy selling it around the world as the latest example of British justice reeling under the body blows of its own inflexibility. A small, rather ironic footnote to the story was that the boy Crew's firm had located in Australia proved not, after all, to be Amber's lost child and the search for him was promptly abandoned. The time limit, set in Robert Martin's will, had run out and his money, swollen by Crew's investments – which were now out of his reach – continued in limbo while Olive sought leave to contest her right to it.

EPILOGUE

![bar]

At 5.30 on a dark and frosty winter morning the Sculptress walked free from the gates of her prison, two hours earlier than the time announced to the press. She had sought and obtained permission to slip back into society well away from the glare of publicity that had surrounded the release of other celebrated cases of wrongful imprisonment. Roz and Sister Bridget, alerted by telephone, stood outside in the lamplight, stamping their feet and blowing on their hands. They smiled in welcome as the Judas door opened.

Only Hal, sheltering ten yards away in the warmth of the car, saw the look of gloating triumph that swept briefly over Olive's face as she put her arms around the two women and lifted them bodily into the air. He recalled some words that he'd had stencilled on his desk when he was still a policeman. *'Truth lies within a little and certain compass, but error is immense.'*

For no apparent reason, he shivered.

Minette Walters has also written two other crime novels. Her first, *The Ice House*, won the Crime Writers' Association John Creasey Award for Best First Novel of the Year and is available in Pan paperback at £4.99. *The Scold's Bridle*, her third novel, is published by Macmillan in hardcover at £14.99. What follows here is the first chapter.

THE SCOLD'S BRIDLE

I wonder if I should keep these diaries under lock and key. Jenny Spede has disturbed them again and it's annoying me. She must have opened a volume inadvertently while dusting, and reads them now out of some sort of prurient curiosity. What does she make, I wonder, of an old woman, deformed by arthritis, stripping naked for a young man? A vicarious lust, I am sure, for it beggars belief that anyone other than her brute of a husband has ever regarded her with anything but revulsion.

But, no, it can't be Jenny. She's too lazy to clean so thoroughly and too stupid to find anything I say or do either interesting or amusing. The later volumes seem to be attracting the most attention but, at the moment, I can't see why. I am only interested in beginnings for there is so much hope at the beginning. The end has no merit except to demonstrate how badly that hope was misplaced.

'In the dead vast and middle of the night . . . How weary, stale, flat, and unprofitable seem to me all the uses of this world.'

Who then? James? Or am I going senile and imagining things? Yesterday I found Howard's offer open on my desk, but I could have sworn I put it back in the file. 'O judgement, thou art fled . . .'

The pills worry me more. Ten is such a round number to be missing. I fear Joanna is up to her wretched tricks again, worse, I wonder if Ruth is going the same way. Blood will always out . . .

ONE

D R SARAH BLAKENEY stood beside the bath and wondered how death could ever be described as a victory. There was no triumph here, no lingering sense that Mathilda had abandoned her earthly shell for something better, no hint even that she had found peace. The dead, unlike the sleeping, offered no hope of a re-awakening. 'You want my honest opinion?' she said slowly, in answer to the policeman's question. 'Then no, Mathilda Gillespie is the last person I'd have expected to kill herself.'

They stared at the grotesque figure, stiff and cold in the brackish water. Nettles and Michaelmas daisies sprouted from the awful contraption that caged the bloodless face, its rusted metal bit clamping the dead tongue still in the gaping mouth. A scattering of petals, curling and decayed, clung to the scraggy shoulders and the sides of the bath, while a brown sludge below the water's surface suggested more petals, waterlogged and sunk. On the floor lay a bloodied Stanley knife, apparently dropped by the nerveless fingers that dangled above it. It was reminiscent of Marat in *his* bath, but so much uglier and so much sadder. Poor Mathilda, thought Sarah, how she would have hated this.

The police Sergeant gestured at the pitiful grey head. 'What in God's name is *that* thing?' His voice grated with repugnance.

313

Sarah waited a moment until she felt her own voice was under control. 'It's a scold's bridle,' she told him, 'a primitive instrument of repression. They were used in the Middle Ages to curb the tongues of nagging women. It's been in Mathilda's family for years. I know it looks awful like that, but she kept it downstairs in the hall over a pot of geraniums. As a decoration it was rather effective.' She raised a hand to her mouth in distress and the policeman patted her shoulder awkwardly. 'They were white geraniums and they poked their heads through the iron framework. Her coronet weeds, she always called them.' She cleared her throat. 'She was rather fine, you know. Very proud, very snobbish, very intolerant and not overly friendly, but she had a brilliant mind for someone who had never been trained to do anything more than keep house and she had a wonderful sense of humour. Dry and incisive.'

'Coronet weeds,' echoed the pathologist thoughtfully. 'As in:

"There with fantastic garlands did she come,
Of crowflowers, nettles, daisies, and long purples,
That liberal shepherds give a grosser name,
But our cold maids do dead men's fingers call them:
There, on the pendent boughs her coronet weeds—"

'Hamlet,' he explained apologetically to the policeman. 'Ophelia's end. I had to learn it for O level. Amazing what you remember as you get older.' He stared at the bath. 'Did Mrs Gillespie know Hamlet?'

Sarah nodded unhappily. 'She told me once that her entire education was based on learning chunks of Shakespeare by heart.'

'Well, we're not going to learn much by standing staring at the poor woman,' said the policeman abruptly. 'Unless Ophelia was murdered.'

Dr Cameron shook his head. 'Death by drowning,' he said

thoughtfully, 'while of unsound mind.' He glanced at Sarah. 'Was Mrs Gillespie depressed at all?'

'If she was, she never gave any indication of it.'

The policeman, decidedly more uncomfortable in the presence of death than either of the two doctors, ushered Sarah on to the landing. 'Many thanks for your time, Dr Blakeney. I'm sorry we had to subject you to that but as her GP you probably knew her better than most.' It was his turn to sigh. 'They're always the worst. Old people, living alone. Society's rejects. Sometimes it's weeks before they're found.' His mouth turned down in a curve of distaste. 'Very unpleasant. I suppose we're lucky she was found so quickly. Less than forty hours according to Dr Cameron. Midnight Saturday, he estimates.'

Sarah leant her back against the wall and stared across the landing towards Mathilda's bedroom where the open door showed the old oak bed piled high with pillows. There was a strange sense of ownership still, as if her possessions retained the presence that her flesh had lost. 'She wasn't that old,' she protested mildly. 'Sixty-five, no more. These days that's nothing.'

'She looks older,' he said matter-of-factly, 'but then she would, I suppose, with all the blood drained out of her.' He consulted his notebook. 'A daughter, you say, living in London, and you think a granddaughter at boarding school.'

'Don't Mr and Mrs Spede know?' She had caught a glimpse of them in the library as she came in, grey faces curiously blank from shock, hands clasped tightly together like petrified children. 'They've been coming in twice a week for years. He looks after the garden and she cleans. They must know more about her than anyone.'

He nodded. 'Unfortunately we've had nothing but hysterics out of them since Mrs Spede found the body. We'll be asking round the village, anyway.' He looked towards the bedroom. 'There's an empty bottle of barbiturates on her bedside table beside the remains of a glass of whisky. It looks like a belt and braces job. Whisky for courage, sleeping pills, then the Stanley knife in the bath. Do you still say you wouldn't have expected her to kill herself?'

'Oh, lord, I don't know.' Sarah ran a worried hand through her short dark hair. 'I wouldn't have prescribed barbiturates if I thought there was a chance she'd abuse them, but one can never be certain about these things. And anyway, Mathilda had been taking them for years, they were commonly prescribed once. So yes, I would rule out suicide from what I knew of her, but we had a doctor-patient relationship. She had severe pain with her arthritis and there were nights when she couldn't sleep.' She frowned. 'In any case, there can't have been many of the sleeping pills left. She was due for another prescription this week.'

'Perhaps she was hoarding them,' he said unemotionally. 'Did she ever open her heart to you?'

'I doubt she opened her heart to anyone. She wasn't the type. She was a very private person.' She shrugged. 'And I've only known her – what? – twelve months. I live in Long Upton, not here in Fontwell, so I haven't come across her socially either.' She shook her head. 'There's nothing in her records to suggest a depressive personality. But the trouble is—' She fell silent.

'The trouble is what, Dr Blakeney?'

'The trouble is we talked about freedom the last time I saw her, and she said freedom is an illusion. There's no such thing in modern society. She quoted Rousseau at me, the famous rebel-cry of students in the sixties: "Man was born free, and everywhere he is in chains." There was only one freedom left, according to Mathilda, and that was the freedom to choose how and when to die.' Her face looked bleak. 'But we had conversations like that every time I saw her. There was no reason to assume that one was any different.'

'When was this conversation?'

Sarah sighed heavily. 'Three weeks ago during my last monthly visit. And the awful thing is, I laughed. Even that wasn't a freedom any more, I said, because doctors are so damn scared of prosecution they wouldn't dream of giving a patient the choice.'

The policeman, a large detective nearing retirement, placed a comforting hand on her arm. 'There now, it's nothing to fret about. It was slitting her wrists that killed her, not barbiturates. And the chances are we're looking at murder anyway.' He shook his head. 'I've seen a few suicides one way and another, but I've yet to see an old woman turn herself into a flower arrangement in her bath. It'll be money that's behind it. We all live too long and the young get desperate.' He spoke with feeling, Sarah thought.

An hour later, Dr Cameron was more sceptical. 'If she didn't do it herself,' he said, 'you'll have the devil's own job proving it.' They had removed the body from the bath and lain it, still with the scold's bridle in place, on plastic sheeting on the floor. 'Apart from the incisions in her wrists there's not a mark on her, bar what one would expect, of course.' He pointed to the lividity above and around the wrinkled buttocks. 'Some post-mortem hypostasis where the blood has settled but no bruising. Poor old thing. She didn't put up any sort of a fight.'

Sergeant Cooper leaned against the bathroom doorjamb, drawn to look at the poor grey body, but deeply repulsed by it. 'She couldn't if she was drugged,' he murmured.

Cameron peeled off his gloves. 'I'll see what I can find out for you back at the lab, but my advice is, don't hold your breath. I can't see your Chief Super wasting too much time and resources on this one. It's about as neat as anything I've seen. Frankly, unless something pretty unusual shows up in the post mortem, I'll be recommending a suicide verdict.'

'But what does your gut tell you, Doctor? The nettles are telling mine it was murder. Why would she deliberately sting herself before she died?

'Self-reproach, probably. Good God, man, there's no logic to this kind of thing. Suicides are hardly in their right mind when they top themselves. Still,' he said thoughtfully, 'I am surprised she didn't leave a note. There's so much of the theatre about this headdress that I'd have expected something by way of explanation.' He began to tuck the plastic sheet about the body. 'Read *Hamlet*,' he suggested. 'The answer's in there, I expect.'

Mr and Mrs Spede hovered in the library like two squat spectres, so unprepossessing and shifty in their appearance that Cooper wondered if they were quite normal. Neither seemed able to meet his gaze and every question required unspoken consultation between them before one would offer an answer. 'Dr Blakeney tells me Mrs Gillespie has a daughter living in London and a granddaughter at boarding school,' he said. 'Can you give me their names and tell me where I can contact them?'

'She kept her papers very neat,' said Mrs Spede eventually, after receiving some sort of permission to speak from her husband. 'It'll all be in the papers.' She nodded towards the desk and an oak filing cabinet. 'In there some place. Very neat. Always very neat.'

'Don't you know her daughter's name?'

'Mrs Lascelles,' said the man after a moment. 'Joanna.' He tugged at his lower lip which drooped oddly as if it had been tugged many times before. With a petulant frown his wife smacked him on the wrist and he tucked the offending hand into his pocket. They were very childlike, thought Cooper, and wondered if Mrs Gillespie had employed them out of compassion.

'And the granddaughter's name?'

'Miss Lascelles,' said Mrs Spede.

'Do you know her Christian name?'

'Ruth.' She consulted with her husband behind lowered lids. 'They're not nice, either of them. The Mrs is rude to Mr Spede about his gardening and the Miss is rude to Jenny about her cleaning.'

'Jenny?' he queried. 'Who's Jenny?'

'Jenny is Mrs Spede.'

'I see,' said Cooper kindly. 'It must have been a terrible shock for you, Jenny, to find Mrs Gillespie in her bath.'

'Oh, it was that,' she howled, grabbing her husband's arm. 'A terrible, terrible shock.' Her voice rose on a wail.

With some reluctance, because he feared an even louder outburst, Cooper took the polythene bag containing the Stanley knife from his pocket and laid it across his broad palm. 'I don't want to upset you any more, but do you recognize this? Is it a knife you've seen before?'

Her lips puckered tragically but she stopped the wailing to nudge her husband into speech. 'The kitchen drawer,' he said. 'It's the one from the kitchen drawer.' He touched the handle through the bag. 'I scratched an haitch on it for "house". The one I keep in the shed has a gee on it for "garden".'

Cooper examined the crude 'h' and nodded as he tucked the bag back out of sight into his pocket. 'Thank you. I'll need the one from the garden for comparison. I'll ask an officer to go out with you when we've finished.' He smiled in a friendly way. 'Now, you presumably have keys to the house. May I see them?'

Mrs Spede drew a string from around her neck, revealing a key that had lain within the cleft of her bosom. 'Only me,' she said. 'Jenny had the key. Mr Spede didn't need one for the garden.' She gave it to Cooper and he felt the warmth of her body seeping into his hand. It repelled him because it was damp and oily with sweat, and this made him feel guilty because he found them both deeply unattractive and knew that, unlike Mrs Gillespie, he could not have tolerated them about his house for even half an hour.

Mathilda Gillespie's nearest neighbours lived alongside her in a wing adjoining the house. At some stage Cedar House must have been one residence, but now a discreet sign indicated the door to Wing Cottage at the western end of the building. Before Cooper knocked on it, he walked along a gravel path to the rear corner and surveyed the patio at the back, neatly bordered by tubs of everlasting pansies, beyond which a clipped box hedge separated this garden from the expanse of lawn and distant trees that belonged to Cedar House. He felt a sudden envy for the occupants. How drear his own small box was by comparison, but then it was his wife who had chosen to live on a modern estate and not he. He would have been happy with crumbling plaster and a view; she was happy with all mod cons and neighbours so close they rubbed shoulders every day. It was a policeman's lot to give in to a wife he was fond of. His hours were too unpredictable to allow him to impose his own yearning for isolation on a woman who had tolerated his absences with stoical good humour for thirty years.

He heard the door open behind him and turned, producing his warrant card from his breast pocket, to greet the fat elderly man who approached. 'DS Cooper, sir, Dorset police.'

'Orloff, Duncan Orloff.' He ran a worried hand across his wide, rather pleasant face. 'We've been expecting you. Dear me, dear me. I don't mind admitting Jenny Spede's howling is a little difficult to take after a while. Poor woman. She's a good soul as long as nothing upsets her. I can't tell you what it was like when she found Mathilda. She came rushing out of the house screaming like a banshee and set her wretched husband off in sympathy. I realized something dreadful must have happened which is why I phoned your people and an ambulance. Thank God they came quickly and had the sense to bring a woman with them. She was really quite excellent, calmed the Spedes down in record time. Dear me, dear me,' he said again, 'we live such a quiet life. Not used to this sort of thing at all.'

'No one is,' said Cooper. 'You've been told what's happened, I suppose.'

He wrung his hands in distress. 'Only that Mathilda's dead. I kept the Spedes here until the police car arrived – thought it best, really, what with them collapsing in heaps about me – mind you, I wasn't going to let my wife downstairs till it was safe – one can't be certain about things – anyway the uniformed chaps told me to wait until someone came to ask questions. Look, you'd better come in. Violet's in the drawing-room now, not feeling too well in the circumstances, and who can blame her? Frankly, not feeling a hundred per cent myself.' He stood aside to let Cooper enter. 'First door on the right,' he said. He followed the policeman into a cosy, over-furnished room with a television on low volume in the corner, and bent over the prostrate figure of his wife on the sofa. 'There's a Sergeant to see us,' he said, raising her gently to a sitting position with one hand and using the other to swing her legs to the floor. He lowered his large bulk on to the sofa beside her and gestured Cooper towards an armchair. 'Jenny kept screaming about blood,' he confided unhappily. 'Red water and blood. That's all she said.'

Violet shivered. 'And Jesus,' she whispered. 'I heard her. She said Mathilda was "like Jesus".' She raised a hand to her own bloodless lips. 'Dead like Jesus in blood-red water.' Her eyes filled. 'What's happened to her? Is she *really* dead?'

'I'm afraid she is, Mrs Orloff. It's only approximate, but the pathologist estimates the time of death between nine o'clock and midnight on Saturday.' He looked from one to the other. 'Were you here during those three hours?'

'We were here all night,' said Duncan. He was clearly drawn between his own perceived good taste of not asking questions and an overwhelming need to satisfy a very natural curiosity. 'You haven't told us what's happened,' he blurted out. 'It's much, much worse if you don't know what's happened. We've been imagining terrible things.'

'She hasn't been *crucified*, has she?' asked Violet tremulously. 'I said she's probably been crucified, otherwise why would Jenny have said she looked like Jesus.'

'I said someone had tried to clean up afterwards,' said Duncan, 'which is why there's red water everywhere. You hear about it every day, old people being murdered for their money. They do terrible things to them, too, before they kill them.'

'Oh, I do hope she wasn't *raped*,' said Violet. 'I couldn't bear it if they'd raped her.'

Cooper had time to feel regret for this elderly couple who, like so many of their peers, lived the end of their lives in terror because the media persuaded them they were at risk. He knew better than anyone that statistics proved it was young men aged between fifteen and twenty-five who were the group most vulnerable to violent death. He had sorted out too many drunken brawls and picked too many stabbed and bludgeoned bodies from gutters outside pubs to be in any doubt of that. 'She died in her bath,' he said unemotionally. 'Her wrists were slit. At the moment the pathologist is inclining towards suicide and we are only asking questions to satisfy ourselves that she did in fact take her own life.'

'But Jesus didn't die in his bath,' said Violet in bewilderment.

'She was wearing a scold's bridle on her head with flowers in it. I think perhaps Mrs Spede thought it was a crown of thorns.' It made no sense otherwise, he thought.

'I *hated* that thing. Mathilda was always *very* peculiar about it.' Violet had a habit, Cooper noticed, of emphasizing words she thought important. 'It must have been suicide, then. She wore it when her arthritis was bad. It took her mind off the *pain*, you know. She always said she'd kill herself if it got so bad she couldn't stand it.' She turned tear-filled eyes to her husband. 'Why didn't she call out to us? I'm sure there's *something* we could have done to help.'

'Would you have heard her?' asked Cooper.

'Oh, yes, especially if she was in the bathroom. She could have rattled the pipes. We'd certainly have heard *that*.'

Cooper transferred his attention to Mr Orloff. 'Did you hear anything at all that night?'

Duncan gave the question long and thoughtful consideration. 'Our days are very uneventful,' he said apologetically. 'All I can say is that if we had heard something, we'd have acted' – he spread his hands in a gesture of surrender – 'like this morning when Jenny started screaming. There was nothing like that on Saturday.'

'Yet you both assumed she'd been murdered by a gang. You mentioned "they".'

'It's difficult to think straight when people are screaming,' he said, reproaching himself with a shake of the head. 'And to be perfectly honest, I wasn't at all sure the Spedes themselves hadn't done something. They're not the brightest couple as you've probably discovered for yourself. Mind you, it wouldn't have been intentional. They're foolish, not dangerous. I assumed there'd been some sort of accident,' he spread his palms on his fat knees, 'I've been worrying that I should have gone in to do something, saved her perhaps, but if she died on Saturday . . .?' His voice tailed off on a query.

Cooper shook his head. 'You couldn't have done anything for her. What about during the daytime? Did you hear anything then?'

'On Saturday, you mean?' He shook his head. 'Nothing that leaps to mind. Certainly nothing unsettling.' He looked at Violet as if seeking inspiration. 'We notice if the bell rings in Cedar House, because it's very rare for Mathilda to have visitors, but otherwise' – he shrugged helplessly – 'so little happens here, Sergeant, and we do watch a lot of television.'

'And you didn't wonder where she was on Sunday?'

Violet dabbed at her eyes. 'Oh, dear,' she whispered, 'could we have saved her then? How *awful*, Duncan.'

'No,' said Cooper firmly, 'she was certainly dead by three o'clock on Sunday morning.'

'We were friends, you know,' said Violet. 'Duncan and I have known her for fifty years. She sold us this cottage when Duncan retired five years ago. That's not to say she was the *easiest* person in the world to get on with. She could be very cruel to people she didn't like, but the trick with Mathilda was not to *impose*. We never did, of course, but there were those who did.'

Cooper licked the point of his pencil. 'Who for example?'

Violet lowered her voice. 'Joanna and Ruth, her daughter and granddaughter. They *never* left her alone, always complaining, always demanding money. And the vicar was shocking.' She cast a guilty glance at her husband. 'I know Duncan doesn't approve of tittle-tattle but the vicar was always pricking her conscience about the less well off. She was an *atheist*, you know, and very rude to Mr Matthews every time he came. She called him a Welsh leech. To his face, too.'

'Did he mind?'

Duncan gave a rumble of laughter. 'It was a game,' he said. 'She was quite generous sometimes when he caught her in a good mood. She gave him a hundred pounds once towards a centre for alcoholics, saying there but for the grace of her metabolism went she. She drank to deaden the pain of her arthritis, or so she said.'

'Not to excess, though,' said Violet. 'She was never *drunk*. She was too much of a lady ever to get drunk.' She blew her nose loudly.

'Is there anyone else you can think of who imposed on her?' asked Cooper after a moment.

Duncan shrugged. 'There was the doctor's husband, Jack Blakeney. He was always round there, but it wasn't an imposition. She liked him. I used to hear her laughing with him sometimes in the garden.' He paused to reflect. 'She had very few friends, Sergeant. As Violet said, she wasn't an easy woman. People either liked Mathilda or loathed her. You'll find that out soon enough if you're planning to ask questions of anyone else.'

'And you liked her?'

His eyes grew suddenly wet. 'I did,' he said gruffly. 'She was beautiful once, you know, quite beautiful.' He patted his wife's hand. 'We all were, a long, long time ago. Age has very few compensations, Sergeant, except perhaps the wisdom to recognize contentment.' He pondered for a moment. 'They do say slitting the wrists is a very peaceful way to die, although how anyone knows I can't imagine. Did she suffer, do you think?'

'I'm afraid I can't answer that, Mr Orloff,' said Cooper honestly.

The damp eyes held his for a moment and he saw a deep and haggard sadness in them. They spoke of a love that Cooper somehow suspected Duncan had never shown or felt for his wife. He wanted to say something by way of consolation, but what could he say that wouldn't make matters worse? He doubted that Violet knew, and he wondered, not for the first time, why love was more often cruel than it was kind.